Praise for "Backlash"

"I loved *Backlash*! I read it in less than three days. Only put it down when I had to. Now, you need to get started on your next book. Your fans are waiting." *L. R., Mississippi.*

"*Backlash* was enjoyable to read on a variety of levels. The characters were well developed. Jacqueline's years in the family business served her well, when she was thrown into managing a terrorist attack directed at her company, soon after taking over as CEO from her late father. Her grit and innovative ways of solving complex issues were evident. The storyline, including special interest groups, reporters, environmental radicals and Washington politics, was easy to follow. Jacqueline was eloquent and human in her approach to protecting her family's corporation against all odds, and I found myself cheering her on, as she took on Washington and her stockholders throughout the book. The storyline flowed, keeping me wondering 'what next?' Author meticulously conducted his research for his book, reminding me of a well-developed Grisham-like novel. Hope another book is in the works." *D. J., Amazon.com review.*

"An 'edge of the seat'er! We need more (real) people like Jacqueline Marie James who will take a stand against some of the idiocy foisted on us by our elected officials (of all parties) to further their own selfish goals. So pertinent to what is going on today in America. But not so political that you can't relate to the characters and get caught up in the emotion of the story. A great read--I didn't want to put it down. Loved it!!! *S. D., Amazon.com review.*

"When is the sequel coming out?" *P. C., Georgia.*

"Didn't have to skip sections for inappropriate language or sexual conduct. This proves a good story can be written without adding trashy content." *S. Y., Amazon.com review.*

"Get Ready for a Wild Ride! *Backlash* can be enjoyed on many different levels. As a page-turner, it keeps you on the edge of your seat from the initial...well, I won't spoil it for you...right up to the denouement. But Backlash has a deeper subtext, almost a platonic dialogue being conducted between the lines, that addresses many of the key political concerns of our time without ever lecturing or slipping into the abstract. As we become engaged by the highly colorful characters, we grapple with the political issues that confront them.

"What's unique is the way in which the author weaves a complex philosophical treatise into a plot that moves as quick as you can turn the pages. You can't help but be transfixed by the unexpected plot twists. It's not until the story is over that you realize that the book has taken on many of the nettlesome issues of our current political discourse. The ride is so fun that you don't realize how much ground you've covered until it's over. What a great read, can't wait for the next one from this author." *B. G., Amazon.com review.*

"Just finished *Backlash* by Gary L. Ivey. It was fabulous!!!! I was so intrigued by the plot...environmental terrorists, murder, politics, moral integrity, a female heroine, hard-core work ethics, and a splash of love made for a great read! (ah...and the evolution/creation thread!)." *L. Z., Facebook post.*

BACKLASH

Gary L. Ivey

IV

First Printing 2011
Published by Lighthouse Christian Publishing

Second Edition 2017
Published by
Studio IV Productions, Kailua Kona, HI 96740

ISBN: 0-9993968-0-3
ISBN-13: 978-0-9993968-0-3

www.backlashbook.com

Cover photography iStockPhoto and DreamsTime.
Design by Gary L. Ivey.

To my wife, Toni, whose fearless

spirit and belief in me inspires me

and cheers me on.

Studio
IV
PRODUCTIONS

CHAPTER ONE

Few things are blacker than crude oil, but this humid Louisiana night almost qualified.

Rising almost 60 feet toward the indigo, moonless sky stood the Gulf Pride offshore oil platform, with bright lights flooding its workspaces and the large black and gold Axiom Oil Incorporated logo on the helipad. A string of bulbs also climbed the derrick that rose another 75 feet. The crane nearby was used to position the heavy pipes that descended through the derrick hundreds of feet below the ocean floor to find and bring up the precious commodity so important to the world's economy. There were literally hundreds of drilling platforms like the Gulf Pride off the coasts of Louisiana and Texas, a testament to the demand for the natural resource that lay beneath the Gulf floor in such abundance.

Because of the bright lights on the platform it may as well have been shrouded in a black velvet curtain, for all that the oilmen could see beyond the railing. The lights made even the explosion of stars above them fade to nothing. Even without the bright work lights, the 60 miles to shore would have prevented them from seeing any signs of dry land.

Almost no light from the platform reached down through the mist to the trackless Gulf of Mexico and that would be unfortunate for the Axiom Oil Incorporated employees this night.

The metal-on-metal sounds and the noise of generators, in addition to the shouts of laboring men, obscured all sounds not already covered by the eternal washing of the waves against the thick cylindrical supports that stretched down beneath the surface. So, none of them heard the approaching inboard motors or noticed when they died about 400 yards away.

The graveyard shift was just beginning its work and the roust-a-bouts, dressed identically in bright blue jumpsuits and yellow hard hats, called loudly to each other as they performed their dirty, dangerous work. Mannie Kowalski, the foreman, goaded the men with jokes or curses, whichever was most effective with these men who were his only companions for weeks at a time. He wiped sweat from his forehead with a red rag that was quickly turning black and returned his yellow hard hat to its customary position, slightly cocked to the left. His lined face gave witness to the years he had spent with little protection from sun reflected off turquoise water and the wind that blew constantly at this elevation.

A length of pipe was gingerly lowered into position by the crane operator, as skillful, gloved hands guided it to its marriage with an identical pipe already stretching down below the derrick. When the pipe was in position, Mannie secured the huge threads himself with a giant wrench and then called, "Clear!" The crane operator pushed a lever to start the pipe on its descent into the deep water as the men on Mannie's crew began to pump "mud" through it. Actually, a commercially manufactured mixture of water, clay, various chemicals and thickeners such as guar gum, the "mud" allowed them to control the flow of the oil, regulating the rate at which it would ascend from the bowels of the earth.

Mannie stepped back and set down the heavy wrench with a "clank!" He wiped his face once again and began idly watching his gang at work. Suddenly, the men were startled by an ear-shattering "BOOM!" and Mannie and the four men with him were all violently knocked to the deck, a couple of them rolling into a wall as the flooring bucked upward, then came down with a loud metal-on-metal crash. Heavy wrenches, sledgehammers, and pipes clattered to the deck amid clouds of dust. Mannie's first fragmented thought was that it must be an earthquake, but then he saw the fire. At the north end of the platform a wall of flames extended above the deck, roaring 100 feet into the air above the startled men.

On an offshore oil platform, few things are dreaded more than fire, so the men overcame their initial surprise and leaped into action. They had often practiced for just such a situation and each of the blue-jumpsuit-clad men knew his job. Automatic sprinklers had already begun to spray the flames, pumping from the endless supply of salt water below the platform.

The men had no time to think about causes of the explosion. They knew they must first contain and extinguish the fire. Investigation and blame would come later.

Some of them deployed hoses to deal with areas missed by the sprinklers and others activated chemical spray units intended for electrical fires. The water was doing the job however, and within minutes the platform was covered with billows of white smoke, illuminated from within by the bright lights.

Mannie coughed in the haze as he counted the yellow hard hats until he was satisfied that all his men were accounted for. He was amazed that apparently no one was injured. He dreaded the paperwork that would now become his main occupation for several days. He would have to fill out forms for Axiom Corporate, the Coast Guard, the Department of Energy, the EPA, and who-knew-who-else.

* * *

Barely a quarter mile away in the darkness, 10 men dressed all in black rested their oars and sent up a silent cheer from two idled cigarette boats as they half stood watching the flames. The dark, polished wood of the sleek vessels blended into the inky waves on this dark night except on their sterns, where the burning oil platform was mirrored in the marine lacquer.

A bearded man with a nine-millimeter pistol strapped to his side raised his hand and, when he had the attention of the others, gestured to the north. The men settled into their places in the two boats and the pilots started the robust inboard engines once again. Within seconds the two marine missiles were hurtling rapidly over the waves, requiring the men to hang on for fear of being bounced overboard. The knowing looks passing between the men was all that was needed to communicate their satisfaction at having struck a blow for The Cause. They would have no nagging thoughts about the prodigious amount of fossil fuel consumed by the speeding cigarette boats or the conspicuous consumerism they represented. The success of this night made it all worthwhile.

The bearded man regarded the growing plume of smoke with disdain as the boats sped away. *The drilling platform is a sacrilege*; a *blight on the seascape*. The great sea was marred by its very existence. Its presence interrupted the harmony of nature and endangered the delicate and beautiful life that flourished under the waves. It was such an ugly contraption, too. It was simply a monument to the selfish wastefulness of the American people. Their desire for convenience was so great that they would rape the Earth's resources without a thought for giving back or preserving the planet for future generations.

At speeds up to 70 miles-per-hour, it wasn't long before the men saw land. Paul Stoddard stroked his beard and looked ahead at the shoreline of Louisiana with its few twinkling lights low on the horizon. They would be staying in a crayfish cabin in a bayou near Cocodrie off Terrebonne Bay for the remainder of the night. It was very remote and he was confident they could not be found even if someone knew to look for them. They would return the rented boats to the marinas tomorrow, then they would drive back to Houston. Part of him wished for a night in New Orleans. It was the ultimate place to celebrate, after all. But that would be contrary to the serious nature of their mission and besides, they all had to be back at work Monday morning, barely 30 hours from now.

The thought of work brought him down a bit. He was thankful that the Cause gave his life meaning. Here he was a leader, a reformer even, changing the world for the better.

* * *

The BlackBerry on the bedside table rang and vibrated insistently. Thirty-eight-year-old Jacqueline Marie James, half awake, fumbled for it. "Yes?" she said automatically into the phone that was never far away. Then she sat bolt upright, wide awake. "Where?... Was anybody hurt?... I'll be right there! Call for the chopper! I'm going out there."

Backlash

Her small, bare feet landed with a jolt on the cool, hardwood floor. Squinting in the sudden, soft light from the bedside lamp, she took less than two minutes to dress in jeans and a denim shirt pulled hastily from the cavernous walk-in closet. The large master bedroom where Jackie slept alone was appointed with cutting-edge contemporary furniture and accessories, all very high end and striking, and there was no clutter. In fact, the room could be said to have been sparse. "Minimalist" might have been a better word.

She pulled her tangled, shoulder-length brunette hair back and secured it with an elastic band, then tossed her makeup bag into the satchel she used as a carry-on when she flew commercial and left by the back door, activating the alarm system as she exited. There would be plenty of time to apply the makeup to her naturally tanned face on the helicopter. The new Chief Executive Officer of the largest gasoline retailer in the country wouldn't go far without makeup, even after being rousted out of bed before two in the morning.

Living alone behind an iron fence as she did, with her backyard garden pool surrounded by tall cedars, no one saw her petite, denim-clad figure on the short walk from her back door to the detached triple garage, which she accomplished at a double-quick pace. She hardly appeared remarkable, with her straight brown ponytail pulled back from her youthful and naturally beautiful face. Her large, dark eyes usually sparkled with mischief and optimism, but were serious and full of purpose now. If anyone could have seen her, few could have guessed that she was one of the richest women in Texas, or the United States, for that matter.

Jackie, as everyone knew her, was born with the proverbial silver spoon in her mouth, but her zest for life and love of adventure had always caused her to work harder than necessary and set ambitious goals for herself. She had always been so wealthy that having a lot of money was not a high priority for her. Some people in her social strata called money "merely a way to keep score", but Jackie focused on money even less than that. If she had taken a more competitive stance few could have kept up, but she did little to flaunt her wealth, beyond the few indulgences she allowed herself, like her horses, stabled at the ranch her father had bought and that now partly belonged to her.

Jackie's father and grandfather had reached the goal of great riches for her. For her part, she tended to think more about accomplishing great things in her profession, which had also been handed down to her by father and grandfather. The fact that she was physically small only intensified her aspirations and at this time of her life she was ideally positioned for greatness, or perhaps great blunders. The events that had positioned her were both fortuitous and tragic, but one's position on the highway of life is rarely entirely of one's own authorship or choosing.

On the way to Axiom Oil Incorporated headquarters in her BMW Z4, Jackie punched a speed-dial number on her cell phone for Wayne Simpson, her waspish personal assistant, to ask him to get together whatever the company had in the way of specs on the Gulf Pride platform. She was fully awake and in command now, able to marshal the considerable resources of the nation's largest gasoline retailer so very recently placed under her control. Then she called Axiom President Benjamin Tyson, who had been her boss in her old job as VP of Operations before she leap-frogged him to become CEO. She also wanted him to go with her to the Gulf Pride.

Next, she called Axiom Legal VP Marcus Williams to alert him, then John Thompson, VP of Exploration and Acquisition, who had been the one that called her with the alarming news. Marcus would get together with the Legal and Insurance departments and John would get a comprehensive report together for the families and notify Media Relations, which would forge the company's version of the facts of the case, as soon as they all knew what the facts were.

By the time she finished those conversations it was three a.m. and she was whipping off Houston's Katy Freeway and into the Axiom parking garage, on top of which the heliport was located, adjacent to the twenty-story Axiom headquarters tower, its mass of black glass and steel barely visible against the moonless sky, except for lights in a few offices looking like so many stars. The pilot had already arrived and was sitting in the helicopter preparing a flight plan for the sudden trip out into the Gulf. Five minutes later Wayne was there, carrying hastily assembled documentation on the platform and anything else he thought Jackie might need. He was in a suit, even at this hour, she saw. Some other time she would have razzed her pinched, type-A assistant about it. Another minute and the soft-spoken, dark-haired President Benny Tyson arrived and they took off on the two-hour flight to the platform.

Jackie was self-conscious as she applied her makeup in front of her male coworkers, but they weren't paying attention to her and had eventually drifted off to sleep while she finished putting on her face.

Has it been only two weeks? Jackie thought. Tears welled up as the boredom of sitting in silence allowed recent events to flood her mind. She had been so happy and her life had been so thoroughly planned. As Vice President of Operations of the company her grandfather had founded in the 1920s, she enjoyed traveling to the company's far-flung installations to exhort the troops and report to HQ on problems as well as progress the company was experiencing around the world. She had a tremendous frequent-flyer account as a result and spent little time in her luxurious, stone-sided home in an exclusive Houston neighborhood.

Two weeks ago exactly, she had been aboard the very offshore platform they were speeding toward now, having been deposited there by this same black jet ranger with the gold Axiom logo on the side. She had worn the blue jumpsuit and yellow hardhat of a roust-a-bout and had sweated in the relentless sun for two days, working side-by-side with the rough, hard men who lived for weeks at a time out of sight of dry land. The work was difficult and dirty, but she had gone to work with enthusiasm, wanting to experience what her employees went through every day. Then the helicopter had returned three days early.

Wayne had emerged from the hatch and announced that she had to return to Houston immediately. She had protested strenuously at first, but his uncharacteristically firm demeanor had told her louder than words could that she needed to do as he said. So, she had reluctantly agreed, excusing herself to change for the trip.

When she emerged from cleaning up, she had been transformed, having indulged her taste for the dramatic. The dark hair that had been crushed under the hard hat was now swaying with her every step in shimmering waves that just touched her shoulders, the ends curled under just slightly. She had worn a red business suit and matching patent leather heels that elicited some low whistles from the oil-smeared workers, but she had seen respect in their eyes. These trips were partly to educate her about the company's far-flung operations, but they were more about management-employee relations.

"Thanks again, Jackie," Mannie had said, shaking her hand as she boarded the chopper.

"No problem, Mannie. You take it easy, now."

"You keep 'em straight at HQ. I've got a pile of stock in this company."

"Count on it," Jackie had replied. Wayne had pulled the hatch door closed and a moment later the graceful helicopter lifted off.

It had only taken minutes before Jackie had grown impatient. She remembered looking at Wayne, who had not raised his eyes since boarding. One of the saucy red pumps hung from her toe as she swung her foot impatiently. "So, what was so important that you had to interrupt my field trip?"

It had taken a couple of seconds for him to answer. "Your father..." he coughed as if to put off finishing the sentence, "...is dead."

Jackie's vision suddenly blurred and she choked, "What? When? How?"

Three hours ago... On the golf course... Apparent heart attack... Couldn't get to the hospital in time....

She heard the answers, but they didn't help make sense of the bottom line: "Your father is dead."

She had stared out the window into the sun beginning to set over the Texas horizon, letting it bake her face. A tear had dragged mascara down her cheek. Wayne had mumbled something useless to prevent silence from taking over, but she couldn't focus on his words.

"Junior" James, as many people knew her father, CEO of Axiom Oil Incorporated for 40 years, had been her hero and mentor. The company was what it was today because of his vision and singleness of purpose. His life knew only the oil business and there wasn't any aspect he had not mastered.

She was his only child and, though she appeared petite and delicate, Jackie had grit about her that made her a match for the most burly rig hand. He had been overjoyed that she wanted to be part of the family business, but refused to get her first job for her, making her apply at a franchised service station under an assumed name, so she would have to prove herself as anyone would. She had begun working while in high school, though as sole heir to her family's fortune, there never would have been a need for her to work at all.

The week after his death had been a blur with the funeral and all that went with it. Homewood Baptist Church had been overflowing with family, friends and Axiom employees of long standing. The service had been held, not in the relatively small sanctuary, but, appropriately enough, in the Donald R. James Family Life Center across the parking lot, because more mourners could be accommodated in the gymnasium that had been built thanks to a matching challenge grant from Homewood Baptist's most famous member. Jackie had entered with her mother on her arm. Florence James barely looked up beyond her broad-brimmed black hat as Jackie eased her along.

Jackie worried about her mother. Florence was a holdover from an earlier time. She had always been the support system for Junior and Axiom, running the estate in Hunters Creek where Jackie grew up, playing hostess to tycoons and politicians and Arab sheiks alike with grace and style. There was no invitation in Houston more prestigious than those engraved cards sent out prior to a James soirée. Yet, though the food and decorations were often continental or exotic, the atmosphere at the James estate was always relaxed and Texas-drawl paced. The former were Florence's responsibility; the latter grew out of Junior's personality. She was the perfect backup to his corporate stardom.

Backlash

Now there was no one for Florence to support. Would she keep the large Tudor house with the roster of cooks, gardeners and maids that were required to maintain it? There would be no rush to answer that question. She could afford to maintain the house as long as she was physically able or interested in doing so.

Jackie looked at Wayne and Benny, sitting across from her in the helicopter. She was glad they could sleep. She looked out the small window beside her at the first orange glow of the sun rising from the dark Gulf water and yawned.

After the funeral, Jackie had experienced a couple of the stages of grief, first angrily questioning God's wisdom for taking her father from her, feeling guilty for questioning God, and then falling into despair and paralysis. But she could not remain there, because it had been only a week ago tomorrow that Wayne had appeared again, this time to startle her out of her mood as she sat motionless on a concrete bench beside her backyard pool.

After some awkward small talk during which Jackie was sure she had insulted him with her petulance, Wayne sat down on the bench beside her.

"Well, I know this is not a good time," Wayne had begun, "but are you going to go up for CEO?"

"Oh, come on, Wayne," she had replied. "Daddy hasn't even been buried a week. I don't want to have to think about that yet."

"I didn't want to have to tell you, but the board is meeting this afternoon."

"To pick a CEO? Already!?"

"I'm afraid so."

"Why didn't they tell me?"

"They'll probably say it was to spare your feelings during this time of personal loss."

"Bull! I've lived in Texas all my life! I know horse hockey when I smell it!"

Wayne had smiled, apparently seeing the fire come back into her dark eyes. "I rather thought you might."

She had crashed the board meeting on the twentieth floor of the black glass tower with Wayne and Gina, her administrative assistant in tow, thinking it would make more of an impression if she had an entourage. She was not a member of the board, but had proceeded to bully Chairman Bud Eldridge into putting off the vote until Friday — *was that just day before yesterday?* — so all qualified candidates could be considered. It was obvious to everyone who had been present that the Chairman wanted the CEO job for himself.

Though her grandfather, a real old-fashioned wildcatter, had founded Axiom in the 1920s and her father had grown the company into a fuel-marketing powerhouse, the company had gone public back in the sixties, so Jackie wasn't guaranteed the Chief Executive job. In fact, she might not have been able to stop the board from voting that day if it hadn't been for one of the members.

White-haired Tom Davis was a wheel in the Texas hospitality industry, owning a chain of medium priced hotels. His signature white suit and black string tie made him look uncannily like Colonel Sanders. It was his insistence that convinced the board to put off the vote.

"But this is not a mom-and-pop operation anymore. There are international problems today," Eldridge had growled at Davis. Thomas "Bud" Eldridge's girth barely fit between the leather-covered mahogany arms of the high-backed chair at the end of the mammoth conference table in the Axiom boardroom. He had known most of the board members for 30 years.

"I've got an MBA from Harvard, Bud," Jackie retorted, "and I've been to every field operation this company has."

"But Axiom is a public company now, not a family business," Eldridge insisted. "There are stockholders to deal with."

"Yes, and an awful lot of them are our employees; employees I've met working my way up the ladder. How many voting stockholders do you know, Bud?"

"I know the big ones."

"Well, don't forget, when the time comes for the stockholders to elect this board in a few months, my mother and I are the biggest of all!"

CHAPTER TWO

In the end, Bud had relented. He knew that Jackie was well liked by the board members and at a time like this she would probably have their sympathies even more than usual. A special meeting had been set for the next Friday to entertain nominations for CEO.

On the fateful day — just day-before-yesterday — Jackie had arrived in the boardroom early, accompanied as always by Wayne, who could do nothing to help her, except be there and watch the voting with acid dripping into his concave stomach.

She had worn a gleaming white suit with a splashy, multi-color scarf, because it would contrast with the dull blue and gray pin stripes of the men who would cast their votes, and because it deepened the natural richness of her bronze complexion, a reminder of the Native American blood in her heritage. To keep from getting a case of the nerves, she had wandered over to the life-size portrait of her grandfather. Donald "Jake" James, a two-fisted Texas wildcatter who built

Backlash

Axiom from nothing in the 1920s, stood tall in front of a Model
T Ford pickup with a black gusher in the background, spraying
through a wooden derrick. A rough wooden sign proudly
proclaimed "James Oil Company", as Axiom was originally
known. A stub of a stogie peeked out from under a salt-and-
pepper handlebar moustache and a wide-brimmed cowboy hat
was cocked to one side of his erect head. One thumb was
hooked in the pocket of his denim overalls and his shirtless,
broad shoulders and labor-hardened biceps completed the
near-mythic image. Jackie barely remembered him as a weak,
stooped, whitehaired man with a rasping voice, but that was a
long time ago and it was the portrait that now survived in her
imagination.

Next to Jake's painting was a smaller portrait of her father.
She choked a bit as she looked at him, looking much as he did
when he used to take her in his arms and lift her to his
shoulders. The heavy, black-rimmed glasses dated the painting
and brought back fond memories of childhood and Christmases
caught on grainy super-8 film.

Where Jake had been rough and ready, Junior was careful.
While Jake was unschooled, Junior was Harvard MBA. Junior
could never have started Axiom Oil, but Jake could not have
run it successfully after its 30th year. Junior helmed the
company through going public, mergers and acquisitions until
it became an international player and the number one gasoline
and diesel fuel retailer in the US, plus retail operations in
Europe and South America. *How fortunate that their
personalities matched the normal business growth arc*, Jackie
thought, a jumble of fragmented memories parading through
her mind.

The board members began coming in and finding seats at
the huge conference table after their 20-story elevator ride from

the lobby. *If there is an old-boy network, this is it,* Jackie had thought. She hoped that there weren't too many of them who still saw her as she appeared in an Axiom newsletter 30 years earlier, mounted on a Shetland pony, dressed in cowboy boots and a fringed buckskin vest, with pigtails coming out of the cowboy hat cocked to one side of her head. She had later graduated to Steeplechase competition and Polo, which had been useful at Harvard.

There were no women seated at the table, but Mrs. Doris Maxwell, the 40-something administrative assistant to the late Junior James, had recorded the meeting on a steno pad from a wingback chair next to a floor lamp over against the paneled wall.

Claude Bowman, interim secretary of the Board since the death of Jackie's father, was chairing the meeting since Bud was a nominee. In fact, Claude had nominated Bud. Seven others had been nominated including Jackie's boss, Axiom President Benjamin Tyson.

Then Tom Davis received permission to speak. "There's at least one more name that we need to include in this list. We still have an heir to the James legacy. If you know anything about Jacqueline James, you know that this business is in her blood and I submit that she's ready to take up where her father left off. She has prepared all her life, coming up through the ranks. She's got the education and the experience. And I believe she's got her grandfather's spirit." Davis looked over at Jackie and smiled. "And so, it's my privilege to nominate Jackie to serve as CEO." Davis then led the polite applause that some, but not all, participated in. Jackie remembered the moment poignantly.

After a tense half hour of voting, Jackie had gone from fourth out of nine nominees through successive votes to be in a two-person race against Board Chairman Bud Eldridge. It seemed that with each vote, the loser's votes went to Jackie and so she had survived.

Jackie had prayed all week looking forward to this meeting that God's will would be done, but now she just wanted the vote to go her way. It might be wrong, but she very much wanted this job.

The folded slips of paper were once again passed to the head of the table and counted. Bowman and Mrs. Maxwell finished counting and then, after whispering something to each other, went through the process again.

Jackie had looked over at Wayne, who was practically catatonic his nerves were so taut. If she hadn't been so nervous herself, she would have laughed at him.

Finally, they had finished the second count and Bowman stood. "Well, gentlemen. This vote demonstrates how great a field we had from within the company. Benny Tyson, our president, was in first place on the first vote. On the next vote Benny and Bud tied for that spot. Then Bud had the lead. And on the final vote, the one that counts, the vote was ten to nine in favor of Jackie James!"

Jackie had been dazed as Wayne lifted her to her feet, giving her a big hug. When the meeting ended, the board members, one by one, had walked over to congratulate her. Benny Tyson was one of the last.

"Jackie, congratulations," he said as he hugged her. "I know you'll do fine."

"I'm sorry Benny. You would've done a great job."

"Oh, don't be sorry. I'll still be around. We'll just switch roles for a while."

"I'm really going to need your help," she said, desperately trying not to cry.

"Absolutely. Count on it," Tyson had said sincerely as he walked away.

Then Bud was there to congratulate her. She hadn't thought how she would handle this moment.

"Well, little lady," Bud looked unsure of what to say for once. "Your daddy would be proud."

"Thank you, Bud. I hope so."

"I know so. Now, we're all in this together, so you just come to Uncle Bud anytime you need anything, you hear?"

"Yes. Yes, I will," she replied, ignoring his condescension. She knew he couldn't help it. Bud had left the room with his head down.

Finally, there was Tom Davis looking at her from several feet away, smiling and leaning on his cane. Jackie didn't wait for him to come to her. She ran and threw her arms around him.

"Oh, thank you, Mr. Davis. Thank you so much for having faith in me!"

"Well, it's not hard. I do see your grandfather's fire in your eyes. You've got a tough row to hoe now, I hope you know."

"Yes."

"But there're a lot of good people around you. Depend on their counsel and you'll do fine."

The kind old man had made his way out of the large conference room, leaving Jackie and Wayne alone. Only then did she let herself cry, and Wayne had been there to take her in his arms.

Jackie began to cry again, remembering. She was glad Benny and Wayne were asleep across from her, strapped into their seats.

* * *

Backlash

At the small airport in Kenner, Louisiana, a Beechcraft Bonanza was being prepared for takeoff in the pink light of morning. Pilot Arthur Beaudreaux would soon head out over the Gulf of Mexico for the second time in two weeks. This time he was carrying a reporter and cameraman who said they were stringers for CNN. *Maybe they are and maybe they aren't*, Arthur thought. They didn't look like anything special, although the video camera was definitely professional. *Maybe they are who they say*, Arthur thought as he glanced at them sipping their coffee and waiting. It seemed a little odd that they had paid with cash.

Beaudreaux had been carrying charter passengers in single-engine airplanes from his base in Kenner, Louisiana since being mustered out of the Air Force in 1973. Usually he ferried businessmen from New Orleans to Shreveport or Jackson and sometimes just up the road to Baton Rouge. Occasionally, well-heeled tourists would hire him to circle the French Quarter for bird's eye views that they would capture on video that would probably never be watched.

Once they were airborne, it would take less than an hour to get to their destination, but it would be a while before he had the plane fueled and checked out for the trip.

* * *

"We're about there, Ms. James."

Jackie started at the announcement of the pilot over the intercom, only then learning she had been asleep. Out the window Jackie could see water turned golden by the rising sun and the billowing smoke of the damaged oil platform silhouetted against the rose-colored sky. Because Jackie had visited this very platform just two weeks before, she regarded the smoke as a personal affront. Wayne and Benny stirred and roused as the pilot took them around the platform in a wide arc for a quick look from the air before descending to the heliport displaying the large gold-on-black Axiom logo.

Jackie looked down and saw Mannie Kowalski running toward the helipad. He had been her foreman as she had worked alongside the roustabouts for a few days in her role as VP of Operations. She believed in the value of every job in the company her grandfather founded and had demonstrated it by regularly spending time in the field.

Jackie was the first out of the hatch of the gleaming black bird, making a beeline for the foreman.

"Mannie, what happened? Is everyone all right?" she shouted over the noise of the still-spinning rotors. "We had a couple of guys bump their heads when the charges went off, but the explosives were right on the water line."

"Explosives? This was intentional?"

"Looks that way."

"I thought it was an accident."

"We assumed that at first, but I've got something to show you."

"We need to call the Coast Guard."

"I just did that, once I was sure it was foul play. They said they'd be here directly."

They hurried away from the noise and wind of the helipad, Jackie following Mannie below where some men readied a small motorboat. It was the equivalent of five stories down to the boat dock.

"So, they didn't do any real damage?" Jackie wanted to know as they boarded the boat.

"You'll see."

"Well, I'm just glad you guys are all right," Jackie said to Mannie.

Backlash

"We'll be back in production before you know it," Mannie asserted. "We pulled some men to do stop-gap repairs until the damage assessment crew can get here, but we won't miss a lick. It'll take more than this to stop us."

"Mannie, let's be sure this rig is safe before you go back into production." Jackie cautioned. "We have no serious injuries as a result of this thing. Let's keep it that way."

Benny and Wayne caught up with them just before they shoved off. The dawn was lighting everything with a blanket of pink haze now and the smoke was still billowing from the side of the massive platform, though not as bad as it had been, Mannie assured Jackie.

As one of Mannie's men started the Mercury outboard, Jackie considered his assertion that the explosions had been purposeful. Who would do such a thing, and why? She looked at Benny, who was gripping the side of the boat as it bounced on the waves close to the side of the platform. He had worked in management at a refinery before being kicked upstairs to corporate. *This might be his first time to an offshore rig*, Jackie thought.

The boat rounded the corner and the passengers could see a series of twisted, blackened cylinders; what was left of the metal supports, with the obvious concentration of the blasts barely six feet above the water line. The three main supports had little real damage. They were about three feet in diameter and the explosives had blown away a hole in each of them, but they still seemed to be doing their jobs. The secondary bracing was another matter, though. There were cross beams, pipes about eight inches in diameter, plus diagonal I-beams, all welded to the main supports. These had all been severed where the charges had been attached to them.

Benny took a tiny digital video camera out of his bag and Wayne simultaneously extracted a small digital still camera from his pocket. They both began recording the damage.

They floated by in silence, looking at the destruction. It was obvious to the most casual observer that this was no accident. There was evidence of multiple explosions, on each of the supports, all along that one side of the platform. They were all about the same height and apparent force. There were no mechanical features of the rig at this level that would have malfunctioned and exploded. What they saw next made Jackie's blood run cold.

"There," Mannie said, "What do you think of that?"

Jackie's mouth fell open as the boat drew close to the main support at the middle of the north side of the platform. Below the damaged area was a message in yellow spray paint that said, "We're Watching You."

* * *

"When we get there, fly around so we can shoot out the right side of the plane, please."

"Right," Arthur said, knowing what to do. He would bank the plane to starboard and let them get a good look as he flew around the platform. He would buzz it from barely 300 feet. Usually TV people preferred helicopters for this kind of thing, but Arthur would demonstrate that fixed wing aircraft could do the job. His experience flying wild-weasel F-1s out of Saigon had to be good for something. Arthur would give them all the time they needed.

It was taking longer than he expected to find it. Some sort of explosion on an oil platform, the reporter had said. There was no shortage of them in the Gulf.

Backlash

Suddenly he thought about the two odd ducks he had brought out two weeks ago. This platform even looked a little like the one they wanted to see, though then his passengers had insisted he stay at 10,000 feet, so it was hard to tell.

Two weeks ago, two very serious men had been sitting in the comfortable aft seats of his six-seat airplane, whispering excitedly above the oil platform, looking down through high-powered binoculars. There were other platforms within sight and they noticed them as well, but they seemed more interested in this one.

"Can you go around again? We'd like another look at it," the tall one had said — "Paul" was it? — after having ignored the pilot for a half hour.

"Sure. No problem." *It's your nickel*, he had thought. Looking back, he remembered seeing the short one writing in a notebook. They were an odd pairing. The tall one was dressed all in flannel and denim, looking like a lumberjack with his bushy beard that had gone out of style in the 70s. Oh! And canvas sneakers and belt.

When boarding the plane, he had briefly noticed that Paul wasn't wearing any leather. The short one, though also dressed casually, was much sharper. His haircut and the mousse he was wearing probably cost as much as Paul's entire outfit and he was looking at a hand-held GPS unit. He was the one who paid for the trip and was obviously in charge, though he had been even quieter than Paul.

Beaudreaux would never put the two men together on the street, but they had huddled together and spoken in hushed whispers like old friends. They had been a couple of odd ducks indeed, speaking to Arthur only to convey short requests. What could be so interesting about an offshore oilrig? Arthur had wondered. They hadn't looked like oil company people. And they had paid with cash, too.

"Is that it?" Arthur Beaudreau asked the men in the aft seats, as he spotted a plume of smoke on the horizon.

"Yes, it must be," answered the one who said he was a reporter.

* * *

Jackie and the others were back on the deck of the rig when the Coast Guard cutter arrived, sounding its loud horn. It pulled up within 50 yards of the damaged oil platform and the skipper used a bullhorn to ask if there was any injured.

"I'm the foreman. Only our pride is hurt!" Mannie answered with his own bullhorn. "Come aboard, gentlemen. We've got our CEO here." Even at this distance, Jackie could see the Captain's head jerk in surprise at that.

"Aye, sir. Coming aboard." And the brilliant white boat slid around to the boat dock. *The word "sleek" must have been coined for a boat like that*, Jackie thought. It was a beauty, and probably fast too.

Once aboard and with introductions out of the way, the Coast Guard officers began questioning Mannie and other men who had been working when the explosion happened. Jackie, Wayne and Benny stood listening to every detail, no matter how minor.

Captain William Hoelzer had grown up in the "Land of 10,000 Lakes", forever in a boat, he said, by way of introduction. Now he commanded a grand boat on a grand "lake", indeed. "Did you have any warning that something like this might happen?" Hoelzer asked Mannie.

"None whatsoever."

"What about you?" Hoelzer turned to Jackie. "Any indicators come in to headquarters?"

"Not at all," she answered. The Captain was as striking as his boat, in his impossibly white uniform. Jackie had to admit, what they said about a man in uniform was true. She was glad her attention was diverted up to the helipad where some of the Coast Guard men were drooling over the Axiom jet ranger.

Suddenly there was a garbled warning on the bullhorn from the cutter. A loud metal-on-metal sound followed. The group Jackie was with looked up, not having enough information to know what to do, but sensing urgency. Then they saw it. The large crane that was used to lift and assemble the drilling equipment was groaning and leaning. Then it was falling. There was no time. Mannie managed a quick warning.

"Look out! The crane...!"

But the crane was already crashing to the deck. Jackie and the others with her were not in danger, but it was terrifying anyway. Men who had been cleaning up after the explosion scurried to this side or that.

When the crane struck the deck, splintered timbers and sheet metal screamed through the air like so many missiles. A tool shed was turned to kindling and the top of a stairway was demolished. Flooring was punctured and left a-shambles. A cloud of dust rose up and obscured the impact for a moment of total confusion. Jackie's ears were ringing from the sound of the crash. She discovered that she was lying on the deck, not knowing if she had ducked, been pushed down or knocked down by the jolt when the crane struck the deck. Raising her head, it occurred to her that the yellow hard hat she was wearing would have done precious little if she had been in the path of the crane. She sat up and looked around, brushing grit from her clothing.

Seeing men running in the direction of the derrick, she looked and saw that the derrick was still standing, but that the crane had struck it and it was now leaning out over the water at a slight angle. Another moment and the huge derrick shuddered and groaned a deafening metallic roar as its weight slowly shifted outward. Rivets began to pop and fly from the girders like so many bullets fired from a rotating automatic rifle, causing men nearby to hit the deck again. Finally, the derrick was at a forty-five-degree angle and could no longer stand the strain. Pipes, bracing and girders all snapped like dry sticks and fell in a cloud of dust into the water below.

The shocked onlookers just stared for several seconds at the empty sky where the derrick had been before anyone moved. Jackie could scarcely believe what she had just seen. She had been relieved to learn that the damage and injury had not been worse when she arrived, but now a new assessment would be necessary. Benny helped her up and they began walking with everyone else toward the damage.

A row of buildings that housed rig equipment had been leveled by the crane. When they arrived at what was left of the equipment buildings, they saw a mass of twisted sheet metal, wood framing and equipment, all looking like they had been broken up and tossed like a salad.

Several men had been bloodied by flying debris but Mannie's quick assessment caused him to sigh in relief that there were no broken bones, only minor cuts and bruises. Then he heard the cry.

"Mannie!" a rig hand shouted. "Juan's hurt!"

Jackie saw him then. A man in a blue jumpsuit and useless yellow hardhat lay crushed under the crane, his body stained with a widening circle of blood. The man who found him reached through the crane and felt Juan's wrist, then looked up and shook his head.

"This just became a murder investigation," Captain Hoelzer muttered. Jackie looked up, thinking she heard the engine of a small plane, but could see nothing through the smoke.

"Better come look at this!" a roust-a-bout called from the edge of the deck where the derrick had been.

Walking carefully the few feet to the damaged edge of the platform, Jackie saw the mangled remains of the derrick and associated pipes, hanging from the edge of the platform. This was a disaster, but then she saw the real problem the rig hand had been talking about.

Through the smoke and haze Jackie saw an area of the water under the platform beginning to darken. No one had to ask what it was.

Oil spill.

CHAPTER THREE

A few minutes after the fateful crane collapse and subsequent derrick destruction and oil spill, Jackie and the others again boarded the motorboat and examined the damaged supports of the platform more closely. There they saw that one of the intermediate supports severed by the explosives was directly under the crane. The base of the crane had apparently weakened with time until its weight had brought it down.

The death of an Axiom employee certainly put a different light on things. Jackie knew that it had happened before, of course. When thousands of people are employed drilling below the ocean, transporting thousands of gallons of volatile fuel across the country, and handling natural gas, there were bound to be accidents occasionally; even fatal ones, unfortunately.

The law of averages was like that.

Several people had been killed in the explosion that caused what became known as the "BP oil spill", although it was always considered an accident.

But to have an employee killed in a terrorist attack! That was unthinkable. What was the world coming to, Jackie asked herself? Who would have done this and was the death of her employee part of their intention?

And the potential problems of the oil spill wouldn't be known until an assessment could be made and a special team could be brought in to try to stop it.

"Mannie, this platform is out of business as of right now!" Jackie said when they had all gathered back on the platform. "Captain, can you take these men to port?"

Hoelzer did a quick head count. "It's only about 60 miles to Louisiana. No need for quarters. We'll just get them out of harm's way. Sure. Let's get the body taken care of first."

"I'll notify the family when we get to port," Mannie said solemnly.

"Thanks," Jackie tried but failed to smile at her friend.

"Let's jack this crane up, then everybody get your gear together," Mannie called out to his men. "We're getting off this barge!"

* * *

Back on the ground in Louisiana, the men who had said they were stringers for CNN went a few miles from the small airport and parked. The one who manned the camera ejected a small flash memory card from the camera and inserted it into a laptop. Within seconds the file was on the computer and in another few minutes the man had uploaded the video file to a server in Virginia.

Next, he sent an email that simply said "Done" and closed the laptop. The other man started the car and turned it toward the ramp onto Interstate 10 past New Orleans and toward Gulfport. The two men knew that the file would be retrieved by the man who hired them and sent anonymously to CNN's Washington D.C. bureau, "over the transom" as it was called, but even without attribution, they knew their footage would be irresistible to the on-air talent and editors eager to beat their competition to the punch.

* * *

For once, Patrick Garrity was early for the Sunday afternoon editorial board meeting. At 40, Patrick was relatively young to be political editor for the Washington Herald, must reading for all those involved in government in the Nation's capital. He tossed his head to one side, returning an unruly, red forelock to its place. Patrick was as Irish as his name, and as Catholic as the nuns at St. Ignatius Catholic School could make him, but that wasn't saying much. Hard work was his religion now, and he had worn out several pairs of shoes on the US Capitol beat.

An even dozen editors and senior reporters sat around the conference table in the too-small room. The scarred imitation-wood tabletop was decorated with rings from countless Styrofoam coffee cups and now-missing ashtrays, casualties of political correctness. Each of the journalists was absorbed in preparations for the meeting, some on cell phones, talking or texting, others reviewing notes or wire service printouts, so Patrick simply nodded "hello" to them as he slipped into an imitation leather chair with chrome arms.

Patrick looked up when Howard Finkel bumped the doorknob with his ample hip for the ten thousandth time as he breezed into the crowded room, his destination the chair at the head of the table. He carried a fat, dog-eared file folder, along with copies of yesterday's and today's Washington Herald, for which he was Managing Editor. Each of the people at the table had a laptop computer, a smart phone with email, and/or a reporter's notebook or newspaper clippings in their own manila folders.

On a nondescript credenza, a 20-inch television was tuned to the Fox News Channel, to which the assembled group was giving varying levels of attention. One of an endless parade of anchors droned dispassionately from a cherry and brushed-aluminum desk.

The TV suddenly went mute by the remote control in Finkel's hand. "Well, people. I know you've heard Axiom Oil has a new CEO. Shelby, I'll know not to pay any attention to your market forecasts from now on."

"I still can't believe it," Shelby Golden shook his head with its abundant white mane. He was Business Editor and the only one at the table in a suit coat.

Patrick remembered that Golden had been adamant that the company wouldn't replace the late Donald James with his daughter.

"I can't believe I skunked you!" taunted Marcia Colter, the Society Editor, a 50ish woman continually fighting her waistline and with makeup and hair that failed in the attempt to appear younger than she was. She had argued with Golden that Jackie was the potential heir to her father's job, even though Axiom was a public company. Patrick smiled at her, silently sharing her satisfaction at puncturing Golden's pomposity.

"Should be interesting to see the politicians line up at the trough now that they know who to talk to," Patrick put in, referring to Axiom's record as a contributor to political campaigns through the years.

"Goldie, you've got the duty on this story," Finkel continued. "I assume there's background data on the new skipper at Axiom?"

"Yeah, plenty."

"And Patrick, I want you to find out about her politics. Where does she stand on green issues, taxes, labor, etc.? Marcia, give me the women's angle. How feminine is she? How does she live?"

"Right, boss," the Society Editor responded.

"What about me?" Science and Environment Editor John Watson interrupted.

"What about you?" Finkel didn't look up from his scrawled agenda. "I don't see a science angle."

"Science and ENVIRONMENT," Watson corrected him. "It's an OIL company."

Patrick smiled inwardly, watching a hot redness creep up Watson's face past his glasses toward the top of his balding head as he realized too late that he had walked up to the line of insulting his boss' intelligence. He didn't dare apologize though, lest Finkel hadn't caught it.

"The politics of the new CEO isn't 'Environment' as far as I'm concerned. Garrity gets it," Finkel's index finger returned his reading glasses to the top of his nose for the hundredth time today, ignoring the slight. "So, what's next?"

"I just can't believe it," Golden mumbled.

"Believe it, Mr. Businessman," Finkel teased. "The glass ceiling just got a great big hole punched in it, even if she is the old man's daughter."

* * *

After the editorial board meeting ended, Patrick decided he would go to The Hill, as the United States Capitol complex was called, to check with several of his contacts in Congress about the progress of their reelection campaigns. It was a presidential election year and several primaries had already been held, so things were beginning to shape up and many of the legislators and their staffs would be in their offices even though it was Sunday. He also would ask about the election of Jacqueline James as CEO of Axiom Oil, which only mattered to him because a lot of Axiom money usually found its way to Washington during an election year. The death of "Junior" James had jeopardized that and the Inside-the-Beltway class were more interested in his replacement than the average Joe in Hoboken.

First going to a congressional office building, he appeared unannounced in the office of Congressman Carl Kellerman, Republican of Colorado.

"Hi, Paula," Patrick smiled at the receptionist. He enjoyed visiting Congressman Kellerman's office, because it gave him an excuse to see Paula. He didn't know if her honey blond hair was natural or not, but it didn't really matter. Just seeing her always improved his day. Not that she would be glad to see him, but she was very nice to look at even if she did treat him like a piece of furniture.

"Mr. Kellerman isn't available today," Paula Cole wasn't smiling back. "Sorry."

"Well, I just wanted to find out how the campaign is going and get his reaction to the election of Jacqueline James as CEO of Axiom Oil."

"That's not in Colorado, is it?"

"They've got service stations there," Patrick's smile was frozen on his face now. Just then, Kellerman appeared, ushering someone out of his office. *Probably a constituent*, Patrick thought.

"Congressman!" Patrick called out.

"Don't have time," Kellerman said with a wave of his hand.

"Just wanted your reaction to Jacqueline James' election at Axiom."

That stopped Kellerman. Axiom had a large storage and distribution facility in Kellerman's district, Patrick had learned. Kellerman put a pudgy finger to his chin.

"Don't really have an opinion," Kellerman said, shaking his head. Patrick wasn't sure if he didn't have an opinion or wasn't sure yet what opinion he should have. As a member of the House of Representatives, he had to face election every two years and so was in perpetual campaign mode. If he had expressed an opinion, it may have been as phony as the congressman's still-dark hair.

"What's it mean?"

"America has lost a great capitalist — uh, make that philanthropist — in Donald James," he began. Both statements were correct, but the second was more politically correct, Patrick realized.

"The election of his daughter to replace him continues a great tradition in a great company and represents an advance for women in America," Kellerman continued, as if constructing a sound bite on the fly.

"Any repercussions for the economy?"

"Probably not. It's a good company. But I'm the wrong person to ask."

"What about corporate contributions with the election coming?"

"Gotta go, Mr. Garrity."

He was gone with another wave of his hand, but Patrick had some quotes he could record into his electronic reporter's notebook after he said goodbye to Paula.

Patrick asked around at several other offices, but didn't get much, and so he decided to go to the Capitol to see who was in the halls.

The first person he encountered was Senator Nathan Taylor, a Democrat from Vermont. Taylor was a classic politician: taller than Patrick, and as slender as a 20-year-old, with a mane of flowing, silver hair cut close below the ears but full on top, as was popular 50 years ago. Too old to be promoted to president, Taylor nevertheless carried himself as if conscious of the power at his disposal as a ranking member of several committees and virtually certain to win a fifth term in November.

"Senator, what is your reaction to the election of Jacqueline James at Axiom Oil?" Patrick asked.

"Who?" replied Taylor, apparently feigning forgetfulness.

"Jacqueline James, new CEO of Axiom Oil."

"Oh yes."

"Any thoughts on the future of the company or the industry as a result?"

"Not really."

Patrick could see the wheels turning in the still very alert brain under all the white hair.

"My hope is the oil industry won't be needed in a few years."

The statement would have struck him as odd if Patrick hadn't known Taylor's record of supporting stringent environmental regulation on the oil and automobile industries and support of Federal spending on research into alternative fuels.

"How will Donald James' death and the succession of his daughter affect the move to alternative fuels?" Patrick asked, still needing something about Jacqueline James before the deadline. "Some good may come even out of this tragedy," Taylor answered cryptically as he turned and walked away.

Tragedy? Patrick thought, as Senator Taylor walked away. He was a bit surprised that Taylor would describe the oil baron's death as a tragedy.

Patrick soon found himself passing the press room on the Senate side of the Capitol, so he stopped in to get a cup of coffee. He said hello to a couple of colleagues from one of the TV networks and went directly to the coffee machine. The coffee was probably already stale, but it would be strong.

In the background, a CNN anchor read the news on one of several TVs on the wall. Patrick barely looked up from his coffee when the familiar musical sound announced a special news bulletin. Garrity was jaded enough to know that breaking news announcements were made about once every couple of hours on the 24-hour news networks whether there was real news or not. But then he heard the news anchor say a word that grabbed his attention.

"... Axiom oil platform experienced some type of explosion or fire this morning. As can be seen from this amateur video just coming in to us, there was extensive damage and possibly an oil spill. We will be updating you as we..."

"Not again!" Patrick heard someone say, and then realized it had been himself. He and the others in the room stood transfixed looking at the shaky images of smoke billowing from a raging fire in the early morning. Suddenly, as they watched, the crane collapsed and pulled down the platform's derrick, which fell into the Gulf waters. After an edit, the video shot changed to show oil beginning to spill from under the platform.

The network TV reporter and his photographer were suddenly both on their cell phones with their bureau. Patrick took his own cell phone in hand and punched the speed dial number for his office. As the phone began to ring, Patrick thought again about Senator Taylor saying, "some good may come out of this tragedy."

* * *

John Watson returned to his office on the outer wall of the Washington Herald building after a conference with another reporter. Like the rest of the editorial offices, it was too small to have much style, but he had put up some pictures: classic Ansel Adams mostly. The stunning black and white images of Yosemite were a pleasing contrast to the yellowing newspaper clippings that dominated the walls of most of the other offices. The pictures served as a fitting reminder of his concern for all things natural and silently underscored his position as Science and Environment Editor.

Watson, dressed as usual in a cotton shirt and canvas loafers, sat down at his computer to check his email. The senior editors didn't come in on Saturday, so he hadn't checked his mailbox since late Friday. Scrolling down through a long list of new messages, John froze when he saw a message from "Mongoose." He looked up to make sure no one had come into his office, then clicked to open the message.

"Those who destroy the earth will be destroyed," the cryptic message began. "Those who build monstrous monuments to consumerism will be brought to their knees. All life is threatened when the seas are polluted. Action will be taken to end America's lust for oil."

Watson looked up nervously, but there was no one around. He saved the message to his hard drive, then deleted it from his mailbox without printing it.

* * *

On the flight back to Houston, after a long day of helping the men secure the platform so they could evacuate, Jackie felt out Benny Tyson about the attack.

"Ever see anything like this?"

"Heck, no! We had some protests a couple of times." Benny had earned his stripes knee-deep in crude in an entry-level job at a large refinery outside Cleveland, Ohio. After business school, he went back to work in the office. He often said his blood was black he loved the oil business so much. "There's some Eco-terrorists out there. This fits their M-O," Benny mused.

"Do you think they meant to hurt our people?" Wayne asked.

"I think they just wanted to send a message," Benny said.

"But if it was the eco-guys," Wayne pondered, "Why would they do something to cause a spill?"

"Good question. Maybe they didn't mean for that to happen." Jackie replied. "Did you call the spill team, Benny?"

"Yeah, the pilot put me through. They'll be out there by the time we get back to HQ. Legal and Insurance will need to be brought in, of course."

"Yeah, I already called Marcus. And there's the PR angle to worry about."

The oil companies had learned many lessons about both containing oil spills and containing bad press after what was known as the "BP oil spill." The Deep Water Horizon spill was an accident, but the press coverage had been brutal. Jackie hoped the public's attitude would be different since they were obviously attacked and this oil spill would not likely be as serious.

The three Axiom executives gradually fell silent and the men dozed, but Jackie stayed awake. She wasn't eager to have to deal with the press on something like this incident. It would certainly be pounced on by some in the media, coming as it did immediately on the heels of her election as CEO. Probably even some people within the company would be eager to see her mess up on something so sensitive. She wondered if it was even possible to keep a lid on it. Hopefully, the top brass at the company knew enough to keep their cards close to the vest. She hadn't wanted to be dealing with things like this right now.

* * *

Later that evening, Patrick arrived home after pounding out the sidebar about the James family and Axiom's political relationships that would accompany Shelby Golden's business section article, even though the news of the oil platform explosion was eclipsing and absorbing the news about the election of Donald James' daughter to replace him, but that was someone else's beat. He parked his six-year-old Nissan Maxima in its usual spot outside his apartment. It was 8:30, neither earlier nor later than he usually arrived home. He had eaten a hearty meat-and-potatoes dinner at the Blue Ribbon Grill, where he was a regular. Often, he met sources there to draw out some key piece of information for a story he was working on.

He turned his key in the cheap, brass lock and went in. Patrick's apartment was a basic two-bedroom, mass-produced flat. There was nothing to distinguish it. The off-white walls were exactly what had been there when he moved in seven years ago and remained virtually bare. The furniture gave no clue as to a plan or direction in style. Patrick himself laughingly thought of his decor as "early garage sale." Since his divorce, much of his money went for alimony and child support, and since he was faithful about sending the checks, he didn't have money for new furniture.

He did have a collection of books, though, nearly covering one wall of the living room in a bookcase that also housed his TV, DVR and basic stereo system. The books were mostly history and biography, and an assortment of vanity books by politicians and journalists, with some political novels thrown in. The remote for the cable-TV box had CNN, Fox News, C-SPAN and the History Channel programmed as favorite channels.

In addition to books and electronics, the shelves featured pictures of his children in simple plastic frames, enlarged to eight-by-ten in the Washington Herald darkroom or, more recently, retrieved from emails and output by the paper's high-end color laser printer. The two girls in the pictures, captured at several different ages, had his freckles and naturally red hair, though Sally, the younger one, was fairer and could have been blond. Both Sally and Elizabeth had blue eyes the color of a mountain lake and just as deep. They had smiled brightly for the camera, but Patrick was always saddened when he looked at them. They were far away from him, in more ways than one. Though Patrick had pictures of their mother, they were not framed or on display.

He picked up the remote control and snapped on the TV, which was already tuned to CNN's Headline News. The first thing he saw was the footage of the smoking oil platform, followed by Donald James Jr.'s funeral in Houston from last week. He watched for a few seconds and the coverage transitioned into the election of Jacqueline James to succeed her father, then returned to the coverage of the oil platform.

"So that's the daughter," he said aloud, as he saw file footage of Jacqueline James. He had seen stills of her from the newspaper's files as he was writing the article. He couldn't tell much about her from the funeral video.

Later in the report they showed file footage of Junior James and his daughter Jacqueline, together at the opening of some service station several years ago. She seemed like a bit of a tomboy, he decided. He fired the remote again and settled down to watch what was left of a documentary about Dunkirk on the History Channel.

* * *

The helicopter set down at the Axiom corporate campus in Houston about nine p.m. Central time and Jackie went directly to her office. She would make an eyewitness report about the incident on the platform and e-mail it to those who needed to know immediately. The company's top brass had company-paid smart phones that ensured they could be reached by voice, text or email at any time or place. A formal report would come later.

Right now, Jackie said goodnight to Wayne, who was carrying an armload of documents from the offshore rig to his office. There he would transfer the pictures he shot from the camera to his computer, ready to be shared with the company's public relations department or the wide world if the Press came calling.

Benny also said goodnight and headed for the parking garage, promising to arrive early tomorrow.

Then his video footage would go to the corporate television studio for copying and archiving for the requests from law enforcement and the media that would certainly come.

What day was it? Oh, yes. Sunday, Jackie remembered. Tomorrow would be her first full official day as CEO. It was a running joke among laborers that Monday was the worst day of the work week, but for Jackie this would be the third black Monday in a row: two weeks ago she woke up the day after her father died. Last Monday, the board met without telling her and might have elected Bud CEO, and tomorrow she would start her new job having to deal with this latest nightmare. She would head for home as soon as possible. She had been up since two a.m. and adrenaline wouldn't keep her going much longer.

CHAPTER FOUR

By 10:00 p.m. Sunday night, Paul Stoddard was back in Texas, after driving with his team from Louisiana in two rented vans, which they returned to the rental agency and parted company. As the sun's rays grew longer on the ground and the shadows expanded into darkness, he turned his 1985 Toyota Tercel down the familiar county road outside Baytown to the entrance of his place.

He guided his aging compact between the brick pillars that marked the driveway to the house he had bought 10 years ago. His prospects had been better then; his career full of promise that wouldn't be realized. The driveway had been a ribbon of gleaming black asphalt then, but was now broken into gray cobbles no larger than saucers, with Johnson grass and other assorted weeds having taken over between the worn twin tire tracks. The drive stretched halfway across the five-acre plot and circled in front of the house like a needle's eye.

Paul stopped the coughing Japanese engine in its usual place before the front steps of the once impressive manse. It was built in the 1920s by a farmer who was possessed by grandiose ideas of his potential in agribusiness on the fertile land east of Houston. Its two-story Victorian façade was designed to inspire awe when seen from the road, though it was, all things considered, a relatively humble home. In the 90 years that had followed the construction of the house, the farm had been gradually sold off to developers in multi-acre parcels until these five acres and the house was all that was left.

Paul got out and carried his duffle bag up the steps to the worn wooden porch that was badly in need of paint. He was quickly inside the front door without a single thought for the house's decaying exterior. Fortunately, the maze of low-hanging, Spanish-moss-covered live oak branches, wild vines, and foot-high grass made the house invisible from the little-traveled country road.

Inside, he set his duffle bag down by the door, turned on a light and was welcomed home by four cats and three dogs of varying breeds, all of which he called by name and quickly caressed as he passed through the entry to a room that had been intended as the dining room, but now was stacked with hundreds of books and cardboard boxes, spilling out of bookcases and onto tables and the floor. Magazines going back many years were arranged in stacks with an organization only Paul could discern. Scientific American and National Geographic were the main mass-market periodicals, but there were scores of other titles. Scholarly journals on mathematics that only academics had heard of were mixed with small-circulation physics journals, "Sierra" and publications of other lesser-known environmental organizations. More cats perched on boxes and stacks of miscellaneous clutter, calling out nasal greetings.

"Here Quark. Come Proton, Isosceles, Copernicus," Paul called them each by name and proceeded along the trail of faded carpet that was the only area of the floor not covered by furniture, books, boxes or litter boxes. The odor of multiple litter boxes and dogs' newspapers would have overpowered most people, but Paul was immune to it. On the wall were several certificates in dusty frames, including a diploma from UC Berkeley that awarded the Doctor of Philosophy in Mathematics to one Paul Lucas Stoddard.

He next entered the kitchen, which was inhabited by still more cats and dogs. Trailing behind him now were virtually all of the dogs and cats he had passed on his trip through the house, meowing and whining and looking at him expectantly. He proceeded through the little-used kitchen and into a mudroom that led to the back of the house. There he flipped a switch that gradually flooded the back yard with purplish mercury light.

As he paused, one of the more eager cats reached as high as it could on his faded jeans, begging. He selected a large feed bag from among a dozen others on a high shelf and picked up a razorblade knife, then opened the back door and left it open so all the animals could follow him as he led the way down the back steps. In the backyard, a score of cats and about 12 more dogs waited. They started an impatient racket as soon as he appeared. More than an acre was divided by chain-link fencing into a series of pens and runs, with several rudely built kennels and feeding troughs. Certain large dogs were separated by higher fences from the general population of feline and canine life that numbered above 50. The yard was stripped of all grass and the bare earth was black with decaying fecal matter.

Paul used the razor knife to slash open the bag of dog food and emptied the entire contents into a homemade wooden feeding trough. It was immediately set upon by numerous dogs that greedily began wolfing down the dry food like so many piglets at their mother's teats.

The cats complained loudly and the big dogs in the separate pen barked their low protests as Paul went back to the mudroom to fetch a second bag for the cats. Soon he returned with a bag hoisted on the shoulder of his plaid cotton shirt and, after a quick slash with the box cutter, thirty-something cats were vying for a position at their own feeding trough. Paul returned to the mudroom for yet another bag for the big dogs. He would repeat this ritual again in the morning, as he always did before going to work. Finally, he used a garden hose to refill several water troughs.

Back in the house, he retrieved his duffle where he had dropped it and went up the creaking stairway to his upstairs bedroom. There he set the khaki-colored bag down on the bed and unzipped it. He reached in and removed three items: an envelope stuffed with receipts, a set of plans for an offshore oilrig, and a semi-automatic, 9-millimeter pistol. All three he placed in a drawer of his nightstand. Drawing another canvas duffle bag out of the closet he transferred about half the remaining contents from the first duffle: several thousand dollars in cash, in neatly wrapped bundles. He then closed the two canvas duffle bags and removed a panel in the back of the closet. He inserted the two bags into the hidden space and quickly replaced the panel.

That done, he walked across the hall to a spare bedroom that hadn't had a bed in it for at least six years. Instead, three metal

Backlash

filing cabinets stood shoulder-to-shoulder in one corner and a large bookcase in the opposite corner overflowed with books and magazines on advanced mathematics, nature science and ecology. In the center of the room, a large gray desk was covered in computer equipment and cables. The mousepad featured a faded picture of the space shuttle and the acronym "NASA" in large block letters. A disheveled, four-inch stack of paper, the produce of an inkjet printer, sat precariously on one corner of the desk. The aging CPU, stripped of its cover, had multi-colored wiring running in and out of it and circuit boards lying nearby, as if it was perpetually being upgraded. An old 17-inch CRT monitor came to life when Paul bumped the mouse as he sat down at the keyboard.

With speed born of habit, he opened a new e-mail document and within twenty seconds had written an enigmatic message and sent it to a group he corresponded with regularly.

The timing could hardly have been better, Paul thought, remembering the unexpected death of the wealthy industrialist and the confusion that must have resulted just as his group carried out their statement against the oil rig. Unfortunately, he knew it would take more than an isolated act of economic defiance to bring about real change. "But things are about to change — exponentially," he said aloud without realizing it. A half-dozen cats meowed their agreement.

* * *

As she arrived at the office on her first full day in her new job, Jackie had not taken a right when she got off the elevator at the twentieth floor like she always had, which would have led to her old office, but remembering that she was moving into her father's office, she had walked straight, past the executive floor reception desk, greeting the receptionist, and through the

48

imposing double doors of the suite of the Chief Executive Officer.

The 12-foot walls were covered in the same varnished wood as the boardroom, with similar sconces on the walls, centered in each of the large trimmed panels. The deep carpet, which she had walked many times before, felt different today as she walked toward her father's office – now hers – passing between two complete sitting areas with oversized couches, chairs, and end tables on which were oil industry trade magazines for those who would wait there for appointments. Finally, she reached Doris' desk, behind which was a room out of site where Doris had every conceivable office amenity with which to provide the CEO with his – now her – every need at a moments' notice.

"Good morning, Doris," Jackie greeted her father's administrative assistant — now hers.

"Good morning, Miss James. How bad was it?"

"Bad. A man was killed while I was there, and we have a spill."

"What? How?"

"Several hours after the attack a support collapsed and the crane fell, taking out the derrick. We're lucky more men weren't hurt. The damage can be repaired. I just don't understand why someone would do this."

"It was deliberate?"

"No question about it."

"Well, you may want to turn on CNN, because that's not the way they're playing it," Doris answered with a deep line etching her forehead, gesturing toward double wooden doors identical to the entrance to the suite.

"What?! How'd they find out?"

Jackie rushed into the inner office – now hers.

Backlash

The office was on the northeast corner of the building and two entire walls were glass, providing a spectacular view of the Houston skyline and the suburbs beyond. The floor-to-ceiling drapes had been drawn back to let in the morning sun, which was filtered through the glass that looked black from the outside. The carpet was a lush blue with the company's golden logo woven into it in the exact center of the room. In one corner sat a table and chairs which could accommodate six for an informal meeting or working lunch.

She took the remote from its cradle on the oversized, ornate desk and snapped on the flat screen TV mounted on the wall to one side of the desk, punching in the cable channel for Headline News. She had to wait a couple of minutes for the story, but there it was, complete with aerial footage of the damaged offshore oil rig with smoke ascending. They replayed the footage as Jackie watched and she was horrified to see that they had video of the crane falling and subsequent derrick collapse, followed by a clear, unmistakable shot of oil in the water.

"Officials at Axiom Oil Incorporated declined to give details of the accident and the extent of the spill," the female anchor read from the TelePrompTer. "We will have an interview with an oil industry consultant later this evening to try to shed some light on what could be an ecological disaster."

"What the — !" Jackie couldn't believe her ears. They were calling it an accident without even talking to anybody at the scene. "Who 'declined to give details?'"

"I have no idea. They didn't call here," Doris shrugged, having followed Jackie into her office. Whoever he or she had talked to, the reporter hadn't persisted to get to anyone who knew anything.

* * *

Paul Stoddard rushed out the front door of his house wearing a dark blue uniform and cap emblazoned with a logo that declared "City of Baytown Animal Control." He jumped into the driver's seat of his rusting compact. He would get coffee and Danish on the way in, as usual.

The crackling AM car radio was tuned to a NewsTalk station and was reporting the explosion on the Gulf Pride oil platform as an accident resulting in an oil spill. Paul Stoddard yawned as he made the last turn before getting to work. He had mixed emotions about the fact that the news reports were calling the events of Saturday night an accident. Part of him wished to take very public credit for the act, but another part recognized that, if it was judged an accident, that would only reflect badly on the oil industry. And besides, that was part of the plan. At least it was a part of the plan on which he had been briefed.

The tired Toyota with fading paint rolled into the fenced parking lot of the Baytown Animal Control Shelter and Paul waited for the end of the report before getting out to go inside and punch the clock after another short night. He reminded himself that this job, no matter how much he hated it, was his cover, in a manner of speaking. He didn't hate the animals, of course, just the situation and his coworkers. But he thought of himself as a sort of spy; a deep cover agent for the forces of Good and Right and the Divine Goddess. It would have to suffice, for now.

Three minutes later he walked into the animal shelter where he had worked for the past six years. He was passing the cages of the animals condemned to death by their longevity at the shelter when a gruff voice stopped him.

"Stoddard! You're late!"

Backlash

Paul turned, though not to identify the voice. He wished he could forget the voice of "Bull" Cahill, his boss for the past six years. Cahill's naturally red, bloated face was made more crimson with the anger that always seemed to be about to boil over. Paul was unmoved by it.

"I went out of town for the weekend."

"So, you can't tell time?"

Paul looked down, biting his tongue, as he always did. "I drove all night to get back for work," he lied.

"So, get to it!"

And with that Cahill turned and left, the dark blue uniform pants making a whishing noise as his thick thighs brushed against each other. Paul sneered at Cahill's shadow on the concrete floor. What a cretin his boss was! How galling to have to bow and scrape to him, day after day! He didn't have to rehearse again the sequence of events that had brought him to this point.

Although doctorates in everything from Geophysics to Computer Science had been common at the Johnson Space Center, Stoddard had shown great promise as a mathematician in NASA's 3,000-strong Aerospace Technology team. Stoddard had been part of a work group that had broken new ground on the space shuttle project after the Challenger disaster. But then he had grown frustrated because of the power plays and political games being played by the team members whose focus should have been the science, instead of budgets and who had the biggest staff. He had begun to make complaining noises that alienated him from his coworkers, so, when a budget-cutting broom went through the department, there had been no one to stand up for him. Jobs are not plentiful for mathematicians who have no interest in teaching, so he took a series of jobs, of which the animal control job was just the latest. Its only redeeming feature was the animals and the fact that he could save many of them. As it happened, he had begun developing more of an interest in the earth than in space, even before his involvement in the space program had abruptly ended.

Paul slid his timecard into the machine until it made its clunking imprint, then went to the yard to check the oil in his truck.

* * *

The television set across the room from the desk of Vermont Senator Nathan Taylor was perpetually tuned to CNN and stayed on much of the time, with the sound muted. Today however, it was turned up loud enough for the aging politician to hear the reporters inhale as they breathlessly reported the events. He leaned forward in his leather, wingback-style executive chair and squinted at the screen as if to memorize the pictures bouncing off satellites and into his office. Taylor had been very vocal during his many years in Washington about his concern for the environment and had been successful in passing several bills and funding programs to turn that concern into action, so the news about the offshore oilrig accident naturally interested him.

The aerial footage of the smoking offshore platform and collapse of the crane and derrick fascinated him, as did the reporter's characterization of the event as an industrial accident. As he saw the spreading dark stain of the oil in the blue water, his thin lips widened in a smile that almost stretched to his white sideburns. A most fortuitous set of circumstances was developing.

When a crisis occurs, someone will invariably say, "There oughta be a law," which is always music to a politician's ears.

Backlash

Men like Nathan Taylor entered public service to help people but stayed in office to rule them. Few experiences could compare to the feeling of knowing that millions of people must obey the words he would put to paper, though Taylor would never say it out loud, of course. People need guidance and he could give it to them through legislation that mapped out the proper way to go on this issue.

The current crisis was a perfect catalyst for the legislation he had been working on. A public outcry was often an important factor in getting legislation passed, since his fellow politicians always became more concerned about representing "the people" as election day drew near.

* * *

The image of the smoking pyre in the Gulf of Mexico was repeated over and over on CNN. E. J. "Bud" Eldridge changed the channel and then changed it back for the umpteenth time on his Texas-size, big-screen TV. Low growling noises came from way back in his throat each time the aerial shot started over. The 65-year-old chairman of the Axiom Oil Incorporated board of directors shifted his 300-pound-plus torso and re-crossed his custom cowboy boots on his favorite leather recliner, its extra-large arms as round as his own.

Anger was mixed with fear and a sizeable portion of frustration as he helplessly watched the blow-dried, mascara'd news readers narrate the story of the accident and subsequent spill with an unspoken accusation that Axiom would somehow be happy about the dark crude escaping into the green-blue water. He didn't know why he watched the news. Anytime he knew anything about a story's background he was amazed at how many details the breathless reporters got wrong. Not to mention the moralizing they didn't quite verbalize. The judgment the viewer was expected to make was always just below the surface. Rarely did he agree with the viewpoint the dandies and bimbos spoon-feeding the news had assumed for him.

For 30 years his fortunes had been tied to Axiom Oil, and this was not the first time something like this had happened. Shortly after Axiom had bought out Bud's company, there had been a tragic fire at the company's refinery in Lawton, Oklahoma. That one had claimed three lives and a dozen more injured. But, ever since the Exxon Valdez had run aground off the coast of Alaska, companies like Axiom were under greater scrutiny. Then came the BP spill, which had admittedly been the worst spill in the Gulf, but it had been an accident after all. Yet it nearly sunk that otherwise strong company.

Part of his frustration was the seeming assumption behind the TV reporting that the Gulf Pride accident was to be expected and should have been preventable. Like there weren't thousands of oil platforms operating safely and efficiently around the world every day. But much that was on the news only served to reinforce the ignorance of the public about things the media chose to ignore; like the massive amount of oil the earth's population demanded each day for everything from airplane fuel to plastic toys. While OPEC and Middle Eastern oil got a lot of attention, there were many large oil fields around the world, from the North Sea to the Indian Ocean, the Russian steppes and north to Alaska.

Bud had built a thriving interstate trucking business in the 1960s and 70s, transporting petroleum products for several companies. "Junior" James had been CEO of Axiom for just 10 years when he made Bud many times richer than he already was by offering to buy him out and give him a seat on the board of what was then a regional oil company. The buyout was part of a strategy that Junior had laid out for Bud that had amazed and excited him. Over the next 30 years Bud would be at Junior's elbow during many more acquisitions as the company purposefully expanded across the country, growing its market share exponentially each time. Bud had sat on the board seven years before he was elected chairman. He was justifiably proud of what he and Junior had accomplished over the past three decades.

The growth had been made possible in large part by Junior's decision to take the company public in the early 1980's. Bud had grown even richer when he helped Junior accomplish this goal. Junior was a much better businessman than he was, Bud willingly admitted, but Junior also depended on Bud as his key team leader. Bud's day-to-day involvement in the operations of the company had long since ended. He now presided over the actions taken by the board, which were certainly not unimportant. Growth was still the primary agenda item at nearly every meeting and the company had continued to gobble up market share to the present day, much to the frustration of competitors Axiom eventually surpassed in each market segment it entered.

For all these reasons, Bud's disappointment was profound that the board had not elected him CEO after he had made it clear that he wanted the job. *What were they thinking, putting Junior's daughter in that important position?* It was fine for her to galavant around playing at surveying operations. Axiom sold a lot of jet fuel because of Jackie's field visits, but how could that little girl lead the company that Axiom had become? Why, Bud had been on the Axiom board almost since she learned to read! Apparently, the sharp businessmen on his board could be sentimental fools when they were caught off guard.

And Junior's death had certainly caught them all off guard. Bud almost felt guilty because he hadn't been in the foursome at the country club that day, but how could he have known? He certainly had played that course hundreds of times with Junior and other captains of industry or politicians or celebrities. Some very big business marriages had been consummated on the lush green ovals of their favorite course.

It should be interesting to watch what happens now, he thought with a tight smile. He would see how Junior's little darlin' stood up to the scrutiny that was coming after this unfortunate incident.

CHAPTER FIVE

Since the story was out now, Jackie would have to make a statement. "Doris, get Charlene Washington on the phone, please." Charlene managed the company's communication program, which included media relations. When Charlene answered, Jackie asked her to come to her office immediately.

"Have you heard what happened Saturday night?" Jackie asked Charlene as soon as she arrived.

"Bits and pieces, yes. Mr. Tyson briefed me."

"Well, if you've watched CNN, you don't know what happened. We need a press release to go out immediately to set things straight."

"If I might," Charlene began, watching for a reaction from her new boss, her flawless, white teeth contrasting beautifully with her milk-chocolate complexion, "You might want to have a news conference. It might have more impact with the broadcast media. They tend to ignore anything they can't point a camera or a microphone at."

"That makes sense I guess."

"Do you want to do the news conference yourself or do you want me to do it?"

"I think I should do it myself. Seems to me I might need to appear so everybody knows somebody's in charge." Jackie looked at Charlene with question marks in her eyes, if not in her voice.

"That's probably a good idea, since this comes when it does. Do you want me to write the opening statement?"

"Yes. I've started a bullet list," Jackie said, handing a copy to Charlene. "Here's what I know so far. You can take it from there. I don't know what to make of the media."

Charlene smiled at her new boss' naiveté. "Too many of them are looking for a Peabody award by finding a huge scandal."

"Seems to me eco-terrorism ought to be scandal enough for anybody."

Charlene smiled again as she left to begin work on the statement.

Jackie wasn't looking forward to doing a news conference but, unfortunately, the horse was out of the barn. CNN's report, as well as its spin, was picked up and duplicated by several other news agencies. *I need to "head this off at the pass" if I can,* she thought. Then Doris buzzed her that she had a phone call.

"It's the FBI," Doris said with an upturned pitch at the end of the sentence.

"This is Jacqueline James," Jackie said into the telephone mouthpiece.

"Hello, Ms. James. This is Special Agent Thomas Shannon of the New Orleans field office of the Federal Bureau of Investigation. I've been assigned to investigate the attack on your oil platform."

"Really? I didn't know the FBI was getting involved."

"Since it was offshore and there was a fatality, we've been called in. What can you tell me that the Coast Guard didn't?"

"You've already been out there?" Jackie was surprised.

"Yes, the Coast Guard gave us a ride."

"Hmm. okay. I don't suppose there's anything I can tell you that the captain doesn't already know."

"Have you spoken to the press?"

"No, but I'm planning a news conference for this afternoon. They're already reporting it as an accident. I'm looking forward to straightening them out."

"If I might, Miss James, please don't tell them about the message that was spray-painted on the platform."

"What? That's the most important part! How am I going to convince them it was a terrorist attack if I can't tell them about the message?"

"I'm sorry, but it may be important to our investigation to keep that part secret, for the time being."

"Mr. Shannon! How can we not share that information when they're out there blaming this on us?"

"I'm sorry, but I'm afraid I must insist. To let that information out could jeopardize the investigation."

This frustrated Jackie to no end, since she knew she could give copies of the pictures of the spray-painted message to the news reporters and all their doubts about the intentional nature of the explosions would be swept away. But for the time being she would cooperate with the FBI and have to put up with the press.

* * *

Science and Environment Editor John Watson looked through his article about the drilling rig "accident" on the second page of this morning's Washington Herald. He thought it should have been on the front page, but managing editor Finkel hadn't seen it that way. It had been an incredibly easy article to write. The hard part was disguising the euphoria he felt at the opportunities this situation presented.

When CNN broke the story, it had caused a sensation in the Washington Herald newsroom, as well as many other newsrooms across the country, Watson suspected. Beyond enabling him to produce copy day after day with his byline attached, Watson could see — or rather, feel — a sea change in attitude of the public toward the oil companies since the explosion and resulting oil spill in the Gulf of Mexico.

An episode like this was bound to happen eventually. The carelessness and neglect of the oil companies was easy to document, at least to his way of thinking. It had been frustrating that more drastic changes had not taken place during and after the BP spill. No one could explain to him why Congress or the President hadn't taken steps to shut down or nationalize the entire industry.

So now, they had another chance. Now everyone would see why it was imperative to wean the world off oil and go to more environmentally friendly fuels.

An article by the business editor yesterday had detailed the election of Donald James' daughter to succeed him as Chairman. Watson didn't know anything about her attitudes on the environment, but mused that this would serve well the people who were working to change things. She would not yet have credibility within the company or with the public, so real pressure could be brought to bear on the giant corporation. Perhaps some real good could come from this.

He laid down today's paper and turned to his computer screen to put the finishing touches on another article for tomorrow chronicling the history of oil spills and other industrial accidents that put the environment at risk. It was turning out to be a good week.

* * *

Promptly at 3:00 p.m. Jackie went to the first-floor theater that Axiom used for large employee assemblies. The media people were there, at least most of the ones Charlene had notified. They were mostly local, since the news conference was announced only five hours before. Three television cameras were set up and the podium was covered with a variety of microphones and mini-cassette recorders. Three portable TV lights cast harsh shadows on the wall behind the podium. There were press packets available to all those present, Charlene's staff had seen to that. Unfortunately, from Jackie's viewpoint, the videotapes supplied to the TV media and stills given to the print reporters both omitted images of the telltale message.

President Benny Tyson was already there. "Are you ready?" he asked Jackie.

"I'd rather be riding," she muttered, referring to horseback riding, one of her favorite pastimes.

"Good luck," he said, appearing genuinely glad he hadn't had the votes to become CEO. Charlene was also there, having served as hostess and guide to the gathered news people. She gave Jackie a "thumbs-up."

Jackie took her place at the podium and held her hand over her mouth while clearing her throat, which didn't really need clearing, but it served to postpone the inevitable. The gathered journalists were attentive as she began her statement.

"Good afternoon, ladies and gentlemen. Thank you for coming. I'm Jacqueline James, just recently elected Chief Executive Officer to replace my late father. Axiom Oil has been in the news over the past couple of days and many, if not all, of the reports have been inaccurate. I'd like to take this opportunity to clear up some misunderstandings that have been stated in the media reports.

"On Saturday night, Axiom Oil Corporation was attacked by persons unknown. One of our offshore platforms in the Gulf of Mexico, the "Gulf Pride", located about 60 miles south of the Louisiana coast, suffered a series of explosions that our preliminary investigation indicates were the result of planted explosives attached to the supports of the platform right at the waterline. I flew to the site myself and saw the damage caused by this vandalism. There is no doubt in my mind after being present at the site that the explosives were set intentionally.

"While I was there a tragic accident happened. The crane collapsed, having been weakened by the sabotage, killing one of our employees and damaging the derrick, resulting in a minor oil spill."

A murmur wafted through the room as the reporters looked up from their notepads and exchanged glances with their colleagues. Jackie paused only briefly.

"The Coast Guard has begun an investigation and other agencies may join as indicated by applicable laws. At this point we do not have any definitive indicators as to who perpetrated this despicable act, but we will not rest until they are brought to justice. We regard this as an act of terrorism against our company and the lives of our employees, and will seek prosecution of the perpetrators by the relevant authorities.

"Until a damage assessment can be done and repairs made, I have shut down the Gulf Pride platform and have moved all Axiom personnel to the mainland where they will be reassigned to other operations. Our spill team is on site to contain the oil and cap the well. We expect complete containment within just a couple of days.

"I will be happy to take questions, now."

The journalists erupted with raised hands and shouted questions. Jackie selected one at random, a rumpled reporter for the Houston Chronicle. He looked at Jackie over the reading glasses sitting low on his nose.

"Ms. James, if this was an attack as you say, why did the initial reports say this was an accident?"

"I have no idea. That report did not come from Axiom. I can only think someone in the media made an incorrect assumption." Jackie was vaguely surprised to see skepticism and perhaps even hostility in the eyes of some of the reporters. But she didn't have time to consider it; there were other questions being shouted and other hands vying for attention. She chose another reporter, an impeccably dressed woman with a Channel 6 logo on her leather-bound reporter's notebook.

"How do you know the explosions were intentionally set and not an accident?"

"As I said, I was there and saw the results. The explosives were attached to the supports of the platform near the waterline, as if they were put in place by people in boats. There are no mechanical aspects of the platform at that level."

"But there are machines and systems on the platform that could malfunction and cause an explosion, are there not?"

Jackie was dumbfounded. It appeared the woman was not convinced. "I suppose there are, but that is obviously not what happened."

"How is it obvious? Won't you have to wait for the investigation into your operation of the platform?"

"There won't be an investigation into our operation of the platform. There is no question about that. The investigation will be to find the people who attacked us, killing a man and causing the spill, and bring them to justice!"

She recognized another hand.

"George Callaway, United Press Houston Bureau. Has this platform had any safety violations in the past?"

"I don't see the relevance of the safety record of the platform."

"If this was the result of carelessness, there might be a pattern."

"Didn't you hear me say that we were attacked? These were planted explosives!"

"Still, what is the safety record of the platform?"

"It is exemplary, though that is irrelevant to this incident!"

Jackie saw the man look down and begin writing, though she couldn't begin to imagine what he would write after their exchange.

"How serious is the oil spill?" asked the next reporter.

"The drill pipe was severed when the derrick collapsed, allowing oil to escape into the water at the Gulf floor level. It did not appear that the pressure was inordinate and, according to the team on site, the spill should be easy to cap. The storage tanks were undamaged and our skimmer vessel is cleaning up as we speak."

"What does the skimmer do?" asked a TV reporter.

"Skimmers use a suction pump to collect the oil that floats on top of the water for disposal."

"Are you using other methods as well?"

"Yes. Containment is accomplished through use of a "boom" that forms a floating perimeter, keeping the oil from spreading on top of the water."

"What about the oil under water?"

There was a lull as the reporters took down her answers then another hand went up.

"What is the name and hometown of the man who was killed?"

"His name is Juan Ortega. His home is in Brownsville."

"Was anyone else hurt?"

"Other injuries were minor."

She chose another raised hand. "Do you expect your company to be sued by the family of the fatality?"

"I would hope not, under the circumstances. We are in contact with the family and will try to meet their needs."

Jackie continued answering questions for another half hour, but when they were done, she wasn't sure some of the reporters now leaving for the visitor's parking lot didn't still suspect she was hiding some accident or covering up something — what she couldn't fathom. There seemed to be more questions about Axiom, its operations, and its record on environmental issues than about the perpetrators. It was almost as if they had come with their minds made up and left with their initial assumptions unchanged. *"You can lead a horse to water..."* she thought incredulously.

* * *

Paul Stoddard was only half listening when the report from Axiom Oil headquarters came on the evening news, up to his elbows in frothy dishwater. He recognized the local reporter and saw from the B-roll video that the new CEO had had a news conference today to say that the explosion at the oilrig had been a terrorist attack. The journalist was not accepting the assertion at face value, and reported it with a question mark in her voice.

The real news to Paul was that one of the oil workers had been killed when the crane collapsed, destroying the derrick, and an oil spill resulted. *It must have happened after we left*, he thought. He reacted to the news of the worker's death with less emotion than he would have if Quark or Neutron, his favorite cats, had been run over by a car. People were dying every day from abuses of Nature by companies like Axiom, after all.

The oil spill was a different matter. The possibility had been discussed and the planners had agreed it would actually improve the chances of the success of the plan, but Paul still felt a twinge of conscience about it.

The dishes finished, he let the dishwater out and wiped his hands on a faded towel. He had already fed the animals out back, so he turned off the TV and headed upstairs as he did most nights to surf the web for news of environmental infractions and to get some good quotes about the "accident" on the offshore platform. That would allow him to write another essay for the website. Then he would send an e-mail to the inner circle of his group and another more cryptic message to a wider circle of interested parties.

CHAPTER SIX

Much later that night, Jackie finished watching a late-night comedian's monologue as she prepared for bed. She hadn't been home long, what with her transition to accomplish and the complication of the attack. Thankfully, the host of the popular show didn't have any jokes about oil spills and she was able to relax and take her mind off the events of the day, if only for a few minutes. When the comedy routine was over, she clicked the "power" button on the remote, silencing the TV and plunging the master bedroom of her spacious, contemporary home into darkness.

She didn't immediately go to sleep. Her mind switched back on and returned to something she had been working on all day, off and on. She could not have put it into words just yet, but it was bothering her and wouldn't let go.

What if they never found the people responsible for the attack on the Gulf Pride? For now, she wasn't thinking about bringing criminals to justice so much as wanting to know

"Why?" Try as she might, she couldn't figure out why someone would do such a thing.

She knew that the terrorists who destroyed the World Trade Center on 9-11 were motivated by religiopolitical ideology, which wasn't unexpected from radicals in the Middle East, even if their methods were a surprise. The hatred of Israel and her allies by some in the Arab world knew no bounds, but to endanger the lives of fellow human beings over an abstract concept like concern for the Environment was beyond her normal thought patterns.

Jackie realized she was not a particularly analytical thinker anyway. She was more of a doer than a thinker. She was always busy. She always had more on her to do list than was humanly possible to accomplish. By getting things done, she confirmed her place in the world.

But this was something that activity couldn't solve — not her own activity at least. She knew the Coast Guard and the FBI were investigating. Perhaps some local police departments along the coast would be involved as well. But nothing Jackie could do would make any difference. So, she was left with shapeless thoughts about an invisible someone who did things she couldn't fathom.

Because of where and how she grew up, she was accustomed to thinking of the oil business in purely positive terms. Axiom provided a commodity people needed. It was dirty, fatiguing, and sometimes dangerous work at virtually every step in the process of drilling, transporting, refining and retailing the oil and gasoline that made the wheels of the world turn. But the people of her company did it because people needed it and their lives were made better for it.

For thousands of years, mankind could travel only as fast as the fastest horse. Now people required only hours to travel distances that once took days or weeks. Easier and faster transportation meant food going to market was fresher; the injured and sick received medical attention earlier; extended families could reunite more often. It was hard for her to see a downside in a product that made such things possible.

While this seemed to Jackie a logical review of obvious facts, she was forced to admit that, apparently there were people who saw the automobile and its fuel as a mixed blessing at best. Several ironies only deepened the mystery of the faceless people who had attacked her employees.

Hadn't petroleum-powered vehicles removed a tremendous burden from the backs of the beasts that had provided muscle for human labor and transportation for thousands of years? And didn't the same type of people who disapproved of automobiles and their fuel also lobby for "animal rights"?

Also puzzling was the fact that those who expressed deep concern for the environment presumably preferred pristine wilderness to urban congestion. Yet they seemed to strongly dislike suburbia. In most cities, commutes lengthened and lengthened as people chose to live further from the unnatural crowding of the urban centers. Wasn't living in the suburbs closer to wilderness living than that of the concrete canyons in the inner city, its inhabitants crowded in tenements like characters in a Charles Dickens novel? And wasn't it the automobile that made suburban living practical? It just didn't add up.

Jackie wondered how anyone could hate a product that brought freedom and empowerment to so many people. How could they disapprove so strongly that they would kill people — intentionally or unintentionally? It was as if they valued humanity less than the rest of nature. She drifted off to sleep with more questions than answers.

* * *

Special Agent Thomas Shannon had difficulty not letting on how sick he had been aboard the Coast Guard cutter when he and his agents had visited the site of the bombing at the now-idled oil platform. He had caught some sideways glances from agents Bouchet and Rice that made him think they were laughing at him behind his back.

They had seen the oil spill and the efforts the company was making to clean it up, but Shannon knew nothing about the technology involved in such a project and that was not his concern anyway.

The 45-year-old Shannon, a former beat cop who took the test and was inducted into the Bureau 10 years ago, was stocky and tough as a street fighter when he needed to be, but had been able to convert his experience on the pavement into the cerebral investigative style of the FBI. So now he was in charge of the New Orleans field office and it fell to him to investigate the incident. There was no doubt that it was an intentional act, but there was little to go on as to motive. He raked his fingers through thinning auburn hair as he sat down at the head of the field office conference table.

"What do we know?" he asked his agents the day after their field trip off the coast.

"The attackers left a message," said the young, green agent Gifford Rice. He was the tallest of the three men, but weighed the least.

"They used some fancy explosives," suggested Tony Bouchet, who was older than Rice, but still just in his early thirties. Bouchet's accent betrayed his Cajun heritage. His hair was black and naturally curly, even though close-cropped. Shannon had more years in law enforcement than both of them put together. He had seen a lot of arson cases and some bomb threats, but nothing like this.

"So, they used sophisticated explosives. What does that tell us?" Shannon pushed.

"They've got some experienced guys working with them," Bouchet ventured.

"And money too. Somebody's bankrolling them," Rice added.

Shannon leaned back in his government-issue gray chair. "Good observations. I think we can rule out a disgruntled employee. It would be too difficult to get to the location," Shannon said, remembering the sick, green nausea he'd felt on the voyage out to the Gulf Pride.

"And there were too many explosives. It had to be a team," Rice said.

"Right," Bouchet agreed. "They had to get it done and get out of there. It had to be a group."

"So what groups have something against oil companies?"

"Environmentalists," Bouchet volunteered the obvious answer.

That seemed to be the conventional wisdom because of the content of the message the perpetrators had left in spray paint. In fact, it was very close to messages left at other scenes of eco-terrorism in recent years. The fire bombing of a ski lodge in Colorado was the largest such incident. Luckily no one was hurt, but there had been tremendous property damage. There had been a number of vandalism incidents in recent years against oil drilling operations in Canada also. And recently, eco-terrorists had targeted car dealerships on the west coast, setting afire whole lots full of new SUVs.

For years, radical environmentalists had obstructed the work of loggers in the Northwest United States, sometimes "spiking" trees so that if a logger cut into one with a chainsaw, he would likely hit a spike and the saw would kick back and injure him.

But the incidents were getting more and more severe. This most recent bombing had the potential of killing or injuring a lot of people. It was fortunate that it hadn't been worse. It also had created an oil spill, which seemed odd that eco-terrorists would do something to cause such a thing.

"So why the oil spill?" Shannon challenged. "Why would they risk that?"

Nobody had a ready response.

"Physical evidence?"

"Nothing we could find, other than explosive residue," Rice said. "They probably used gloves and nobody saw anything. Nobody even heard boats."

"Yeah, and we can analyze the residue, but that probably won't tell us much more than we already know," Bouchet added.

"So, we've got to go at it another way," said Shannon. "People who use explosives like this have to buy them on the black market or make them themselves, in which case they have to buy the raw materials. In the latter case, there's going to be records. We're pretty sure they did it from boats. Boats have to be bought or rented. They have to leave the shore from a specific location at a specific time. People who sail in boats have to drive to the shore and leave a vehicle behind. People see things, hear things. We've got to talk to people; people who saw something; people who know something."

"Yeah, 'cause we sure as heck don't know anything!" Bouchet quipped, but Shannon wasn't amused.

* * *

Backlash

"The events of last Saturday night are a wake-up call for all Americans who care about the Environment."

In the Senate chamber, Senator Nathan Taylor of Vermont had the floor. "Careless companies like Axiom Oil, which take the earth's resources but give nothing back must be dealt with in no uncertain terms. Again we are faced with the ecological disaster posed by an oil spill. We don't know how bad it will be, but we have seen how the entire Gulf of Mexico Coast can be affected. From Texas to Florida we may be faced with the death of thousands of sea animals, birds and fish, and a massive and expensive clean-up operation will again be required. When are we going to face the fact that we must wean ourselves off oil and find other sources of energy?" He paused for effect and surveyed the chamber.

"I have been working on legislation that is now obviously urgent. In order to reduce the demand for gasoline, the primary reason for our continued exhaustion of the earth's resources, this legislation will increase Federal taxes on gasoline to a level that will force the discontinuance of all unnecessary travel. On the other hand, it will reward those who use mass transit, because buses and commuter trains would be exempt from the new tax. Alternative renewable fuels such as ethanol and hydrogen will also be exempt," he paused again to allow the impact of his proposal to hit his fellow Senators.

He glanced at the gallery and saw a familiar face. The very-well-dressed man had black hair combed straight back and he was hanging on Taylor's every word. Though the man's face was expressionless, Taylor knew he was excited about what he was hearing. His presence meant the pieces would be falling into place. With the man was a beautiful, young woman that Taylor had not seen before; a tall blonde who looked like a magazine model. But the man in the gallery always had beautiful women around him, sometimes more than one at a time.

"Other exceptions would logically be natural gas, electric and hybrid vehicles. We all remember what happened in the 70s and again just a few years ago. When the price of gasoline went up, people changed their habits. They drove less. They bought smaller cars. They conserved.

"We must take action if we are to protect our environment, because to preserve the Environment is to preserve our futures. My committee will be making Senate Bill 1407 available for evaluation by this body later this week."

Taylor didn't go into much detail in his oration. That would come later. He was experienced at shaping opinion in Washington and he knew his chances of passing his bill were better if he aroused sympathy for the general idea before revealing the details.

The intent of his legislation was to punish the oil companies by adding a new two-dollar-a-gallon Federal gasoline tax. This would be in addition to the present 18.4-cents-per-gallon Federal tax and the various state and local taxes that amounted to as much as 25 cents per gallon in some states. At the same time, the bill would only allow the oil companies to raise their prices by $1.00 to a maximum of $6.00 per gallon. There was currently a cap of $5.00, which had been passed by Congress to stop the price increases that began in the previous decade, when fuel prices approached $7.00 in the West before falling again. This new $6.00 cap would force the oil companies to forfeit some of their obscene profits and provide a windfall for the Federal Treasury. Taylor's staff had produced a report showing that, at current gasoline usage levels, the new tax would result in $400 billion per year in new money coming into the treasury. He had a long list of friends and contributors who could use that money to help restructure American society in line with their values.

The American people would be very grateful to him when they realized that he was fostering a revolution that would make life so much better — in the long run at least. Some people in Congress were bound to oppose the bill when they saw it would increase the price of gasoline by at least a dollar a gallon. *Better to keep them in the dark as long as possible*, he thought.

* * *

In retrospect, Jackie supposed she should have known the reporters wouldn't leave. In fact, in a vacant lot across from the Axiom headquarters, a sort of RV park was forming, with several satellite trucks and a variety of vans and recreational vehicles to support the various reporters, who ranged from local little-known weekly newspaper columnists to national TV network reporters. "News Gypsies", Axiom President Benny Tyson called them. In some cases, it was a business reporter who was dispatched to Houston; others were some variety of environmental news writer. The aggregate affect was that the reception desk of the Axiom headquarters was besieged by constant requests for interviews.

As it turned out, Jackie's news conference had only served to muddy the water, since the media had already decided on the slant it preferred for this story. On Wednesday, more newspaper articles and TV reports appeared recalling stories of past oil company transgressions that resulted in oil spills and straying into tales of more general industrial ecological crimes. Some news outlets implied through loaded questions or the arched eyebrows of news anchors that Axiom was covering up something and that the official "terrorism" story from the new

CEO was a smoke screen. Others began to focus on Jackie as a newfound celebrity. Coverage ranged from exalting her to the status of feminist icon for breaking through the corporate "glass ceiling" to depicting her as automatically suspect by virtue of her wealth and inheritance of power.

Jackie was distressed by all this and met with Benny Tyson and Media Relations Director Charlene Washington to try to decide how to respond and how to contain the damage. They sat around the small cherry conference table in a corner of Jackie's office.

"It's impossible to grant individual interviews to all those requesting them," Charlene said. Her department was fielding the requests and she was feeling the pressure as much as anybody.

"And we can't have just anybody giving out information," Benny put in. "We need to manage it."

"So how do we do that?" Jackie looked at them, her eyes pleading, though her voice was steady.

"Well, my department can turn out press kits and updates," Charlene said. "But I think we need to have additional news conferences."

"You're probably right," Jackie winced. It did appear that the media wasn't taking the company's statements at face value.

"Should several of us take turns?" Benny asked both of them.

"That might be a good idea," Charlene replied. "It would prevent the press from focusing on one person."

"Sounds good to me," Jackie sighed. "So long as we all stay on the same page."

"That's for sure," Charlene agreed, speaking from experience. "These reporters make their living getting spokespeople off message and into deep water."

Backlash

"Some of them won't be satisfied until they get an interview," Benny predicted.

"Let's put them off until we have something substantive we can tell them," Charlene suggested. "Then we'll pick and choose who we give the interview — or interviews — to."

The prospect of more news conferences nearly drove Jackie to distraction, but she realized that refusing to talk to the press would only make things worse. The reporters continued reporting, even if they didn't have anything new, and that led to very public idle speculation that could only hurt Axiom.

That afternoon, Charlene circulated a photocopied memo to the members of the press that had laid siege to Axiom announcing a news conference for the next morning.

They set the news conference early — seven a.m. Central time — so some of it might make it on the morning news shows. Of course, with CNN, Fox News and MSNBC, and any number of news-oriented websites, there was no such thing as a news cycle. They would cover the entire news conference live, then they would continue talking about it for hours. Maybe days.

They worked late to get material together and then got up early to be there for the news conference. Jackie and Benny were there and Charlene led the conference.

The general statement was virtually identical to the first news conference, since there wasn't really any news, but the reporters scribbled in their notebooks and scratched their chins thoughtfully anyhow.

* * *

Jackie sat alone in her king-sized Scandinavian bed with a spreadsheet printout in front of her and sipped a mug of hot chocolate. Her days since becoming CEO had been filled with concerns about the damaged oil platform and the fatality, plus the PR problems it had created. So here she was, reviewing company financial reports at 10 p.m. at home, because she would have been busy enough at work, even without these unexpected events.

Across the room, the 42-inch LCD TV droned on endlessly, just so the big empty house wouldn't be totally quiet. Jackie was paying it little attention until the late news came on and the lead was a story about the proposed gas tax. "Senate and House committees rushed to complete legislation on a new two-dollar-a-gallon gasoline tax today and both committees narrowly approved the measure," the local news anchor read. "The bill is designed to reduce the nation's dependence on oil. Only one-dollar of the two-dollar tax would be passed on to consumers. Debate on the bill will begin on the floors of the House and Senate next week."

Jackie's mouth fell open and she set the mug down hard on the nightstand. "I can't believe they're doing that! Two dollars a gallon!" She grabbed the phone.

"Yes, let me speak to Benny, please.... This is Jackie James.... Benny, this is Jackie. Did you hear the news?... Right. What's it going to do to us? Yes, could you get Dennis to do that first thing tomorrow? Make this first priority. I never thought they would do it... Yeah, let me know as soon as you've got it and we'll get everybody together."

She hung up the phone and stared at the TV, her anger slowly turning to concern as she turned the news over in her mind.

* * *

The attack on the Gulf Pride and the introduction of the Petroleum Independence Act focused the nation's attention on the oil industry once again. The nation's news organizations compared notes and produced great volumes of copy about the industry, the history of oil spills, and the threat to clean air posed by fossil-fuel burning vehicles. It seemed every major newspaper led with separate stories on the Gulf Pride incident and related Environmental issues.

The Washington Herald was no exception. John Watson and the reporters in his Science and Environment Department brought out virtually every piece of information they had in their extensive background files about the oil industry and its history of abuse of the earth. Reading the pieces they produced, one would have assumed the reporters rode bicycles to work, but that was not the case, of course.

Patrick Garrity and his political reporters went into overdrive when the attack in the Gulf generated legislation on Capitol Hill. He DVR'd C-SPAN around the clock and had his political reporters scanning the Congressional Record, trying to follow the rapid developments. He marveled that something like this could happen and privately wondered what a dollar-a-gallon spike in the price of gasoline would do to the economy.

Patrick gave his reporters the task of cataloging the Federal laws and regulations dealing with oil exploration and transport, gasoline refining, and automobile emissions. It was a monumental task, but since it was all in the paper's morgue, each new law having been reported when it passed, it was simply a matter of pulling it all together and putting it in a form that made sense.

Patrick's office was cluttered with old newspapers, thick research files, and copies of the Congressional Record going back several years. There were pictures on the wall of a very young Patrick with Ronald Reagan and Bill Clinton. A few framed yellowed newspaper clippings traced Patrick's career as a reporter for the New York Times, first as a young reporter

earning his stripes on "man-bites-dog" stories, then covering
state politics in Albany.

Patrick was just starting his day. The gas tax bill was being
"fast-tracked" and insiders on Capitol Hill were predicting it
would be out of committee and up for debate in both chambers
as early as next week. He sat pounding the keys of his computer
writing an article for the afternoon edition, when the phone
rang.

"Garrity... Yeah, Howard. Be right there."

He saved what he was working on and took a gulp from his
ever-present coffee mug. Then he stood and walked across the
building to the managing editor's office. Howard Finkel was
staring at his computer when Patrick knocked. Without looking
up, Finkel gestured "come in." Patrick took a seat and
momentarily Finkel turned his chair to face him.

"I want you to go to Houston."

"Houston?"

"I want you to cover the reaction of the oil companies to the
new gas tax Congress is talking about. Especially Axiom's new
Chief Executive Officer-ette."

"Why me?"

"It's political now. That's your department."

"Can't I just call or send one of my reporters?"

"This is big. I want you on the ground. I've already gotten
your ticket. It's waiting at the airport."

"When's my flight?" Patrick blinked at the suddenness of it
all.

"Four hours. Better go pack."

"I guess so."

* * *

Backlash

The Boeing 757 jet was full on this flight to Continental's hub in Houston and Patrick was jammed into a coach seat toward the back of the plane. Patrick closed his eyes while his mind paged through the responsibilities he was carrying. There was a lot going on in Washington and he was a bit surprised that Howard had sent him on this trip. He had turned the article he was working on over to one of his reporters, who would have no trouble finishing it for the afternoon edition and he would be in constant communication with them via cell, email and text.

From his briefcase, he withdrew a file folder containing a collection of clippings about Axiom, including several pictures of Jackie James at different times in her life. The pictures were from all over the country — in fact the world — as she had appeared at various company installations in the performance of her duties. She had an easy smile that looked genuine, even though many of the pictures were obviously posed by company PR photographers. He returned the file to his briefcase and closed his eyes again, deciding to doze for the remainder of the trip if at all possible.

When the plane touched down at Houston's Hobby International Airport, he found the rental car counters and picked up the car Howard's secretary had reserved for him. By now it was about six p.m., so the only thing to do was find the hotel listed on his itinerary and try to get an interview tomorrow. Taking I-45 toward downtown, his directions told him to turn on I-10 West, also known as Katy Freeway. He had never been to Houston before so he slowed to check out the skyline. He was sure it was a big deal here, but he had lived in New York City, so it would take a lot more skyscrapers than this to impress him. He drove for several miles looking for his exit until he passed Loop 610. Suddenly he saw the twenty-story black glass building with the gold Axiom logo covering the upper floors. Across the street he saw a parking lot full of TV satellite trucks and all the clutter that goes with a media encampment. He breathed out slowly. Getting an interview tomorrow would be difficult if not impossible.

CHAPTER SEVEN

Vermont Senator Nathan Taylor leaned back on the black leather rear seat of the Lincoln Town Car limousine in which he rode to Capitol Hill each day. Washington was a beautiful city at night. Countless floodlights made the white marble monuments jump out of the darkness and reflect in the many pools and fountains. Each reflection called up the ghost of statesmen long dead and enhanced Taylor's self-esteem as one who had inherited their mantles.

He was on his way to 1600 Pennsylvania Avenue. President Robert Ryles had agreed to his demand for an audience. He had been to the White House on many occasions during his four terms in the Senate. Since Presidents were limited to two terms and often didn't get reelected for that many, Taylor had virtually dealt with a different president during each of his six-year terms. He didn't have to worry about reelection to a fifth term. His seat was considered "secure" by the Democrat Party leadership. He would have to go through the motions until November, but it would be largely a formality. Vermont voted

Democrat in virtually every election. The '84 presidential election was the only exception in recent memory, when the state joined the rest of the nation in voting for Ronald Reagan.

Today, he was on a mission to get a commitment from President Ryles to sign his Petroleum Independence Act. He suspected Ryles would be reluctant, but Taylor believed he could persuade him.

The driver stopped at the guard booth at the entrance to the White House grounds. Taylor was expected and so they were waved through. The limo stopped at the side entrance where visiting dignitaries were usually routed. The driver opened the door for Taylor, who struggled a little to get out of the low back seat. The white-haired pol walked through the door and was checked in by a serious Secret Service agent. A young Marine in crisp dress blues was assigned to escort him to the Oval Office. He could have easily gone there himself, but it didn't hurt his ego to be ushered in by this respectful youngster.

As the Oval Office door closed behind him Taylor realized he was alone. He walked to one of the twin couches in the middle of the room and sat down, only to stand again, because Ryles came in with his executive assistant.

"Thanks, Mary," Ryles said, dismissing her.

"Nathan!"

"Mr. President."

"How's Jane?"

"I wish I was doing as well as she. She can spend money faster than any woman I know."

"Don't be so sure," the chief executive laughed as he sat across from Taylor on the other couch. "So, what brings you here? I suppose you'll want to talk about the gas-tax bill," said the president, getting right to business. "Do you really think it has a chance of passing?"

"Yes sir, I do. The events of recent days demonstrate the necessity of changing the country's habit where oil is concerned."

"And bringing a pile of tax money into the treasury to boot."

"Yes, and that money can be put to good use in researching alternatives to petroleum."

"Now Nathan. You know where I stand when it comes to government getting people to change the way they live. I'd rather let the alternatives come about and let people adopt them of their own free will."

"But research requires funding, and the gas tax will both fund research and encourage people to use the alternatives that are available."

"Well, I've thought about it and I don't like the way things are shaping up. To raise the price of gasoline by at least a dollar when we are going into the vacation season; how can that be good politically?"

Taylor had not forgotten that it was an election year for Ryles, too. In fact, it was part of his contingency plan. "Mr. President, I think there are enough people who understand the problem that it may be the best thing you could do politically. Our polling suggests that people are appalled by another accident in the Gulf and concern about our dependence on oil is at an all-time high."

"I'm sorry Nathan," the president was standing as if the meeting was ending. "I just don't think it's the right thing to do. I'm not going to be able to sign your bill."

Taylor was still seated. "In that case, Mr. President, I have just one thing to say: Hutchinson's Island."

Taylor disguised his glee as Ryles face went white and he sank back onto the couch. Then he appeared to recover.

"What do you mean by that?"

"You know what I mean, sir. I have a complete report of what happened on a weekend there five years ago, when you were still in the Senate."

Taylor had given him place and time. That should be enough to convince Ryles he had information that could damage him. "I also know the name of the young woman who was with you on the cabin cruiser belonging to a campaign donor in Ft. Pierce." Taylor didn't have to tell the president the effect a strategically placed leak would have six months before the election.

Ryles put his head in his hands. "You wouldn't," he mumbled.

"I don't want to, Bob. But this bill is something I've been working toward my whole career in public service. I want your commitment that you will sign the bill."

After a full 15 seconds, the president whispered bitterly, "You've got it."

* * *

The red compact rental car stopped in front of the gleaming modern high-rise and Patrick Garrity looked up at the black glass and steel monument to Jake James. He then drove to the visitor parking lot.

After parking, Patrick looked across the street at the press encampment. Three television reporters were standing in a row barely 20 feet apart with their backs to the Axiom tower as their images and voices were transmitted through three separate video cameras to three separate satellite uplinks to three separate networks. Other reporters talked on cell phones or pounded on laptops under temporary awnings. Patrick expected he'd be joining them soon, but he would try for the interview first. If he was successful, it wouldn't be the first time saying, "I'm from the Washington Herald" had opened doors.

Backlash

He walked into the spacious lobby fresh from a good night's sleep in a medium-priced chain motel, carrying his scuffed, brown leather briefcase. There hadn't been time for him to call ahead, but he knew Howard would have done that. He stepped up to the desk and greeted the receptionist.

"Patrick Garrity, Washington Herald, to see Ms. Jacqueline James."

The receptionist looked at him over narrow reading glasses as if he had just asked to borrow a million dollars.

"You and about a thousand other people!"

"My office was supposed to have called," Patrick continued bravely. *I do have experience with receptionists.*

"Look," she said, handing him a photocopied sheet of paper. "Here's the latest release. The daily news conference is at eleven." Just then the phone rang with an anemic "beep-beep" and the receptionist answered cheerily, "Axiom Oil Incorporated... One moment please."

Patrick wondered if he should try again, but could see from the standard news release in his hand that the company wasn't being very open right now. It was three hours until the news conference. Perhaps he would join his colleagues across the street and see what he could pick up in the meantime.

* * *

"I don't get it, Dennis. How do they expect us to make a profit?" Jackie was meeting with 10 of her top brass in Axiom's mahogany-paneled conference room. She was speaking to Dennis Trask, chief financial officer.

Trask was not what one expected in an accountant. His broad shoulders would have looked even more formidable if not for his protruding belly, but the effect was to make him look like a retired NFL linebacker. He was tall — at least six foot three — and had a large balding head and red face whose main feature was a thick handlebar mustache he kept neatly waxed. Jackie could imagine him spending weekends playing an outlaw at a Wild West theme park somewhere.

"I don't think they're too concerned about how we'll make a profit, Ms. James," the CFO answered more formally than usual.

"Don't they understand what a hardship this will be on the people that have to buy gas to go to work?"

"I don't think they care about that either. They just want to save the world, or 'The Earth,' I guess."

"The government is under a lot of political pressure from environmental groups," John Thompson, VP of exploration and acquisition, put in, also more formally than usual. *Ordinarily he would have said "the green guys" instead of "environmental groups,"* Jackie thought. She wondered if his usual name for them was an allusion to "little green men from Mars."

"But what do they hope to accomplish with this?"

"They want to force people to stop using gasoline, I guess," President Benny Tyson volunteered.

"So, what are people supposed to do for transportation?"

The people at the table looked at one another, stopped momentarily by the latest of their new boss' questions. They were all familiar with the efforts to replace the internal-combustion engine with other technologies, and they all knew the reasons it hadn't happened yet. As promising as solar power, electric power, fuel cell or some kind of gasoline-electric hybrid might be, there were always limitations that caused the vehicles to be less than practical for the mass market. Either the vehicles couldn't go fast enough or they couldn't go far enough or, in the case of experimental solar vehicles, they wouldn't go at all if there was a stretch of cloudy days. A solar-powered car that could go as far and as fast as a gasoline car would need to be two highway lanes wide and as long as a semi-trailer truck to have adequate collection surface.

As for hybrids, which were already being marketed, the lackluster improvements in fuel economy were somewhat offset by higher sticker price and the $300-to$400 battery replacement cost. The kicker was that, in an accident or fire, the potassium hydroxide used in the special batteries became a serious hazardous material requiring a special "Class D" fire extinguisher. That had to frustrate the Environmentalists! A car that had half the power and half the range of an internal-combustion-engine car, but cost twice as much just wouldn't fly in the market.

Fuel cell technology held out great promise and California had tried to set up fueling stations, but a nation full of them would require large quantities of hydrogen to be available at service stations. The men at the table knew something about transporting and marketing fuel. Hydrogen was dangerous and difficult to store and dispense; in its pure gaseous form, hydrogen was much more volatile than gasoline. Using "reformers", hydrogen could be produced from various hydrocarbon raw materials including petroleum products, but the byproducts were as objectionable – if not more objectionable – than the exhaust of modern internal combustion engines, and so far, the hydrogen produced by such processes hadn't been pure enough.

Axiom had done its own research with each of the technologies, just so there wouldn't be any unpleasant surprises. The Axiom executives knew there might come a time when the company would have to change with the new technologies, if the efficiency obstacles could be overcome. And even if alternatives to petrol fuel were perfected to the point of being widely available and marketed at competitive prices, the need for petroleum products would still be great for lubrication, plastic auto parts and hydraulic brake fluid. And that was just for automobiles; it didn't even touch the need for heating oil and petroleum used in manufacturing everything from asphalt pavement to binders in pharmaceuticals to synthetic fabric.

"It looks like they would wait until practical alternatives are available before doing something like this," Benny said.

"That would imply that the government was logical," Thompson laughed.

"Maybe we ought to stop selling gas for a while so the environmental lobbyists can't drive to Capitol Hill!" Jackie joked, causing wry laughter to go around the table.

Then she asked, "Is there anybody we can talk to in Congress about this?"

"Our lobbyists have their favorites, of course," Benny said. "They say they were blind-sided by this just like we were."

"See if they can get a read about the bill's chances from somebody in Congress."

"Right away," Benny said as he made a note to himself on his pad.

They discussed the situation for another half hour, but didn't really solve anything, since the company could do little to stop a vote in Congress besides making political contributions and Axiom had already done that, by the bucketful. For some reason, this train seemed to have left the station. The assembled executives agreed to think about the issue and meet again next week. Then Jackie dismissed them to do the work they already had on their desks before all this started.

Although she had plenty to do, she would have to once again meet with Charlene and prepare for yet another news conference. The recent events in Washington did nothing to encourage the "News Gypsies" to leave. She had been naïve to think they would lose interest and go away, but that had been her hope: that if she or Charlene or Benny told them roughly the same thing every day, the reporters would decide there was nothing newsworthy and would fold their tents and steal away.

But now there WAS news and Jackie was sure there would be questions about the proposed gas tax. Charlene, in their now-daily meeting, advised simply saying they didn't have enough information to formulate a response, which was true, after all.

* * *

FBI Agent Tony Bouchet sat down at his desk at the New Orleans field office. It was piled high with notes and files with a system only he knew. He noticed a new pink "While-You-Were-Out" note taped to his computer monitor. He pulled the note loose and read it. It asked him to return a call from Arthur Beaudreaux. He might have information about a case, it said. *That's strange*, he thought. *Why would his father's cousin have information about a case?*

The number was on the note, so he immediately called it, expecting to get an answering machine, but Arthur came on the line.

"Hello. Beaudreaux Aviation."

"Bonjour, Arthur, is that you? It's Tony."

"Tony, mon ami. Merci, for calling me back."

"What's up, cousin? The note said you had something about a case. What do you know about my cases?"

"Not to worry, Tony. I don't know your cases, but something happened the other day that I thought I should tell someone about and naturally I thought of my little cousin who grew up to be the big, important FBI agent."

And Arthur proceeded to tell Bouchet about the odd pair he had flown out to see the Gulf Pride Oil Platform two-and-a-half weeks earlier. Agent Bouchet was indeed interested.

"One of the guys was tall and had a beard. He wore all cloth, no leather, not even his belt. The other one wore his hair slicked back and was a real dandy, a sharp dresser. I heard on the news that the company said it was a terrorist attack, but the news guy thought it was an accident; the oil company's fault. When I flew the reporter and camera guy out there, I wondered if it was the same platform."

"Did they sign anything?" Bouchet asked as he feverishly wrote down every word of Beaudreaux's story.

"The first guys? No, they paid with cash and I just took them where they wanted to go."

"Arthur, you did the right thing by calling. This information could be very helpful to us. I'll let you know if we have other questions. Thank you very much. Give my love to your sainted mother."

"Adyeu, Tony. We need to go crawdad fishing soon."

"Sounds good to me. Adyeu."

Bouchet hung up the phone and sat back in his chair, hardly believing the conversation he had just had. He didn't see Arthur but perhaps once a year, but they had known each other all Bouchet's life. When Tony was a toddler, Arthur had been the older cousin of Bouchet's father.

It could be nothing. Indeed, Arthur wasn't sure it was even the same platform, but if they were casing it when they chartered his plane, then Arthur might have just given him a description of the people who attacked the oil rig. When the import of Arthur's information had sunk in, he jumped up and virtually ran to the nearby office of his boss, Special Agent Thomas Shannon.

Backlash

He knocked on Shannon's open door and was nodded in. "You're not going to believe the phone call I just got," Bouchet began.

* * *

After the dismissive treatment he experienced from the receptionist, Patrick left his rental car in Axiom's visitor's parking lot and walked across the street to the press encampment. He had been in these sieges before, during high profile trials or during scandals like those that seemed to crop up as regular as the changing season, with politicians mixed up with young, nubile interns, the politician refusing to answer press questions, which just made them sure he was hiding something. There was something of that atmosphere here now. Presently he saw someone he knew.

"Patrick, I didn't expect to see you here!"

"My boss says it's political now, so here I am," Patrick smiled as he shook hands with Diedra Baumgard, reporter for Newsweek magazine. They had worked together briefly at the New York Times, although much of the time he had been in Albany following the state legislature. Diedra was older than Patrick and was a respected reporter and columnist.

"Yeah, it'll be interesting to see what line they try to feed us today," she said with a bored expression.

"What's the buzz?"

"Management claims they were attacked by terrorists. Most of the guys think something else is behind it."

Patrick knew "the guys" were the other reporters. On a big story, there was always cross-pollination as reporters sat around together waiting for something to happen or for their deadlines when they would have to file their stories. After exchanging a few more personal pleasantries with Diedra,

Patrick excused himself, having seen Bernie Maitland across the way. Bernie had been an intern at the Herald several years ago.

"Bernie! Hey, man! Long time no see!"

"Mr. Garrity! How are you?" Bernie had lost the boyishness he'd had 10 years ago and put on several pounds.

"So, what are you doing now?"

"I'm working for the Dallas Morning News; state beat."

"Good for you. I just got in. What's going on?"

"Well, you know about the bill in Congress I'm sure."

"Yeah, that's why I'm here."

"Of course. We haven't heard anything from management about that yet. It was starting to get a bit boring. There hadn't been anything new for a couple of days. I guess the news conference today will be different."

"Yeah, maybe. What do you think of their story about the terrorism?"

"I don't know. At first it just sounded like a scam, but they haven't wavered," Bernie shrugged. "Maybe it's even true. The Coast Guard won't allow any reporters or photographers to get close to the site, so that hasn't helped."

Patrick enjoyed seeing his old colleague again and they soon began talking about more general things. Before he knew it, it was time to go across the street for the news conference.

The auditorium was already crowded with reporters when Patrick and Bernie arrived. TV cameras lined the back wall and there was a noisy locker-room atmosphere as the reporters joked with each other. Patrick knew that there was also suspicion and competition just below the surface. Even now, some of the journalists were on cell phones to sources or to their editors, trying to get an edge that would allow them to be the ones that asked THE pointed question that split the story wide open. Patrick wondered if he should have called his office for the latest from Capitol Hill, but he figured Diedra or Bernie would have told him if something big was up. He'd call after the news conference.

Patrick placed his mini-cassette recorder on the podium among the many microphones with their brightly colored logos declaring the network or local TV station to which they belonged. Once more he thanked the news gods that he was a print reporter and wasn't shackled to a 30-pound TV camera and a microwave truck.

Promptly at 11:00, a trio of Axiom management types strode in, followed by an assistant carrying photocopied news releases. Patrick recognized Jacqueline James from the pictures in the file in his briefcase and from the video he'd seen on TV. She was shorter than he'd thought she'd be, but people were always different in person than they looked on TV. She was also more attractive than she had appeared in the pictures, he decided. Still pictures couldn't show how a person moved and that could be an important clue to personality. She stepped to the podium, took her watch off her wrist and laid it in front of her.

"Good morning, everyone. We have a handout for you. Pick one up on your way out. I don't have any prepared remarks this morning, so we can go right to your questions."

And they were off and running.

"What is your reaction to the new gas tax proposed in Congress yesterday?" a reporter asked the obvious first question.

"We have not seen the actual legislation, yet," Jacqueline began. "We have only heard what's been reported in the media. Naturally we are distressed that Congress seems to want to hurt the people who buy gasoline. However, until we are able to learn the details of the bill, I can't comment on it directly."

She swept a small hand through her dark, shoulder-length hair and pointed at another reporter.

"The intent seems to be to discourage people from buying your product by increasing the price by a dollar a gallon. An additional dollar per gallon will have to come out of your profits. How will Axiom respond?"

Patrick saw that she was expecting the same question to be asked again in a different way and wasn't rattled by it. She already knew the game.

"We haven't had time to formulate a response. Our liaisons in Washington will be relaying specifics to us as they learn them and I suppose we will have to assemble all the facts before we can know how we should respond. Naturally, we aren't happy that Congress appears to want to punish us, when we haven't done anything wrong."

Patrick wondered if she had intentionally tweaked the reporters in the room, since many of them would regard Axiom as having done wrong simply by trafficking in oil. Perhaps she was that naïve, or perhaps she was that spunky, he couldn't tell which. He did notice that she carried herself well, though, and didn't seem intimidated by the scrutiny that was focused on her. As the news conference continued for the half hour allotted, very little was accomplished as the reporters used their questions to relay what they knew about the proposed new gas tax and Axiom's petite CEO steadfastly refused to give them much information, other than the statement of general disappointment she had expressed 30 minutes ago.

Finally, the allotted time expired and Ms. James thanked the reporters for coming, almost sounding sincere. Patrick hadn't asked any questions, having just gotten there and figuring out right away that there wasn't any real news to report yet. The press' suspicion of negligence on the part of the company was growing tired as management kept to their terrorism story, and if the FBI was involved, as was indicated by the photocopied handout, maybe Axiom was telling the truth. This would frustrate the reporters, Patrick knew, and they wouldn't easily forgive the company for denying them a scandal.

The CEO was right, the gas tax bill had appeared out of nowhere and they really hadn't had time to formulate a response. He could guess what might be the off-the-cuff remarks in the boardrooms somewhere upstairs. Perhaps there would be news tomorrow.

Patrick made his way forward to retrieve his recorder, like a salmon swimming upstream through the waves of reporters headed out the back door. TV producers and cameramen were retrieving their microphones as they did every day at this time. About the time that Patrick got to the podium, a big, bearded tech in an "I'm-With-the-Band" T-shirt grabbed his microphone and knocked Patrick's mini-cassette over. It slid down the desk of the podium and bounced across the carpet, coming to a stop at the feet of Jacqueline James, who had come back into the room through the door behind the podium. She bent down and picked up the recorder and locked eyes with Patrick.

"Is this yours?" she asked him.

"Yes, thank you," he said taking it from her outstretched hand.

"I forgot my watch," she said, taking the small, jeweled timepiece from the podium where she had left it and replacing it on her wrist.

Patrick realized he was staring dumbly at her when she smiled and started to leave. Then he came to his senses and became a reporter again. "Ms. James, could I ask you something?"

"The news conference is over."

"I know, I'm Patrick Garrity, Washington Herald. I just wanted to know how you're liking your new job."

She didn't extend her hand, so Patrick didn't extend his, though he would have liked to shake hands with her. It never hurt to establish a personal connection with people you were reporting on.

"I haven't really had time to do my actual job yet. I'll probably like it just fine when I can get to it."

She smiled again and turned to leave once more. Patrick couldn't think of anything else to say, so he watched her disappear through the door. There was something about her he liked; he just wasn't sure what it was.

CHAPTER EIGHT

That wasn't the attitude of his peers, however. About the middle of the afternoon, he went to lunch with Diedra.

"Can you believe that woman? Standing there and refusing to answer our questions like that," Diedra said, her lips stopping just before another forkful of chef salad landed on her tongue.

"I didn't see anything we haven't seen a thousand times in a thousand other news conferences," Patrick answered.

"Maybe, but I would just like to see what's really going on upstairs right now. I bet they're sweating bullets."

"And I suppose you're glad?"

"What's not to like? A fat corporation that's made its money preying on people and abusing the Environment? Maybe it's about to get its comeuppance."

"But what will a sudden dollar-a-gallon jump in gasoline prices do to the economy right before the summer travel season? Isn't that a problem?"

"It will force people to take public transportation," Diedra said, echoing the line that had become the battle cry in Congress as the gas tax bill was being pushed through committees.

"You can't take public transportation to grandma's house or DisneyWorld," Patrick argued. "I think this bill could be a little hasty."

"Still it would be fun to see them get theirs," Diedra smiled grimly, her dark eyes hard as granite.

Suddenly Patrick remembered Jacqueline James' eyes as she smiled and handed him his mini-cassette. The contrast was striking. He realized right then that what he liked about Ms. James was that she seemed genuine. It was just a gut feeling, but he couldn't help thinking that, even if she was misguided, the Axiom CEO at least believed what she said and said what she believed. His colleagues in the news business might be too cynical to accept it, but Ms. James might be a force to be reckoned with, if for no other reason than she believed in herself. Sure, she was green now, but she was learning. If she was as genuine as she appeared, she might just be telling the truth about the terrorism, but no one in the news media seemed to be interested. That was incredible, now that he thought about it.

As soon as he could, he excused himself and headed back to his hotel where he fired up his laptop and went on the Internet to research eco-terrorism. He was surprised how little he knew of the incidents of eco-terrorism and how much there was to research. Except for the Unabomber's mail bombs, it seemed no one had ever died as a result of the terrorism, but there seemed to be an escalation of terrorist activities. Patrick wondered why these violent acts against private property hadn't been more widely reported.

* * *

Special Agent Thomas Shannon's navy Ford Victoria slid a few inches as he braked to a stop in the shell-and gravel parking lot of the Timbalier Bay Marina near Port Fourchon, Louisiana. Another identical blue Ford was already parked in front of the salt-corroded sign that read "Boat Rental." Shannon was met by agent Tony Bouchet, who had discovered this marina after calling a long list of coastal harbors from Biloxi to Beaumont.

"Bonjour! We think we got 'em."

"They rented the boats here?"

"One boat," Bouchet said, looking toward the water, he pointed at a low, streamlined cigarette boat, its dark, varnished wood mirroring the afternoon sun. "It's designed for speed. Great for making a getaway."

"The rental was the right time frame?"

"They picked it up the day of the attack, kept it overnight and brought it back within 24 hours," Bouchet grinned. "Wouldn't want to pay for a second day, Patron!"

"Right," Shannon's smile was brief. "How'd they pay?"

"Cash, of course. Owner thought that was unusual."

"How many?"

"Two showed up, but they rented five life jackets."

Shannon smiled bigger this time. "Good job. Got a good description?"

Bouchet waved his notebook. "I got it all down. Maybe good enough for a composite. Both American. One was tall and thin, with a beard," Tony gave Shannon a knowing look as they both wordlessly recalled Arthur Beaudreaux's phone call.

"What about their vehicle?"

"The owner didn't see what they were driving, so we're canvassing the surrounding slips to see if anybody saw anything."

"Have you dusted the boat?"

"Yeah. There's hundreds of fingerprints. It gets rented at least once a week. I doubt any of the prints are our guys. They almost certainly used gloves, but we'll run 'em anyway. C'est la vie," Bouchet said with a shrug.

They had continued to walk down to the dock until they stood next to the long boat that looked like it was speeding over the water even when it was tethered to the pilings. It had just enough room for six, a bit cramped, but there was a small cabin in the bow. *Bouchet is right*, Shannon thought. If the perpetrators were smart they didn't leave any prints or other evidence, but they would collect and run the prints anyway. They would also check for fiber evidence and traces of the explosive that was used at the oilrig.

Just then two men approached, one fit and lean in a navy knit shirt with "FBI" on the breast pocket and the other short and beefy in bright yellow shorts, a turquoise-and-white Hawaiian shirt and a white captain's hat. His flip-flops made a "thunket-thunket" sound on the planks of the dock.

"This is Mr. Tinker. He thinks he saw the vehicle," Agent Gifford Rice said, pointing to the other man and nodding hello to Shannon.

"Special Agent Thomas Shannon," he said, extending his hand for the Hawaiian shirted man to shake.

"Bob Tinker," the 60-something man said in a vaguely Michigan-sounding accent, extending his hand to Shannon and Bouchet in turn. He had a couple of days of white stubble on his sunburned face. "My boat is the 'Betty Jean' over there," he pointed to a nearby slip, close to the shore. The "Betty Jean" was a cabin cruiser, about 30 feet long, bow to stern, Shannon guessed as he glanced that direction.

"You saw the men who rented this boat last Saturday?" Shannon asked.

"I saw them bring it back on Sunday. I was kicked back with a Bud, watching the Tigers get trounced on the dish, and I saw the van waiting for them."

"What time was that?"

"About one, one-thirty. The game had just started."

"Somebody picked them up? They didn't leave the van overnight?"

"Guess not. The van was a rental. Sat right over there for about 45 minutes before the guys dropped the boat off." Tinker pointed to a corner of the parking lot. He went on to describe the van as a red, long-wheelbase Dodge and told the agents which rental agency's logo was on the fender. Bouchet added the new information to his notebook.

"Did you see who was driving?"

"Yeah, he looked like an old hippie. Had long straight hair pulled back in one of those ponytails. Salt-and-pepper. There were others in the van, too."

"How many?"

"I don't know, two, maybe three. They stayed in the van the whole time with the engine running and the AC on, I expect. Didn't think much about it, but I did notice the ponytail guy driving. And one of the guys on the boat had a beard."

"Thank you, Mr. Tinker, you've been very helpful," Shannon shook his hand again. "We'll contact you if we need to know more." He turned to Rice. "You got his numbers?"

"Will do, sir," Rice answered, taking a notebook out of his pocket with which to record Tinker's contact information.

"Hey, what did these guys do?" Tinker probed.

"We can't talk about the investigation," Shannon said, as he and Bouchet eased away from them.

"Yeah, I guess not," Tinker said, obviously disappointed. He gave his contact information to Rice, then ambled back to the "Betty Jean" on his short, bowed legs.

Shannon, Bouchet and Rice compared notes on everything they knew. The description given by the marina owner matched the description of the tall, bearded man Arthur Beaudreaux had flown out to see the oil platform. There had probably been five altogether, but only two took the boat out. Since the men rented five life jackets, the boat must have picked up the men in the van somewhere else to avoid being spotted and they left the van elsewhere to avoid its being connected to the boat. The suspects had rented the boat with cash, but they couldn't have rented the van without a credit card and that meant there would be a paper trail. It might be their first break.

* * *

The next morning, Patrick rose early. Knowing it was an hour later in Washington, he made a phone call to an agent he knew at the headquarters of the Federal Bureau of Investigation. "Sam, it's Patrick Garrity," he said when Special Agent Samuel Jorgensen came on the line.

"Yeah, what's up?" the Fed asked warily. They were not friends by any means, but Jorgensen had been willing to talk to Patrick off the record in the past.

"What can you tell me about the investigation into the attack on the Gulf Pride oil platform in Louisiana?"

"I don't know what you're talking about."

"Don't you watch CNN?"

"Occasionally."

"Do you not know about the incident or do you not know anything about the investigation?" Patrick knew enough to ask a question that couldn't be answered with "Yes" or "No."

Backlash

Enough time elapsed before Jorgensen answered to tell Patrick that he knew something and was trying to decide what to tell him.

"You know we don't talk about ongoing investigations."

"So, there is an investigation," exulted Patrick. It was a small victory, but he had confirmed Axiom's assertion that the incident was being treated as a criminal act. "Can you tell me if the investigation has shown conclusively that it was a terrorist attack?" Again, there was a long pause before the answer came.

"We're certain that it was an attack, yes."

Gratified by his success, Patrick pressed further.

"What proof do you have, and can I quote you?"

"That's all I can tell you, Garrity, and no, you can't quote me. This is deep background, as always."

"Gotcha. Thanks Sam. You've been a big help," and Patrick hung up the phone.

So, it was true. The FBI was investigating. They only got involved when criminal activity crossed state lines. The attack on the Gulf Pride had been in international waters and a man had died. The FBI's involvement ruled out an accident. Patrick hadn't gotten an answer to his question about proof, but no answer was almost as good as a "Yes" in this case. That put a whole new complexion on what was going on in Congress. Could it be that the members pushing the gas tax bill didn't know what the FBI knew?

Now he really wanted to get an interview with someone inside Axiom. There would be another news conference at 11:00 a.m. today, but he'd prefer not to alert his competition by asking a pointed question that would only send them all scrambling to get the same information he had. No, he needed to talk to someone in the know, and he would like for it to be the petite, dark-haired CEO with the sincere eyes.

Patrick's experience had been that a company like Axiom hunkered down and clammed up in a situation like this, so it would probably keep its no-interview policy in place. To give himself a chance, he got to the auditorium early for the daily news conference and sat on the front row where he could make a beeline for the exit door that Jacqueline James would use when the news conference was over.

* * *

President Robert Ryles hated himself for what he was about to do. Yet he hated Nathan Taylor more for forcing him to do it. He had regretted the weekend in Florida so many times. He thought it was under wraps, yet he should have known that if people know something they will eventually talk about it. He wondered if Barbara told someone. Women did tend to talk to each other and, even when sworn to secrecy, their friends could hardly resist passing on such juicy information. The young campaign worker, Barbara, had been sweet, lovely and willing, looking at him as a hero or perhaps she was just seduced by power. Either way, her attentions were irresistible for his ego as he geared up for his presidential campaign. The wealthy donor may have known what had happened because it had happened on his yacht, but he had looked the other way. Maybe he had talked. Or maybe some Marina employee had seen them leave and remembered his face when it later turned up on TV at the party's convention or in the debates.

At any rate, he would be finished if it got out. The lessons of Bill Clinton's dalliances and Hillary's support for him was irrelevant in Ryles' case. He had run convincingly on a family-values platform. He really believed it too, but that day four years ago his libido and ego had overcome his principles.

Backlash

Ryles wondered how much Taylor really knew. He hadn't said much, but the little bit he had said had been breathtakingly accurate and the implication of political and personal damage was loud and clear. There was no love lost between Ryles and Taylor, with Ryles being a conservative from Wisconsin and Taylor a liberal from Vermont. They had crossed swords in the Senate about welfare reform, dairy price supports and other issues; Ryles taking the hands-off approach and Taylor always favoring government "help"; what Ryles called intrusion.

But this Saturday morning, Ryles would have no choice but to support Taylor in a bill he was certain was a mistake. It went against his principles, but he couldn't risk a revelation that would shatter his wife and children just when he needed them — and the voters — to support him in his bid for a second term.

He rose from the large desk in the Oval Office, having finished reviewing the speech one of his best writers had written for his weekly radio address and walked out into the hall. The door opened for him as if by magic, held by a Secret Service agent who always knew where the president was and where he would go next.

Without a word, the agent escorted him to the studio where he always recorded the address when he was in town. He entered the soundproof booth alone and sat down facing the microphone in front of the double-glass window. He waved at the technician on the other side, sitting at a console covered in scores of little buttons that were meaningless to Ryles.

"Mornin' Dale."

"Good Morning, Mr. President."

"Are we ready?"

"Whenever you are, sir."

* * *

The time was drawing near when Jackie would have to once again go down into the "vipers' den" as she had taken to calling the auditorium where the press gathered each day for its briefing. Once again there was little news to give, but at least the news conferences had reduced the requests for interviews to a trickle. The events in Washington only added to the pressure being applied by the reporters as they grilled her each day.

Today, even though it was Saturday, Charlene would give the opening statement and Jackie would stand by to answer questions if she was needed, which seemed unlikely, since the company still had no official response to the proposed legislation and it was too soon to know more about the investigation into the attack. There would be no news conference on Sunday. Jackie had put her foot down about that.

Charlene appeared and together they walked to the elevator and descended to the first floor, taking a back hallway to the back door of the auditorium, which had become their routine.

Inside, the room was full as usual and Charlene went to the podium while Jackie sat in a chair to one side. Charlene's assistant had passed out a news release and was now standing at the back of the room.

"Good morning," Charlene began. "I have an opening statement and then we will take questions." Then she began reading from the prepared statement.

"While we still do not have specific information about the proposed legislation now before Congress regarding a new gasoline tax, Axiom takes the position that such a tax would be detrimental to the economy and to the American people in going about their business. It would hurt the poor most of all and would severely hurt many if not all businesses, not just oil companies.

"For this reason, Axiom management urges our political leaders to defeat this ill-considered bill. Coming as it does at the beginning of the summer travel season, a variety of industries could be adversely affected.

"Now, for your questions," Charlene said, having finished the written statement. "Yes," Charlene pointed to a reporter.

"Have you heard that President Ryles announced in his radio address this morning that he will sign the bill if it reaches his desk?"

Charlene caught her breath and shot a look at Jackie, who shrugged. "We had not heard that," Charlene admitted, lapsing into PR-speak. "We are disappointed to hear it. We will get a transcript of the message as soon as possible. We can't comment until we read the message." She then recognized another reporter.

"You encourage the defeat of the bill, but what will Axiom's response be if the bill passes?"

"It's too early to tell. We frankly don't see how such a bill could pass. We're believing that cooler heads will prevail."

"But what if it does pass?" the reporter insisted.

"Then we will take action at that time."

And so it went. There was no need for Jackie to answer any questions. Charlene handled the news conference just fine. Jackie decided she would skip some of them next week. Even with the president's promise to sign the bill, perhaps the media frenzy would lose some steam as the days passed with nothing else happening since it would take a while for Congress to pass the bill, if it passed at all.

Eleven-thirty came and Charlene declared the news conference over. Again, no real news had been made except Axiom had called on Congress to defeat the bill, which was really no surprise to anyone and could even appear self-serving.

Jackie had stood and started toward the door when she saw someone coming toward her. It was the reporter whose recorder she had picked up yesterday.

"Ms. James. I'm Patrick Garrity of the Washington Herald. We met yesterday." He extended his hand for her to shake and reflexively she did. "I wanted to tell you, I've done some digging and I believe you about the ecoterrorism."

"Really?" Jackie said warily. Inside she was thinking, *What took you so long?*

"Yes, I talked to a contact at the FBI this morning and I was wondering if I might ask you a few questions — in private."

Jackie looked at him through narrowed eyes. Could this be a ruse just to get an interview? So far, she hadn't granted that to anyone, though many had requested it.

"Why should I give you an interview?"

"Because I agree with you that Congress is about to make a big mistake. I'm a political reporter, Ms. James, but I think something more is going on than meets the eye."

Jackie considered herself a pretty good judge of character and, as she looked into Patrick Garrity's clear blue eyes, she decided maybe she could trust this reporter. Reaching into a pocket of her navy suit coat, she took out a business card and on the back wrote "Bar T Steakhouse" and an address. She handed the card to him.

"Meet me here at eight tonight."

"Okay. Thank you!"

Jackie turned and hurried through the door, hoping she hadn't just made a mistake. Charlene joined her as she waited for the elevator.

"What was that about?" she asked.

"I just agreed to an interview."

"Who is he?"

"Political reporter for the Washington Herald."

"Do you think that's wise?"

"He's talked to the FBI and he believes us that the Gulf Pride was a terrorist attack. I think he might be able to do us some good if he prints an article that proves we were attacked and not negligent. Most of these reporters don't seem to want to believe that."

"I hope you're right," Charlene said without looking at Jackie.

"Me too," Jackie answered.

CHAPTER NINE

The Bar T Steakhouse was a raucous place with loud country music on the jukebox and cowboy boots galore. The décor was rustic and purposely garish. The bar was crowded with men and a few women in blue-collar clothes. Jackie James entered, decked out in fringed shirt, jeans and shiny cowboy boots, stopping at the first table.

"Hey Duke!" She slapped a blue-collar man on the back then looked at his friends. "I hope all of you know to take Duke's stories with a grain of salt. He tends to 'Texas-size' everything." All those at the table laughed, including Duke, a weatherworn giant of about 60.

"Hey, Jackie, sorry about your dad!" Duke said in a booming voice. "He was a good man!"

"Thanks. We'll all miss him. Good to see you." Then she looked up and surveyed the room.

There he was, the reporter from Washington D.C., looking as out of place as could be in a sport coat. *He'd probably never owned a pair of cowboy boots in his life*, she thought. She walked over and he stood as she sat down. The glass of iced tea in front of him was half finished, even though she wasn't late.

"Hungry?" he asked, touching the menus propped up between the saltshaker and napkin dispenser.

"I'll just get an iced tea like yours," Jackie answered as she made a small gesture with her hand that was picked up without a word by a petite waitress with a bouncy ponytail behind the bar. Less than 15 seconds later she set a big glass of iced tea in front of Jackie.

Almost subconsciously, she wondered why Patrick hadn't ordered beer. The Bar T certainly had a plentiful selection and she had heard that reporters as a class were serious drinkers.

"You must come here often," Patrick said.

"This was one of my father's favorite places. I came here with him a lot." Then, determined to keep the conversation businesslike, she changed the subject. "So, you said you believed we had been hit by terrorists. How come you're different from all the other reporters?"

"I have a source at the FBI in D.C. He wouldn't tell me too much, but he did confirm that they are investigating, which tells me they believe criminal activity is involved. Any clue who did it?"

"If the FBI knows, they haven't told me," she said glancing at him sideways, unsure of how much to say. "I guess they're just getting started."

"I did some research and found out about a group called the 'Earth Liberation Front' that has committed arson several times up in the Northwest. Do you think they might be involved?"

"Like I said, the FBI hasn't said anything yet. Sounds like a suspicious group, but we're not in the Northwest. I hope you're not too disappointed that I don't know more." She looked at him for some reaction in his expression, but his face had not changed.

"Is there anything you can tell me by way of proof that it was an attack? You went to the site, right?"

She paused, realizing that not answering quickly was an answer in itself. She may have already revealed enough that he would eventually find out what the FBI had told her not to tell the press.

"I'm new to all this," she said finally. "Can I tell you something — what do you call it — 'off the record'?"

"Yes, of course. If it confirms my suspicions then I'll know that I'm looking in the right direction."

She paused for a moment as she struggled to justify what she had wanted to do for days. She had to tell someone the key piece of information that would clear Axiom of suspicion and direct everyone's attention to the perpetrators where it belonged. She hoped it wouldn't damage the investigation, but this reporter's acceptance of the premise that the company had been attacked was too seductive to ignore.

"Okay, but you can't print this yet, because the FBI doesn't want it to get out until they get a line on the outlaws."

Patrick smirked and Jackie blushed because she knew he was amused by her use of the word "outlaw." Sitting here in the Bar T Steakhouse it seemed a perfectly appropriate word to use, with its rough-hewn paneling and six-gun-and-lariat motif; in Houston, where the state police was still known as Texas Rangers, with all the Old West lore that name conjured.

"Okay, but you're the one out of your element here," she chided him, sitting there in his turtleneck sweater and tweed blazer. "Where are you from anyhow? I get the feeling you're not from these parts." He did laugh this time as she put some extra twang in the words "these parts" for his benefit. She

decided she felt comfortable with this man, even if he was a
reporter and from—?

"Boston, originally," he said with a lingering smile. "And I
lived in New York for several years. Then wound up in D.C."

"Boston, huh? I thought I heard you drop an "R." Did you
know I went to Harvard?" She pronounced Harvard as
"Haaahvaaahd."

"No joke?" He appeared genuinely surprised while ignoring
her exaggerated, imitation New England accent. "And I went to
NYU. I guess the grass is always greener somewhere else, huh?"

"Well, I went to Harvard because my Daddy did."

"And please pardon me for not telling you I'm sorry for your
loss."

"Thanks," Jackie said softly, watching his blue eyes for
evidence of sincerity.

"I went to NYU for the journalism school."

"Harvard Business."

"Right. So, what were you going to tell me?"

"Off the record?" she held up an index finger as if to pin him
down, not quite pointing at him.

"Off the record, until you tell me otherwise."

"Okay. The terrorists left a message."

"A message?"

"Yeah. It was spray-painted on one of the supports of the
platform. It said, 'We're watching you'."

"No joke? I'll be...! Did you know that message has been left
at some of the other terrorism incidents?"

"You're kidding!" She wondered if he was pulling her leg, but
she didn't have to wonder long. He reached into his briefcase
and withdrew a printout from a website showing a picture of a
white pickup with exactly the same message on it in black
spray-paint. In the background was a row of charred buildings.

"I can't believe it," she said.

From then on they were like old friends who shared a secret. She opened up and told him all she knew about the attack. When the waitress with the bouncy ponytail returned, they ordered steak and potatoes and black-eye peas, and later, black bottom pie and coffee. They talked about Boston and Congress and the oil business and the New York Times until it was almost time for the Bar T to close.

"So, are you married?" she smiled mischievously.

"Was. Didn't work out."

"I'm sorry," she answered, meaning it and suddenly wishing she hadn't asked.

"What about you?"

"Nope. I never slowed down long enough." She deftly changed the subject to something that would be more comfortable for them both. The truth was she had been engaged once.

She had dated often in high school and college. Then, in grad school she slacked off some with the rigors of Harvard. After joining the family business, she worked hard and dated regularly enough. Then she met Arturo. He was a Mexican-American with the darkest possible black hair and eyes to match. She decided the phrase "tall, dark and handsome" had been coined for him. She had fallen hard for him in her twenty-eighth year. They dated for about two years, and then he asked her to marry him. She enthusiastically agreed and she and her mother planned a wedding fit for royalty. Then suddenly, three weeks from the wedding date, Arturo had apparently gotten cold feet. He disappeared with just a note and no forwarding address. Jackie made every effort to find him, but he didn't want to be found.

Backlash

Jackie had then thrown herself into her work, soon becoming Vice President of Operations and using her job as an excuse to be on the go all the time. After that, anyone wanting to date her would have had to lasso her and tie her feet together like one of her rodeo calves.

"You sure you don't want me to print the information about the message?" Patrick asked as he sipped the last of his coffee. "Seems like it would really help your case."

"You don't know how much I wish I could let you do that, but the FBI says it's important to the investigation to keep that quiet for now."

"But that would make it clear that you were attacked and not negligent like some reports are saying."

"I know, but I can't. I'd like to shout it from the rooftops, but what I want more is for the people who did this to be caught."

Patrick looked down at the dark crust that was all that was left of his pie and frowned.

* * *

On the way home alone in her BMW, Jackie smiled as she thought how she and the redheaded reporter had laughed together about self-important politicians and editors and chairmen of the board. It had been a long time since she sat with someone she liked and laughed so.

* * *

It had been a week since the successful attack on the oilrig. Paul Stoddard was taking this weekend easy, tending to his animals and repairing a kennel. He had also worked on his website and answered some email, including a congratulatory message from his Washington D.C. contact, who indicated there might be more missions in the future.

Meanwhile, he saw the reports of the proposed gas tax legislation and was gratified. He felt that he had done something positive and was part of a movement that would be able to really change things for the better. Everything seemed to be falling into place the way his contact had said it would. The president had even promised to sign the gas tax bill, a turn of events that surprised most people, because he usually took the side of the special interests. This time was different, Paul knew, feeling smug that he could sit in his living room in Baytown, Texas and have a better feel for what was going on in Washington than some of the insiders did.

And best of all, the spinners were doing their jobs so that most people still thought the incident at the drilling rig had been an accident. He was sure that there was an investigation, but they had been very careful, using cash as much as possible and had split up and taken care to not appear as a group. It had been inconvenient to travel several miles from their base cabin in the bayou to rent the boats and from different marinas, but it had allowed them to leave the vans in the wilderness instead of parking them overnight at the marinas where they could be spotted and identified. His training had been thorough on those points. He was confident they had not given law enforcement a trail to follow.

He was pleased with the way his organization had developed. It had started as an Internet bulletin board for people wanting to do something about the flagrant abuses of Mother Earth. He had identified and screened participants who lived in the Houston area, meeting them one by one, testing their commitment to the Cause. Meanwhile the website that grew out of the bulletin board caught the attention of a national group that had a Washington D.C. office. Over a period of months, with funding and training from the national group, Paul and carefully selected associates had picketed embattled companies suspected of environmental violations, performed relatively small harassing activities at refineries and even swelled the ranks of anti-death penalty demonstrators at the state penitentiary at Huntsville. He had hoped they were being groomed for bigger things.

The bombing of the oilrig had been their first truly violent mission, and Paul suspected it had been a test. If they had been caught, the authorities would have had difficulty tying them to the national group, so the Cause would not have suffered. Paul had no qualms about being a sacrificial lamb for the Cause, but since everything had turned out well and had set up the proper circumstances for the other piece of the puzzle, he was certain his group would be given more to do. It was only a question of when and who would be the next target.

* * *

The plane was only about half full on this Sunday morning. *It was a late night*, Patrick thought as he covered a yawn and stretched as much as the coach seat ahead of him allowed. Then he smiled, remembering how much fun the evening had turned out to be. He had gotten his interview, but it seemed he had gotten something more. He had thoroughly enjoyed the time at the Bar T Steakhouse and he felt she had enjoyed herself too. He didn't dare think she could become his friend, though the prospect was very appealing. Her sharp wit and flashing dark eyes would have been attractive even if her dark hair hadn't framed her face so nicely.

Then he blinked a couple of times and sipped at the Styrofoam cup of coffee the flight attendant had brought and shamed himself for thinking there could be any kind of lasting connection between them. He, the cynical newspaper reporter, could hardly relate to her, the corporate heiress, long term. He didn't dare consider what her net worth might be, though he was sure he could find out, since someone at the Herald had almost certainly done the math since she became CEO and was thrust into the thick of this controversy. And besides, he had never been to Houston before and might never return again.

The information she had given him about the message from the terrorists was not conclusive, he knew. Some disgruntled employee could have done it, and covered his tracks by making it look like a terrorist incident. Patrick had learned about "We're watching you" on the Internet after all, so anyone could know about it. Still the scope and expense involved in acquiring and delivering plastique explosives 60 miles off the coast would seem to rule out a former employee with a beef. Usually a shotgun was the weapon of choice for someone like that.

And besides, oil companies were prime targets for the Earth Liberation Front and their ilk. Patrick didn't feel strongly one way or another. He knew there were environmental problems with oil and the products that were made from it, but at present he didn't know of a good substitute. He wouldn't be involved in the research into technologies to replace oil, even as a reporter. That was John Watson's field.

That afternoon, Patrick drove from Dulles directly to the Herald to transfer his notes to his computer and then to transform them into an article that could run in Monday's morning edition. Finkel was not there, but Patrick had been gone for four days and he needed to produce some copy. He had accomplished what he was sure others had failed to do: he had gotten a one-on-one interview with the Axiom CEO.

The fact that he was sworn to keep mum about the best information she gave him was really starting to eat at him, however. By printing the information, he would actually be helping her, or he should say, helping Axiom Oil. Usually when he wrote something someone didn't want printed, it would not help them and they expressed their feelings about his revelations in no uncertain terms. This time, the interviewee gave him information that would actually help her case and yet she didn't want it revealed. Just because the FBI said, "Pretty please." He wondered if she was playing him, expecting him to print the information in spite of her definite prohibition.

Yes, he could see that. Perhaps their meeting was just an elaborate leak. Was she really much more sophisticated than he thought? The memory of her musical laugh and dark, sparkling eyes made it difficult for Patrick to be objective about her motives and about what his course of action should be.

Finally, he decided to put it in the article. The information was too hot. She must have intended for him to write about it. That was it, he reasoned. It was all set up so she could leak the information she really wanted out there. And so, he wrote a paragraph about the message, placed high enough in the article that no editor would cut it out. He was able to strongly infer that terrorists were involved without saying something he'd have to prove.

Then he continued with the rest of the information. Two news conferences and his own research, plus the knowledge of which pond to fish in, enabled him to write something that would spin the national coverage in a new direction and that was always fulfilling for a journalist.

But soon he was stuck. He needed a statistic on oil spills to fill in a blank about the concerns of environmentalists. He could look it up on the Internet or make a phone call, but decided to get up and walk the 20 yards to John Watson's office. He would probably be working, even though it was Sunday, since there was a news frenzy going on and the subject matter was his passion. John had memorized statistics like the ones Patrick needed and could spout them at a moment's notice. Patrick would still get a second source of course, but talking to Watson would give him a starting place.

Watson's door was open, but he wasn't there. *Perhaps John is in the john*, Patrick mused, knowing that his pun wouldn't be appreciated by anyone but himself. Without intending to, Patrick looked at Watson's computer monitor. His email program was open and something stood out as if it was red and blinking. The most recent message, as yet unread, had the subject line: "Mission Accomplished: One Oil Hemorrhage Stopped." The message was from "Mongoose."

Patrick turned to see if anyone was watching him through the office door. No one was. Though his curiosity was raging, he couldn't bring himself to open someone else's mail, at least not while he could be caught. When Watson didn't come back in the next couple of minutes, Patrick gave up and went back to his office, deciding he must have been in a meeting or out to lunch.

The rest of the afternoon, Patrick turned the subject line of John Watson's e-mail over in his mind while he worked on other things. "Mission Accomplished" it had said. And who was "Mongoose"? *A mongoose is an animal that attacks and kills the deadly cobra; a furry, rodent-like animal that overcomes a poisonous snake*, Patrick thought. "One Oil Hemorrhage Stopped" the rest of the subject said. Was it talking about the offshore drilling platform that was now shut down? Jacqueline James had convinced him the incident had been sabotage or a terrorist attack. Could Watson be corresponding with the terrorists? If that was the case, why hadn't he mentioned having such a source? But Watson was insisting that it had been an accident. Did he actually know it was a terrorist incident and perhaps even know who the terrorists were? Was he protecting them?

These disturbing questions continued nagging at Patrick after he turned in the article and left the Herald building for his nightly meat and potatoes at the Blue Ribbon Grill.

He didn't have much of an appetite tonight. Usually, by the time Patrick arrived at the Blue Ribbon, he was ravenous. Tonight though, he kept thinking about the email. By now, he was convinced that Watson was in sympathy with an environmental terrorist group and was communicating with them. His reporter's instincts told Patrick there was something there. His reporter's ethos also rebelled at the idea of Watson's knowing something about a big, breaking story and not disclosing it.

But maybe he had disclosed it to Finkel and they were waiting until they confirmed the information before breaking the story. *But, that doesn't ring true*, Patrick thought. He sensed that something was going on and, as a sometime investigative reporter, the lure was too great to resist. He paid his check and drove back to the Herald.

* * *

Do all basements smell like this? Patrick wondered. The Information Services Department occupied about half of the basement of the Washington Herald building. There was a time, not so long ago, when the newspaper didn't even have a computer, before Patrick got there. He could remember pounding out his articles at the New York Times on an IBM Selectric typewriter. Back then the Herald basement had been storage for the vast quantities of paper produced by the reporters' typewriters, the paper now replaced by electronic storage on multiple large hard drives.

Like so many hooded druid priests, the IS Department employees ministered to the large server at the center of the company network, continually presenting offerings of hardware upgrades or software patches, ever tweaking and fiddling with the server and the web of coaxial cable through which it was nourished by the hundreds of daughter computers throughout the building. The young acolytes religiously performed backup rituals to preserve the information stored in the server's RAID. The server resided in a glass inner sanctuary here in the basement that was climate controlled, fire proof, and access controlled, with the keypad combination changed weekly. If a major flood or fire hit the basement of the Herald, the server would survive, but the people would be on their own.

Patrick wondered who would be working on Sunday night and if they would be cooperative. What he wanted to do was not really ethical. In fact, it could get him fired. But he felt he was on the trail of a story and that had justified some borderline activities in the course of past investigations. The problem was, even newspapers that did investigative reporting didn't like being investigated themselves.

The paper was pretty much a 24-hour-a-day operation, so there were several of the nerdy IS guys in the basement. Some of these bottom dwellers probably preferred working at night, Patrick supposed. He spotted a guy that looked barely 20 and assumed he might do some hacking on his own time. The tattoos, prickly hair and pierced ears, nose and who-knew-what-else gave that impression anyway.

"Hi, I'm Patrick Garrity, political editor," Patrick held out his picture I.D. badge like the ones all Herald employees wore. The Pierced Boy didn't seem impressed. "I wonder if you could help me? One of our editors is gone for the day and I'm up against a deadline." Both halves of the statement true, they just weren't actually related. "I need to access his computer."

The various computer users — editors, reporters, graphic artists, etc. — could access their own computers and certain common files on the server, but they couldn't access files on another user's computer. To share, the users had to put files in a common area. Of course, someone had to have access to everyone's computers and it was the Information Services Department that was entrusted with the sacred passwords.

"You need a file from a dude's computer?" Pierced Boy asked.

"Yeah," Patrick shrugged, pretending it was no big deal. "I guess he forgot to put it where I could get it."

"Who?" asked the boy, turning his pimply face toward the monitor, where he entered a password and then pulled up a list of all the computers on the network.

He looked eager to demonstrate his prowess.

* * *

It was nearly 10 o'clock before Patrick arrived home.

He wasted no time sliding the flash drive into his laptop's USB port. In the directory for the disk he could see seven e-mail messages that Pierced Boy had copied from John Watson's computer. All of them were from "Mongoose." The messages hadn't been in Watson's e-mail folder, but had been saved to another location on his hard drive. That fact had only delayed finding the files by a few seconds, thanks to Pierced Boy's skill. That the emails had been moved further heightened Patrick's suspicions about Watson's relationship to "Mongoose." There didn't seem to be any emails from Watson to "Mongoose" however, so maybe their communication was one sided. *Still,*

Watson should have made the contacts known, Patrick thought.

He opened the earliest message. Its date was six weeks ago. Patrick had never seen such obtuse writing. It was almost poetic, but what in the world was it talking about? "Those who rape the Mother..."? "The sulphurous haze will clear from their mind-skies..."?

Patrick kept reading and gradually a profile of the writer began forming in his mind. Then he realized something. If Watson received the first message six weeks ago, he had to have prior knowledge that the incident at the offshore platform was going to happen. *In fact,* he thought as he checked the dates on the emails again, *Watson had received a relatively clear warning just six days before the incident.* It wasn't enough to discern time and place, but, once you learned to decipher "Mongoose's" writing, it wasn't difficult to realize what the email had predicted.

Now what should he do with this information? Patrick wondered.

Suddenly, he thought about the paragraph in his article that told of the spray-painted message on the oil platform. What if his revelation of that fact did indeed short-circuit the FBI's investigation? Ordinarily he wouldn't care, but if people he knew were somehow involved, that meant there was a conspiracy that was much larger than local "Green" harassment. If there was a Washington connection, that could be a much bigger story.

He suddenly realized he would rather not have the information released too soon either. But he had already put the article on the network for Howard to review. He would have to make one more trip to the Herald, even though he was bone tired. He didn't know if it was ethics or his own desire for the

Backlash

best story that made him do it, but he went back to the newspaper and took the paragraph out. He got back to his apartment after one a.m.

CHAPTER TEN

As she sat down at her desk, Jackie felt "worn to a frazzle", as her father would have said. The long days had taken their toll, with so much to do, coming into a new job with unexpected events like the attack on the offshore rig taking so much time. The latest report indicated the well was capped and repairs were underway.

Thankfully, the spill had not gotten far and had done almost no damage to the ecology of the Gulf.

Now came the nightmare of the proposed gas tax. She felt that the first meeting of the upper management had yielded nothing useful in dealing with the situation. She usually felt rested and energized on Monday morning, but that was not the case today. Not even going to church yesterday had refreshed her. Usually she could count on the rousing songs and contemplation of the eternal to bring her back to center, reminding her of what was ultimately important. That was not the case this week, however.

Some people probably saw her as a contradiction.

Backlash

She was a member and supporter of Homewood Baptist Church, as well as some denominational schools and hospitals, but Jackie's discipline — other than Business — was Science. As an undergraduate at the University of Texas, she majored in Petroleum Technology and minored in Geology. Without exception, her professors had been atheists or at least agnostics, and had taught Evolution as an assumed fact. It was even worse at Harvard, though it wasn't as obvious in her business courses.

At Homewood Baptist on the other hand, the pastor and the members were believers in a personal God who created the earth in six days. Some of them believed that the earth was only six thousand years old. In college, Jackie had been able to compartmentalize, giving the expected answers on tests, while being active in the Baptist campus ministry.

Since then, she hadn't thought much about it. She used her knowledge of Geology to talk to the men in the field who were doing the hard work of bringing up the crude. They didn't talk about the "Mesozoic" or the "Paleozoic" layers in terms of time periods so much as distances into the earth.

Yet Jackie knew that the idea of the earth's history extending back billions of years was anathema to the gentle ladies and godly men of Homewood Baptist Church. For them, the idea of a Special Creation of the earth and its billions of species of life in a six-day period presented no problem at all. God could do anything He chose to do, in any time span. That's what made Him God.

For her professors, and presumably for the True Believers in the Environmental Movement, God was not a factor. Only that which was observable was fact; anything else was myth, with the possible exception of those who indulged in New Age mysticism of some sort.

Having been educated on both sides as she was, Jackie realized that Evolution as a theory of origins was no more observable or provable than the Creation story. No one had been there and written an eyewitness report in either case, unless you say that God reported His Creation in the Bible through inspiration. Duplicating the circumstances for the origin of life as Darwin had theorized them in a laboratory was impossible, since setting up an experiment including an environment totally devoid of organic matter required the involvement of intelligent scientists, who then could be seen as "creators." And no one could wait for billions of years to see the experiment to its end. Conclusions drawn from the fossil record were often drastically revised with each new major discovery. Anyone who examined it could see that science today differed greatly from the theory of origins Darwin had conceived.

Her professors easily ignored and even ridiculed the Bible, however. The problem with using the Bible to prove something to a non-believer was that all they had to say was, "I don't believe the Bible," and there was little more to say. Of course, once a person decided to believe in a God, the Bible, as well as Nature, confirmed his or her faith in ways her professors would never understand, Jackie believed, but until they took that "leap of faith", it was easy for them to ignore the Bible and its worldview.

The professors had invested their confidence in the earth with its fossil and archeological record. To them, this was the record that counted, although Jackie saw that it too was subject to interpretation. It all depended the assumptions with which one began.

There are important differences between the two worldviews, she thought. For the believer, mankind was the capstone of Creation, the crowning achievement of what God called "good." Adam, the first human according to the Bible, was given "dominion" over the earth. For the Evolutionist, mankind was simply the most recent in a long, long chain of meaningless mutations that resulted in a new species. In fact, the human race was regarded by some as a definite negative for the rest of Nature. There was no inherent superiority to the human race in that scenario. The theory of origins one chose greatly affected his or her worldview.

Far from negating concern for the environment, belief in God caused people of faith to be conscious of their stewardship of the earth and its creatures. Jackie thought she even remembered a text somewhere that said, "God will destroy those who destroy the earth." *That is pretty strong stuff!*

There had been a time in the early days of the oil boom when unsightly derricks had sprung up everywhere in the rush to reap the millions of dollars that came to anyone lucky enough to find the ugly, messy stuff. Drillers had let oil foul streams and ground water. Jackie figured her grandfather was probably guilty of such things, but the situation had changed radically since then. New technologies made it unnecessary to erect a forest of derricks to harvest large quantities of oil. The crude beneath thousands of acres could be brought up with one strategically placed well. And there were measures in place that ensured the oil wouldn't escape into the ground water. At least, most of the oil was contained.

Of course, the human factor, like the intentional sabotage against the Gulf Pride, or human carelessness, like the drunken tanker captain of the Exxon Valdez, or a blowout like the BP spill in the Gulf, was impossible to prevent with new technology or company policies. The Valdez experience had led to many improvements in the way the industry handled its product and the way it handled crises, but no company could foresee a terrorist attack like the one on the Gulf Pride.

Why would anyone, even if they didn't regard their fellow human beings to be a special part of Creation, be willing to take people's lives in the name of environmental concern? Was this eco-fanaticism a descendent of some nature religion? *They would probably object to the characterization of their concern as a religion, but anyone who would blow up an oilrig populated with innocent people is more of a fundamentalist than any of the members at Homewood Baptist Church,* Jackie thought.

She looked at her calendar. She would have an executive meeting and another meeting with Charlene and Benny to plan the morning news conference. There would not be enough time for all she needed to do. She fortified herself with a gulp of black coffee and went to work.

* * *

Carl Kellerman, the representative from Colorado, almost ran toward the House Chamber. He was still in good shape at 52, owing in large part to his career as a running back at the University of Colorado. Training in the Flatiron Mountains had been very good for his endurance. Today he wasn't running to catch a pass, but to try to argue down a vote.

Kellerman had never seen a bill sail through the House of Representatives like this one. Usually bills languished in committee for weeks — or months — before coming to the floor. But this morning his aide had informed him that debate was beginning on the gas tax bill. *What in creation is the rush?* he wondered to himself.

The bill was being pushed by liberals in the Republican-led House, but it seemed to be powered by rocket fuel. Kellerman wondered if the Republican leadership was asleep at the switch. To him it seemed an ill-considered move to take an action that would almost certainly increase gasoline prices by at least a dollar a gallon right at the beginning of the summer vacation season. What were they thinking?

Kellerman rounded a corner on the polished marble floor, managed to avoid slipping, and continued toward the entrance to the House chamber. He slowed to a trot and went in to his seat. The representative from the fourth district of California was speaking.

"...and this measure will solve that problem. We have an opportunity to greatly impact the quality of our air and water by passing this bill. It will move our country toward independence from the noxious gas and oil compounds that threaten our very existence. We must pass this legislation for the sake of our children and grandchildren. Thank you, Mr. Speaker. I yield back the balance of my time."

Kellerman watched as the next representative to speak also extolled the virtues of the gas-tax bill. He hadn't had a chance to read it yet, it had come up so fast, but he'd talked to his colleagues on the Committee on Energy and Commerce. The things they had told him were not comforting. It appeared that there were members who wanted to punish the oil companies by imposing a new two-dollar gas tax and only raising the price cap by one dollar. *That is nuts*, thought the representative who had come to Washington on the wave of 1994 and the Contract With America. Even a high school economics student should realize that taxing corporations only increased prices for consumers, because corporations didn't pay taxes. They only collected them from their customers through inflated prices and passed them on to Washington.

In the case of gasoline, the Federal, state and local fuel taxes were included in the price. Other goods had sales taxes added after the price was set. But all goods and services had taxes hidden in the price that most people forgot about. Businesses had income and other taxes levied against them just like individuals and the only place they could get the money was to inflate the prices of their products. As a result, by some estimates, the price of every product or service was increased by as much as 30 percent because of hidden taxes.

Requiring oil companies to pay part of the new tax out of profits would force the companies to cut production or jobs or both, Kellerman reasoned. So intent were the supporters of this bill to hurt the Big Oil Companies that they didn't mind forcing the price of fuel up by one dollar, and that would hurt the consumer.

Usually the occupants of the "lower" house were more sensitive to the plight of the common voters, since they faced election every two years. It was a curse placed on them by the Constitution that forced members of the House of Representatives to be in perpetual campaign mode. The fact that Senators served for six years allowed them many luxuries not afforded Representatives. They could often pass unpopular legislation because, at most, one third of them would be facing election within the short attention spans of their constituents.

But the supporters of this bill were on fire. They seemed not to care about the electoral ramifications. Kellerman hadn't prepared an argument against the bill, because he didn't know it would come to the floor so soon. He couldn't get his name in to speak today anyway. As morning turned to afternoon, there were a few who spoke against the bill, but they were as unprepared as he would have been.

An aide to one of his fellow representatives from Colorado came in and told his boss that the Senate had just passed its version of the bill. Word spread rapidly on the floor. The political balance of the Senate was much closer than that of the House, and the Democrats were in charge. Still it was a surprise that the Senate had acted so quickly. They were supposed to be the "deliberative body."

Kellerman grew really worried when a fellow Republican from New Hampshire spoke, throwing his support behind the bill. His speech wasn't as enthusiastic as some had been, but he was supporting the bill, nevertheless. Kellerman began to fear that the bill could pass. And the president had already promised to sign it.

* * *

Dennis Trask, Axiom chief financial officer, and Jorge Rodriguez, comptroller, sat fidgeting in the two red leather chairs facing Jackie James' cluttered desk, having been summoned there ten minutes ago. She returned to her office from a conference with Doris.

"Dennis, I got your memo and it made no sense. Spill it!"

"It's simple, really. The Senate has voted a new two-dollar-a-gallon gas tax and the House looks like it will follow. If it does, the president says he will sign it. My projections show there's no way to make a profit on gasoline and diesel during the fourth quarter."

"I don't get it. We have to make a profit. Don't we just have to raise the price per gallon equal to the new tax?"

"Only problem is," Jorge explained in his soft Hispanic accent, "if we raise the price to the new price cap, we estimate it will cut our revenues by 60 percent. People won't buy as much gas. Plus, the new law only allows us to raise our prices to one dollar above the current price cap, so somewhere between 50 cents and a dollar will come out of profits, depending on the state."

"And our overhead wouldn't change that much," Jackie completed the thought, "even though we would be spending less on crude, refining, transportation..."

"Our infrastructure has a lot of fixed costs," Jorge said, as he showed her a colorful chart printed on legal-size paper. It showed a red "Revenue" line submerged below "Expenses" for the foreseeable future. "So, with lower sales, our unit cost would be even more. That's why we don't see any way to make a profit."

"Is that true as long as the gas tax is in place?" Jackie asked, her eyebrows raised as the full impact of what they were saying hit her.

"I suppose it's possible that things would adjust over time," Dennis said, ever the diplomat. "Maybe people would change their overall spending habits to get back to buying gas at current levels, eventually."

"Or maybe they'll adjust their lifestyles and won't ever buy as much gas again," Jackie replied, showing her practical side. Dennis was skillful at getting people to come to their own conclusions so he didn't have to break the bad news too roughly.

"Hmmm," Jackie leaned back in the red leather wingback executive chair that was becoming molded to her backside. Her trademark impish smile teased her face. "Too bad we can't just refuse to pay the tax!"

"Right!" the two men laughed.

It's good to make jokes at a time like this, Jackie thought. It meant that she could see past the bad news to the possibilities that might fix the problem. She had never been an "either-or" person, but was a "multiple-possibility" person, seeing more than one solution to every problem. It made a person a lot more positive — and successful.

"So, are you telling me that we will lose money with every gallon of gas we sell?"

"By the fourth quarter," Jorge nodded, "all our projection models indicate that, yes."

"And the more gas we sell, the more money we lose?"

"We can't make the projections come out any other way," Dennis admitted.

"What about all our other products and services — the convenience stores, the auto repair shops, the motor oil and additive sales, do they keep making money?"

"All those things are tied to cars being on the road," Dennis explained. "If people are buying less gas, they'll be driving less and that means they'll be using less oil, needing their cars repaired less often... It's a domino effect."

"Perhaps the greens finally got their wish to force people to work close to home and use mass transportation," Jorge put in. They all knew there were people out there who wanted to force other people to live their way. Something in Jackie fumed at the idea of a select group of people forcing other people to live according to their rules. It smacked of Fascism. *Why can't they live and let live; let nature take its course?*

"Is this true for the other companies — our competitors — too?"

Dennis and Jorge looked at each other as if they hadn't anticipated this question. "I suppose so," Dennis answered. "But they may not see it. We almost missed it."

Jackie leaned back in her chair and looked at the ceiling. Suddenly she stood up. "I've got an idea! I want you do another projection and this is how I want it to go."

When she had finished her explanation, they left to do what she had asked, *looking like they had been "hit with a stupid stick"*, she thought, remembering something her grandfather used to say.

She sat down at her desk and said aloud, "Lord, help us!" It was part exclamation and part sincere prayer. She had been praying about the situation, but it didn't seem to get better. It seemed to her that her options were being taken away one by one. The great thing about being an optimist, though, was that there was always another option. If the door was locked, she would find the key. If there was no door, she would go through a window. If there was no window, she would rent a chainsaw.

CHAPTER ELEVEN

Congressman Kellerman was finally able to make a speech on the second day of the debate on the new gas tax bill. "The Petroleum Independence Act" as it was officially known, seemed unstoppable, but Kellerman was determined to speak against it anyhow. When his name was called, he stepped up to the simple lectern.

"My fellow Representatives," he began, "Being from Colorado, I am acutely aware of the importance of preserving and protecting the Environment. Some of the most beautiful landscapes and most precious wildlife in our country are in my state." He looked up to see if anyone would dispute what he said, but the other congresspersons were either listening with blank faces or talking to aides.

"But, living in Colorado, I have also seen many excesses of environmental concern in my own as well as neighboring states. I have seen people's land taken from them because someone from the EPA or the Army Corps of Engineers declared a part of their property to be a 'wetland'. I have seen a child arrested in the name of the Endangered Species Act for bringing a bird feather to school! I have seen thousands of acres of private land turned into a "National Monument" by Executive Order, without financial remuneration to the people affected. "This new punishing gas tax is just the latest abuse of power on the part of this government in the name of the environment. I will oppose this bill for several reasons. First, the practical consideration: Every member of this body faces re-election in five months. Do we really want to double our constituents' gasoline expenses just in time for summer vacation? Although that is the least important consideration, there are others.

"The second problem I would mention is this: Inherent in this bill is the notion that we here in this exalted body have the right — no, the obligation — to dictate what products our constituents buy, how much of it they buy and how often. My friends, this smacks of an arrogance I can scarcely fathom. I believe it was Jefferson who said, 'The government that governs least, governs best.' I submit to you today, my friends and colleagues that this bill does not govern 'least'. Rather it governs 'more'. In fact, I would go so far as to say it governs 'most'.

"But thirdly and most importantly: To keep our collective arrogance in check, I would like to remind you that there are laws that are not enacted by this body; laws that we cannot repeal or amend. Laws that we all must obey or suffer the consequences. I'm speaking of natural laws, economic laws, and — dare I say it? — moral laws. Have we considered the effects this action may have on a host of segments of our society? Have we considered the ramifications on our economy; on transportation; on the conveying of goods to market? Have we considered the strain this capricious Act will have on the personal finances of the people we are supposed to represent? Have we considered the shortages that may result, not just of gasoline, but also of other basic commodities? Have we considered the social upheaval when people are unable to afford fuel to go to their jobs?

"And finally, have we considered the moral component?" Kellerman took a deep breath. His speech was on the home stretch and he wanted to make this point strongly. "We are not gods on Olympus, manipulating the lives of poor, ignorant peasants. We are not Caesars, deciding who lives and who dies with thumbs up or thumbs down. We are not even kings, ruling by divine right, pulling the strings of our subjects to suit our latest whims. We are the representatives of the people in a government that is 'of, by and for THE PEOPLE'.

"For years we have tried to manipulate the social structure of this country through the income tax code. I have always been against that, but it is too useful for too many members of both houses of Congress. Now we are proposing to try to change people's behavior through another tax on a commodity. I, for one, will vote against this bill for the reasons I have stated, but most of all, I will vote against this bill because, the people I represent deserve to be allowed to make their own decisions — about this and many other things. I urge you, if you are thinking of voting 'yes', to reconsider. Reconsider your role in this. Reconsider your constituents and their interests. I urge you to help me defeat this ill-considered bill. Mr. Speaker, I thank you for this time."

There was some applause as Kellerman returned to his seat, but it died quickly, and the next speaker obviously tried to rebut Kellerman's points without referring to him directly. Kellerman looked around the room and did a head count. It didn't look good.

He had talked to his colleagues among the Republicans and had been surprised by their reaction. Many of them seemed to hang their heads but said they would vote for the bill. There had been too much publicity about the offshore platform incident, they said. They had suffered the slings and arrows of a press that called them anti-environment before, and they didn't want it to happen again; not with the election coming so soon.

Debate continued through the dinner hour. Kellerman wanted to leave but didn't dare for fear the vote would be taken. Sure enough, at nine o'clock, the Speaker called for the vote. It took about an hour for everyone to vote and no one left the House floor until the result was announced. Kellerman saw on the tally board that, of the 435 members, only 392 were present. That meant that 200 would need to vote for the bill if it was to pass. The Republicans had a slim 10-vote majority, so if just seven or eight of them voted with the Democrats, the bill would succeed — assuming the Democrats would vote as a unit.

Finally, the vote was tallied; 212 for, 180 against.

It was the height of irony then that, within an hour after the news was released about the passage of the bill, Kellerman heard another news bulletin appeared on the radio that the oil spill had been contained and all the oil that could be recovered had been picked up by the skimmers. Not one globule of oil had reached the coast.

* * *

Jackie sat behind her desk as Dennis and Jorge nervously finished their presentation using hastily printed database reports and projection models. "This is hard to believe," Jackie said as they finished. "It looks like we could actually pull this off."

"I didn't say that," Dennis hastened to say. "I said the numbers work. Pulling it off PR-wise would be another thing."

"And, it's not my field," Jorge said timidly, "but you'd better run this by Legal, right?"

"Yeah, we don't buy a toilet brush around here without running it by Legal," Jackie admitted with a bitter smile.

"Are you serious about this?" Dennis asked.

"I don't know. I need to talk to some more people. Can you guys keep this under your hats? I'm very serious about keeping this secret until the time is right. How 'bout it?"

Dennis and Jorge looked at each other.

"Yes, ma'am."

"Of course. Absolutely."

"All right," Jackie continued. "I want you to polish these figures and make a full-fledged presentation out of it. Eventually we're going to have to show this to several groups of people and it's got to look good, okay?"

"We'll get right on it."

"Right away, ma'am."

"Great. Good work, gentlemen. I'll look forward to seeing something more finished as soon as you can get it done. And remember, mum's the word."

Dennis and Jorge excused themselves and headed out of Jackie's office.

Jackie picked up the phone and punched "Intercom."

"Doris, get Joe Jemison on the line. He manages the Savannah, Tennessee, store. Thanks." Momentarily Doris came back on the intercom to say that Joe was on the line. "Joe! Jackie James... Yeah, it was really unexpected... Well, I appreciate it... Listen, Joe, I need to run something by you."

* * *

Patrick arrived back at his office after witnessing the House vote to approve the Petroleum Independence Act. He had already sketched out articles that told the story of the vote either way it turned out, so it would just be a matter of selecting the right one and adding details.

So, there would be a one-dollar increase in the price of gasoline at the pump. Actually, it could be more than that in some places, because, though the cap would now be $6.00 per gallon, prices were currently well below $5.00 most places. In states where state and municipal taxes were low, the price could nearly double! That would yield almost-European price levels and Patrick was certain some people would be happy about that. It wasn't his department, but Patrick wondered how the nation would fare with this punitive increase in the price of such a basic commodity as gasoline. The bill included diesel fuel, so over-the-road trucks would be affected as well.

Everything in the country moved on trucks, so no one would be untouched by the price increases in all kinds of goods that were sure to come. Congress hadn't set price controls on anything else.

He thought momentarily about Jackie and wondered how Axiom would react now that the new gas tax had been enacted. Congress had made a point of adding a two-dollar tax and allowing the oil companies to only pass on one dollar of it. That would likely wipe out the profits of most of them. And there was no cut-off date for the new tax. It was permanent.

He still hadn't told anyone about the emails he had found on John Watson's computer. To him they proved beyond all doubt that the attack on the Gulf Pride was a conspiracy and that John Watson might even be part of it. But John had been a colleague and coworker for several years now. *How can I just turn him in?*

Backlash

It was possible he knew nothing, but it was also obvious that Watson regarded them as sensitive, since he saved the emails to his hard drive where most people wouldn't think to look.

Then there was the issue of his own breach of company policy and ethics by copying private files from a coworker's computer. *If I'm wrong about Watson, I could wind up out in the cold.*

Finally, he knew what he had to do.

* * *

Jackie was moving in high gear. The news that the House had followed the Senate in passing the new gas tax made her plan all the more urgent. She cancelled the daily news conference so she and her executives could focus on the issue at hand, promising the press through Charlene that they would have a response soon. She gave Doris a list of people she needed to talk to. Some of them were in the Axiom headquarters building. Some were in the field in very different time zones. On top of that, she wanted an emergency meeting of the Board of Directors set for four p.m. Jackie knew Doris could pull it off if anyone could.

She met with Marcus Williams from Axiom's Legal Department at about 10 a.m. There were real legal concerns with the course of action she was proposing, but on reflection, Marcus decided the potential problems could be handled. Jackie asked him to outline a complete contingency plan.

Shortly after Marcus left, Doris came in to tell her that a Mr. McAlister was returning her call.

"Thanks Doris. I'll take it." She picked up the phone. "Bret! How are you?"

"Jackie!" Bret McAlister answered. "It's good to hear your voice. Sorry about your pop. He was a great guy. And congrats on your new job!"

"Thanks Bret. You still keeping the wheels rolling?"

"You know it. You still remember how to shift a Peterbilt?"

"How could I forget, after you taught me? Where are you?"

"I just stopped at a truck plaza outside Lawrence, Kansas, on my way to Kansas City to drop my load. What do you need from me, boss lady?"

"I need your opinion about something," and she laid it out for the tanker truck driver the way she had for the others, with one twist.

"So, do you see what I'm trying to do with this?" she asked when she had finished.

"Yeah, I can see you're in a bind. Do you think you can pull it off?"

"That's why I'm talking to you. I need to get the union perspective and you're a steward now."

"Well, I can't answer for the whole union, much less all the unions you deal with, but I'm a little concerned that some of the guys won't see the light."

"What if I tell them the government is management, Axiom is labor, and we're striking the government?"

McAlister had to laugh at that. "Well, Jackie dear, that might just do it."

"And besides, you'll be getting full salary and not working — at least not as much."

"Yeah, I hear you. I'll do what I can with the rest of the guys."

"I appreciate it. The hardest part of this is going to be making everyone understand what we're doing and why."

"Well, you've got your work cut out for you, I'd say."

"I can't do it without people like you helping others understand."

"Okay, Jackie. I've got your back."

"Thanks Bret."

When she hung up she checked with Doris to see if the board members were going to be able to come to the emergency meeting. Then she ran her finger down a list of major stockholders and picked a name she felt she could call for his opinion.

* * *

Most of the board members had responded that they could come to the emergency meeting. Jackie had invited a number of the vice presidents to be there also. There would not be an official vote on Jackie's plan at this meeting. That would wait until everybody could sleep on it. It so happened that some regional managers were at headquarters for one reason or another and Jackie made sure to invite them to sit in as well.

The men and women gathered in the large, twentieth-story conference room, pouring coffee and water as the meeting was about to begin. Some of the people didn't know each other that well, as the VPs almost never met with the Board of Directors.

Jackie entered breathlessly, followed by Dennis Trask and Jorge Rodriguez, the latter carrying a laptop computer. Jorge plugged in the computer to a connector in the table and Dennis flipped a switch on the wall lowering a video projector from the ceiling. Jackie called the meeting to order.

"Ladies and Gentlemen! Your attention, please. It's good to see all of you." She waved at a couple of people who were there from across the country.

"Thank you for coming on such short notice. We have some matters to discuss that will impact our company very greatly, both immediately and long term. I'd like to get right to those issues.

"I don't have to tell you that there have been some recent developments in the Federal government that will greatly affect us. Just how much they affect us you may not know. I've asked Dennis and Jorge to make a presentation of some information they showed me a couple of days ago so you will understand the problems we are facing."

Dennis stood to address the group as Jorge controlled the computer-generated slides projected on the permanent screen at one end of the room.

"Good afternoon everyone. I hope you've got some strong coffee, because you're about to need it." He had said it with a smile on his face, so there was a ripple of laughter as he had intended, but everyone was alert and paying close attention now. Jorge dimmed the lights so only the sconces on the walls were illuminated.

"It came to our attention a few days ago that we had serious problems with our projections when we factored the new two-dollar-a-gallon gas tax rate into them. We estimate a drop of 60 percent in gasoline consumption nationwide. While our expenses for crude would drop accordingly, our infrastructure would have to remain in place. When you add in the fact that the recently imposed retail price cap only went up one dollar per gallon, as much as one dollar a gallon would come directly out of profits. We cannot see any way to make a profit on gasoline sales after this tax goes into effect in the fourth quarter."

"What?" several people gasped. "How is that possible?"

Jackie watched their reactions in the darkened room.

"I think you better redo your charts!" Jackson Benson, Senior VP for retail sales said loudly. "That's nonsense!"

"The charts are right, Jackson," Jackie said. "Finance has done it to death."

"Do you mean to tell me that my division can't make a profit?"

"Retail can make a profit by continuing to sell food and other things in our convenience stores and keeping our repair shops open," Dennis continued. "But something's got to give if we're to make a profit on fuel. We estimate a drop in fuel revenues of 60 percent when the new tax kicks in."

"But if people aren't coming to my stores to buy fuel, what makes you think they will come to buy 'tater chips and Co'Colas?"

"That's a consideration we've built into the projection model. There will be a drop in all sales if people are buying less gasoline."

"Can other sales compensate for the loss on gasoline?" Mike Swenson, regional VP for the Midwest District, asked. "What about motor oil?"

"There could be some compensation," Dennis answered, "but remember, the intent of the new tax is to discourage people from driving their cars. If they're not driving as much, they won't need to change their oil as often."

"And remember this," Jackie said, helping the reality to sink in. "We're not just talking about the fourth quarter. This will be the situation from now on — or until the tax is repealed. Retailing gasoline is our biggest single source of revenue. If that goes south it will drag everything else down with it. But I had an idea. Dennis, show them the new projections."

* * *

Patrick had tried multiple times to reach Jackie by phone. He had gotten to know Doris' voice when he heard it, but the message was always the same: "She's in a meeting." By turning on the charm and veiling his growing frustration, he had learned that the daily news conference had been cancelled today. That made sense. The management would be scrambling to figure out what in the world to do now.

He made sure Doris had his office, home and cell numbers, saying Jackie could call anytime, day or night. He tried to make Doris understand that he had something really important that he must tell Jackie, but he knew that any one of the reporters camped across from the Axiom building had probably said the same thing twice a day for a week.

His cell phone finally rang about eight p.m., but she could just as well have called his office phone, because he was still there. It would likely be a long night for him and his department.

"Jackie! I mean, Ms. James!"

"No. Call me Jackie," she answered.

"I'm so glad you returned my call. I've got some information for you about who attacked your offshore operation."

"You know who did it?"

"Not exactly. I'm really betraying a trust here, but I just feel like you should have the information."

"What's that?"

"I could lose my job for telling you this, so I'd appreciate it if you didn't say anything about where you heard it."

"No problem. What do you have?"

"I think one of our editors here has been getting emails from someone who knows something about the attack. He's Science and Environment editor."

Jackie thought a minute before responding. *An editor at the Washington Herald has information about who perpetrated the attack?* "How do you know?"

"That's where the betrayal comes in. I accidentally saw one of the emails and got our computer guys to make a copy of them for me."

"How many are there?" she asked, her heart beginning to pound. "Can you send them to me?"

"There are seven and they appear to predict the attack and then take credit for it after the fact."

"Who they are from?"

"I don't know. The sender calls himself 'Mongoose'."

Jackie again took a minute to think about this new information. "Patrick, you need to give this to the FBI."

"Oh, I don't know... ."

"What do you mean, you don't know?"

"Well, I'm just not used to handing information over to the police. A reporter can't become part of the story."

"Yeah, but won't it be a better story if they catch the people who did it?"

He had to admit that was a good point. And perhaps he could use this to get some more information from her. "Okay, that's true. I guess I could pass that much along. I could get in some trouble over this though."

"Not as much trouble as you'd be in if I get the FBI to subpoena you."

Wow, this lady is tough! She looks like a small, delicate woman, but bargains like a Turkish market vendor. "Okay. If I do this, what can you give me?"

"What do you mean?"

"I want a scoop. I want an exclusive on what you are going to do to deal with the gas tax."

"Well," she slowly began while she was still thinking. "I suppose that would be okay. I'm not quite ready, but if you turn over what you have to the FBI, I'll give you your scoop."

Gary L. Ivey

"It's a deal."

"Okay, I'll have to call you when our board has voted on a policy in response to the new tax law. You might need to come back to Houston."

"Okay, I'll have to run that by my boss, but there shouldn't be any problem." So, he would be going back to Houston!

She then dialed the number for the New Orleans FBI office and, on a three-way call, Patrick told Special Agent Thomas Shannon about the emails from Mongoose. Shannon was understandably excited and asked him to forward the emails on to him. Even though he was feeling guilty and conflicted, Patrick did so from his laptop at home that very night.

* * *

The next morning was Friday, May 21st. Jackie hadn't slept much, spending most of the night struggling and praying about the Board of Directors meeting that was first on the agenda. How much she wished her father could advise her on what she should do. She had cried when she thought about him and then she tried to put herself in his place. She decided that he might have done what she was about to do. Certainly, Jake would have. *He would have bit down on his cigar and told the board what he expected of them.*

She arrived at the boardroom early, getting there even before the Danish, orange juice and coffee arrived from the company cafeteria.

She couldn't see a good outcome to the new gas tax, no matter how Axiom responded. She had decided that her plan was the correct one morally because it might result in changing the government's position, but she couldn't predict all the consequences that might descend from the decision. If the board voted not to do it, it might weaken her as CEO, but that

153

was the least of her worries. The long-term viability of the company and honoring the trust placed in Axiom by customers, employees and shareholders were her responsibilities now. The effect of the government's new tax on the company and the millions of people who depended on it was difficult to predict, but the government had made it plain it wanted to hurt those millions of people.

Eventually a few people began drifting into the boardroom. Jackie put on her game face and greeted them warmly. Chairman Bud Eldridge arrived, looking uncharacteristically subdued.

"Good morning, little lady."

"Mornin' Bud. A big day."

"Yeah. Are you sure you want to do this?"

"I'd rather it all went away, actually."

"Well, it does look like we're durned if we do and durned if we don't."

"That's about it. Do you have any feel for how the vote will go?"

"Not a bit. We'll just have to see what happens."

By nine o'clock, the room was full. Upper management had joined the board again, although they wouldn't vote.

"Let's come to order," Bud said, though he didn't really need to. The assembly was unusually solemn, lacking the usual good-old-boy, back-slapping greetings. "I want to thank each of you for going the extra mile in being here for these called meetings. You have before you the outline of the plan that was presented yesterday. If we do this, we gotta vote it now, since there are a lot of details to work out and we've got just a little more than a month. Any further questions or discussion?"

"I hope you've thought the legalities through!" shouted Claude Bowman.

"Marcus?" Bud looked around for the head of the Legal Department.

Marcus Williams was a bulldog of a man; short and squat, never without his thick glasses. Though he didn't look imposing, he was one of the keenest legal minds in the state and Axiom paid him accordingly.

"Ms. James presented the plan to me yesterday morning and my team has looked at it from all angles," the head of Legal began. "We think we're covered. Of course, anybody can sue at any time for any reason."

"I just think you better figure some stockholder's going to try to sue or get an injunction," Bowman insisted.

"That's a real possibility," Marcus admitted. "But I think we can deal with it."

"I have made it a point during the last 24 hours to talk to a lot of people," Jackie put in. "Both employees and stockholders. When I have made them understand what's at stake they agree it's the only way."

"Can a judge or the Federal government force us to abandon the policy?" Bud asked Marcus.

"A judge could issue an injunction, but we would immediately appeal it. My team hasn't been able to find any existing law that could be used to force us to sell any product. We're only talking about three months, so I think the moratorium would be over before a case could be fully adjudicated." Marcus' words sounded more certain than his tone, which didn't appear to reassure some people in the room.

"What's the long-term effect on customer loyalty if we do this?" a VP asked.

"Some people might not like it," Jackie admitted. "But what will be the long-term effect if the new tax is allowed to stand?" She didn't have to finish the thought, because they had seen the numbers. It might take months or even years, but eventually the company would be bankrupt if they submitted to the tax.

"What about our employees?" asked a Regional VP from the Midwest. "The plan says we keep paying them. Is that realistic?"

"Most of them will still be working," Dennis Trask answered. "We'll still refine oil, transport oil, and sell motor oil, fuel oil, oil for plastics manufacturing, and so on. We'll still be selling natural gas and asphalt. Our stations will still do oil changes and sell air filters and fan belts. Then there's the soda pop, food and souvenirs we sell in our stores. There may be a few people with nothing to do, but most will still be busy."

"And this is just domestically," Jackie pointed out. "Sales in other countries won't be affected at all, because there is no big tax increase we are fighting anywhere else. In fact, we might need to look at having some of our domestic employees work elsewhere for the three months." She looked sideways at President Benny Tyson, whose look told her he hadn't thought about it, but would check on the logistics.

"Can we lay some people off, at least temporarily?" The question came from the regional VP from the Northwest.

"I'd like to be able to tell everyone we won't do that," Jackie said. "I think we owe that to our people and it will help ensure their support."

"Will this deplete our cash reserves?" Tom Davis asked from the end of the conference table opposite Bud.

"It will make a dent in them, all right, but it won't deplete them," Dennis Trask replied. "We just have to remember that if we maintain the status quo, our reserves will also be depleted — by the tax."

"That's right," Jackie chimed in. "This is about maintaining long term profitability by influencing public policy. When the government does something that affects us, we have traditionally just anted up the money it took to comply. This situation is different. There's no way we can comply and survive. So, we have to do something about it. Congress made a tax law that can bankrupt us and we have no recourse. We can't choose not to pay the tax. Unless we get creative."

The meeting continued for another two hours, with every conceivable scenario being explored. Between Jackie, Dennis and Marcus, most of the questions were answered convincingly, and the members reluctantly agreed to vote. Doris passed out blank pieces of paper she had prepared for this purpose and returned to the wing-back chair against the paneled wall.

When the votes were counted, with 21 voting members present, 12 voted for the plan. Like it or not, Jackie's plan was a "go."

CHAPTER TWELVE

The FBI field office had experience with mobsters, since New Orleans seemed to attract them more than other cities of its size. But this offshore drilling rig case was not like anything Thomas Shannon had seen before. He had heard about eco-terrorism, but hadn't seen any up close, much less been responsible for the investigation. Beginning his career as a beat cop in Chicago, he had seen arson cases that were perpetrated by organized crime and some bomb threats, but nothing like this. He had a forensic team working on the evidence from the scene and from the rented boat, and others trying to create a profile of the perpetrators.

Tony Bouchet's cousin had given them an excellent description of the duo he had flown out to the platform, and the appearance of one of them had been confirmed by the marina owner. The witness who had seen the van had been helpful, giving a good description of the vehicle and its driver. He had also named the rental agency, but hadn't noticed the license plate, so Shannon didn't know where the van had been rented.

A quick check determined that no one had rented a red Dodge van at the New Orleans rental agency the weekend of the attack. If it wasn't rented in New Orleans it could have come from anywhere. That meant they would have to obtain the records of all the company's locations in the country.

Actually, they would start by drawing a circle with a radius of 250 miles or so and get those records first, since it seemed reasonable that the people who perpetrated the attack would be at least somewhat local. But a 250-mile radius included parts of five states. Beyond that, they really didn't have much to go on, so he was glad when the call came from Axiom headquarters.

The new CEO had called and introduced a reporter from Washington with a story about another reporter at the Washington Herald who was getting e-mails from someone who called himself "Mongoose." The e-mails that the reporter forwarded to Shannon were strange, but incriminating. Shannon had his tech guys attempting to trace the e-mails. It wasn't as easy as it might seem, since "Mongoose" had attempted to hide his identity and location by going through a number of forwarded e-mail accounts. It had only been yesterday afternoon when he had turned the search over to the tech, so he was surprised to see him this morning.

"I think we got something, boss," Agent Clarence Jackson laid a piece of paper in front of Shannon, a smile lifting the corners of his neatly trimmed goatee. Shannon looked up from his desk at Jackson, a light-skinned black man in his late twenties who stayed up-to-the-minute on Internet protocols like HTTP, FTP, SMTP, and a host of other alphabet soup Shannon avoided at all costs. In past years, Government investigative agencies were always on the cutting edge technologically, but today they struggled to keep up with developments in the private sector. Things had changed a lot in police work since Shannon walked the south side 20 years ago. He preferred shoe-leather investigative work to the high-tech approach that was so hot now.

The paper Jackson laid on Shannon's desk was a printout of registration information for a website called "motherearthknights.org", listed in the name of the "Knights of Mother Earth." The address for the organization was Baytown, Texas, near Houston.

"This guy Paul Stoddard is the website owner," Jackson said, pointing to the pertinent line in the printout. "The address is probably a house or apartment rather than an office. You ever hear of the Knights of Mother Earth?"

"No, but there are a lot of groups I've never heard of. What's on the site?"

"The website content is fairly bland. Just some hand-wringing over various ecological problems, some animal rights info and an invitation to join in working for cleaner air and water. The site does have a place to sign up for a newsletter. I figure that's where you get the real info about the group. I signed up through my personal ISP."

"Good. Maybe we can get a match on the writing style if it's the same guy."

"Yeah. The site also has a '10-most-wanted' list of companies guilty of pollution."

They both laughed at that, since the "most-wanted" idea had originated with the FBI. Whoever had committed this crime wouldn't make the FBI's list, but it was funny anyhow.

"So, is Axiom on the list?"

"Yeah, but it's only number six."

"Hmmm. Work up a profile on these 'Knights'," Shannon told Jackson. "I'll run it by Washington — and the Houston field office. Maybe they've run into them before. It may just be some guy with a website. Do we know the e-mails came from this Stoddard guy?"

"Him or somebody with access to his e-mail account."

"When you've got everything together, I'll get the Houston office to stake out this Stoddard guy and, when the time comes, we might pick up several people who were involved. Anything on the site about funding?"

"It asks for donations. Must be a non-profit. I'll check that out, too."

"Good. I doubt if the oilrig attack could have been funded from donations alone. Talk to the forensic accounting guys about doing an estimate of the amount of money required to finance the job. That might help us trace the money to some other people who were indirectly involved."

"I'm on it, boss," Jackson was already out the door.

Shannon thought the "Knights of Mother Earth" name was a little corny, but the group did fit the profile.

That Washington reporter sure gave us a break.

* * *

The daily news conference had been delayed because of the board meeting and Jackie could see the reporters were in a surly mood. She wasn't in a great mood herself, having just committed the company to a course of action that many doubted would lead to a good conclusion. But at times one had to take a stand, even when the issue was not exactly clear-cut, she insisted to herself. Her company, her employees and her stockholders — even her customers — were under attack and that demanded a response. Whether their chosen course of action showed courage or foolhardiness would only be known in hindsight.

Backlash

When three o'clock arrived, Jackie stood at the podium. "Good afternoon. Thank you for your patience. I and the company's Board of Directors, along with many of our top managers, have met today, making decisions about our response to the new gas tax. I know you are anxious to hear about that response, but I am going to have to wait until next week because we still have a lot of work to do."

An audible groan went up from the reporters crowded into the auditorium. A few of them shouted questions that were more like demands for information. Jackie held up her hand and continued with her prepared remarks.

"I also need to inform the people that will be impacted by the new policies before releasing those policies to the press. So, we will not be having any more news conferences here. We will instead have a major news conference on Thursday of next week in Washington, D.C."

There were a few additional groans, but there were also quizzical looks on many faces.

"We will notify you of exact time and place for this news conference. I'd like to encourage you or someone from your organizations to be there. That is all for now."

Jackie turned and began walking toward the back door of the auditorium. Charlene was already holding it open for her. The reporters were shouting questions, but Jackie kept walking without looking back. When she was through the door, Charlene twisted the lock just before someone tried to open it to follow them. Jackie and Charlene traded a relieved look and hurried to the elevator.

As the afternoon wore on, the cars, RVs and satellite trucks that had been camped across the street gradually melted away. Like a queen in her castle, Jackie watched from her twentieth-floor office as the siege ended and the attackers withdrew.

Perhaps they could have a few days of peace before she ignited a new firestorm. She told her staff that they would not have to work Saturday this week, but to plan on long days at the beginning of next week.

* * *

Late that night, Jackie called Patrick Garrity at home and told him to be in Houston on Wednesday if he wanted his scoop, then to be back in Washington on Thursday for the news conference. He thanked her and told her he would try to get in sometime on Tuesday and would let her know when he was in town.

When she left the office on Friday night, she vowed to forget the burdens of her office until Monday morning. *It will be the beginning of a busy week*, she thought grimly, *as though the previous weeks were spent in a hammock with a glass of lemonade.* There was only one way to keep from thinking about business.

* * *

Saturday morning at seven a.m. found her at the family horse farm near Hempstead, wearing jeans and a dark cotton shirt with white piping and fringe in the classic cowgirl style. She was soon galloping across the open ground on Sable, a high-spirited chestnut, the thick heels of her cowboy boots braced against the stirrups. It was the kind of place where one could let a horse have its head and not worry about being swept off by a low-hanging branch.

She had learned to ride here before she learned to read. It was a classic Texas ranch in terms of its size, once having been a working cattle ranch, complete with the branding and breeding of fine beef cattle and a full complement of rough cow hands, a foreman and a cook. Today it was the province of a lone caretaker-groom and just a few horses. Years ago, it was used often as a retreat for Axiom management and Jackie had spent entire summers exploring the vast acreage on the back of a gentle mare. In recent years, she had spent less time at the horse ranch, which was known as the "Bar-X", homage to the name "Axiom." The groom who cared for the three horses the family owned also maintained the grounds and few buildings, which consisted of the stable, large vehicle shed, and the bunkhouse, a spacious if Spartan home outfitted for entertaining and sleeping 20 guests. The rest of the property was untamed and largely neglected except for the perimeter fences. The land was mostly flat enough to almost see the curvature of the earth, except where two creeks had cut out a four- or five-foot gully at the bottom of which lay a ribbon of precious, cooling water. Soaring cottonwoods and drooping willows hugged the banks of the creeks in stark contrast to the expanse of open prairie around them. Everywhere was soft prairie grass and Indian Paintbrush vied with Bluebonnets for space on the rich earth.

Her broad-brimmed straw hat had long since been blown off and was hanging against her back by its chin cord, allowing her hair to be blown straight back. The wind in her face and the scent of bluebonnets temporarily swept away the burdens and concerns she faced. Jackie yielded to the change in rhythm as Sable shifted to a trot of her own accord. She also yielded her weary mind to random thoughts that came and went. She stopped herself more than once from thinking about work, but she decided that thinking about a particular person was not work exactly, and therefore permissible.

The time she had spent with Patrick Garrity at the Bar T Steakhouse had been the highlight of the past few weeks. She couldn't decide if it stayed in her mind because there had been so few times of unmixed pleasure since she had been installed as CEO or if she was really feeling something for him. She knew she was attracted to him, though they were from very different worlds. He was, after all, one of the "news gypsies" she had been so glad to send away. But she had told him he should return to Houston and he had agreed. She knew, as he must know, that the trip was really unnecessary, but she wanted to see him again, and this seemed to be as good an excuse as any.

He was different from her in other ways: he was East, she was West; he was North, she was South; he was City, she was Country — at least she was Country today, atop this gleaming, strutting mare with hardly a sign of civilization in sight.

Her mind idly wondered what he thought of her. He was a journalist and, more often than not, journalists were suspicious of corporate management. Certainly, that was the impression she got from the reporters who had come to her news conferences. Like most women, she wasn't entirely confident that she was attractive. She did her best to look her best, but there was only so much a woman could do with make-up, hair-color, and clothes. It was especially difficult for a professional woman because one needed to be feminine while being businesslike. It was easy for one to cancel out the other. She didn't know Patrick well at all, so she had no idea if he liked women in positions of power. Most reporters tended to be liberal, which meant they would give lip service to the idea of women in managerial roles, but that didn't tell her what a specific reporter might think deep down.

She smiled when she thought again of the pleasure she had felt in his company, while finishing the black bottom pie, the hot coffee adding to the flush of her cheeks as she laughed at his jokes and tried to top them with her own. She missed that.

Backlash

It had been many years since — she pushed the thought out of her mind, but it was insistent.

Memories of Arturo still brought her pain, though it was muted by the years. Surely someday she could think of him without the heaviness in her chest. Except for the fact that they were both Catholic — at least Jackie assumed Patrick was Catholic — Patrick and Arturo had almost nothing in common, which might be a good thing. Arturo was dark, of Mexican descent, with Latin good looks that made women swoon, but he was also a dreamer and notoriously unreliable. Leaving without saying goodbye was merely the final affront Jackie had suffered from him, because he was constantly late or blowing off appointments. In her moments of cold logic, Jackie was glad she hadn't married him. He had probably spared her a lot of grief by disappearing.

Patrick was as different from Arturo as two people could be. His red hair and ruddy complexion left no room for doubt as to his heritage, and although Jackie wasn't certain, he must be very responsible to hold a prominent editorial position at a large newspaper. He had said he was divorced, but Jackie hadn't probed to learn the reasons. She decided she wouldn't conclude anything about that until she knew more. She didn't think Patrick was as handsome as Arturo, but as they say, "looks aren't everything." That didn't mean she thought Patrick was unattractive; far from it.

She reigned in Sable when they got to one of the creeks, walking her through a lush carpet of Bluebonnets and letting her drink her fill under the boughs of a cottonwood. With her mind still in neutral, Jackie wondered if socializing with Patrick might be a conflict of interest.

Her mind was suddenly transported back as she watched the creek gurgle past her under the low-hanging willow branches.

Many times she had stopped at this spot with her father, when he would ride his favorite stallion and she would struggle to keep up on a tired, old mare. They were an imposing picture, the large, muscular horse and her father sitting tall in the saddle, his broad shoulders thrown back and a wide felt cowboy hat cocked to one side of his head. His hair had been coal black and his skin bronze owing to the fact that his grandmother had been full-blooded Cherokee from Oklahoma. The American Indian in the family's heritage probably accounted at least somewhat for their fiercely independent spirits.

The little creek was deeper here and so they stopped when they crossed it at this spot, instead of jumping it as they did where the stream was narrower or splashing through without slowing where it was shallow. It was a good place for watering and catching one's breath and contemplating important things. A tear escaped each of Jackie's eyes, which gazed unfocused into the flowing water, seeing the scene as it had been 25 years earlier.

* * *

Doris worked on travel arrangements and screened the phone calls that seemed to multiply by the hour. There were hundreds of details to coordinate and Jackie thought Doris might have made a good circus juggler. Wayne seemed to be everywhere and then just where she needed him with just the right piece of information. He always seemed to have the facts or could locate them in the nick of time. Charlene had just left Jackie's office to flesh out the statement that Jackie would make on Wednesday to the employees. The PR staff was also charged with creating information packages that would have to be printed and delivered overnight to 3,000 retail outlets, 17 regional offices and numerous refineries, distribution centers and drilling operations. Jackie, Benny and Dennis had sketched out the contents of the packages after the vote was taken last week, and Charlene and the other writers in her group had smoothed them out and turned them into well-designed documents on humming Macintosh computers. If that wasn't enough, they were rushing through production an extra issue of the stockholders' newsletter, with its own explanation of the plan that the board had voted, and the same information was duplicated on the company's employees-only website.

On top of all this, urgent e-mails and duplicate faxes were being sent to the top managers at each of the company's locations to alert them to Jackie's live satellite address to the employees on Wednesday. This project had been turned over to the MIS department, since they could pull e-mails and fax numbers from the company databases and send out the messages around the clock automatically.

This afternoon Jackie would meet with Marcus Williams from Legal to review the employee packets in order to catch any legal misstatements the executives and PR staff might have made in the text of the statement to the employees or the packets they would send out. He would also walk Jackie through the document his staff had prepared spelling out the details of their policy. *It will probably be 14 pages of tiny type*, Jackie thought, knowing the lawyers in the Legal Department. It was only halfway through Monday and she was already tired.

Lunch would be a sandwich at her desk again. Saturday at the Bar-X had been refreshing and Sunday at Homewood Baptist Church had been a blessing as well, but now it was back to work and there was no postponing it. Tomorrow, she would meet with President Benny Tyson and CFO Dennis Trask, who would be accompanying her to Washington, D.C. for the news conference. They would each read part of the statement at the news conference because it was important to present a united front to the world. She would also meet with Bud, to keep the chairman up to speed on the details of the plan and the promotional efforts.

He has been surprisingly docile during the whole ordeal that began with the bombing of the Gulf Pride, Jackie thought. Perhaps it had so shocked him that he had been unable to cause her any trouble. She had certainly expected Bud to challenge her, since he was undoubtedly still smarting from his loss of the CEO job to her. Even when she had revealed her plan, he was passive and simply let the board vote without any particular comment one way or the other. *I wonder if his cooperation and support can continue forever.*

* * *

Patrick Garrity arranged with the ponytail waitress to sit at the same table as before. He didn't know how long he would have to wait before Jackie would arrive. He knew she had a lot going on right now, but she had agreed to meet him to give him his scoop. Patrick only hoped getting out ahead of the rest of the media would atone for turning in John Watson, should the word get out. He was certain something really big was afoot and his article would appear at least a day before anyone else's. Not even the 24-hour television news channels could beat him this time, assuming Jackie James came to the Bar T Steakhouse like she had promised.

On the flight from Washington, he had looked forward to seeing her tonight, almost as much as he relished the idea of getting the promised scoop. He wasn't sure which was more enticing: the prospect of skunking his competition or getting to sit across the table from Jackie again.

Backlash

He slowly sipped his iced tea, not knowing how long to make it last. It had been his drink of choice ever since he had stopped drinking, though the difficult decision to stop hadn't brought his family back to him. Perhaps he could never get them back, but he knew better than to have even one beer. They had hammered that into him in the program.

He had called Jackie from the airport to let her know he was in town. A half hour passed, then another, but he was not anxious. He had been in this situation many times. Busy, powerful people often had difficulty making appointments, because there were so many demands on their time and attention. And right now, nothing else mattered. He used the time to sketch out a couple of articles with different angles depending on what direction the Axiom policy announcement took, or at least what he thought the possibilities were.

Suddenly, she was there, coming through the front door, causing a commotion as people recognized her and she spoke to first one and then another, calling some by name. Behind her was her assistant, Wayne, carrying a briefcase. Patrick had seen him once at the Axiom headquarters building. When she had greeted a number of people, she stopped and spoke to the entire room.

"Can I have everybody's attention please?" she shouted.

But she already had it. Somebody pulled the plug on the jukebox and the room was suddenly very quiet. "I've got a favor to ask. I need to talk to all the Axiom employees in the Longhorn Room for a minute. Employees only, no spouses or anything, okay?"

Then she turned and looked at Patrick and motioned for him to follow her into the Longhorn Room. As Patrick watched in amazement, about a third of the people in the restaurant stood and followed Jackie toward a banquet room with the words

"Longhorn Room" burned into a knotty pine plank over the door.

Once inside, people settled in around tables as Jackie waited for it to get quiet. They were an assortment of people, young and old, male and female, employees at the local Axiom distribution center and refinery, Patrick surmised. The common characteristic they shared was their blue-collar talk and work clothes.

"First, I've got to ask you to swear that nothing I say will go out of this room," she said. "It's very important that no one who is not employed by Axiom find out what I'm about to tell you and that nobody here let it slip. That includes wives, husbands, sweethearts, children, everybody. Anybody got a problem with that?"

People looked around at each other, wondering what was coming. The old man Jackie had called "Duke" when Patrick had been there the first time broke the silence: "You tell us what it is, honey. I'll make sure nobody tells nobody nothin'!"

Jackie smiled. "There is one exception to this rule," she smiled as she looked at Patrick, who had already felt suspicious sideways glances from the assembly. "I've invited Patrick Garrity of the Washington Herald to be here. He's going to be breaking the story of what I'm about to tell you as part of an agreement I won't go into here."

Patrick didn't look around to meet the eyes that were then trained on him. He was certain that they weren't sure they liked having a reporter among them. He simply froze a smile on his face and looked at Jackie, who continued quickly enough.

Jackie made her presentation to the group without the help of visual aids. Patrick listened without making too many notes. That would come later. He couldn't believe what he was hearing. He certainly couldn't have predicted this approach.

"So, does this make sense?" Jackie asked after outlining the basic plan. "Any questions?"

A young man in a white T-shirt and heavy boots raised his hand. When Jackie recognized him, he stood and put one hand in his jeans pocket. "If we do this, how do we know it won't backfire and people will refuse to buy anything from us after it's over?"

"Well, that's a great question. I give you my word that I'll promote this like crazy to let the public understand what we're trying to do. In a way, we're doing this for them, too. It will benefit everybody in the long run. But I guess the short answer is we don't really know how people will react. I'm just being honest with you, now."

That seemed to satisfy the man and he sat down. A 50ish, heavyset woman raised her hand. "Yes, ma'am," Jackie said.

"Can the government force us to back down?"

"That's an excellent question. Our Legal Department can't think of any law that we'd be breaking by NOT selling something, but we could be sued. Of course, we have two or three nuisance suits going all the time anyway."

A ripple of nervous laughter went from table to table in the Longhorn Room.

"That's good enough for me," the woman said.

"Ms. James," said a tall, thin man in worn jeans and cowboy boots. He spoke with a slight speech impediment that appeared to be the result of botched dental work. "I'm a tanker driver and so I'm Teamsters. What's my union going to say about this?

"Well, you'll be getting paid for doing nothing, so that ought to suit the union just fine!"

The hard-working people laughed again, this time at the expense of the tanker driver, who chuckled in spite of himself.

"I'm sorry. I'm not making fun of you," Jackie took a few steps toward the union man. "That's a very important consideration. I hope that you will realize, and will help your leadership realize, that the best thing for the union workers is that Axiom be profitable. No question it will be a tough sell. I've thought about it. I'm open to your input. I need it quick, though. The Board of Directors has voted the plan you just heard and my staff is writing the policy. Tomorrow I'll do a teleconference to announce it to our employees everywhere. We have to move fast because the government has moved fast."

"Ain't that the truth!" Duke agreed.

"If you have ideas or suggestions, I'd prefer you write them down and get them to me at HQ. You can email them if you like."

Patrick didn't say anything during the meeting, knowing he would have time to ask his questions in private. He had a great many questions to ask.

The meeting broke up then, feet shuffling and chairs scraping on the floor. He returned to his table and waited while Jackie said goodbye to her employees. They were no longer boisterous, but several of them shook hands with Jackie and whispered to her. She responded to each one by nodding and smiling. Finally, she dismissed her assistant, who left the restaurant. Only then did she walk over to where Patrick was sitting. She sighed heavily as she sat down.

"Whew! What a day!"

"It must have been. Was this plan your idea?"

"I guess, but it took a lot of people to formulate it."

"What happens now?"

"Tomorrow, I do a teleconference so the employees know what's happening. You'll be there as part of your scoop. Then

Thursday, we go to Washington and do a news conference on your home turf."

"I'll be there with bells on!"

Then he asked her about specifics of the plan. He got the dates and the ground rules. She answered his questions over steak and butter beans, washed down with bottomless glasses of iced tea. Once he had written down the pertinent details in his reporter's notebook, they relaxed and talked of more mundane things: of travel to Washington, D.C., where she had been many times with her father. Patrick knew that Donald James Jr. had made frequent pilgrimages to the Capital.

"So, you know the town?" he asked.

"Yeah, pretty well. Daddy said he went there to visit his money."

Patrick laughed with her at that. He didn't need her to explain what Junior James had meant. Axiom Oil Corporation was a major contributor to political parties and to politicians through its Political Action Committee and many lobbyists. Also, considering his wealth, Donald James' personal income tax and capital gains liabilities had probably been astounding.

As the evening wore on, they found much more to laugh about and Patrick was surprised that she seemed in no hurry to leave. Perhaps she needed this respite from the pressures that were on her, although as he memorized her smiling eyes and the soft, dark curls that just touched her small shoulders, she didn't seem to be under pressure at all. Had he walked in and sat down 10 minutes ago, he might never have guessed this petite woman with the easy laugh was capable of hatching a plan that would certainly shake the halls of power to their foundations.

CHAPTER THIRTEEN

In the 1980s, someone had suggested that corporate communications could be enhanced by the creation of a company satellite television network. Junior James embraced the idea, not because he wanted to be on TV — he didn't — but because he realized the importance of the personal touch, and there was no more intimate mass communication medium than television. It was the next best thing to being there, and with almost 100,000 employees he couldn't "be there" with all of them.

The network represented an investment of several million dollars, but Junior felt it was well worthwhile to be able to address each of the tens of thousands of Axiom employees on the closed-circuit network. Anyone who stumbled across the satellite channel without the proper decoding equipment would just see snow and hear static. But those with the Axiom "black box" could tune in anytime night or day and see presentations in straightforward English by someone at corporate headquarters, usually on videotape; but, live when circumstances warranted.

To operate the system, the company employed several production technicians and had built a production studio at the Houston headquarters. An automated system played training videotapes or displayed text around the clock and a schedule was published on the employee website.

A by-product of the network had been that many of the Axiom employees felt like they knew Junior personally, and so there was a high degree of trust of the company's management.

Occasionally, Axiom management did live teleconferences and today was one of those days. In the relatively small corporate TV studio, Tom Sheridan, Axiom's corporate television director, supervised his younger assistants. Tom was in his late 40s and was wearing the corporate uniform of long sleeved shirt and tie, though the sleeves were rolled up and the tie loose. The Axiom Logo hung on the "cyc" wall and an oil derrick prop gathered dust in one corner. A news-anchor-style desk and chair sat in the middle of the room.

Jackie entered the studio, followed by Doris, Dennis, Benny and Wayne, carrying Jackie's briefcase. Then Charlene Washington, the PR Director, came in. Last through the door was Patrick Garrity, who had met the others upstairs in Jackie's office before they came down.

"Good afternoon, Tom."

"Yes. Good afternoon, Ms. James. We're ready for you right here." Tom gestured to the lone chair behind the desk. Jackie walked to it and sat down.

"Thanks. Wayne, you've got the drive, right?

"Yes, here it is."

Wayne took a flash drive from his pocket and handed it to Tom, who called to his female assistant:

"Amber, load this in the TelePrompTer, please."

Amber took the drive through a nearby door into the control room. Jahmal, the other assistant, took his place behind the camera and adjusted the controls so that Jackie's image appeared on the monitor. Momentarily the first words of the speech appeared on the mirror in front of the camera. Tom brought over a lavelier mic and clipped it to Jackie's navy suit coat.

"So, I just look there and read?"

"That's right. You want to try it? We've got about 15 minutes before you go on."

"Yes, I probably should." Jackie said and then started reading from the prompter.

"Friends and fellow employees of Axiom Oil: I'm Jackie James, CEO of Axiom. You're accustomed to seeing my father on these broadcasts, but as you know, he passed away suddenly last month." She swallowed hard at that. Maybe she wouldn't struggle through this part during the real thing now.

"I have become chief executive in his place and look forward to a bright future as we work together to provide energy to the world... ." She stopped reading and looked at Tom. "Okay, that's pretty easy."

The young man behind the camera gave the "Okay" sign to Tom. Amber signaled through the control room glass that the mic level was good.

"You'll do fine," Tom reassured her. "You're a natural. Now if you'll excuse me, I've got some last-minute things to do in the control room."

"Sure. Go ahead."

Tom went through the same door Amber had gone through.

"Well, here goes nothing." Jackie said to her entourage.

* * *

The cafeteria at the Axiom Oil Refinery in Gary, Indiana was filling up with workers in coveralls and hardhats, slapping each other on the back and laughing, their noisy talking reverberating off the concrete block walls. A large TV set had been placed on a cart at one end of the room. The workers took their time finding seats in small groups of friends and coworkers.

* * *

Meanwhile, at an Axiom Service Station in New York City, Manager Jim Powers entered the service bay and shouted to three mechanics: "Hey! It's time for Corporate TV!"

"Do we have to?" one of the mechanics complained.

"What's such a big deal we gotta drop everything?"

"Come on, youse guys," the manager chided. "This must be important or they wouldn't have told us to watch it LIVE."

"Yeah, what're you complaining about," one of the other mechanics scolded his coworker. "How often d'ya get paid to watch TV?" The men laughed as they left the service bay.

* * *

Jackie studied the speech on the printed pages she would only need if the TelePrompTer failed. Tom came back into the studio.

"We've got one minute. Are you ready?"

"Yes. Let's do it." Jackie gripped the papers in her hand, betraying her nervousness as well as her concentration.

Tom put on a headset and spoke into the mic. "Ready out here, Amber." He looked at Jackie. "Stand by." He listened, then held up his hand. "Okay, Ms. James. We're on in ten, nine, eight, seven, six," then he began counting down with his fingers. "Five, four, three," silently Tom continued the countdown with his lips and fingers: two, one, then he pointed to Jackie. She took a deep breath and, looking at the camera, began reading as the TelePrompTer rolled, staying just ahead of her.

* * *

At an offshore oil platform south of Newfoundland, a large satellite dish sat high on one corner, pulling in the signal from 23,000 miles above the equator. "Friends and fellow employees of Axiom Oil," the voice said from the TV in the galley. "I'm Jackie James, CEO of Axiom. You're accustomed to seeing my father on these broadcasts, but as you know, he passed away suddenly last month." About 30 workers strained to see the face on a 32-inch TV set. "I have become chief executive in his place and look forward to a bright future as we work together to provide energy to the world."

* * *

In Anchorage, Alaska, it was 10 a.m. and the boardroom at the Axiom Regional Office was full to overflowing as about 25 executives and secretaries sat crowded around a conference table, watching a TV set built into the wall, where Jackie's face and voice was the center of attention: "This is my first televised message to you, though I have met many of you during my visits to your facilities in my former capacity as Vice President of Operations."

"I love this company," Jackie continued on the TV. "As you know my grandfather was 'Jake' James, a no-nonsense Texas oilman who built Axiom from nothing in the 1920s. My father followed him and Axiom became the multinational corporation it is today. Both my grandfather and my father are gone now, but it is my intention to carry on their tradition of quality and service.

"I still own part of the company, but most of you are also part owners of Axiom. I know some of you who have worked for Axiom since before I was born. You have thousands of dollars — some of you, tens of thousands of dollars — of Axiom stock. That's your retirement, your security. You have helped build this company and have earned every dollar of the high value of that stock. Some of you have just started to acquire ownership in the company through our investment plan, and I'm sure you are happy to be associated with a strong, stable company.

"It means your future will be predictable and secure. Some of you belong to unions, but you understand that the profitability of Axiom is what drives your wages and especially your benefits."

* * *

Back at the studio in Houston, Jackie turned a page in her printed script, even though she wasn't reading from it. "Unfortunately, my first message has to inform you of a threat to our company. As you know, we were attacked by terrorists recently. The Gulf Pride offshore platform was bombed and one of our workers was killed. We don't understand the motivation of people who would do this terrible thing, but you can rest assured that an investigation is going forward and I believe we will eventually know who the guilty parties are.

"This has led to a great deal of news coverage and now has prompted Congress to enact a brand new gasoline tax in addition to those already in place. The speed with which Congress approved the new tax shocked us all.

"All this comes after we have spent years complying with more and more Federal government regulations on a variety of fronts. We understand the need for safety regulations and we don't question them. We also care about the environment — about air quality, clean water, and the oceans. We all breathe the air and drink the water after all, and we know that we must plan for a healthy future for our children.

"Accordingly, we have cooperated with the efforts of the government to modify the way we acquire, refine and transport petroleum products, spending millions to modernize our facilities and retool our methods, so that we have been honored with a number of awards for our compliance with ever stricter standards and our innovation to improve our 'green' stance as a corporation.

"Increasingly though, the regulations take the form of environmentally motivated strictures that are poorly supported scientifically and only serve to increase our overhead and reduce profits. That reduces your income and security. It makes your future less certain."

Jackie's face was no longer on the screen. A series of bar and pie charts illustrated the numbers as she continued speaking and Amber made the changes in the control room according to the script. "Simultaneously, our corporate income taxes have crept up and up until they are at the highest levels they have ever been. In fact, they are now triple what they were when my father began his career. Then there's the taxes that are added to the price of every gallon of the gasoline and diesel fuel we sell. When my father began to lead Axiom, those taxes amounted to less than a penny per gallon. Today they range from 25 to 40 cents per gallon, depending on the state. Inflation could account for some of that, but it's still about a threefold increase. These increases must be passed on to the consumer and that places a hardship on our customers. When gas prices are artificially high due to tax increases, people buy less gas, and we have to lower our profit margins to stay competitive. That comes directly out of the profits of this company and that affects the value of the stock which most of you own.

"The most recent new gas tax, which just passed in both houses of Congress, increases the amount of tax we have to convey to the Federal government by an incredible two dollars per gallon! It is being sold to the country as an effort to reduce gasoline consumption and thereby reduce air pollution. This has naturally created a crisis situation for us. Our financial people are among the best anywhere, and they all tell me the same thing: this new increase in the Federal gasoline tax has made it impossible for us to make a profit on motor fuel unless we raise our prices significantly — in fact we would need to more than double them. Unfortunately, the politicians in Washington saw to it that we can't do that. They limited our increase to only one dollar a gallon above the previous cap. Depending on the area of the country you are in, that means that we will be selling gasoline at a loss of somewhere between seventy-five cents and a dollar for every gallon we sell, even if we immediately go to the new price control limit."

Jackie's face appeared on the studio monitor again, as Amber switched back to the camera shot of Jackie. "In light of all this, our board has voted to take an unprecedented action. It was my idea and I will accept full blame if it doesn't work, but it has been supported by our financial managers and voted by the board." Jackie quickly glanced at Dennis and Benny, who looked a little peaked. "Before I outline our plan, I want to stress to you that we are not planning layoffs during the time we put this plan into action. That was something that was discussed and rejected by the board. But we will have to all work together to pull this off. So, I hope you will listen carefully to what I am about to say."

Jackie looked down at the paper in front of her and took a deep breath, then looked back at the camera. "The action we have decided to take is this: during the fourth quarter of our fiscal year, July through September, we will sell no gasoline or diesel fuel, neither retail nor wholesale. We would lose money on every gallon we sold, so we won't sell any."

Jackie could almost hear the gasps and vocalized questions across the network, so she paused before going on. "I know you have questions, but wait until I have explained the whole plan.

"We have many other things that we sell. Retail motor fuel sales represent about 40 percent of our revenue stream. The other 60 percent is made up of convenience store sales, auto repair and parts, motor oil and additives, and the sale of petroleum products for manufacturing and asphalt for paving.

"Also, let me point out that this moratorium is only in the United States. Our operations will continue full speed ahead in the other countries. There will be no interruption of revenues in that segment of our business.

"Let me hasten to reassure you again that during this three-month period no one will be laid off. Everyone will continue to work. Those who work at our 3,000-plus gas stations will continue to sell everything except motor fuel. Also, you as Axiom employees will be able to purchase fuel to get to and from work. And everyone will continue to be paid. Everyone except, that is, for me. I have elected to forego my own paycheck and stock dividends for those three months. My grandfather and my father have taken care of me so that I can do that. That money can go to the bottom line, to be sure that all of you can put food on your tables during this time.

"In talking to our labor union representatives about this experiment, I presented it this way: Axiom's relation to the Federal government is much like management's relation to labor. We can't control what the government does, but what they do can affect us radically. So, one way to look at this is that Axiom Oil Incorporated going on strike against the Federal government of the United States. The union guys seemed to understand that."

She smiled her impish smile, then continued. "In other words, during this time, we will not be paying the gasoline tax, because we will not be selling gasoline. You can be sure, Washington will notice. That is why we are calling this boycott — that's essentially what it is, a boycott — 'Operation Backlash.'

"Simply put, we want Congress to repeal the gas tax. We hope our moratorium will make them re-think what they have done. If they do not respond, we will have to re-examine our long-term strategy.

"So, what will be the results of our action? You can be sure that we have formulated plans for every contingency we can foresee. We can't be sure, of course, what will happen. One probable result of the tax, as well as our moratorium, will be a shortage of gas and diesel. The other companies may be unable to meet the demand, but the market will force the price up to the limit across the country. Another possible result is that we might lose some customers after we start selling gas again. My hope is that we can make the public understand why we are doing this and they will come back to us.

"It may well be that many people will be angry at us because they don't understand the issues at stake. Perhaps some of YOU will be mad at me, but I hope that you can understand that we must defend ourselves and preserve our viability as a company. We believe the market should be allowed to speak. The government has tried to prevent the market from behaving normally by instituting price caps and punitive taxes.

"Ours is a strong company and we can boycott the market for three months and not be hurt by it long term, but if a company like ours doesn't make a profit year after year, it will eventually cease to exist. Nobody would loan us money. Nobody would buy our stock. Many people wouldn't buy our product because their faith in us would be shaken. If we failed to make a profit year after year, many of you would seek employment elsewhere because you need to work for a strong company with a bright future.

"Too many people in Washington don't understand what I'm telling you, but you do, because it's your life that's involved.

"It might seem phony for me to call the employees and stockholders of Axiom Oil Incorporated a 'family.' After all, we're a public corporation with tens of thousands of employees, thousands of locations and millions of customers. But the first Axiom employees were MY family. And I still think of many of you old timers that way. So, I want to do right by you and I, along with my advisors, believe this is the best course of action.

"Information packets have been sent to all our locations that will give you details of this plan. I and other members of Axiom management will be giving a news conference in Washington, D.C., tomorrow to announce the plan to the public. I know I'm asking the impossible, but I need all of you to say nothing to your family or friends until after the news conference.

"I'm sorry to be beginning this way, but the circumstances were not of our making. I will update you again before the beginning of the fourth quarter and you can be sure that we will be running our PR mill overtime so that the American people know what we are doing and why. Please be strong and pray for your management and our nation as we seek to respond to this situation. Thank you and good day."

Backlash

* * *

On the plane back to Washington, Patrick was glued to his laptop, except for the approximately 30 minutes at the beginning and ending of the flight, when passengers were required to turn off their electronic devices so they wouldn't interfere with the plane's controls. He had to file his article by eight p.m. Washington time for it to appear in the morning edition. He had the transcript of Jackie's teleconference to the employees and a copy of the statement she would make at the news conference in the nation's capital tomorrow.

He had started a couple of articles based on angles he thought he might take, but the actual story was so different from anything he'd expected that his efforts were of no use. He would have to start from scratch. Thankfully, he had plenty of material and it was directly from the horse's mouth, so he didn't have to worry about fact checking or reporting something he wasn't supposed to. He had gotten full access and the scoop he was promised. His article would create a sensation and ensure a good attendance at the news conference tomorrow morning.

He wrote pretty much what Jackie had told him and what he had observed, relating in some detail the impromptu meeting of employees at the Bar T Steakhouse, the teleconference and the board meeting in which the policy was voted. The article included photos of Jackie, President Benjamin Tyson and CFO Dennis Trask, supplied by Axiom Media Relations. He was a little uncomfortable because the article was an uncritical relaying of Axiom company positions, but at this point there was no reaction to report, because the moratorium hadn't been announced yet and he still believed in the fundamentals of journalism. He wouldn't editorialize in a news article. In fact, his article would be the first public announcement of the moratorium, unless you counted the teleconference that announced it to tens of thousands of Axiom employees. When there was reaction, he could report it, and he was certain there would be a reaction.

One thing he would leave out of the article was his growing fascination with Jackie James. Again, they had closed down the Bar T Steakhouse last night. She had seemed to enjoy their time together as much as he did, but to date, their contacts had all been dictated by their jobs. He wished he could know if she thought about him beyond using his position to get the word out about her moratorium. If that was all he was to her, it wasn't a total loss, since he was using her as well, to gain an advantage over his competitors.

The article is coming along well, Patrick thought. He should be able to have it finished in time for the deadline with no problem. He had e-mailed Managing Editor Howard Finkel that he had a scored a major coup.

Patrick was sure it would ingratiate him to his boss.

* * *

The next morning, Patrick Garrity parked his car and walked to the Commerce Department Building where the news conference was slated to take place. The day was already hot on this Monday morning in June and he was glad it was set for nine a.m. rather than later in the day. As he approached, he could see the TV cameras setting up on the front steps of the Commerce Department building.

Because of the flurry of news coverage about the new gas tax and Patrick's article, which had just hit the streets, the news conference was well attended by inside-the-beltway press, Patrick saw. Multiple video camera crews, led by carefully coiffed TV reporters, waited with the more casual print journalists and still photographers. They looked at Patrick with a mixture of admiration and cynical jealousy for the scoop he had pulled off. He joined the gathering throng, greeting his photographer, Sanjay, who was already there.

Patrick saw Jackie, Axiom CFO Dennis Trask and President Benjamin Tyson standing off to one side talking to each other and occasionally looking at the gathering news people. Momentarily, they started for the podium.

It was time.

Jackie went to the podium first. Holding a copy of their joint statement, she stepped up to the podium and its forest of microphones. "Thank you for coming. I'm Jacqueline James, chief executive officer of Axiom Oil Incorporated. With me is President Benjamin Tyson and Chief Financial Officer Dennis Trask. We have a joint statement and then will take questions." She began reading from the paper in her hands.

"We are here today representing the number one company in motor fuel retailing, with 30 percent share of the nation's gasoline and diesel fuel market. Axiom Oil Incorporated has operations across the continent and in several foreign countries. Our company has seen remarkable growth from its inception, proving that our management understands what is required to mount a successful business venture."

Then she looked up. "With me is Benjamin Tyson, President and Dennis Trask, CFO of Axiom. They will assist me with our statement. First, President Benjamin Tyson."

Jackie stepped aside and Tyson went to the podium with his copy of the statement, continuing where Jackie left off.

"Good morning. With the recent increase in the Federal tax on gasoline and diesel fuel and the combined effects of price controls, government-mandated wage levels and other factors, our financial personnel have demonstrated that we cannot make a profit for the year unless we take drastic action during the fourth quarter. Our responsibility is to conduct business activity that will make a profit for the owners of our company — our shareholders."

Benny in turn stepped aside to make way for Dennis. "When a particular activity ceases to be profitable, we cannot continue that activity. Our company is involved in a wide variety of business activities with multiple revenue streams. We have decided to cease one of those activities for three months. It is our intention to sell no gasoline or diesel motor fuel at the retail level during our fiscal fourth quarter, which begins July 1."

Patrick thought he saw Dennis gulp as he stepped away from the podium and Jackie returned to it. The start date was just over three weeks away. The journalists suddenly erupted with questions, the mention of the date serving as a signal to unleash their pent-up curiosity.

Jackie raised her hand in the universal signal for "stop" and waited for silence.

"We'll take questions when we have finished reading the statement. Thank you." Then Jackie continued with the last paragraph of the statement.

"This moratorium on motor fuel sales will not affect other sales of petroleum products for manufacturing. It will not affect heating oil or natural gas supplies. There are many other companies that have retail outlets for gasoline. They will continue to sell fuel, since they are not a part of this moratorium. We are confident that after the moratorium, conditions will have improved to the point that we can resume gasoline sales. Now we'll take your questions." She looked up at the reporters, who again erupted with questions. Jackie pointed at a reporter and the rest became quiet.

"What about fuel for over-the-road trucks?"

"Diesel fuel is included in the moratorium, since it was included in the most recent tax increase." She turned and pointed to another reporter.

"Won't this create shortages and drive the price of gasoline up too high for most people to be able to afford it?"

"Ordinarily, I'd say 'yes,' but Congress has capped the price of gas so it can only go to $6.00 per gallon."

"But isn't the price of gas too high as it is?"

"I believe the whole point of Congress' recent increase in the gas tax was to drive the price up so people will use less gas because it is thought to be harmful to the environment. We don't want to raise our prices, but we would have to in order to survive. Rather than raise our prices to the consumer, we decided on another solution: the moratorium."

"You can't do that! People need gas!" another reporter exclaimed without being recognized.

"Yes, we can do it, and we have. In fact, we have no choice."

Finally, Patrick raised his hand and was recognized. "Ms. James, would you say your moratorium is primarily aimed at Congress?"

Her eyes bore into him like a laser, but the corners of her mouth went up as if the two of them were sharing a secret everyone else had missed. "Mr. Garrity, I believe? You are very perceptive, but it's much bigger than that." She turned to address the group. "I think you'll find detailed answers to these and many other questions in the press packets that are available at the table to my right. We thank you for your time, today." She gestured to the black and gold press packets stacked on a table to one side of the podium. The executives and their aides turned and made a beeline for a couple of limousines parked at the curb. Some of the reporters followed, shouting questions, but the news conference was over. Some of the news people opened their press packets and begin to devour the contents.

Patrick watched Jackie until she was in her car. *What a gutsy lady she is! This ought to make some people sit up and take notice,* he thought, struggling not to laugh out loud. Then he made his way to the table and picked up one of the last press packets, though he already had most of the contents.

CHAPTER FOURTEEN

Having just arrived home from work and fed his animals, Paul missed the first part of the report of the Axiom news conference on the six o'clock news. When he finally turned the TV on for noise while he prepared his own supper, he was suddenly mesmerized by the breathless female reporter, standing in front of the Commerce Department in the nation's capital.

"... Ms. James used the word 'moratorium' to describe the action the company is taking in response to the gasoline tax. Apparently, the company's management believes it can modify public policy by this means. We will find out what effect it will have when the company stops selling gasoline on July first."

Paul's mouth fell open as he tried to replay the woman's words in his mind to be sure he had heard right. Axiom was going to stop selling gas beginning July first? What astounding good news! That was exactly what they wanted to happen, wasn't it? Then he began to have second thoughts. *Wait a minute, What are they trying to do?* A company like that wouldn't just stop doing its main business activity like that. If only it was that easy!

The newscast had gone on to other stories, so he turned off the TV and picked up the phone, dialing a number he had memorized after hearing it one time. He had no need of phone books or contact lists to remember phone numbers. For Paul, as a mathematician, numbers had almost mystical relationships to each other and he memorized all sorts of numbers without trying.

"It's Paul," he said when the man answered. "Did you hear the news?"

"You mean Axiom Oil's news conference?" the voice on the other end of the phone said, sarcasm dripping from every syllable.

"Yes, they're going to stop selling gas. That's good, isn't it?"

"They're only stopping for three months. I went over to Commerce for the news conference and, believe me, it's not good. Or maybe it won't matter, I don't know. Just know they aren't doing it out of any concern or change of heart. They're doing it to screw us!"

"How does this screw us?"

"I'm not really sure. They may be trying to garner sympathy and get the public to demand the repeal of the gas tax."

"But it's already passed."

"And it can be repealed if the gutless wonders in Congress get a few angry phone calls and letters! I'll have to go hold their hands; maybe spread some cash around," Paul's Washington connection said, more to himself than to Paul.

"Is there anything I can do?"

"I'll let you know. I hate to admit it, but I didn't see this coming. I'll figure out something in the next few days and let you know. Meanwhile, don't call us, we'll call you."

"Okay, okay." Paul hung up the phone, a vague sense of dread weighing on him as he leaned back on the magazine-covered couch. A cat jumped on his lap and he stroked its arched back absent-mindedly.

* * *

The man in the Italian sports car made a show of noisily hanging up, but it was impossible to slam down a smart phone to hang up the way one could with a landline phone. A bigger demonstration would be dangerous while driving anyway.

"Something wrong?" asked the supermodel-thin woman in the low passenger's seat.

"Just work," Marvin Borelli answered with a scowl. She tugged at her short designer skirt, but didn't ask him for details. The phrase "useful idiot" came too easily to mind anytime he talked to one of the many locals he had recruited across the country to carry out his "projects." They were such babes in the woods, so wide-eyed and clear-minded about "The Cause." Many of them were fairly dangerous true believers and couldn't see the larger agenda. They were committed and so did what they were asked with the scantest of justification, which was just what Marvin needed.

He seemed to wipe away the frustration clouding his mind and smiled at his leggy companion for the evening. "Where shall we dine?"

The woman, only recently turned 21 years old, looked at him mischievously. "Where will the most people see us?"

Marvin was accustomed to nightly dinners at Washington, D.C.'s finest restaurants, with beautiful, young women at his side, wooing the most powerful politicians in the world with cash, opulent gifts and personal favors, paying for it all with the vast sums of money that flowed into the Nation's capital through people like him from special interest groups across the political and ideological spectrum. He sped about town in his Maserati GranCabrio, known and sought-out by all the power brokers. At 32, he was dashing in expensive clothes and jewelry, with black hair moussed and combed straight back. Marvin was regarded as something of a wunderkind and tended to believe his own PR: that there was nothing he could not accomplish; no amount of money he could not raise for the right payoff.

Borelli ran his own company, Borelli Partners LLC, but in actuality there were no partners. Borelli was an independent Government Relations Specialist. His specialty was lobbying Congress for non-profit environmental groups like Champions of Mother Earth, his biggest client, and other similar but smaller groups. He had personally written legislation on behalf of members of both houses of Congress that had brought about real change in the way vast industries disposed of waste and tooled their factories. He had contributed to policy at the EPA and other agencies that transformed the respect paid to environmental concerns, however grudging it might be in certain quarters.

In many ways he, Marvin Borelli, was smarter and more powerful than the doddering old fools who greedily sopped up the money he offered so they could afford to campaign to obtain the votes that would return them to the banks of the Potomac term after term to do it all again.

The couple arrived at the agreed upon restaurant and, after entrusting the GranCabrio to a valet, made their grand entrance, turning heads across the dining room as they knew they would.

* * *

"You might want to see this, Patron," Agent Tony Bouchet startled Thomas Shannon, who was sitting at his desk lost in thought.

"What's that?"

"Just got some phone traffic from the tap the Houston field office got a warrant for. Our boy Stoddard's calling Washington."

"You don't say? Who's he talking to?"

"I don't know him, but from the sound of the conversation, I'd lay odds he's a player," Bouchet handed Shannon a transcript of the conversation.

"This looks very hot," Shannon said as he scanned the sheet. "Find out who this guy is. Washington probably knows him. They'll get a warrant and soon we'll find out who else this guy talks to," Shannon said, handing the transcript back to Bouchet.

When he was gone, Shannon pondered the implications. The transcript sounded like Stoddard was being directed by the person he had called in the Nation's Capital. Stoddard had asked if there was anything he could do, as if he would follow the order whatever it was. If the "Knights of Mother Earth" were being directed by someone in D.C., that would throw an interesting light on the events they were investigating.

* * *

Jackie had been warned that this might happen. The formal summons had come soon after she arrived back in Houston following the Washington news conference. She would have to go back to answer questions before the Senate Commerce, Science and Transportation Committee next Monday. She decided she would take Dennis Trask and Marcus Williams with her, to answer any specific financial or legal questions respectively. Wayne would go too, to prompt her with pertinent facts that he was so good at ferreting out. It was a bother to have to go back there, but she figured it would also give the company an opportunity to get the word out about the purpose of their moratorium. Some of the politicians might even support the action they were taking — the ones who had voted against the gas tax. But even they were probably worried about what would happen as a result of Axiom's bold plan.

* * *

Alec Kincaid the Third stomped into his office, muttering something under his breath. Even he wasn't sure what it was he was saying. It was more guttural grousing than articulate speech. He slammed his ostrich briefcase down on the brown leather couch, strode on long, slender legs to his massive walnut desk, and plopped down in his wingback executive chair without removing the jacket of his $2,000 suit, sweeping a hand through his full head of curly umber hair. Hitting a key on the keyboard, he woke up his computer and opened a boilerplate form, which he immediately began modifying, his thin, manicured fingernails clicking on the keys at machine-gun speed.

What were they thinking? he asked himself. Listening to the news on the radio during his 45-minute commute, he had heard the coverage of the Axiom Oil news conference from the day before. He had been boiling over ever since. He had owned Axiom stock for nearly 15 years. He did well as a $500 per hour corporate attorney, serving the greater Chicago area — indeed most of the Midwest. He had bought the stock over a period of years, so now he had roughly eight-hundred-thousand-dollars worth. It wasn't his only holding of course, but Axiom had always done well for him, so he'd recommended it to many of his well-heeled friends. But what was this nonsense about not selling gasoline during the fourth quarter? *How does a gasoline company not sell gasoline? How do they think that will help the stock price?*

He'd call several of his friends and get the ball rolling. With luck, he'd have enough signatures to file — let's see, today was Thursday — he should be able to file by Monday, three weeks before the start date. They'd be sorry they concocted such a dimwitted scheme when they learned of his class-action lawsuit!

* * *

After flying to Washington for the second time in a week, Jackie, along with Dennis, Marcus and Wayne entered the Senate Committee Room where they had been instructed to appear. A committee aide came out of nowhere, showing them where to sit, how to use the microphone, and pointing out the water pitcher and glasses. The three managers sat at the table and Wayne sat directly behind them, ready to prompt or to supply any materials they might need from his briefcase that was bigger than some luggage.

It was about fifteen minutes before the proceeding was to begin and Senators were gradually coming in, throwing their suit coats on the backs of their chairs, since in June, the central air had a hard time overcoming the Washington heat in the crowded room.

Jackie looked at them one by one. Wayne had put together a who's who of the men and women on the committee, their party affiliations, how they voted on the gas tax, and their general attitude about business, labor issues, the environment, ad infinitum. Most of it had been helpful and she was glad that she actually recognized many of the committee members faces and remembered a little about their voting profiles.

Each Senator had a couple of aides sitting behind him or her and there were committee staffers crowded into the room doing their jobs. One thing Jackie learned from Wayne's briefing materials was that Senate committees had their own staffs and office space, apart from the Senators' personal offices and staff. Further contributing to the growing claustrophobia of the room was the press. Perhaps as many as 30 news people sat or stood along the walls.

Jackie saw that Patrick Garrity was there. Of course, he would be, since he was the Political Editor of the Washington Herald. She resisted the impulse to wave at him fearing it might jeopardize his journalistic integrity somehow.

Several television cameras were stationed around the room to pick up various angles. The one in front of the Senators was pointed right at Jackie and seemed to be operated by remote control.

Jackie recognized the chairman of the committee, Dodge Drummond, Democrat from Ohio. She remembered he was pro-union, which might be bad.

Drummond rapped his gavel and the meeting began.

"Let's come to order, please. Come to order. Thank you." He looked squarely at Jackie. "Ms. James, thank you for coming to respond to the questions this committee would like to ask you today."

"Thank you, Senator," Jackie dipped her head slightly to speak into the microphone. "I appreciate the opportunity."

"I think you know why you've been asked to come here today. Your industry is an important part of the commerce and transportation infrastructure of this country."

"Yes, sir."

"By way of introduction, could you briefly give us an overview of your company's recent actions and what you hope they will accomplish? Then I'm sure my colleagues will have some questions."

"Yes, sir I'd be happy to. Senator, we have taken this action for one reason. After looking at our projections, adjusted for this new tax and the reduced revenue that will result, our financial people concluded that we will lose money on every gallon of gasoline we sell during the fourth quarter. So, as a business decision, we have decided to suspend the sale of that product until the beginning of the first quarter of the next fiscal year. I'd like to have my Chief Financial Officer, Dennis Trask, share some figures that will clarify the issue."

Dennis cleared his throat and began speaking through his thick mustache.

"In the course of revising our projections in light of the new gasoline tax which passed Congress recently, my staff brought to my attention the problem that we face going forward with gasoline sales for the remainder of this fiscal year."

Jackie watched as he talked, partly reading from the piece of paper in his hand. His voice was deep and confident and she was proud of the impression he must be making.

"In running the numbers every way we could think of, we could find no way to make a profit on gasoline sales while the new fuel tax is in place. Since about 40 percent of our overall revenues comes from fuel sales, we found that we will be in a dire position if we sell gasoline during this fourth quarter of our fiscal year. That's July 1 through September 30.

"That being the case, we have made a decision to place a moratorium on fuel sales during that three-month period only. After that we will sell gasoline and diesel fuel once again."

"Mr. Trask," Senator Drummond interrupted. "What do you hope to accomplish by this stunt?"

"Begging your pardon, Senator. It isn't a stunt. We are doing it because it makes good business sense."

"How can it be good business sense to stop selling what you sell?" He looked at his fellow Senators with a sly grin, as if to mock this big yokel from the oil patch.

Jackie looked at Dennis as he measured his words.

"Sir, I'm an accountant by trade. I'm paid to worry about the bottom line. That means that if the bottom line has a red number on it, I need to remove something above the bottom line until that bottom figure can be black."

Jackie smiled as she watched Dennis struggle to keep his trademark diplomacy intact.

"It became clear that the only way to break even after July 1 was to stop selling gas, because we will lose money on every gallon if we continue to sell it. There's an old joke among business people, Senator. It says if you're losing money, you make it up in volume. But the reason it's funny is that if you're losing money, selling more volume just causes you to lose more money!"

"But don't you realize people depend on gasoline?" Drummond asked.

"Of course, that's why we sell it. Because people will pay for it, and that enables us to earn a profit."

"Profits aren't as important as people's needs."

"The needs of which people, Senator?" Marcus Williams had remained silent as long as he could.

"All people. Everyone needs gasoline. Don't you care about them?"

Marcus looked at Dennis and he gave him a "go ahead" look, so he continued. "Senator, I'll tell you whose needs we are required to care about. There are 100,000 people on Axiom's payroll. If Mr. Trask and I and the rest of our top management don't ensure our company makes a profit, we may have to lay some of those people off. They won't be able to buy food, much less gasoline.

"Then there's another group we have to be concerned about: the stockholders of Axiom Oil."

"I don't think you need to worry about your rich stockholders."

"You know better than that, Senator," Dennis joined in the conversation again, risking making the politician angry, but he was already headed that way himself. "A lot of Axiom's stockholders are small investors. Many are also employees. The quality of their retirement hinges on the value of the Axiom stock. They're not rich. Many of them have worked faithfully for decades. They have a right to expect that their investment will be sound. I seem to remember that this body had a lot to say when Enron's employees' 401k's went south."

"But it's your job to provide gasoline for people who need it."

"No, Senator." Now Jackie had to respond. "Our job is to make a profit for the owners of Axiom Oil. We sell gasoline to make a profit. Every business does what it does for one primary reason: to make a profit. When an activity stops being profitable, a company has no choice but to stop that activity, whether it's selling gasoline or vacuum cleaners door-to-door."

"That seems awfully crass."

"Not at all. The company that conducts its business any other way won't last long. Our employees have to eat and put children through college. There's nothing wrong with that."

"But it's your civic duty to be concerned about the needs of all people."

"What about your civic duty?"

"What do you mean?"

"You're a United States Senator. The people elected you to represent their interests in the government."

"And I do!"

"I beg to differ, Senator. You use the power of government to influence the market. You levy huge tax increases to try to change people's buying habits, rather than letting the free market decide. The free market is nothing more and nothing less than the people and their needs."

"Sometimes people want things that aren't the best for society at large."

"How can you presume to know what people need better than the people themselves do? You should not be making those decisions. The people should be allowed to make their own decisions in a free market. That's what freedom is."

Nathan Taylor raised his hand to the chairman.

"The chair recognizes the Senator from the state of Vermont," Drummond said, appearing glad for the relief.

"Thank you, Mr. Chairman. Miss James, I'd like to expand on a point that the chairman made. That sometimes the people want things that aren't the best for society as a whole. Your product pollutes the earth and the air. It would be better if we didn't use it. We humans need to end our domination of Nature."

Jackie didn't answer immediately. She didn't follow the Senator's reasoning at all.

"Senator," she said, letting her natural Texas drawl come through, "You're gonna have to run that one by me again. What do you mean, 'our domination of Nature'?"

"Your business depends on the extravagant use of the earth's resources," Taylor said, warming to his topic. "That means that you are using Nature for your own ends."

"Yeah, so what?" She regretted saying it immediately, but she stared into Taylor's eyes without flinching.

"I don't think it's morally right for humans to dominate and use Nature."

"I thought humanity was PART OF nature. But that's beside the point. Senator, how did you get to this hearing?"

"Uh... Why, in a car."

"And what kind of fuel did that car use?"

"Mmm... I think we're getting off track, here."

"No, we're not. If you're not willing to answer the question, I'll answer it for you. You got here in a gasoline-powered car. If you had come in a horse-powered wagon, you wouldn't be here yet. Or would even a horse-drawn wagon qualify as 'humans dominating Nature'?"

"You're missing the point. The point is our lifestyles need to change. We are consuming the earth's resources at an alarming rate. Someday we will run out of oil."

"Senator, nobody knows the projections better than those of us in the oil business. We have thoroughly explored all the alternatives. For now, nothing is as cheap and efficient as oil."

"And there's another issue," Taylor continued, choosing to ignore her answer. "We live in a consumer-driven society. America consumes a disproportionate share of the earth's resources. Your company sells most of your gasoline to Americans. Is that not right?"

"Axiom is an American company. In the beginning, we only sold in Oklahoma, Texas and Louisiana. But we have grown, until today we have retail outlets in 14 countries, besides the U.S."

"Yes. And most of those countries are industrialized, not the less fortunate nations of the world."

"I don't know what you're getting at."

"Don't you think the poorer countries deserve gasoline too? Why have you concentrated on selling your product in the rich countries?"

Jackie was incredulous. "Oh, I don't know. Could it be because they're the ones with the CARS?!"

A ripple of laughter went around the room. Even Taylor's aide had to cover his mouth and cough, Jackie saw.

"Don't be insolent with me," Taylor replied, his face growing red.

"Forgive me Senator. I meant no disrespect, but I don't know how to react to you. You sound like the politicians who go to third world countries talking about putting the Internet in school classrooms when they don't even have electricity! Why are you even talking to me about what countries we're in? That's really none of your business!"

"Now you're insolent!"

"I'M insolent? How many shares of Axiom stock do you own, Senator?"

"Why none, of course!"

"Well, as soon as you buy some stock you can come to a stockholders' meeting and vote on our company's expansion plans! But I'm telling you this, and I want you all to hear it: My board, which is elected by Axiom's stockholders, makes the decisions about business strategy and they don't appreciate your trying to control us from Washington. My stockholders vote in elections, too, Senator."

Taylor looked like he might burst a vein. "You're aware that we can go to court to force you to continue selling gasoline?"

This was the cue for Marcus to speak again.

"You would force us to operate at a loss?" Marcus began. "I don't know for sure what law you would use against us, but I can assure you we will defend ourselves."

Backlash

"It will not serve you well to threaten us," hissed the Senator.

Marcus kept his tongue, though Jackie could see he was seething inside. Jackie said nothing for a moment, then turned to Wayne and whispered, "Give me the folder." He responded like lightning placing a two-inch think manila folder in her small hand.

"Senator," she began as she leaved through the thick folder. "I believe Axiom Oil has contributed to your campaigns about eight times: four House races and four Senate campaigns," she said as she paged through the well-organized file. "We have also contributed the legal limit to the campaigns of most of the Senators on this panel. Do you know why we did that, Senator?"

"I suppose because Axiom regarded me as the best man for the job."

"Wrong, Senator. Wrong answer, because in each of those eight elections, we also gave money to your opponent."

Jackie saw his back straighten and his eyebrows go up as if he had been hit on the behind with a two-by-four.

"Don't act so shocked. We play both sides for one reason: because this body, the Senate as well as the House — in fact, this whole town — has the power to shut us down. With the stroke of a pen you can put us out of business. With a few paragraphs of legislation you can make it impossible for us to survive. It doesn't even have to come from Capitol Hill. There are bureaucrats in the Department of Energy, OSHA, EEOC, Commerce, the IRS and EPA that can write rules that you, the elected representatives of the people, don't get to vote on and the president doesn't sign, but nevertheless have the force of law. For a company like Axiom, those regulations can cost millions, even billions, of dollars in increased overhead and compliance expenses and they don't add a single dollar to our bottom line. If we fail to comply, these agencies can slap us with fines in the millions of dollars per day, and if we still don't satisfy them, they can send armed men to our offices and take our records. So, every election we give money to you and to just about everybody else in this town. It's protection money, Senator. So you'll remember us when it's time to pass legislation that might hurt the thousands of people who work for us and depend on the paychecks they earn from Axiom Oil Incorporated.

"But right now, I'm not sure it has been money well spent, because I'm not feeling very protected."

"Our responsibility is to protect the rights of all Americans," Taylor began. "Not just..."

"Not just the ones who pay you?"

"You're out of order!" Drummond broke in.

"Why? Because I'm telling the truth? How many times have you ridden on our Lear Jet, Senator Drummond?"

"I, uh..." Drummond stammered.

Jackie looked down at the file Wayne had put together. "Don't bother trying to remember. I have the records right here. I know how many times you've eaten at Washington restaurants on my nickel, courtesy of the couple of dozen lobbyists we have to keep on the payroll to appease you and others like you. I know when you went to Scandinavia ostensibly to encourage international trade, but we paid for the trip, because we have drilling interests in the North Sea. We keep track of those things because the IRS requires us to. Mr. Trask oversees an army of CPAs to calculate the expenses we incur because we have to deal with Washington. It's a cost of doing business."

She slammed the thick file down on the table causing most of the people in the room to jump, then act like nothing had happened. "I can enter all this in the record of this hearing if you'd like."

CHAPTER FIFTEEN

Patrick had been scribbling in his reporter's notebook, but he just about lost it with Drummond's response. It was hilarious to see how Jackie handled these self-important gasbags. Patrick had grown tired of listening to them years ago. It seemed they always had some hidden agenda that contradicted what they said publicly. Jackie's southwestern candor must truly be shocking to them.

He had his portable recorder running for backup to his notes, so he stopped writing for a minute to watch the fireworks.

"I didn't think so," Jackie continued. "But there is a limit to the expenses we can afford. Eventually there has to be a backlash."

An audible collective gasp went out into the room. Patrick could see that the people in the room were stunned by the word "backlash." He watched as the men at the elevated desk struggled to recover.

"Are you threatening us again?" Drummond asked.

"No, Senator. I'm not threatening," Jackie pushed the file folder to one side and raised her eyes again. Patrick marveled at how focused and in control she was.

"I'm not threatening, but I'm promising you that we will not roll over. My father did everything according to the rules you made, but the rules keep changing and we've got to do what's best for the Axiom family."

"Senator Taylor, you may continue," Drummond said, apparently hoping he could get some traction.

"Thank you, Mr. Chairman." Taylor leaned back and whispered something to an aide, then listened for the answer before continuing. For the first time, Patrick focused on the aide sitting behind Taylor. He was a bit striking, because he wore his hair moussed and combed straight back. He also had a large gold and diamond ring on each hand. Patrick hadn't seen him before, though he thought he knew most of the senior staffers in the Senate. Come to think of it, he dressed much better than most Senate staffers, Patrick noted.

"Ms. James," continued Taylor. "I don't think you see the full import of your actions. This is an ill-considered move on your part."

"I assure you we have given this every consideration. In reality, we're just doing what you said you wanted."

Patrick smiled again as the white-haired man's jaw dropped.

"I, I don't understand."

"Don't you see Senator? You won. You wanted less gasoline consumed. You said it was harming the environment. You got your wish. We surrender. Have it your way."

Jackie raised her open palms in the universal posture of surrender, but the impish grin Patrick had seen before was straining at the corners of her mouth.

"I'm very serious when I say, I'm giving you what you wanted. You just don't get to hurt my company and the people who work for me in the process!"

"You can't do this," Taylor struggled to find reasons. "Your company is colluding. That's illegal!"

"Colluding with ourselves?" Marcus responded incredulously. "If we were setting prices with other companies; that would be illegal. Only you — the government — can set price controls legally. But we're not fixing prices. We're happy to let the prices do whatever they want. We just have to stay out of the marketplace until the end of our fiscal year. Then we'll be right back in there competing again."

"But what about the taxes?"

"We're taking this action in response to the new tax," Jackie answered.

"I know that! I'm talking about the tax revenue that will be lost because of this! What about that?"

"We will pay every dollar of taxes we owe," Dennis asserted.

"But you won't owe any gasoline taxes if you're not selling gasoline!"

Patrick watched as Jackie's eyes narrowed. He could tell she was enjoying the horror that was dawning on them.

"Did you just now figure that out?" she said.

* * *

A few minutes later Jackie and her entourage fought their way through a sea of journalists, cameramen, microphones and flashing cameras, down the Capitol steps to their limo. Finally, Jackie stopped and turned to face the reporters.

Patrick watched her answer the reporters' questions from the top step of the Capitol, shaking his head at the audacity of this relatively young woman with so much responsibility. What was it about her that made her willing to take on the whole Washington machine? She was definitely made of stern stuff. Patrick was sure there were some Senators wondering what had just hit them.

He wanted to join her; to go off and celebrate her triumphal appearance before the self-important Senatorial committee, but he couldn't let himself be seen fraternizing with her while she was at the center of the political firestorm he was charged with covering.

* * *

Once they were finally in the limo with its dark windows, Jackie buried her head in her hands for about five seconds until the urge to cry had passed.

"That was amazing, Miss James," Dennis was the first to speak.

"Did I do okay?"

"Okay? You had them on the run. They probably thought they could run roughshod over this little woman from South Texas. Boy! Were they in for a surprise!"

"You were awesome," Wayne confirmed softly.

"I should have let you talk more," Jackie said to Dennis.

"I think your passion was much more compelling than my spreadsheets," Dennis said. "I was there if I was needed."

For a moment, they rode quietly thinking about the exchanges in the hearing. It had been quite a rush.

"But we've got to remember one thing," Marcus broke the silence.

"What's that?" Jackie asked.

"These guys always have the last word."

"Yeah, I know."

* * *

Jackie put Benny Tyson in charge of getting the word about the moratorium to the American people. He met with Charlene Washington and her lieutenants in Media Relations to plan an ad campaign that included newspaper ads and televisions spots. The sound tracks of the TV spots would also be turned into radio spots for the widest possible distribution.

They had to use the ads to explain what they were doing and why. Once Benny and PR had hammered out what they needed to say, they brought in the ad agency the company had under contract to make the message interesting enough that people would pay attention and understand.

After the company's Washington news conference, the subsequent coverage was prolonged by the appearance before the Senate Commerce, Science and Transportation Committee. The fireworks there made good TV and so sound bites from it were heard over and over on the broadcast news and panels of pundits on the 24-hour news channels argued about the exchanges for a week. All the media coverage complemented Axiom's public relations efforts nicely and soon it was difficult to find anyone who hadn't heard of the moratorium.

* * *

"But why are you doing this?"

Jackie's mother said the words without talking louder, but Jackie knew she was upset, because the pitch of her voice always went up when she was really upset.

"We have to do something to try to get Congress to change its mind about the gas tax."

"But isn't there already a gas tax?"

"Yes, there are several, but this is a new tax that is added to the existing ones. Dennis tells me we can't make a profit as long as the tax is in place." Jackie didn't need to use his last name to identify CFO Dennis Trask to her mother. He had been to the James Estate on many occasions.

"But how will it help to stop selling gas?"

"It's the only way we can think of to deny the government what they want and make them rethink what they've done."

"I don't know if it's good to rebel against the government."

Jackie knew her mother retained a pre-Watergate attitude about the wisdom and character of the Federal government. She honestly believed that there was something wrong with questioning the motives of people in government. To Jackie, the people in government were just people, subject to prejudices and pressures like everyone else. But in addition, their immense power demanded constant scrutiny. She knew her father had been more realistic than her mother, hiring lobbyists to prevent the public servants in Washington from damaging his company, his employees, and his customers. Of course, her mother had never worked for Axiom and probably was blissfully unaware of the millions of dollars the company had sent to the Nation's capital. The Axiom money train still traveled from Houston to Washington, but something was different this time. The money hadn't made a difference.

"Well, this is what my advisors agree we should do and the board has voted to do it."

"You wanted this job. I hope you don't live to regret it."

"Me too, Mom. Me too."

* * *

The morning sky was the color of salmon and the texture of mother of pearl. Twenty acres of tall corn stretched toward the Iowa sunrise as Pete Breitbach walked the 50 yards from the farmhouse to the barn. After checking the local farm report on

TV, he had switched channels to CNN while he finished his eggs and bacon. They had the story about the Axiom gasoline moratorium and it had set him to thinking.

He walked around the corner of the faded red barn and under a rusted tin roof overhang where a tarp covered something. He untied a rope and pulled the tarp off into a dusty pile, revealing a contraption that looked vaguely like a moonshine still. Pete leaned back and chewed on a piece of grass. The farmer's teenage son, Kyle, appeared just then.

"Hey, Pop. What's up?"

"Well, son. I didn't think I'd ever need this again when the price of gas went so low, but now I'm thinking I might need to get it working again."

* * *

The sun rose on July 1, just like every other day. One hundred thousand Axiom employees went to work as they always had. At a New York City Axiom service station, the fluorescent lights came on at five a.m. as usual, but there were neon-orange signs on the gas pumps saying "No Gasoline For Sale" in large black letters. Details about the moratorium were contained below in paragraphs few would read, but Axiom's Legal department had insisted that the wording be there. Padlocks secured the nozzles to their cradles on the gas pumps, which were turned off in any event.

Manager Jim Powers unlocked the door from inside the station and turned the "Closed" sign around so it read "Open." He looked out at the morning traffic, but no cars were stopping. Across the street, cars were crowded into a competing gas station. Powers had never seen anything like this. He had been an Axiom station manager for 25 years. In fact, he was one of the first black station managers, a beneficiary of Affirmative

Backlash

Action. Over the years he had made the Axiom Northeast regional managers glad they promoted him, since his store was always in the top ten in the district. He understood what the company was trying to do with the moratorium, but it sure seemed strange to be opening the station without intending to sell gas.

Then, as Powers watched, a car pulled in and stopped at a pump. A young woman was driving the car with three young children. She was obviously frustrated and in a hurry. She ignored the sign and tried unsuccessfully to take the padlocked pump hose from its cradle. The manager walked out the door.

"Sorry ma'am, we don't have any gas."

"What? Why not?"

"We ain't selling gas right now. Hadn't you heard?"

"No. What are you talking about?"

"You must not watch the news. Axiom won't be selling gas for three months, until October." Powers saw a look of despair and panic pass over the young woman's face.

"But why?" she asked, her lip quivering.

"The gas tax increase made it so we can't afford to sell it. We don't make any money."

Tears started down the young mother's face. "But I've got to have gas to take my children to daycare and get to work." She held up an Axiom credit card, "I'm running on fumes and yours is the only card I've got."

"You can pay cash at any station," Powers suggested gently.

"I don't have cash and I don't have time to find an ATM!" She was definitely crying now.

Powers thought a moment, then said: "You wait right there."

Powers walked back to the station and went to the repair bay. There he found a gallon gas can that was used by the mechanics to clean grime from auto parts. He took the can to

her car and poured the fuel into the gas tank opening. She held
out the Axiom credit card.

"No ma'am," Powers said, gesturing 'stop' with his palm.
"I'm not allowed to sell gas, but I guess I can give it away. That
will get you to an ATM to get some cash and you can get some
gas somewhere else."

"Why, thank you so much."

"Don't worry about it," Powers smiled, "Just come back
when you've got more time and use that credit card to pay for
something in the store."

"Oh, thank you! I will!"

The woman got back in her car and drove away.

* * *

Patrick sat in his usual booth at the Blue Ribbon Grill,
glancing occasionally at the television behind the bar, which
was tuned to CNN with the sound barely audible. The reporter
was telling how prices were up a dollar a gallon or more across
the country due to the gas tax. He started listening when the
anchor mentioned the gasoline moratorium.

"After the first day of the Axiom Oil moratorium on gasoline
sales," a TV reporter on location in New York began, "the only
effect appears to be the crowding at the other stations. It's too
early to tell what effect the higher prices will have on those
stations that are selling gas.

"One good-news story to come out of the bad gasoline news
is from New York City, where an Axiom station manager gave a
gallon of gas to single mother Sherry Cole, whose only credit
card was for Axiom. She was late for work and the free gallon of
gas let her get her children to daycare and then to an ATM
before going to work."

The report cut to an interview with Sherry Cole. "I don't know what I would have done if he hadn't given me the gas. I'm definitely going back to buy something else." Then a man came on who the words on screen said was Jim Powers, the station manager. "It just seemed like the decent thing to do. She hadn't heard we weren't selling gas."

Suddenly the bar patrons cheered and applauded with some laughter mixed in. Patrick noticed their reaction and wondered if people were reacting the same way across the country.

* * *

The Sherry Cole story was repeated in newspaper articles and passed around on social media. It just seemed so out of character for a gas station to give away gasoline that it captured the whole country's imagination. The irony was only enhanced by the fact that it happened in New York City, not a place usually known for kindness to strangers.

First thing Friday morning, Wayne brought Jackie a copy of USA Today with an article about the incident and she immediately called Marcus and Charlene to get their input on how they could capitalize on the publicity.

"What do you think about this? Is there a way we can build on it?"

"It does appear to be a good opportunity from a PR standpoint," Charlene agreed. "What exactly do you want to do with it?"

"I don't know, could we say we'd give a gallon of gas to anyone who needed it?" Jackie asked, really not sure what she wanted.

"Can we afford that?" the lawyer asked, even though that was not something that usually concerned him. It was enough to not sell gas, but to begin giving it away was a real stretch.

"I guess we'd have to limit it to places where there wasn't another gas station close by or something," Jackie said, hoping Marcus could give her some guidance.

"I suppose I could write a policy that would work without bankrupting the company," Marcus mused. "If we said there couldn't be a competing station within, say, five miles and the customer had to be running on empty. We'd have to be sure the front-line people understand the limits of the policy." Marcus explained that the five-mile limit on the policy would cause it to only apply in rural areas where Axiom was the dominant gasoline retailer. Undoubtedly there would be some who would try to abuse the policy, but the public relations value of the gesture could be tremendous.

"And we'll have to explain it to the public," Charlene warned. "Otherwise there might be more frustration than good will out there."

"How would we get the word out?"

"Well, we could spend a bundle on TV commercials of course, but there might be a better way," Charlene tapped her chin with a rose-red fingernail. "I think we might be able to get free news coverage if we do it right."

The next day was Saturday, usually a slow news day, but it was Fourth-of-July weekend. Charlene placed full page ads in the New York Times and the Washington Herald explaining that all Axiom service stations would GIVE a gallon of gasoline to anyone who was running on empty when there was no competing gas station within five miles. As Charlene predicted, CNN, Fox News and the Big Three TV networks all ran reports on the new policy after the newspaper ads appeared.

July 4 was Sunday, so there was a three-day weekend with the usual picnics, ball games and fireworks displays. There was scarcely a gathering across the country where the Axiom

"Gallon Giveaway" wasn't discussed. In some cases, there were arguments about the motivations behind the moratorium and the gas tax. The buzz was mostly positive for Axiom, as Jackie had hoped it would be.

* * *

Monday was the third day of the three-day weekend and Paul Stoddard, like most Americans, had the day off. He used the time to putter around out back and then, when the afternoon heat and humidity became unbearable, he went inside and, after fixing himself an avocado-and-tofu sandwich, sat down to watch the local news. It was mostly patriotic folderol about concerts, ball games and fireworks displays over the weekend. Paul had just about had his fill and decided to change the channel when a reporter started asking people attending a parade what they thought of the Axiom "Gallon Giveaway" program. Paul turned up the volume.

"I think it's cool," said one young dad holding the hand of his three-year-old daughter who was licking a snow cone. "It shows the company cares about people."

"Why do you think Axiom is not selling gasoline?" the reporter asked.

"Well, I don't know all the history, but there ought to be a limit on how high taxes can go. I figure it'll cost me another ten bucks a week to drive to work because of the tax."

The shot changed to show two women being interviewed by the reporter.

"What do you think about the 'Gallon Giveaway'?"

"I think it's great. At least you know you can always get enough to get part way to where you need to go," one said.

"Right," said the other with a self-conscious grin, obviously a woman of few words.

"What about the moratorium?" the reporter probed.

"I don't use Axiom anyhow, so I guess it don't matter."

Next, the reporter found an older couple. The man wore a wide-brimmed, straw cowboy hat.

"Well, I think the company is real smart to do it that way," the man said. "People gotta notice when a company gives anything away."

"What about the fact that the company isn't selling gas?"

"I don't blame 'em. They gotta make a profit. I think maybe the gov'ment maybe went too far this time. It don't matter to me, that much. I don't go nowhere, no way."

"He's retired," his wife put in.

Paul scowled at the bumpkins, their butchery of the language and their simplistic notions. The reporter had finished his interviews and was looking at the camera, wrapping up his report.

"It appears the "Gallon Giveaway" program has a lot of people talking here at the Fourth Parade in downtown Houston. Most people felt it humanizes the company. Not everybody understood the moratorium, but some saw it as a reaction to the government's gas tax, which seems a little ironic here on the Fourth of July. Back to you in the studio."

Paul slapped the couch, causing a cloud of dust to rise in the shaft of afternoon sun coming through the window. It was not supposed to happen this way! *Axiom is supposed to be a pariah because of the "accident" and the gas tax. But people aren't blaming the company. They are actually giving Axiom credit for caring about people!*

* * *

After the three-day weekend, the late-night talk shows had a field day with the "Gallon Giveaway" policy, since it was great fodder for joke writers. One show featured a map of the nation with red flags denoting Axiom stations that were close enough together that a family could plan their vacation driving from station to station getting a gallon at a time. Soon Axiom's policies were the talk of the nation around water coolers, on talk radio and between innings at baseball games. People who hadn't been paying attention to the news of the moratorium now learned about it through the news of the give-away program and the word-of-mouth it generated.

The new wave of publicity brought new requests for interviews, this time from the popular media, and the emphasis was on Jackie personally.

On Wednesday, after the long weekend, Jackie was returning from a meeting when Doris Maxwell came into her office with a stack of phone messages.

"Miss James, may I disturb you for a moment?"

"Sure, Doris."

"I thought you would like to see some of these messages. They are from people all over the country, thanking you for the "Gallon Giveaway" program."

"Really? How many do you have there?"

"This is just a representative sampling. I'd say our receptionists have logged about 300 calls and emails the last couple of days."

"What's the score?"

"Most are positive. Here's one: 'Thank you for your giveaway idea. It shows not all corporations are big and impersonal. I don't know if I'll need to use it, but it's nice to know it's there if I need it.' It's signed by a single mom in Montana."

"That's the kind of thing I was hoping for. They're not all positive though, are they?"

"No, I've got a sampling of the other kind, too. They are mostly from people who think the policy is too good to be true."

"Okay. Leave them here and I'll look through them. I won't have time to answer them. Do we have someone who can? Don't say you'll do it. You don't have time either!"

"I can give them to the PR Department."

"Yes, good."

"I also have a number of requests for interviews from news agencies. I know we weren't doing any interviews, but these are different. One magazine that wants to do a cover story on you."

"What magazine?"

"PEOPLE."

"Really?"

"Yes, apparently the popular press has discovered you, thanks to the "Gallon Giveaway" program. I guess a lot of people are interested in you."

"I guess that's good."

"I think so. What do you want me to tell them?"

"Do they want to do it here? I don't know that I have time for a trip right now."

"You could tell them it needs to be here. Then they'll just have to do it here, if they want the interview."

"Yeah," Jackie mused. "I like the way you think, Doris. Tell them I'll do it if they want to come to Houston."

CHAPTER SIXTEEN

There was no easy way. Thankfully, the security guards were easy to spot and avoid. They were just "rent-a-cops"; not much of a problem. T2o see her when she left the office, Paul had to leave his car in the visitor's parking lot and walk into the employee parking deck. *This "moratorium" is Jacqueline James' idea*, Paul Stoddard thought, *and she is personally selling it to the American people.* She was actually popular and people were cheering her on! That was NOT the result that had been planned when everything was set in motion. *By now she should have been vilified as the criminal she is. Not held up as some sort of folk heroine!* He wondered what time she left work. He looked at his watch. It was 5:30.

Paul took a chance that she would come out on this level. The parking deck had three floors, but he assumed she would park on the lower floor, because, being underground, it was the most remote. As he walked through the garage, he saw several cars that might be hers. Gas-guzzlers of various descriptions; high-dollar road hogs that called to mind all that was wrong with America's wasteful, narcissistic consumer society. Then he spotted it. One parking spot near the elevators had a new sign that read "Jacqueline James, CEO." Parked between the yellow lines in front of the sign was a sports car, a BMW. That fit. The sporty green Z4 convertible reflected the mercury vapor lights of the basement garage like a mirror. Jealousy warmed the back of his neck as he thought how unfair it was that someone like her, who didn't have a doctor's degree like he did, could drive a car like that, profiting as a merchant of death. Now that he knew what to look for, he could go back to his car.

He wasn't sure what he would do, once she came out. He just figured information about where she lived might be important at some point. Having information like that before it was needed would make him all the more valuable to The Cause. He was also curious to see how this woman lived. In some ways, she defied explanation. She was a poster child for the privileged classes, born with the proverbial silver spoon in her mouth, and yet, she somehow came off as populist. People seemed to love her, but that just made Paul more determined to find a way to turn the tables on her.

Another hour had passed before she showed up, the green sports car darting suddenly from the parking garage exit. Paul turned the key in the ignition and his old Toyota rumbled to life with a cough and struggled to follow as the little roadster zipped toward the street.

In the waning light of dusk, he memorized the shape and proportions of her taillights so he could keep her in view, following from three or four cars back as she drove onto the ramp to Katy Freeway and headed west. Paul made a point of settling in a different lane so as not to be right behind her. She helped him by signaling her intention to exit, so Paul was able to get off, too. Coming down the ramp, he was behind her with no other cars in between, but it couldn't be helped. He slowed so she could pull away from the stop sign at the end of the ramp before he got there. She had gone right and Paul had to let another car pass before he could pull out, which was exactly what he wanted. He slowed again so when she turned off the main road, she wouldn't notice that he was following her.

Soon she did just that, turning into a subdivision, if that's what one called an assemblage of multi-million-dollar custom dwellings. Paul was thoroughly disgusted by the pretentious ostentation, but he was fascinated in spite of himself. There were faux Roman villas and French chateaus, neo-Tudor and Georgian houses, all with impeccably manicured lawns, *undoubtedly kept by illegals from Mexico and paid slave wages*, he thought. Most of them had brick or stone fences around them with wrought-iron gates and security cameras. The street names all had some relation to merry old England: Sherwood Forest Way, Maid Marion Lane, Nottingham Court. *It is all so gauche*, Paul thought.

He was looking at the wealth-on-display so intently that he almost missed it when she turned on another street. It was growing dark, but Paul wasn't going to turn on his lights until he had learned where her house was. Then she turned into a driveway. He drove on by, watching as she passed the left side of the house to a triple garage on the side. The house was a large, contemporary ranch. This was a surprise. He had figured her for a two- or three-story, red brick Colonial with white pillars; or maybe a white Antebellum plantation house, perfect for a slave master. Instead, the house was low with stone siding. It looked more natural than what he expected.

He made a mental note of the address as he continued past. After a block, he turned around and passed the house again. Warm light now illuminated the draperies shrouding large plate glass windows that made up much of the front of the house. He tried to define the front of the house into living areas: foyer, living room, and bedroom.

* * *

In his office in Richardson, Texas, just north of Dallas, Gerald Tokalas, President of Petrocom Energy Limited, waited impatiently for the clock to strike ten, when the meeting would begin. The 58-year-old executive had felt a sense of foreboding beginning about the time of the announcement of the new gas tax. It had happened so fast that his company hadn't had time to act. The Axiom moratorium was worrisome, as well. Some of his executives saw it as an opportunity to grab Axiom's market share. As the third largest gasoline retailer in the United States, the idea of capturing part of Axiom's market was very attractive, but Tokalas still worried, the white hair on his temples moving with each surge of blood through his constricted arteries. Axiom was saying it couldn't make a profit with the way the new tax was structured. So, what made his executives think they could conduct business as usual and expand their markets as well? Tokalas was afraid they were headed for problems.

This morning's meeting was with the Operations VP and Comptroller of the company. Tokalas wanted them to project the effects of the new tax on their bottom line. They probably should have done it a month ago, but it had all happened so fast. The two men arrived and the three of them sat at a conference table. Tokalas' administrative assistant, a plump woman with reading glasses pinched low on her nose, took minutes.

"I think we just need to stay the course," said Phil Snodgrass, vice president of Operations, his baby blue eyes wide with optimism. "After all, we didn't get hit with an attack or accident or whatever it was. We're bound to get additional business because of this hare-brained moratorium."

"I hope you're right," Tokalas said.

"Of course, I'm right. This is a great opportunity for us. We can adjust to the tax. Sure, it's a drag, but we've adjusted to tax increases before."

"But this one's different. We can't pass it all on to the consumer. George, what do you think?"

George Adams paused before speaking, as was his way. He was charged with overseeing the finances of a large corporation and the large responsibility seemed to translate into a ponderous way of moving and talking. "We can increase our market share," he began. "And we have survived tax increases before. I guess the only question is, how different is this one?"

"I just think it's an opportunity," Snodgrass interrupted.

"Do we have new projections?" Tokalas asked Adams, ignoring Snodgrass' exuberance.

"No, but we can do them," Adams answered.

"Fine, do it as soon as you can get them to me. I've got a bad feeling and I hope it's nothing."

"You just worry too much," Snodgrass grinned.

"I hope you're right," Tokalas didn't smile back.

* * *

"And Terry in Maplewood, Missouri, you're next on the Tim Chapel Show."

"Tim, I like what Axiom is doing."

"Tell us why, Terry. America wants to know."

Chapel imagined millions of radio listeners leaning closer to the speakers of car radios or slowing the pace of their evening jog and turning up the radio apps on their IPhones to hear what

Terry in Maplewood, Missouri would say next. The Tim Chapel Show was a nationally syndicated talk show that served as a direct line to the national dialogue on current events.

"I think it's time we told Congress where they can stick their taxes."

"So, are you feeling sorry for poor little Axiom Oil Corporation, Terry in Maplewood?"

"No, it's not that. It's that Congress is trying to punish the oil companies and in the process they're punishing all of us. How can a person making minimum wage afford to go to work now, paying $6.00 a gallon for gas?"

"I guess they'll just need to flip hamburgers closer to home," Tim Chapel said as he hung up on Terry in Maplewood. "Bill in Highland Park, Texas. What do you think?"

"I think we gotta do something different."

"What does that mean?"

"We gotta find other fuels and other means of transportation. If this gas tax makes people take mass transit that's good."

"But, Bill, you live in Dallas, Texas, right? That's where Highland Park is, right?"

"Right."

"So, you've probably got a decent public transportation system there. What about the small towns where they don't have public transportation? And those people often have to drive further to get to work, shopping and entertainment. What about them?"

"Well, not everybody can, but maybe it will make some people change. And maybe more cities will start public transportation."

"Yeah, but how many years does that take? There have been small communities that tried to start public transportation services that were stopped by — guess who? — the Federal Government. Why? Because the government wanted all the buses to be equipped for the handicapped — the Americans With Disabilities Act strikes again — and those small communities couldn't afford to equip ALL their buses for the handicapped and the government wouldn't let them have a few special buses, so they scrapped the program. Bottom line, Bill, public transportation systems are extremely costly to build and maintain and they never make money.

"Roger in Dover, Delaware, you're next on the Tim Chapel show. Make it count."

"Hi, Tim. Love your show."

"And I love your town, Tim. I used to work at a little station there in Dover that I won't mention because they don't carry my national show, but I really enjoyed living there for three years back in the 90s."

"Thanks, Tim. I agree with the previous caller that said it's time to send a message to Congress that they just can't keep putting new taxes on us. In fact, I think we've gotten back to the point where we were 200 years ago and it may be time to throw the tea in the harbor again."

"What do you mean, Roger? Are you joining the Tea Party?"

"I have been to some Tea Party events but that's not what I mean. When the Bostonians threw the tea in the harbor, they were making it impossible to pay the tax because the commodity that was being taxed couldn't be sold. I think that's what Axiom is doing. Congress wanted to grab a big pile of tax money from the oil companies and Axiom said 'no' the only way they could. They prevented the product from going to market so the tax wouldn't be collected."

"Hmmm. Roger, I think you may have just expressed what's going on better than anybody has, including Axiom itself."

"Yeah, in fact, I think I'm going to join Axiom in not paying the tax, just to show them!"

"How can you do that? Don't you have to get to work?"

"Yeah, I don't know how I'll do that yet. Maybe I'll telecommute."

"Yeah, I guess a lot of people could do that, if their bosses would let them." The talk jockey leaned away from the microphone and shouted, "Hey boss man! Can I telecommute? I'll just phone it in!" Chapel erupted into uproarious laughter very amused with himself.

* * *

Most of the time Bull Cahill's face was red either because he was Irish or because he was on the verge of a temper tantrum, but today, Paul Stoddard thought his boss actually looked a bit pale. He was also less angry and almost appeared deflated as he sat low in his creaking office chair.

"You wanted to see me, Mr. Cahill?" Paul asked from the doorway, having found a note on his timecard.

"Yeah, come sit down." When Paul was seated in front of the desk, Cahill continued, "I'm sorry, Stoddard. I tried to call you before you left home. You can go back home if you want."

"What? I don't understand."

"I'm not laying you off or anything. It's just that, well, we don't have any gasoline, so I can't send the trucks out."

"But can't we just buy more gas?"

"The County Commission sets the monthly fuel budget for the Shelter and, because gas costs almost six bucks a gallon now, we've already spent our budget for the month. So, I can't send the trucks out until the first of next month. You'd think the yahoos in Washington would've exempted local government services from the blasted gas tax!"

"So, do I get paid?"

"How many personal days do you have?"

"Four left for the year."

"Then you'll get paid for four days, I reckon. Sorry. I'll call you if anything changes, but for now, don't come in until the first of the month."

Paul was still stunned by his conversation with his boss when he started the engine of his car and pulled out of the Animal Shelter parking lot to head back home. One thing that surprised him was that he could never remember Bull Cahill saying, "I'm sorry" about anything. That was worrisome, because it made Paul wonder if things were really worse than Cahill made it sound. Could the county increase the fuel budget or would they lay off workers when they couldn't put them to work driving county vehicles? Paul gripped the steering wheel as he repeated in his mind his boss' question about why Congress hadn't exempted local government services. What about police, fire and ambulance services that the county provided? Presumably they were faced with the same budgetary problem, and they would surely receive priority over Animal Control. And if there were layoffs, an hourly worker like Paul would be among the first to go.

His personal days off would only cover him for the rest of this week, then he would miss a week's pay before the end of the month. And there were four more months before years' end when he would be allotted a fresh supply of personal days off. He wondered if his Washington contact had foreseen this. This was one more thing that was that Axiom woman's fault!

* * *

Roger in Dover hadn't forgotten his conversation with Tim Chapel on the radio, in which he had said we wanted to find a way to join Axiom Oil in refusing to pay the gasoline tax. In his mid-50's, Roger had always been a student of American history and thought he had a pretty good grasp of what the country's "Experiment in Liberty" was all about. To him the gas tax was one more in a long line of government abuses of individual liberty.

As it happened, Roger was already active in talking about his love of liberty before he called the Tim Chapel show. He had a blog called "Freedom Post" where he would periodically write short missives about this or that in the news, whenever something raised his ire.

His little blog was one of thousands on the web, of course, but he had garnered a small following, with a few other blogs linking to his, just as he linked to others of like mind. He also supplemented his exposure with Facebook and Twitter posts and links, with several thousand "Friends" and "Followers", respectively. It had become his main hobby, taking more time than he really had to devote to it. Frequently he had considered pulling the plug, but now he wondered if he could use it to do some good.

So, he posted a short opinion about the Moratorium, including the idea he had spontaneously voiced on the Tim Chapel Show about finding a way to not pay the tax. The post garnered a few responses at first, neither less nor more than his usual response. But then a reply from Washington State set his blog on fire. A woman in Seattle wrote in all capital letters:

"I CAN'T BELIEVE YOU ARE PROPOSING WE SUPPORT AN OIL COMPANY AGAINST THE GOVERNMENT! DO YOU HATE THE EARTH THAT MUCH? YOU PEOPLE ARE ALL ALIKE; JUST CATERING TO YOUR FAT-CAT SPECIAL INTERESTS! WHY DON'T YOU GO SWIMMING IN THE

Backlash

GULF SO YOU CAN CHOKE ON THE OIL YOU LOVE SO MUCH!"

What happened after this was posted surprised Roger. He had never seen so much activity on his blog. The traffic grew exponentially as people put links to his blog on their own, on their Facebook pages and copied it to their email address books. It became a free-for-all as people argued back and forth, calling each other bitter, sometimes profane names. Alarmed, Roger posted another message, saying:

"Please everyone, take a step back and BREATHE. Let's do something constructive. Let's think of ways we can avoid paying this tax legally." That was all it took.

Soon Roger's blog and Facebook "wall" were filling with ideas, not all of which were legal, unfortunately. Besides a couple of replies that simply recommended stealing gasoline, there were the obvious ideas of taking public transportation, carpooling and telecommuting. It was the next day before the really creative – and legal – ideas began to appear.

* * *

"Hello America! Are you awake?" Tim Chapel shouted into the microphone as his raucous theme music blared behind him. "Oh my, the Blogosphere is ablaze right now and, at the risk of sounding, ahh, braggadocios, it started right here on my humble program. Yes siree, America is having an old-fashioned rhetorical brawl about the gasoline tax and Axiom Oil's moratorium in response to it. Some are saying hooray for the Feds in sticking it to the nasty, greedy oil companies; they deserve it. Others say the gas tax really sticks it to all of us, making it more difficult to afford to get to work, get goods to market; indeed, to function at all.

"So, one of my illustrious listeners, one Roger in Dover – too bad his name isn't "Dennis." Then it would be "Dennis in Dover, Delaware" – hey, Roger, what's your middle name? Oh well. What was I saying? Oh yeah. So, Roger in Dover says to me, 'I think I'll find a way to join Axiom in not paying the tax, because that's what they are doing. They're refusing – legally – to pay the tax.'

"So, Roger has this blog called "Freedom Blog" or something and he writes about it and stirs up one major hornets nest. And now there's a bunch of people joining him in thinking of ways to avoid – legally – paying the gasoline tax.

"What? What's that I hear you say? How do you legally avoid paying the tax? Well, it's really easy you see; you just don't buy gasoline. No purchase, no tax. Easier said than done I hear you say. You're right, I say. You have to get creative.

"Here's an email from a creative fellow named Cyrus in Wynot, Nebraska. 'Why Not Nebraska?' I always say!" Chapel cracked up at his own pun and eventually continued.

"Cyrus — who has the perfect name for a wheat farmer in Nebraska, don't you think? — Cyrus has started riding his bicycle to work at the grain elevator. It's four miles, but he says he's getting a lot more exercise than before. Might even lose some weight! Hey, Mrs. Cyrus will probably like that! And think of the stories he can tell his grandchildren. 'I had to ride a bicycle 40 miles to work! In the snow! Up hill!'

"Then there's Brenda in Colorado Springs, who sent this: 'I decided to take both weeks of my vacation, all my sick days and all the personal days off I have left during the moratorium. I'm going to sit home from work with a bucket of bon-bons and let the tax collectors stew in their own juice!'"

Tim Chapel laughed uproariously at that, even though he had previously read the email, having personally selected it for reading on the air.

"So, will this make any difference? Not if it's just Roger and Cyrus and Brenda. But if a lot of people did this kind of thing, it could really make a statement. Hey, the graybeards in Washington are counting on a windfall of tax revenue from this gas tax. Who knows if they will really use the money for alternative energy? This is getting interesting!"

* * *

The doorbell rang and Brenda Campbell pulled on her pink slippers, not knowing who would be at the door in the middle of the day. Clutching her bathrobe modestly, she opened the door to see a blond woman with a microphone and a bearded man with a large video camera.

"Are you 'Brenda from Colorado Springs?'" the woman asked. Then Brenda saw the large red number in a circle on the microphone and instantly recognized the logo of a local TV station.

Brenda stammered, "I don't know. What do you mean?"

"Did you email the Tim Chapel Show that you were staying home from work to protest the gas tax?"

"Uh, yes, I did," Brenda said, still not sure whether to continue talking or close the door and hide.

"Mind if we ask you a few questions for the six o'clock news?"

* * *

The Colorado Springs TV station's piece on Brenda Campbell was picked up by Fox News and played around the clock, creating a sensation. Pundits from both sides of the argument debated loud and long the relative merits of what Brenda was doing. Mostly, conservatives thought it was funny and liberals were angry.

One of the pundits, in the midst of a heated exchange, called Brenda's work stoppage the "Bathrobe Boycott." The term was repeated by others and soon spread like wildfire on the Internet as some people laughed and others fumed.

The next week Fox followed up and reported that they had checked with some large employers and found a strange increase in the incidence of people calling in sick, taking sick days and even simply being absent from work. Except for the AWOL employees, those taking sick days, personal days and vacation were acting according to the companies' policies, although the increase was noticeable.

CHAPTER SEVENTEEN

Paula looked up as she forwarded an incoming phone call to a staffer to see Patrick Garrity grinning at her.

"Is he in?"

"Yes, and he's expecting you," she said, all business as usual.

She ushered Patrick into the inner office of Colorado Representative Carl Kellerman.

"Ah, hello, Mr. Garrity," Kellerman extended his hand as soon as Patrick stepped through the door. "I'm not sure what you want to talk about."

"Isn't Brenda Campbell that's been all over TV one of your constituents? What do you make of what seems to be happening across the country?"

Kellerman paused, knowing he was on the record and so chose his words carefully. "I think my constituent found a clever way to express her dissatisfaction with the Petroleum Independence Act, which I voted against."

"So, this is, as has been said, 'throwing the tea in the harbor' as concerns the gas tax?"

"Exactly. I don't know what we expected. Adding so much to the price of gas was bound to get people up in arms."

"Congressman, staying home from work in your bathrobe isn't exactly torches and pitchforks. Do you think this really indicates wide-spread anger out there?"

"Well, I actually think it is in the tradition of nonviolent resistance to government tyranny."

"Brenda Ghandi?" Patrick couldn't help himself. The whole thing was just too funny.

The unflappable congressman continued seriously. "Several residents of my district have written letters to me about their plans to, uh, boycott, so my staff is contacting them and letting them express their sentiment. I've talked to some of them myself. We haven't reached all of them yet, but, yes, I think there is some strongly held feeling out there that Congress went too far this time."

"What kind of things are they saying?"

"They're saying we've reached the same point where we were when those Boston patriots dumped the tea in the harbor. Something's got to change."

"Do you foresee anything happening to change the gas tax?"

"It's too early to tell. It depends, I suppose, on how many members get this kind of communication from their constituents and how strongly worded the letters are," Kellerman smiled. "It isn't easy to reverse a law that's just been passed. There are reasons why members voted for it and they are not easily reversed."

* * *

Before Patrick finished his article on the growing "Bathrobe Boycott", word had crossed the wires that people all over the country were taking time off, saving their gasoline and saving their money.

Patrick had to laugh as he watched the reporting that followed the revelation that the "Bathrobe Boycott" was intended to send a message to Washington. One such report on a national TV news magazine showed a reporter questioning a woman who was literally in her bathrobe. The reporter's tone of voice betrayed bewilderment that the woman was not supportive of the gas tax. "But don't you think we need to find alternatives to gasoline?" he asked.

"If there are practical alternatives, let the market decide. Don't punish the American people this way," the woman insisted. "I think that Axiom woman — what's her name? James? — she's doing the only thing she can do." Not all interviewees agreed, of course. Some felt Axiom was a big greedy company taking advantage of people by keeping its gasoline to itself, but a surprising number on the various news shows seemed to "get it".

* * *

"Unbelievable!" Paul Stoddard slammed down his beer bottle on the coffee table as he heard the woman on TV say Jackie James had done the right thing with the moratorium. "It's not supposed to be that way!" he shouted at the flickering black-and-white image. Fuming, he got up from the couch and left by the front door, getting into his Tercel and driving down the driveway, through the brick pillars and out onto the road, his headlights parting the gathering darkness. He turned west toward Houston, though he could hardly see, he was so angry. *Couldn't they see that she is a criminal, a polluter — a killer! How could anyone agree with what she is doing?* "If there are practical alternatives, let the market decide," she had said!

What stupidity! Stupidity like that was why people shouldn't be allowed to decide what fuel they used! People needed to be led like dumb animals, which is all they were after all. "The Market!" What an absurd notion! It was simply the expression of the lowest common denominator. "The Market" gave the world soap operas and tractor pulls, Disco and professional wrestling. What was needed was leadership, not "The Market"!

It took him about 45 minutes to reach the west side of Houston, fuming every mile about the TV interview that had set him off. Before he knew it, he found himself turning into the subdivision where she lived. For a moment, he felt a bit foolish for driving all the way over here. What was he going to do? He decided to just drive past and see if there were lights on at her house.

He gave scant notice to the large houses along the way, set back from the street to emphasize their importance to anyone taking time to look at them over the imposing fences that kept the world at bay. Instead he faced forward, turning on the street whose name he had memorized, until he knew he was close. He took his foot off the accelerator and allowed the car to decelerate as he coasted by the glass-and-stone, single-story home. There were lights on in the house, so he then wondered what he would do next. He felt a trickle of sweat run down his chest as he decided what he wanted to do.

Half a block beyond Jackie James' house, Paul parked on a stretch of curb where two houses faced away on perpendicular streets so he wasn't blocking any driveways or sitting in front of anybody's house. He got out of the little Toyota and walked back toward her house on the sidewalk, ducking under a low-hanging willow branch and turning into her driveway. Like the other houses, she had a fence and a gate, but the fence was decorative and presented no real obstacle as he slipped over it.

He quickly moved to put a large evergreen tree between himself and the street, in case anyone came along on the sidewalk and wondered why he was skulking about.

He skirted the side of the house, walking toe-first, soundlessly on the concrete driveway. The three-door garage was behind the house and separate from it, so the driveway extended well past the back of the house. Once in the back yard, Paul hugged the rough-hewn stone siding and eased along the wall until he reached the door that provided access to the back of the house. There was no window in the door and so he went past until he was beside a small window that must be in the kitchen. He cautiously peaked inside. It was the kitchen, which was dark except for light coming from other rooms. He continued to move along the wall, moving out around a darkened bay window, watching his step in the moonlight to avoid tripping over a garden hose. A shaft of light extended from the next window he reached. Slowly he leaned away from the wall to peer inside.

It was a living room, or perhaps a family room, it was hard to tell. Paul reasoned a house like this would probably have a formal living room and then a separate...

Oh my! There she is!

She came out of a hallway that must go to the bedrooms. Paul ducked down, then realized that her eyes would be adjusted to the light inside and it would be unlikely she would see him if he stayed back and to the side. So, he stood up again and looked through the large plate glass window. The drapes were open most of the way and so he was able to see the wide expanse of the room. It was a large room with high ceilings, edged with heavy molding. In the center, a kidney-shaped trey ceiling with indirect lighting sent a soft glow throughout the room. It was sparsely furnished with odd, contemporary furniture. Probably designer fixtures and very expensive, he groused to himself. She sat on a nonsymmetrical loveseat with solid purple upholstery. The floors were wood in a very light finish Paul had never seen before.

He relaxed a little, thinking, *So this is how a wealthy industrialist lives. No big deal.* He watched for several minutes before he saw that she was staring at a laptop. What was she doing, he wondered? Was she working at home at 9:30 p.m.? Before long he found himself getting bored and figured he would just slip away and go home. He did have to go to work tomorrow, after all. Oh! *No, he didn't!*

Then, suddenly she stood again and faced the window. Paul had to jump back and stand hard against the rock wall. Out of the corner of his eye he saw the drapes close. Another couple of seconds and the soft glow of the drapes in the window went dark. Apparently, she had left the room. *Does that mean she is going to bed?*

He paused for a moment, not knowing what to do. Then he remembered his anger and inched further along the wall of the house until he reached another small window, which he deduced was a bathroom. Varnished shutters were closed tight with only the thinnest columns of light escaping around and through them. He moved on to another large curtained window that he figured would be the master bedroom. Just beyond the window was a set of double doors which opened to a raised stone deck which stretched across the yard to the spa at the edge of the pool. Water cascaded from the spa into the pool, making a soothing sound and the pool filter hummed softly inside its enclosure. Paul climbed the stairs onto the raised deck.

The curtains were closed on the double doors as well, so there was nothing to see. He would simply head back. He was very close to the side of the house opposite from where he started and he decided he could more easily make the full circle around the house and head back to the front fence than go back the way he came. He descended the stairs on the other side of the deck in the darkness.

Suddenly, a bright light blinded him and he stumbled, knocking over something metal — a shovel? It noisily fell to the ground, scraping against the stone siding as it fell. Panicking, he ran around the corner to get out of range of the motion-sensing light fixture and collided with a prickly cedar. Thrashing through the branches, he finally got past it and sprinted toward the fence, his heart throbbing and his skin cold, suddenly drenched with sweat. He did not look back until he was safely over the fence. Another light came on, flooding the back yard. A dog barked at a neighbor's house and others took up the cry across other fences. He began slowly walking away from the house, away from his car. He wouldn't walk back in front of the house until much later that night; not until the residents of this posh neighborhood had decided all was well and had gone to sleep.

* * *

The state of Georgia had one of the lowest state fuel tax rates in the nation. As such it had always enjoyed some of the lowest gasoline and diesel prices in the country. With the introduction of the new gas tax all that changed, however. With average prices for the "regular" grade hovering at $4.30 per gallon on June 30, it was a real shock to the citizens of the state when the price became $6.00 overnight. Immediately the state capitol switchboard in Atlanta lit up with calls from people who were certain they were being gouged and demanding that their elected representatives do something about it.

Elected officials cannot resist acting when the voters are up in arms, even if the problem was created by other elected officials. So leading legislators asked for a meeting with the governor. It was a small meeting, behind closed doors under the gold dome of the capitol building within site of the intersection of three major interstate highways.

"What can we do?" asked a state senator from Gilmer County. "We can't lower the taxes on gas. They're already as low as they can go."

"It's Washington that's done this to us," the governor said, as if he despised the District of Columbia and would never consider running for an office that might force him to go there.

"We have to make Axiom Oil sell gas," said another senator from Augusta.

"What difference would that make? It's the tax that's boosted the price," reasoned the governor.

"Well, we have to do something," said a senator from suburban Atlanta.

The politicians around the table knew it was true. They had to do something, even if it was wrong; even if it didn't solve the problem. They had to be perceived to be acting on behalf of the people. Results didn't matter as much as perception. On election day, perception always trumped everything else.

* * *

Bret McAlister pushed the perspiration-ringed straw cowboy hat back off his forehead. He knew about the custom of taking one's hat off indoors, but it might have been easier to get him to take off his jeans. But that would have been as difficult, since the well-worn Wranglers were secured to his trim waist by a belt buckle that was easily five inches across and featured a 3-D panorama of cattle on the range. He wore the hat constantly as he drove his route across Eastern Colorado, Kansas and Missouri. His home base was in Colorado Springs and he had driven a tractor-trailer rig for Axiom Oil for two-and-a-half decades. A few wisps of graying hair stuck to his forehead, immobilized by the sweat that was inevitable in the July heat here on the prairie where there was little forest cover from the merciless summer sun. The hotel banquet room's central air conditioning labored in vain to overcome the Oklahoma heat.

Bret wasn't the only truck driver in the room with his cowboy hat sitting stubbornly atop his head. The cowboy hat was appropriate, because over-the-road truckers had inherited the cowboys' mantle as nomadic American heroes, fiercely independent and resourceful.

The Axiom Teamsters Union members had been summoned to this Oklahoma City hotel ballroom to decide the union's reaction to the company's moratorium. The truckers depended on the union to fight their battles for them, since they were rarely in one place long enough to deal with the company they worked for. The union was large, second only in membership to the National Education Association. The International Brotherhood of Teamsters bargained with literally hundreds of companies who employed commercial drivers of all kinds, from courier services to large transport shippers and even including warehouse workers. The products they carried ranged from eggs to nuclear waste, from furniture to corn syrup. It was not too much to say that the entire country moved on trucks.

McAlister listened to the speeches being made by the union bosses; men who had driven for a variety of companies and were accustomed to thinking entirely in terms of management (bad) and labor (good).

"We must respond to this crazy thing management has done," one of the thick-necked, barrel-chested Teamsters bosses said as he closed his impassioned speech, his deep voice booming over the cheap PA system in a New Jersey accent. "Action like this moratorium puts union jobs at risk, but besides that, it is an obvious attempt to 'stick it' to our representatives in Washington, who have always supported us. We can't allow Axiom fat cats to play fast-and-loose with our jobs!"

Funny, McAlister thought as he listened to the veteran labor leader. *I don't remember you getting a paycheck from Axiom.* And what was that about support from our representatives in Washington? Was that what this was about? Was the union supposed to help Washington bring Axiom to its knees from the inside?

There was applause as the man finished his speech and another union man, the moderator for the meeting, took his place at the podium, saying that the union leadership was recommending a work stoppage against Axiom, but of course there would be discussion before a vote was taken. He directed the assembly's attention to two microphones that stood in the aisles for questions or comments. McAlister was immediately on his feet and walking toward one of the microphones.

He was third in line to reach the microphone, but since there were two microphones, he might end up being sixth in line to speak. Both mics had several people lined up, eager to contribute to the discussion. As the men began speaking, some asked questions about the nature and duration of the "work stoppage" and others commented about the advisability of the plan. McAlister saw that a couple of those who spoke were not sure a strike was a good idea. Then it was his turn.

"I'm curious, just how is this moratorium hurting us Teamsters?"

"Anytime a company does something irrational like this there is danger that jobs will be cut."

"But the company has promised no layoffs will occur," he had seen Jackie's news conference in streaming video on the company website.

"And we really believe the company, don't we?"

The line got a laugh from a lot of the men present, but McAlister wasn't laughing.

"Yeah, actually I do believe the company. You see, the CEO is a good friend of mine who's ridden with me and worked dispatch for several months back about 15 years ago, and so if Jacqueline James says it, I believe it's so."

A few people clapped at that, enough that the bosses on the platform looked at each other uneasily.

"Not only that, but she's the only one not getting paid during this moratorium. I know because I know her, that she never asks anyone to do anything she's not willing to do herself, and that's saying something for a girl that's had more than your usual good fortune. She's got a tremendous responsibility and she's doing what she's doing for us, I think. I've been with Axiom for 24 — going on 25 — years. All that time I've been getting Axiom stock and the company's matched it. I traded some of it in for some other stock, but I've still got a lot of it. It's worth about four times what it was when I got my first shares. That's after the '70s oil crisis and the '87 stock crash and all the blood on Wall Street recently.

"I figure in about three years, I'll hang it up and my dividends and retirement will be more than I'm making now. Irene and I might cruise the Caribbean, or we might stay home and plant a garden, I don't know. Of course, if the company doesn't do well and the stock price falls, then my retirement won't be as good. In case you guys have forgotten, when your paycheck comes every two weeks, the logo on it is Axiom's, not Teamsters'!"

He watched the reaction from the crowd and saw they were thinking about what he was saying. Many of them had stock, too.

"In case you forgot, this moratorium thing is an effort to keep the company solid. The bozos in Washington wanted to punish the company we work for and that means they want to punish us."

"Surely, you're not identifying with management," one of the leaders said into the podium microphone.

"Yeah," said several voices in the audience. "What about it?" someone else asked. "You tell 'im!" still another shouted. McAlister waited for them to finish so he could go on, but the moderator then thought it necessary to speak.

With McAlister still standing at the mic, the moderator went on at length about the innate strength of management versus the vulnerability of labor to the unpredictability of the market economy and the greed of fat cats with corner offices. They always got their golden parachutes, he reminded them, while those who did the real work got left holding the bag. McAlister knew the moderator could make the speech in his sleep and soon had most of the crowd cheering and on his side. He could see the wind change as surely as a Kansas whirlwind snaking across Interstate 70.

When he could speak again, Bret McAlister looked around at his brother truckers. "I'm just saying the company could have used this as an excuse to lay a bunch of us off and they would have been justified, but instead they kept everybody on and gave us busy work to do so we wouldn't go stir crazy like I always do during a strike. I just don't think a strike is a good idea because it might hurt the company and we'd just be hurting ourselves. They are doing this to protect our jobs!"

The room erupted in noisy shouts and arguments as strong feelings became verbal shotgun blasts, some men shouting their disapproval of McAlister's opinion and others loudly coming to his defense in brief, colorful retorts. As he walked slowly back toward his seat, all eyes were on him. Suddenly three large men impulsively left their seats and stood in the aisle, blocking McAlister's way to his seat, their massive, sunburned forearms folded across their chests. He could hear the moderator trying to gain control of the situation from the podium, but no one was paying any attention to the stage anymore.

"Come on boys, I just want to sit down," McAlister shouted above the racket of the crowd as he looked steadily at the three men blocking his way.

One of the men motioned "Come on" with one hand. McAlister took a step forward, thinking maybe he meant to let him through, but the man drew back his fist and aimed it at McAlister's jaw. Quick thinking saved Bret from the blow as he leaned to the right enough for the fist to miss by a fraction of an inch. But this only left him open to a crashing left hook from the second man and a surprised McAlister staggered back as his jaw exploded with pain. The third man was also rushing toward him, but he was stopped cold when a young man from the crowd jumped over a row of chairs and collided with him, apparently coming to McAlister's defense. The two rolled on the hotel carpeting, punching and wrestling. The watching crowd roared in anger and in support of one side or the other as the situation degenerated into total confusion.

More men joined the fracas, punching and kicking and throwing folding chairs reminiscent of an Old West saloon brawl. McAlister steadied himself and raised his fists in a defensive posture. But a sudden blow to the back of his head sent him sprawling forward as his eyesight and awareness dimmed like the fade-to-black at the end of a movie.

* * *

Two reports sat on the desk of Gerald Tokalas, President of Petrocom Energy Limited. One was current crude-oil prices from OPEC. The member countries had imposed another price hike, because the gas tax gave them cover and because they could.

The other report was a projected Profit/Loss statement for Petrocom for the month of August. Tokalas sat looking from one to the other, realizing that the full story could only be found by merging the two and allowing for additional factors not accounted for in either report.

The first report told him that his profit margin would be squeezed between the OPEC price increase and the price cap imposed by the United States Government. That was the reality even before considering the new gas tax. An indication of the effect of the tax was found in the projections of the other report, but even that wasn't the whole story. It assumed consumption levels would remain the same in the face of the new tax, but Tokalas knew that wasn't realistic. The government was pretending people would go right on buying gasoline at pre-tax quantities, even though, in some parts of the country, the price had nearly doubled. *News reports focused on the wonderful things that would be done with all the money raised by the tax, which was nothing but a revenue transfer from his company to the government*, Tokalas thought darkly.

But he had seen the other news of the "Bathrobe Boycott" and so he knew that the downturn in gasoline sales which common economic sense told him would come, was being abetted by purposeful and enthusiastic cutbacks in fuel consumption in some quarters.

As he considered the totals on the projection report, he could see profits slipping, even with the optimism of his accountants. The trend was most certainly downward, but when he considered the slowdown in consumption that was now beginning, Tokalas saw red ink washing over the projections.

What options did he have? To stop the downward trend, he could do two things: decrease overhead by instituting layoffs and/or closing stations, or increase revenue, which meant selling more product. Probably both tactics would be necessary. However, one worked against the other. Increasing sales while reducing sales outlets would be difficult indeed. It was like trying to increase the speed of a sailboat while furling its sails.

He now fully understood what Axiom was doing with its moratorium. By not selling gasoline for a time, the company cut its cost of goods sold, and didn't pay the punishing tax. It didn't matter that they lost the revenue, Tokalas realized, because the tax wiped out the revenue as it came in. This was not an income tax. It was a dollar-amount levy. Petrocom was expected to remit two dollars to the Federal government for every gallon of gasoline sold, regardless of the price the market allowed them to charge. Of course, the price cap further defeated the market by ensuring that part of that two dollars could not be passed on to the consumer, even if the consumer would pay it, and that seemed doubtful.

Looking at his own projections, he saw what Axiom must have seen early on: Petrocom was losing money with every gallon of gasoline it sold. While many of his executives chattered about grabbing Axiom's market share, his company was slowly sinking beneath the waves of red ink. The more of its product Petrocom sold, the faster the company sank.

Drastic action was needed, and soon. The initially baffling path Axiom had chosen didn't seem open to him, so he would have some hard decisions to make.

CHAPTER EIGHTEEN

Straw and fine dust blew across the blacktop as a pickup pulled off the highway into a Petrocom Energy gas station in Schleswig, Iowa. Pete Breitbach stopped at a pump and got out to fill his tank. He had come into town for supplies and was running low on the diesel fuel for his fifth-wheel pickup. He kept a large tank of fuel behind the barn, but had allowed it to get low, so he had decided to fill up when he came to town.

"Sorry Pete," Tom Keswick said, coming out of the station. "We're closed. I haven't had a chance to put the sign up."

"Closed? What do you mean, closed?" Pete looked around and squinted at the pumps.

"The company shut us down. Said they're having to close 'marginal stations'. I never knew we were 'marginal'," Tom shook his head.

"Why?"

"I guess the gas tax is hurting the company."

"So, are you out of a job?"

"Looks that way. They said I might be able to get on at a station in Ft. Dodge."

"Well, good luck, Tom. In the meantime, what am I supposed to do for fuel?" Pete didn't need to remind Tom that the only other station in town displayed the black-and-gold logo of Axiom Oil, but it wasn't selling gas.

"I guess you'll have to go to Ida Grove. Sorry," he said again.

Pete wasn't sure he could make it to Ida Grove, even with the free gallon of gas he could get at the Axiom station.

Just then an eighteen-wheeler pulled into the station and stopped at the diesel pumps.

"Guess I'd better get that sign put up," Tom said.

* * *

Ben Donner had managed an Axiom service station in Atlanta for eight years. During that time, he and his wife had started a family, calling their son "Benjamin Jr." Ben felt his future was very promising and he worked very hard to ensure he would do well in his career. Every morning he arrived to open the station at 4:30. Today was no exception. He was accustomed now to not selling gas and was using the time to have his employees spruce up the place in preparation for the day when they would have customers again.

There were few cars on the street at this hour. Actually, a couple of nearby bars had only just closed, but within the next half hour, a trickle, then a flood of commuters would wash by his station. He looked forward to the day that they would stop again. Georgia had the lowest state and local gasoline taxes in the nation, so the pump price had consistently been as much as 50 cents below the highest prices in the country. But that had all changed when the new Federal gas tax went into effect. Overnight, the price of gasoline and diesel fuel had skyrocketed from just over three dollars a gallon to the cap of $6.00 for the highest grade. The citizens of Georgia were understandably outraged. Some blamed the government's new tax, but many blamed Axiom. That didn't make a lot of sense to Ben, since Axiom wasn't selling gasoline for $6.00 per gallon, but people didn't always think things through.

Out of the corner of his eye he saw a vehicle turn onto his corner apron of concrete. He turned to look, expecting to have to tell some early-bird commuter looking for coffee that he wouldn't open for another hour. To his surprise the first vehicle was followed by two more.

His background as a member of the 1st Cav in Desert Storm left no doubt that he was looking at two Bradley Fighting Vehicles and an armored troop carrier from the Georgia National Guard. Shortly a tan-fatigue-wearing lieutenant was striding toward the front door, accompanied by three non-coms with M4A1 rifles at the ready.

"What the heck!" he wondered aloud.

* * *

"This is more like it!" Paul Stoddard said aloud as he watched the report on his black-and-white screen. The National Guard had been called out in Georgia and Axiom gas stations all over the state had essentially been forced to end their petty moratorium. With relish, he watched the video of armed vehicles and men using bolt cutters to remove padlocks from gas pumps.

Usually he didn't see the news until evening, but today he was home, on unpaid leave from his job, so he saw the first bulletin when it was broadcast at nine a.m. Texas time. The network report had interrupted a game show, which was no big loss. Barely five minutes into the report the phone rang.

"Are you seeing the news?" asked the voice on the other end of the line. It was his Washington benefactor.

"You mean Georgia?"

"Yes. I think I see an opportunity here. Are you available for a job?"

"Absolutely," Paul answered, trying not to sound too excited. He could really use the money that would come with the job.

"You'll have to go to Georgia."

"I got nothing else to do."

* * *

Jackie stared at the calendar on the wall of her office. It was Axiom's employee calendar and featured gorgeous, glossy photography of Axiom installations in exotic places around the globe. Today, Jackie didn't care about the pictures, however. She was looking at the page that was titled "July", trying to will it into September, but the days of the moratorium were crawling by. It was still two days before she could flip the page to August.

All things considered, the moratorium was going well. Jackie and her able staff had been able to get the word out and explain their position and the reason they weren't selling gasoline for three months. There had been serious discussion in the national town square about the roles of business and government, of profits and taxes. Jackie thought the company had fared well in public opinion, at least as well as could be expected.

The situation in Georgia was strange, with Axiom employees pumping gas at gunpoint. The state's action in calling out the National Guard had indeed started the fuel flowing again at the company's stations, but Jackie didn't see it making any difference in the larger scheme of things. She just hoped the tactic wasn't contagious in other states.

The lawsuit was worrisome, but Marcus and his team were handling it. It was in the discovery phase, but a hearing had been scheduled. Although Jackie was named personally in the class action suit, Marcus had assured her she wouldn't need to appear. Still, the prospect of a long bitter lawsuit wasn't pleasant.

And the union dust-up had been distressing. Again, she had expected some trouble from that quarter, but she had tried to "head it off at the pass." She had used the company jet ranger to make a day trip to Oklahoma City after the fracas there and she had visited the Axiom drivers that were hurt in the hospital. She especially felt bad about Bret McAlister. Apparently, he had stood up for her in the meeting and had gotten a concussion for his trouble. She had visited the others as well, though some of them were obviously not sympathetic with the company policy.

The brawl had broken up the meeting so no vote had been taken. Some of the Teamsters leaders still wanted a strike, but it looked like there wouldn't be time for them to meet again and implement it. Bret had told her he thought the strike would have passed if they had voted. His speech, while not swaying the majority, did succeed in preventing the strike indirectly, thanks to the ensuing melee. Jackie couldn't figure out what a strike would have accomplished anyhow, since they were already not working, but they were getting paid. If they went on strike, Axiom wouldn't pay them anymore. She couldn't understand the reasoning of those who wanted to strike.

Thankfully, she was now enjoying a bit of a lull after the crush of activity that had begun when she took the reins of the company and continued through the attack on the Gulf Pride, the gas tax and Axiom's moratorium. For a couple of months, she had barely gotten weekends off, much less been able to take any personal days. Thank goodness she hadn't gotten sick! There would have been no time for that. But now she was able to relax a little. Dennis had his finger firmly on the pulse of the company's financial picture and gave her regular reports. Charlene and her staff kept information flowing through the pipeline using a variety of company newsletters and news releases to the public media.

The calls for interviews had largely faded away, which didn't mean Axiom wasn't in the news. The company was always in the background of the continuing coverage of the results of the new gas tax. Some reports made an effort to show the research into alternative fuels and modes of transportation, telling in glowing terms how much money would be produced by the tax for the research and development that was required before the alternatives could survive in the marketplace. But, Jackie thought as she scanned the headlines in the Houston Chronicle, the reports of billions in tax money going to Washington were greatly exaggerated. One article, deep in section C, laid it out pretty well.

People weren't driving, it said. Estimates were that total miles driven would be down as much as 30 percent for the quarter and pleasure driving was down perhaps 60 percent. The hospitality industry was in freefall. Resort locations that usually had their salad days during the summer were like ghost towns. Although aviation fuel was not included in the tax, gasoline used by rental cars and taxis was, so people were just staying home. The shopping malls across the country were beginning to voice concern and stage sales to induce people to come and shop, but people seemed unwilling to part with their money, uncertain what the future would bring. The article mentioned that many companies had inaugurated programs where their employees could work 10 hours per day, four days per week, thus saving 20% of the miles usually driven.

Technology was also playing a role. Internet shopping sites reported a spike in sales when the tax went into effect. Suddenly "teleworking" was a concept on everyone's lips, the article said. Some employers were making it possible for some employees to work from home as many as four days per week, coming to the office only one day, using that day for committees. What with Intranets, call forwarding, instant messaging, e-mail, and computer teleconferencing software, people could really work at home.

Real estate brokers reported an 80% increase in inquiries into in-town apartments, houses, and lofts by people wanting to live closer to work. There had been an increase in people using public transportation, since the Petroleum Independence Act had exempted diesel fuel sold to transit systems for buses or trains.

People were hunkering down, reasoning that if gasoline was going to cost $5.50-to-$6.00 per gallon from now on, their lives would have to change. Existing carpool programs were deluged with requests from people wanting to join and new programs were being formed to meet the need. One good byproduct of the tax was that traffic in most cities had been greatly reduced.

Another paragraph in the article was a concern, though. It said Petrocom Energy was laying off 10,000 people and closing 300 gas stations across the country. Jackie knew without reading the rest of the paragraph that Petrocom had been forced to cut back on production because the tax was biting into their profits. She wondered how long before production cutbacks became real shortages.

* * *

"Where's the bread?"

"All we got's on the shelf, Owen."

Owen Brewster frowned and hooked a thumb through the strap of his overalls. "There ain't no bread on the shelf."

"Then we ain't got any," replied Tom Keswick, the newest employee of the Schleswig, Iowa, Super Grocery. Keswick was the former manager of the now closed Petrocom filling station.

"How does a grocery store not have bread?"

"Since the new gas tax, the bakery cut its runs from Des Moines. They only come once in 10 days now instead of every week. We'll have bread next week."

"Hmmf," Owen muttered, as if to say, *What's the world coming to?*

"I guess Eileen'll just have to make bread again. She used to do it all the time."

"Yeah, I'm sorry Owen," Keswick said, with all the sincerity a person could muster when the problem was entirely out of his ability to solve.

"How're you liking your new job?"

"It's okay. I'm enjoying it."

"How'd you manage to get a job in town?"

"The guy who had this job lived 15 miles away and couldn't afford to make the drive every day, what with the tax and all. So, he quit."

"You think Petrocom will ever reopen the station?"

"I have no idea."

"Yeah, well. That's the way the cookie crumbles. Take it easy, Tom."

* * *

July was almost over. At least it was for the Grove Harbor Hotel and Resort in Myrtle Beach, South Carolina. *In fact,*

Backlash

Hotel Manager Dave Martinez thought, *the whole summer might as well be over, judging from the reservations on the computer screen in front of me.* Most years at this time it was almost impossible to get a room in Myrtle Beach, which was far enough north to avoid the worst of the summer heat that afflicted Florida, and had amenities like golf, the beach, and nightlife.

Much of the vacation traffic to Myrtle Beach was by automobile, located as it was not far off Interstate 95, the main artery from the Northeast to Florida. It was just a long afternoon drive from inland cities like Charlotte and Raleigh in North Carolina, Atlanta and Augusta, Georgia and Chattanooga, Tennessee. As a result, the city swelled with regional vacationers from spring through the fall months. By December Myrtle Beach was a ghost town, because it was too cold for the beach and the golf course.

This year was shaping up differently, however. With the gasoline tax, reservations were down — could it be? — 70 percent! And there was no indication that things would change. Why would it, unless the gas tax was repealed? Some first-class hotels might be doing better, but his was a medium-priced hotel and Martinez figured his middle-class clientele had been hurt the worst by the outrageous increase in gasoline prices.

At least it didn't matter that the wholesale food company had cut back on deliveries to stock the hotel restaurant. Very few travelers ate there these days anyhow.

How could he continue to pay his maid staff when there were so few rooms to clean? How could he continue to pay waiters and cooks when so few meals were being served in the hotel dining room? He hated to think of laying off any of his employees, they needed to be able to feed their children.

* * *

Jackie had been neglecting her mother, so she forced herself to take the evening off and go with her to the mall. Florence James was a veteran shopper, being completely familiar with all the best brands and why they were better quality.

Jackie's mother grew up during Camelot, the idealistic years of the Kennedy administration. After the American GI's saved the world from Fascism in the 40s and took the economic world by storm in the 50s, the United States of America became the greatest country that had ever existed, at least by most measures. In the 60s, the Kennedy administration had seemed to embody the limitless hope and promise of a country that stretched from sea to shining sea and could defeat Depression and despots at the same time.

Jackie knew the story by heart. Florence James had watched Jacqueline Kennedy giving the TV tour of the White House, showing new drapes and china on the scratchy black-and-white screen, and determined to name her daughter Jacqueline — if she had a daughter someday, of course. If Jackie had been a son, he would have been Donald R. James, the third. That was assumed.

Jackie knew she was nothing like what her mother had expected. She had no interest in drapes or china. Her mother had patterned her own life after Jackie Kennedy, playing host to politicians and captains of industry in the sprawling neo-Tudor estate west of downtown Houston. She had painstakingly furnished the house as if she were the first lady redecorating the White House. But Jackie James would not be following in those footsteps.

As they glided along from Lord and Taylor to Neiman Marcus, Jackie was growing impatient, carrying several bags of her mother's purchases. She had never cared for shopping. Not

that she didn't have good taste, she just found other activities
more rewarding. For Florence, like a lot of other people,
shopping was recreation, and the things she bought defined
her. She knew all the most obscure, exclusive lines of china and
furniture, clothing and perfumes. Jackie, with her business
background, realized that much of the reputation of these
products was the result of careful positioning in the
marketplace by advertising professionals and there might be
little real difference in quality between the exclusive designer
names and the more common — and much less expensive —
alternatives. But, expense was not something Jackie's mother
needed to worry about, so Jackie was inclined to let her have
her fun. Anyway, it gave them an excuse to do something
together.

"I want to see about some new sheets for the downstairs
guest room," Florence said.

"The Blue Room?" Jackie asked. The James estate had so
many rooms that they often remembered them by their
dominant color scheme.

"Yes, I'm thinking a floral that will work for Fall and
Winter and will bring out the yellow in the wallpaper."

"Good idea," Jackie said, not really paying attention.

"Where is everybody?"

"What? What do you mean?"

"There's nobody here. Usually the mall is crowded in the
evening."

Jackie looked around. Sure enough, the mall did look empty.
Malls were the hangouts of teenagers with new driver's licenses
and of families with children constantly outgrowing their
clothes. Malls were the new town square, the meeting place for
the community. But tonight, there were just a few people in the
hallways or in the stores as they passed. As Jackie and her

mother walked along the concourse, boutique owners looked out at them with hollow boredom.

"You're right. Where is everybody? You don't suppose they're staying home to conserve gas?"

"If they've had to spend all their money to get to work, I guess they wouldn't have any to spend here," Florence answered. She had stopped walking, as if something was dawning on her. "I see now why you wanted to boycott the government. How are people going to make it with this tax?"

"I don't know, Mom. I don't know."

"People need to be here, buying things so these shop owners can stay afloat."

"That's right." Jackie was surprised to hear her mother draw a conclusion about the relationship of free enterprise and the economy. She could see a light dawning in her mother's clear face.

"Somebody should have thought this tax through."

Jackie dropped her mother's packages in a jumble on the shiny mall floor and embraced her while Florence was still processing it all.

"My sentiments exactly," Jackie said, choking a little.

* * *

Pete Breitbach looked up from "gassing" up his John Deere 50-series combine when he heard the sound of a vehicle bounce over the cattle guard into the barnyard. He recognized Owen Brewster's Ford F-250 pickup from the sound. "What's he want?" Pete muttered, as he straightened up and looked toward the approaching truck.

Owen was Pete's next-door neighbor, just a half mile away. Usually Pete was glad to see him, or any of his neighbors, but right now he wasn't sure how he'd explain the fuel in his elevated tank.

"Hey, neighbor!" Owen called out as he dismounted the two-ton Ford. "You still got diesel? I ran out last week. My corn's gonna burn up if I can't get it harvested soon."

Supplies of diesel fuel at the nearest station were failing to keep up with demand lately.

Pete didn't say anything and Owen noticed a small puddle under the John Deere. "Hey! That don't look like diesel," Owen said, bending down and putting two fingers in the puddle then raising them to his nose. "Don't smell like diesel, neither. What you got here?"

Pete grimaced and hesitated before spilling the beans. "It's Bio-Diesel."

"What?"

"I make it from vegetable oil."

"You make it? Here?"

"Yeah, right over here," Pete said as he walked toward the barn. Owen followed, his eyes wide with interest. Pete led him around the corner to where his son Kyle was pouring the thick, dark brown oil-and-water mash into the funnel-shaped opening at the top of the still.

"Why this looks like a moonshiner!" Owen exclaimed.

"It is, kind of. It makes alcohol fuel."

"Where're you getting the vegetable oil?"

"From restaurants, mostly. Lard works too."

"Is that a fact?" Pete could see the wheels turning under old Owen's hat. "How much you got?"

"We're making enough to get by."

Owen looked at the still and then at a hose running to a 50-gallon drum. Liquid was running through the clear hose at a pretty good clip.

"That stuff work?"

"Yeah. Actually, it kinda cleans out your engine and I can feed the dregs to the cattle."

"How much you want for it?"

"What? Oh, I hadn't meant to sell it," Pete said. He had intended to use his still just to provide alcohol fuel for his own use, but it didn't seem neighborly to say so.

"I'll give you six dollars a gallon for all you got there!" Owen said pointing to the drum.

"I don't know, Owen... ."

"Eight bucks! Eight bucks a gallon for 50 gallons," Owen said as he reached for his wallet from the back pocket of his worn overalls. He pulled out four one-hundred-dollar bills and laid them on a three-legged stool. "I gotta get my corn in, Pete. Your tank is filled over there. Sell me some fuel!"

Pete looked at his son, who was grinning like his face would break.

"Okay, Owen. I'll sell you 50 gallons, but don't tell nobody, 'cause I can't make enough for the whole county."

"Bless you Pete, and your boy too. Hey, will this work in my car?"

"Nope, not unless it's diesel. Gotta modify a gas carburetor to take alcohol," Pete replied. Ironically, both Pete and Owen sold a lot of corn to Ethanol producers but they didn't have the ability to produce it themselves. Pete had learned a fair amount about alternative fuels back during the gas shortages of the 1970s. Then the shortage ended and it was cheaper and easier to just buy petroleum-based fuel.

When the 50-gallon drum was full, Owen closed the tailgate of his Ford pickup and drove away.

Soon word spread and other farmers wanted to buy the biodiesel. Pete looked at his costs and decided he needed to charge $9.00 per gallon to cover his expenses and to pay Kyle to do the work. People grumbled but they paid it.

CHAPTER NINETEEN

"Are you smoking more, but enjoying it less?" It was a line from an old TV commercial he had heard when he was a boy in the 50s. There hadn't been a cigarette commercial on TV for decades now, so it sounded politically incorrect, yet it seemed to express what Dennis Trask was thinking this morning as he went to his regular meeting with the CEO. He just substituted one word so his jingle would be "Are you working more, but enjoying it less?"

Dennis Trask had a good staff and so producing the financial reports was all but automatic. It was true that a tremendous amount of work went into the Information Systems and the Corporate Intranet that made it possible to "push a button" on his computer and generate the reports. That was always the way with push-button convenience. Somebody had to do a tremendous amount of conceptual work and engineering before someone else could "just push a button."

For Axiom Oil financials, data entry people all over the country entered the raw data for the system to shape into reports. They had come a long way toward automating the data entry process, with systems in place that allowed sales data to be uploaded from the stores across secure Intranet connections directly into the company's servers in Houston. The Information Systems Department occupied fully three floors of the black and gold Axiom headquarters, and there were more computer people in the district offices, ranging from data entry to network specialists. Axiom had recently created the position of Chief Technology Officer as testament to the company's growing dependence on computer communication and data management. This was especially true for Accounting.

Of course, one of the problems with push-button accounting was that one was tempted to just trust the numbers. The old saying "numbers don't lie" was itself a lie as far as Dennis was concerned. He knew that the numbers could be made to appear to say any number of things. It was only through carefully and persistently testing and questioning the reports that landed on his desk that he could get a real, and therefore valuable, picture of the financial viability of the company. Of course, there were established accounting procedures and standard reports, but there were a thousand ways to manipulate the numbers and change the outcome. He was constantly goading his staff to refine the parameters of their reporting and forecasting so he could know what was happening and what to expect.

Ordinarily, the job gave him a great deal of satisfaction, but as his jingle said, he was working harder, but finding less satisfaction during the moratorium. The numbers were not good this week. When they had decided to go down the road of the moratorium, they had known they would forfeit the revenue from gasoline sales. They had also known there would be a decline in other sales, because most of their revenue depended on people stopping to buy gasoline. However, they had been

optimistic enough to hope that some people would still stop for soda and chips or a cup of coffee and a deli sandwich. Wasn't it reasonable to think they might still get oil-change business in their stations that did repair?

But the numbers showed a steady downward trend. It was small consolation that the sales of other oil companies, not to mention retail in general, were down across the board, according to the Wall Street Journal. His figures thus far for fourth quarter, projected through September 30, had Axiom's revenues down by 60 percent. Not the 30-to-40 percent in his original projections, but a staggering 60 percent! Needless to say, there would be no profit this quarter. Worse, even though the company would begin selling fuel again in a few weeks, the gas tax would ensure that there would be no profits for the foreseeable future. They had promised not to lay anyone off during the moratorium, but Dennis feared the company would not be able to continue that policy once the moratorium was over. Something had to give.

To add insult to injury, the financial pages of the Nation's newspapers were watching Axiom's stock price more closely than usual. Dennis had hoped, along with Jackie and the Board of Directors, that the public relations efforts would forestall a drop in stock prices, but that, too, had been overly optimistic. From an average stock price of 78 5/8 for the previous 12 months, the stock price had required only a month to drop to 61 7/8. That amounted to a loss in valuation of more than 20 percent. One-fifth of the value of the company was gone in 30 days! Again, it was small consolation that all stocks were down, at least somewhat.

"Hello, Miss James," Dennis said as cheerfully as he could when he was ushered into Jackie's office. *She looks tired*, he thought. The spaces under her eyes were darker than usual and her usually round, red cheeks appeared flat and washed out.

"Please tell me you have some good news, Dennis."

"The Astros are 20 and 16."

"Very funny."

"I'm afraid that's about the best I can do." Dennis took a stapled sheaf of papers from a manila folder and laid it on Jackie's desk. She picked it up and looked at the rows of numbers as he continued. "As you can see, the news isn't good. Revenue is down 60 percent in our new projections."

"Ouch! That's worse than we thought."

"Yes, I'm afraid there are a lot of factors we hadn't counted on. People's spending patterns have changed more rapidly and more drastically than we expected."

"Are other companies getting our market share?"

"Some, but it appears they aren't getting it all. Industry revenues are down overall. Long and short: people aren't driving."

"We knew there would be a drop off."

"Not like this. The business tracking services are reporting that most people have cut out all pleasure driving, and a lot of people are changing how many days per week they work, so they don't drive as much."

"I guess maybe the environmentalists are getting their wish, then?"

"Could be."

"Have we messed up, Dennis?"

"I don't know. What else could we do? The numbers wouldn't be any different without the moratorium, thanks to the tax."

"Yeah, we'd just be sending the money to the government, instead of not ever getting it in the first place like we are now. I just needed to be reminded."

Dennis looked at her as she pushed a dark lock off her worry-lined forehead. He had known her for many years, since she was a very young woman. They were not really friends, just coworkers. She had been his boss' daughter, full of the fire of enthusiasm for her work and life. She now was in the full flower of womanhood and had been through a baptism of fire during her first month as Chief Executive. It had taken its toll. She was as subdued as he had ever seen her.

"I know I don't have to tell you the status of our stock," he said, barely louder than a whisper.

"Lord, no! I can't avoid seeing the price every day. I guess we have to remember we're not the only ones."

"That's right. There is one small ray of sunshine. Our corporate income tax liability for the quarter will be down substantially!"

"Well, I guess we have to take good news where we can find it!" She finally laughed and he was relieved that he could lift her spirits at least a little.

* * *

Patrick grinned at the computer screen. It was quite a piece of reporting if he did say so himself. Of course, he had to share the credit with Shelby Golden, Financial Editor for the Herald. But it had been his discovery.

The Congressional Budget Office had done a confidential forecast showing the effects of the downturn in the economy on revenues to the Federal government. While no one was saying anything publicly, those on Capitol Hill who had seen the report were truly alarmed. Patrick had asked around, knowing that the CBO would be doing such forecasts and had found his usual sources to be very tight lipped, while insisting that everything was fine.

Of course, that just sent him into investigative mode and he eventually found someone who believed him when he pretended he already knew about the report, so they talked. Then, by leaning on another source like he never had before, he obtained a copy of the report and it was off to the races.

"CBO Report Predicts Deficit $900 Billion Greater Than Earlier Projected" the headline read, front page, above the fold. "The Washington Herald has learned of a Congressional Budget Office forecast predicting that total projected revenues from taxes will be down as much as 30 percent during the current calendar year, due to the slow economy which, the report predicts, will be dragged down further by layoffs and reductions in sales.

"The report, which represents a drastic revision of previous forecasts, singles out the Axiom Oil Inc. moratorium as a major loss of revenue for the government, as much as $20 billion of the total tax revenue shortfall, due to a loss of revenue to the company during the time it is not selling gasoline. Axiom management launched the moratorium, which is to last three months, as a protest against the large Federal gasoline tax hike instituted in the Petroleum Independence Act."

The story went on to explain how the tax, and to some extent Axiom's moratorium, was slowing the economy more than anyone expected. With reduced economic activity, tax revenue was reduced as well. The already-weak economy, after the War on Terror and the real estate market collapse, could hardly stand the blow of the new gas tax, the article explained. There was no area of the economy untouched by the effects of the tax, since everything people bought arrived on over-the-road trucks,

which used diesel fuel included in the new tax. As a result of increased shipping costs, wholesale prices on literally everything from food to building materials had increased as much as 20 percent overnight. This meant that profits were greatly reduced, if not eliminated, for all companies that manufactured and shipped hard goods. Since there was a reduction in "income" — the profits that represented revenues minus expenses — there was necessarily less income tax to be paid by these companies. An increase in wholesale prices meant a corresponding increase in retail prices, and that meant consumers' budgets were pinched, causing them to cut back on spending, leading to a downturn in sales, further constricting profits in the retail sector, reducing demand for manufactured goods, resulting in an accompanying decrease in projected tax revenue by all businesses. It was like an elaborate arrangement of dominoes, the first of which were knocked over in Washington D.C., successively knocking over dominoes across the country in random patterns, then returning to Washington, where the final dominoes would fall.

The people in Congress who had voted for the gas tax hadn't counted on a reduction in revenues, in fact they were expecting just the opposite, the article said in a section Patrick had written. Some legislators had even been quoted in the press saying something like an additional half-a-trillion dollars per year would be raised through the gas tax. Instead, they were looking at a 900-billion-dollar shortfall for the next calendar year. The gas tax was being paid by the oil companies other than Axiom, but the layoffs, business cutbacks and zipped-up consumer wallets had effectively negated the gas tax revenue by reducing revenues elsewhere.

Patrick could easily predict the reaction that would follow the article's release in tomorrow morning's edition of the newspaper. There would be denials from people in Congress, who would offer alternate explanations that might even sound plausible to the uninitiated or gullible. There would be endless discussion on the 24-hour TV news networks and the news-talk radio stations. Other newspapers and magazines would launch their own investigations. Patrick had no doubt that the major points of his story would be born out in the end. *The bottom line*, he thought to himself, *was that Congress had over-reached and the gas tax had backfired.* Foolishly they had thought they could institute a punishing tax on a vital commodity and there would be no price to pay. They didn't seem to understand that taxing any activity reduces the amount of that activity which takes place, and therefore the amount of tax revenue is reduced.

Patrick changed the word order to clarify the meaning of one last sentence and saved the article, then posted it on the network where it could be edited by Managing Editor Howard Finkel. From there it would go to Typesetting and Layout to be incorporated into the rest of the paper, a copy of which would land on Patrick's doorstep before six a.m. tomorrow morning.

* * *

"So, do you deny the statements of this story?"

"Absolutely. There is no validity to the reckless charges made in this piece."

"Are you saying there is no CBO report that predicts a budget shortfall?"

Senator Dodge Drummond didn't answer immediately. He looked at the TV camera through narrowed eyes and the corners of his mouth turned downward.

"Let's just say the article in the Herald this morning greatly exaggerates the negative aspects of the report."

This time the Morning Show hostess paused before speaking into the camera in her New York studio.

"So, what does the report say?" she said. A lock of blond hair fell across her forehead as she earnestly leaned forward.

"That report has not been released as yet and the Herald should not have published this article."

"But it's out there now, Senator, and I think a lot of people would like to know if there's anything to it."

"People don't need to worry," Drummond insisted to the camera in the small Washington TV studio, listening to the voice from New York on the flesh-colored earpiece. "The Petroleum Independence Act will be providing a tremendous revenue stream that can be used to move our society from dependence on oil to cleaner, more efficient forms of energy and transportation."

"So, you don't think the gas tax is causing a downturn in the economy?"

The elderly statesman smiled now, "The issues are much more complex than that. The economy doesn't change overnight. And the money that is collected from the gas tax will be spent on research, so it will be going back into the economy. So, everyone should go about your business; keep buying gas, take your vacation trips..."

"Senator, haven't you been a strong advocate of alternative fuels? Are you really encouraging people to buy gasoline?"

"It is vital that people go out there and buy gas," Drummond almost shouted. "We need the money for research into alternative fuels!"

"Do you find it odd that your Republican colleagues are cheering on the "Bathrobe Boycott" and you, who have always pushed concern for the Environment, are encouraging people to buy gasoline?"

"Huh? Why, uh. What?"

"Thank you, Senator, we have to leave it there because of time," said the Infotainment anchor, as she turned to face a different camera and the cheerful theme music began playing. "Next on the Morning Show, Tom Cruise is here talking about his new movie and then we'll look at back-to-school fashions, so don't go away."

* * *

"Hello America! Are you awake? Wow! Have you people seen the article in the Washington Herald this morning?" Tim Chapel said into the microphone as the bumper music for the nationally syndicated "The Tim Chapel Show" was faded out by the radio engineer on the other side of the double-glazed studio window. "If you don't get the Herald, you can read the article on the Herald website."

Chapel went on to give his listeners a rundown of the main points of the story, reading selected paragraphs, which he had marked with a yellow highlighter on the pages he had printed for himself off the newspaper's website.

"This article appears to confirm the worst fears of yours truly, Tim Chapel, and the callers to this program who said the Petroleum Independence Act was a bad idea. If this article is half right, our economy is about to take a nosedive and it's all because of this tax.

"Now, many of you, because of this program, are taking time off work and finding ways to conserve gasoline. The "Bathrobe Boycott" continues — all to communicate your disapproval of the tax. And now it appears that you, the listeners of the Tim Chapel Show, may be smarter than those people in Congress who are supposed to represent us.

"Now, it looks like Congress itself, in this CBO report, is saying that the gas tax will be bad — not just for the economy — but for the government! Of course, there are already Senators and Congresspersons out trying to spin this story the other way. They are saying the article accentuates the negative. They are saying the article exaggerates the impact of the tax on the economy. They're saying the R & D they will spend the money on will counteract the reduction in sales the article talks about. Of course, they are saying that! They know that if the economy takes a hit after people see this article, they will blame Congress and the tax they passed! And I know I don't need to tell the listeners of this program that there is an election coming in barely three months!"

* * *

"All rise!"

The crowded courtroom erupted in noisy activity as the judge entered and those assembled obeyed the bailiff and stood to their feet. Marcus Williams, head of the Axiom Legal Department clapped a bulging file folder to his thick torso as he laboriously stood up behind the dark walnut defendants table. With the other hand, he pushed his thick glasses to the top of his nose.

At the other table, Alec Kincaid, the Chicago corporate lawyer and Axiom stockholder was representing the class of participating Axiom stockholders who objected to the moratorium on gasoline sales.

When the white-haired judge had entered the courtroom and was seated, the rest of the people in the courtroom sat again. Marcus looked over at Alec. Under other circumstances they might have shared a drink and laughed about self-important executives and the messes they made for themselves from which high-priced attorneys must extricate them. But today Alec saw Marcus as the enemy and they were in a Chicago courtroom, where Alec had home-field advantage.

Marcus was accompanied at the table by two of Axiom's lawyers, both specialists in litigation, plus a legal intern and two paralegals. Back in Houston, the rest of the staff would work on the suit as needed, communicating with Chicago by cell phone, fax, text message and e-mail.

Marcus had delayed this day as long as he could. He had filed motions and demanded documentation from the plaintiffs in the discovery phase, but the hearing before the judge had finally come. This was part of the process of certifying the class in a class-action lawsuit. Alec's job was to convince the judge that the participating Axiom stockholders were a "class", with a common grievance against the company that could best be dealt with in one civil action instead of individually. Marcus' job was to convince the judge that there was no basis for certifying the Axiom stockholders as a class. If he succeeded, the case against Axiom would be dismissed without going to trial.

Marcus' strategy was basically one of negatives: There was no basis to the suit because there was no law that prevented Axiom from selling nothing. And because the moratorium was only for three months, there would be no permanent effect on stock prices. Failing that strategy, there were ways to stretch a suit such as this so that it took longer than the three months of the moratorium, after which, the suit would be largely irrelevant.

"Mr. Kincaid, you represent the aggrieved class against the defendant, Axiom Oil Incorporated?" Judge Samuel Feeney asked, his reading glasses almost sliding off the tip of his nose.

"Yes, your honor."

"And you are a shareholder yourself?"

"Yes."

"You don't feel this fact represents a conflict of interest for you?"

"On the contrary, your honor. It makes me intimately involved with the plight of the class in this action."

"You've been in my court before, have you not?"

"Yes, sir. I represented Chrysler Corporation in a suit a couple of years ago."

"So, this time you're suing a company rather than representing one?"

"That's right, your honor."

"Mr. Williams, you represent the company?"

"Yes, your honor."

"You are an employee of the company?"

"Yes, I am the Vice President for Legal Affairs for Axiom Oil Inc.," Marcus pronounced the last word as "Ink" and then wished he had said "Incorporated" but the judge seemed not to notice or care. Marcus began to relax, since the judge had already taken a couple of jabs at Alec Kincaid. Maybe Judge Feeney could be fair, in spite of Kincaid's home-field advantage.

* * *

Patrick Garrity entered his apartment and set his briefcase down by the door. He had skipped the Blue Ribbon Grill tonight and had stopped for Chinese takeout instead, but at the moment he was too tired to even open the little white cardboard boxes of rice, sweet-and-sour chicken and Oriental vegetables. So, he dropped the sack on the kitchen counter and sat down on the couch, taking the TV remote control and snapping it on. He changed the channel to avoid watching a commercial and landed on C-SPAN, which was showing tape from the Senate from earlier in the afternoon. Patrick recognized Vermont Senator Nathan Taylor at the lectern.

"This situation has reached a critical point. A point where action on the part of this body is no longer optional, but an urgent necessity," Taylor's voice said from the small TV speaker. "All across this great land, people are suffering due to the corporate greed and intransigence of companies like Axiom Oil Incorporated, who, rather than doing what was in the best interest of the people, chose to hoard their supplies of motor fuel during this time of shortage."

Suddenly Patrick wasn't tired anymore, grabbing a piece of junk mail to take notes on.

"This has always been the way of such corporations," Taylor continued on videotape. "To act in their own self-interest and the devil may take the rest of the country. But this cannot be allowed to stand. The entire energy sector is in disarray. Shortages, layoffs and the development of a black market have created an untenable situation. It is time that we, as the elected representatives of the people, acted on their behalf to stabilize the economy and regulate the country's vital commodities, specifically oil."

"What does that mean?" Patrick said aloud to the TV. He didn't have to wait long to find out what Taylor meant.

"I have long felt that there was a problem with allowing a necessary commodity such as oil to be controlled by a few tycoons, who can set the prices as they will, or even withhold the commodity altogether, as we have seen recently. It has been my contention that oil is much too important to be left in the hands of a few private citizens to be exploited for their own benefit.

"Therefore, I am introducing a bill later this week that would bring the management of the oil companies under the direct oversight of the Department of Energy of the Federal Government. Known as the "Energy Sufficiency Act", it will ensure that no private company can hold the nation hostage as Axiom has done, ever again. The Department of Energy will closely control and coordinate the business activities of all the oil companies in the interest of all the people instead of just a privileged few. Indeed, we may find we do not need multiple oil companies at all. This needless competition just creates confusion and disruption in the marketplace. We must never again allow the captains of industry to hold our economy for ransom as is happening now."

"By everything that's holy!" Patrick exclaimed loudly in the otherwise empty apartment. "He's talking about nationalizing the oil industry!"

Patrick continued watching. There was initially a stunned silence in the Senate chamber as Taylor closed his notes and began limping to his seat. Then a few Senators clapped until the level of applause reached a respectable level. Patrick muted the television as the Senate moved on to other things. For a while he stared at the screen without comprehension of the dancing images, trying to digest the meaning of what he had just heard.

So, the Federal government was going to try to take over the oil industry! Surely it would never fly. But then, many had said the same thing about the gas tax bill Taylor had written.

CHAPTER TWENTY

"Your honor, I'd like to place this into evidence as plaintiff's exhibit 15."

"It's the Wall Street Journal," Judge Feeney looked over his reading glasses at Attorney Alec Kincaid as he laid a newspaper in front of the Judge. Watching from the defendant's table, Marcus Williams thought the judge might be getting impatient with Kincaid.

"That's right, your honor. Specifically, it is this morning's stock prices. I have highlighted the price of Axiom Oil Incorporated stock."

Judge Feeney looked through the reading glasses this time at the tiny type on the 10-column page. Kincaid had marked one line with a yellow highlighter. "So, what is your point?"

"If your honor will note, there is a figure for the year to the right of the column, showing that the stock price is down almost 20 points for the year. That's a 25-percent loss in the value of the stock. I and the stockholders represented in this class action contend that the moratorium on gasoline sales has precipitated this loss in value for the stockholders."

"Mr. Williams, would you like to respond?"

"Thank you, your honor. Yes, I would like to respond. Mr. Kincaid seems to be forgetting that I and each of my associates at this table, not to mention all the executives and board members who voted for the moratorium, also own Axiom Oil stock. Mr. Kincaid seems to be saying that these stockholders, including myself, intended for the stock price to fall and are happy that it has. This is ludicrous on its face. My Axiom stock is worth exactly the same amount that Mr. Kincaid's and the other plaintiffs'."

"I do not doubt that the management of the company didn't want to see the price of the stock go down," Kincaid answered. "My assertion is that management has behaved recklessly and irresponsibly in voting to conduct the moratorium and the stockholders have been hurt by it. The losses suffered by the members of the plaintiff class alone amounts to more than $15 million dollars!"

"That is only if you sell," Marcus said. "If you hold the stock, I believe you will see its value rise to its previous level and beyond, if the company's strategy is successful."

"But we can't know that the stock price will go back up, can we?"

"No, that is the nature of the market. When you buy stock, you know there is a chance the stock may go down in value. Every public company's prospectus says so in bold letters, but if you would like, I can enter Axiom Oil's stock prospectus into evidence."

When Kincaid didn't respond, Marcus continued. "Your honor, I wonder if there is also on Mr. Kincaid's exhibit a chart showing the Dow Jones Average for the year?"

"Yes, I feel sure there is," the judge strained through his glasses to find the chart at the top of the left-hand page.

"If I might be so bold, since you have the exhibit, could you tell us what it says the Dow Jones Average is for the past year?"

"Why yes, that would be good to know, wouldn't it? I see here it says — my goodness — the Dow is down 19 percent!"

"Thank you, your honor. I believe what we should conclude from this is that the entire market is down at present for a host of economic reasons that have nothing at all to do with the Axiom moratorium."

"I would disagree, your honor," argued Kincaid. "It would be just as valid to argue that Axiom's irresponsibility has depressed the entire market, causing untold billions of dollars in losses to the Nation's economy."

"All right, I get it," Judge Feeney said, cutting Kincaid off. "Mr. Kincaid, what about Mr. Williams' question: do you plan to sell your Axiom stock?"

"At some point, I would think so, yes."

"Are you more likely to sell now, when the value is down, or at some point in the future when the value goes back up?"

"Well, of course I would prefer to sell when the value is up, but..."

"Then I'd advise you not to sell right now."

Marcus had to cough to keep from laughing out loud. Somehow, he managed to maintain his solemn mask as the judge continued.

"We'll recess for two hours for lunch, then we'll come back and see if we can't move this process along." And with that he banged his gavel once sharply and stood to leave. Everyone in the courtroom stood with him, their breath taken away by the abruptness of it all.

* * *

"Mr. Kincaid's presentation of the loss of value of Axiom shareholders' stock is irrefutable," Judge Feeney began when court reconvened that afternoon. "There may even be some basis for his assertion that the apparent collapse of the stock price has affected the whole market. It is true that the stockholders are at the mercy of the actions of management and those actions can affect the investments of shareholders."

Judge Feeney looked over his reading glasses at the courtroom full of plaintiffs, defendants, and press people. Marcus Williams listened carefully, knowing that judges were good at sounding like they were deciding in favor of one party, when they would ultimately find for the other.

"However, the only greater gamble than the stock market is Las Vegas and its many imitators. Mr. Kincaid and the plaintiffs he represents claim the managers at Axiom purposely hurt the value of the company, Mr. Williams maintains that those very managers own more stock than any of the plaintiffs and would not have purposely hurt themselves. Mr. Williams also argues persuasively that the activities of the government may have required Axiom to take the action of the moratorium to preserve the value of the company and that without the moratorium, the stock price might have suffered even more."

Marcus was feeling good as he charted the judge's course through the logic of his decision.

"Therefore, I find that the management had every right to institute the moratorium and that by so doing they were not trying to hurt the stock value. Mr. Kincaid, you still may have recourse to unseat the board by a vote of the stockholders according to the bylaws of the corporation, but I find the plaintiff's complaint has no merit and cannot justify certifying a class in this matter. I find in favor of the defendant. Case dismissed."

Three quick raps of the gavel and Judge Feeney was out the back door of the courtroom. Marcus was jubilant but didn't allow it to show.

Outside he gave a restrained, canned speech to the press who dutifully wrote his words in their notebooks, recorded them on small recorders or large television cameras. "We are glad for the outcome and we always knew we would be vindicated. We are also confident that our company's value will be restored as soon as the gasoline tax is repealed and the country's business can be conducted on a realistic footing once again."

* * *

Ben Donner parked his classic 1966 Chevelle SS behind the Atlanta Axiom station he managed and unlocked the back door. Inside he did what he did every morning, first scooping fifteen teaspoons of coffee into the workhorse Bunn coffeemaker in the break room and filling it with water. By the time he turned on the lights, opened the front door and policed the convenience store, the coffee would be ready.

He grabbed a broom and large dustpan from the janitor closet with which to sweep along the glass at the front of the station. It was always hard to see dirt in the questionable fluorescent light, but soon the sun would come streaming in and he would likely be too busy to sweep up the dirt then. Since the National Guard had been called out, it was business as usual, resulting in Georgia stations being the only Axiom stations to sell gas in the country. The soldiers would arrive at six a.m.

When he reached the front of the store, he once again cursed the architect who put the only light switch at the front of the building behind the counter. This morning, something caught his eye and he broke his usual pattern. Instead of feeling his way behind the counter to turn on the lights, he walked to the front door and looked out at the first pink blush of dawn in the Eastern sky. A few early-bird commuters' headlights led their way to work. He then took the keys from the clip on his belt and reached to unlock the front door.

It would be his last act.

Suddenly a pickup with off-road suspension and large mud tires sped onto the station lot. Ben didn't have time to wonder about it. Two men in rough work clothes rose up in the pickup bed and threw several flaming bottles at the front of the building and the pump islands. One of the men had a beard. The pickup never slowed down and was gone as quickly as it came. Ben watched wide-eyed as the Molotov cocktails burned a flaming path from the gasoline pumps to the store window where Ben was standing. He blinked as the flames climbed up a pump hose. Before he could blink again, a red, yellow and black gasoline-vapor-fueled explosion shredded the roof over the gasoline pumps and rose 100 feet into the early morning air. A wall of fire blew out the nearly 500 square feet of glass at the front of the store, knocking Ben backward, smashing him against a shelf unit which held candy and fruit pies, his back and neck snapping on the steel and plywood. He never heard the loud boom that marked the explosion. A second explosion buckled the concrete apron over the underground storage tanks and upended a pump island in a cloud of red dirt and concrete dust. The entire property was in flames.

In the street, a car slammed on its brakes and spun around. The driver got out and watched in disbelief as the service station he passed twice every day was destroyed before his eyes. A full 30 seconds elapsed before the shocked commuter thought to call "911" on his cell phone.

Soon a traffic helicopter was circling overhead giving descriptions of the disaster to residents of the city on radio and television. Video from the chopper was picked up by television news departments first in Atlanta, then by the Networks, Fox News and CNN, so before the day was over, the whole country would see the thick black column of smoke which obscured the sun just coming up beyond Stone Mountain. Television news trucks and newspaper photographers arrived to record the damage and the efforts of firefighters to tame the blaze.

Once the fires were extinguished and it was safe, it didn't take the police and arson investigators long to determine the cause of the explosions. The broken bottles and gasoline residue on the concrete told the story plainly enough. Ben Donner's body could not be identified, it was too badly burned, but horrified station employees informed the police who it must be when they arrived for work.

* * *

Jackie and other staffers watched in horror as the news media played and replayed the tape of the smoking gas station. There was anger and grief in the black tower with the gold logo as they watched on TVs in the first-floor theater, the twentieth floor boardroom and in various executive offices throughout the building. Secretaries cried as they saw EMTs carry the body bag to an ambulance that would have no need to hurry.

Again, Jackie was challenged with the questions of who would do such a thing and why? At least this time there was no confusion in the media about whether it was an attack or an accident. With a heavy heart, she prepared to make a quick trip to Atlanta. There wasn't anything she could really do, but she felt she should make an appearance. She would take a check with her for Ben Donner's family. It would be above and beyond the benefits they would receive as survivors.

After the initial coverage of the firebombing and the tragic death of the manager, the reporters began to conjecture about the motives of the attackers. The journalists reasoned that whoever did it must have blamed Axiom for the gasoline shortage. Jackie couldn't think of an argument against that theory.

She and Wayne were on a Continental flight to Hartsfield-Jackson International Airport by one o'clock that afternoon.

* * *

At almost the same time, a Delta flight left Atlanta bound for Houston's William P. Hobby Airport. Paul Stoddard hadn't used his real name on the ticket, but a false name supplied to him by his Washington benefactor. The same name appeared on a driver's license and the credit card with which he'd purchased the ticket.

In the waiting area at the gate, Paul had heard on the suspended TV always tuned to CNN that a man had died in the explosion at the gas station. He felt less this time than he had when he heard that a man had died in the aftermath of the oilrig attack. Perhaps only these extreme measures would convince the merchants of death of the serious danger their product posed to the health of the Earth.

Before boarding, he had used the cell phone that had also come from Washington to call and report, though it was hardly necessary, since CNN's world headquarters was barely five miles from ground zero. His contact could hardly have missed seeing the video of the pillar of smoke on the news. Still, it was good to report that Paul and the local activists who worked with him had gotten away undetected.

Throughout the flight he pretended to sleep, keeping one of the Delta-blue blankets pulled over most of his face. The fewer people who could remember seeing him in Atlanta today, the better off he would be.

* * *

Nothing of any import would happen in the Senate Chamber for the rest of the afternoon, so Senator Nathan Taylor decided to leave a little early. Perhaps he could beat the rush to his favorite pub where he usually hung out with other career government employees who frequented the place. He had called for his car and headed toward the door. He wouldn't go back to his office in the Hart Senate Office building. Anything that needed his attention there could just as well wait until tomorrow.

The news of the explosion at the Axiom service station in Atlanta was uppermost in the minds of people everywhere and Taylor reasoned that the time was nearly right for him to unveil his next piece of legislation: the law that would allow the Federal government to take control of the oil industry. He had prepared the ground with his earlier speech and now, with the attack, his fellow legislators might be convinced the action was necessary. He grew almost giddy at the prospect of having a part of controlling the multi-billion-dollar industry.

During the BP oil spill there had been calls for the Federal Government to take over the company, but BP stood for "British Petroleum" so there were international considerations that kept the proposal from going forward. Axiom however, was a thoroughly American company.

As he exited onto a portico of the Capitol building, he noticed three Capitol police officers watching nervously as a group of demonstrators walked in a circle shouting slogans and waving their signs. "Stop Fed Takeover of Oil Cos.," the signs read cryptically. The demonstrators were chanting, "Freedom now; Stop the Fascist takeover." They were down at the base of the steps, occasionally looking menacingly toward the Capitol building. Taylor scowled at them from his safe distance, though a chill went through him in spite of himself.

One of the police officers said something into a two-way radio and continued watching. Then, seemingly from nowhere, another group of demonstrators arrived, disembarking from three large passenger vans. They too had signs, but theirs said things like "Stop Big Oil from Killing Planet Earth." The new demonstrators set up a few yards from the first group at the base of the stairs.

The three Capitol police officers looked at each other and discussed options. When two additional officers arrived in a squad car, the three officers began gingerly walking down the stairs toward the demonstrators. One of the two who had arrived in the car tried to silence the demonstrators with uplifted hands, but they paid no attention.

Then it began. Like at the battle of Lexington and Concord, no one knew who fired the first shot, but the two groups suddenly began hurling verbal missiles at each other. The Capitol police officers were horrified as they hurried down the stairs to see the two groups moving closer together, voices growing louder and language more abusive with each second. Finally, one demonstrator pushed another just as the five officers arrived on the scene. They rushed in, shouting to the people to move apart and settle down. One of the officers stumbled as he tried to restrain a demonstrator and fell backwards, landing hard on the pavement. The other officers, mistakenly thinking he had been knocked down, drew their nightsticks and began using them to drive back the activists who had now become rival mobs. Demonstrators defended themselves with their signs and other policemen went down.

It was only seconds before more Capitol policemen arrived to finally subdue the demonstrators, many of whom had wounds from nightsticks or signs that had bashed their heads. The worst offenders were arrested and taken away in Capitol Police squad cars.

Taylor was horrified as he watched the melee, deciding to wait in the shelter of the portico before descending the stairs to his waiting limo and driver.

* * *

"A truck driver was attacked and knocked unconscious yesterday, when a crowd of people looted the truck, which contained bread and pastries bound for a South Los Angeles supermarket." Jackie stopped midbite through a bagel and cream cheese and focused on the morning news anchor. "The truck was emptied of its contents in about 10 minutes. One of the looters was overheard to say they hadn't had bread at the store for over a week, and they didn't want to risk missing this shipment. A spokesman for the bakery to whom the truck belongs confirmed that the company has cut back on its delivery runs to conserve gasoline. The driver is in satisfactory condition at a local hospital."

Jackie began chewing again, having gotten the gist of the story. She knew Axiom's moratorium was not the reason for incidents like this one. People could get gasoline; it was just very expensive. That meant businesses that depended on goods being transported to market had their expenses greatly increased. Something had to give. At times like this, people got desperate. There were so many factors over which most people had no control. That was one reason for the boycott, she realized: to maintain control of the business by withdrawing from the activity the government had sought to control.

The fact that the truck driver had been attacked made no sense whatever, but then mobs never thought logically, did they? The newsman went on to say that there were shortages of all kinds of things all over the country, due to the high price of gasoline and the resulting expense of getting the goods to market. There didn't seem to be a solution unless the gas tax could be repealed or the country could adjust to higher prices for everything.

"In a related story, another Axiom Oil service station was vandalized last night," the anchor said, as video of a Detroit, Michigan, Axiom station, covered in spray-painted graffiti, appeared on the screen. "Oh, no!" Jackie said aloud, though she was alone in her kitchen. The reporter on the scene was talking now. "The damage is only cosmetic, but it serves to illustrate the frustration many people feel concerning the gas tax and the Axiom moratorium."

"At least no one was hurt." Jackie said with a sigh.

* * *

Claude Bowman is a very proper man, thought Bud Eldridge as they waited for their salads to be brought to them. Though a native Texan, Bowman, treasurer of the Axiom Board of Directors, was not a horseman and made a real effort to banish all traces of the slow, twanging drawl that was characteristic of the Sunbelt just west of the Mississippi.

Nevertheless, he had been Bud's best friend for many years. They had much in common, even if Bud did purposely enhance his "good-old-boy" accent and occasionally wear cowboy boots, whereas Claude thought such things were undignified. *Perhaps that's why we make a good team*, Bud thought.

One thing they both believed in however, was Axiom Oil Incorporated. Their years on the board had made them intimately familiar with all aspects of the company. Junior James' death had been as personal for them as if he had been a brother.

So, when they met for lunch on the top floor of a downtown Houston hotel, it was inevitable that Axiom would be discussed.

"I tell you Claude, I don't know how much longer I can keep quiet. It's all just going to heck in a handbasket."

"I know. I never thought things could get this bad this quickly. We're going to have to do something."

"Right. We've got to get rid of her."

"I was wondering if you were thinking it, too," Claude lowered his eyes and his voice as he said it, as if someone nearby might hear and turn him in for sedition.

"I been thinking it, but I just look like a sore loser if I say anything. Pretty soon it won't matter, though. There won't be any company to save."

"Right. Can we get the stockholders to vote her out?"

"Well, one problem is, she is about 25 percent of the votes, with Flo anyway."

"Yes, and I don't figure we could sway her mother."

"But if we could...." He knew he didn't have to finish the thought for Claude.

* * *

Later that same day, Bud called Florence James and she agreed to talk to him. By three o'clock he was there at the front door of the James Estate in Hunters Creek.

"Bud, how are you?"

"Doing well, Flo. How 'bout you?"

"Just as well as I can."

"We all miss Junior. They won't make another one."

"No."

She answered him flatly, without volunteering to pursue the thought any further, but looked down at her lap as if she was uncomfortable talking about him.

"I was wondering about something. How do you think Jackie is doing, as CEO I mean."

"Oh, I don't know. She seems to be enjoying it."

"But what kind of a job do you think she is doing?"

She looked up with question marks in her eyes now. "Why do you ask? Is there a problem?"

"Well, I hate to say anything. You know how I love you and Jackie, but I don't know about her leadership. This moratorium she rammed through, it's just not turning out well."

"How do you mean?"

"Well, for one thing, have you looked at the stock price lately? It's dropping like a late season apple. That can't go on long or we'll be in serious trouble."

"I did know about that, though I don't follow it too closely."

"Yeah, well. You've got things to do; the house and all. That's why I thought I'd come and ask you about it. I'm thinking we might have to do something drastic to save the company."

"Like what?"

"Well, I hate this worse than you can imagine, but we might have to remove her from the CEO job."

He watched her reaction and it was if he could see the wheels turning in her head. *Bless her heart, Florence James is the salt of the earth and as good-hearted as any woman could be, but she is a little slow on the uptake sometimes.*

"Don't you have to have a vote of the stockholders to do that?"

"Yes. I hate it, but it may be the only way."

"And if you succeed in removing her, you would end the moratorium?"

"Yes, it would be the first thing I'd do. I probably couldn't do it without your votes, Flo. That's why I needed to come talk to you."

She looked at him with eyes suddenly bright and wide. "So, you want me to vote out my daughter from the job she loves in the company my husband built. Bud, you've been around a long time and I love you and your family, but you have made a mistake if you think I will vote against Jackie. I happen to think the moratorium is an excellent idea. The whole country is going through a bad time, thanks to the gas tax, and Jackie is the only one standing up to the government. I know enough to know that things will get better if and when the tax is repealed and this moratorium is the only thing happening that has a prayer of getting the government to change its mind."

"But, but I didn't think you wanted Jackie to be CEO in the first place. I thought you'd want her out of that job."

"I want Jackie to be happy and she wants the job. Lord knows, I don't understand it, but that isn't the issue. As for the moratorium, I support it. I won't be voting to unseat Jackie!"

Bud left the Tudor mansion stunned. He had thought he knew Flo James well enough to play her on this, but she had suddenly found conviction and he wasn't sure why. He could still call for a vote. Jackie and her mother together owned about 25 percent of the company. They were personally losing a lot of money, so Bud couldn't understand Flo's unwillingness to go along. With her votes, he would have had a chance. Without them it seemed unlikely that he would succeed. There were employees and stockholders who favored the moratorium. If the other 75 percent split down the middle, he had lost already. When he arrived at home, he found that Fed Ex had delivered an overnight letter from Chicago that perhaps turned the whole situation around.

CHAPTER TWENTY-ONE

She had never done it before. Not even when she was working behind the counter at an Austin convenience store while a freshman at the University of Texas. She tried justifying it to herself, but she didn't have much experience at excuse-making either. Nevertheless, she did make the call. Doris accepted her claim to illness at face value. She would have little trouble rearranging Jackie's schedule, since the company's managers had cut back on meetings during the moratorium. The reports were too depressing.

Of course, if she were a man, she would be out on the golf course twice a week. It was just considered part of doing business, but she had never gotten into the game. She preferred her horses when she needed time outdoors. She had so little time for them these days. So, she drove to the "Bar X" on a Tuesday and saddled up Sable, her favorite mare. Once they were out in the pasture, she let Sable have her head. The mare was obviously as glad to be out as Jackie was to be there.

Riding always cleared her head and allowed her to see the big picture again. Unfortunately, she didn't like what she saw today. The attack on the station in Atlanta was still fresh in her mind. The visit with Ben Donner's family had been very difficult. Some in the media blamed her personally for everything from his fiery death to the shortages of food. Though the shareholder lawsuit had been dismissed, the bad taste lingered. She didn't think she was the type to require that everybody like her, but it wasn't pleasant being so much in the public eye, when it was easy to point the finger of blame her direction.

Self-doubt was not usually a problem for Jackie and so she wasn't sure what her feelings meant. As she melded her body into Sable's galloping rhythm, she wondered if she had made a fantastic mistake. Who was she to take on the entire United States government, anyhow? She had been so certain the moratorium was what the company had to do, but had she been wrong? She searched in vain for some positive indication, but couldn't think of any. Both within and without Axiom Oil Incorporated, the news was almost universally bad.

She reined Sable to a stop at the familiar turn in the creek under the cottonwood trees and let her drink her fill. She dismounted and knelt in the wild grass on the creek bank.

"Lord, I don't know where to go from here," she began praying aloud. "I thought I knew what I was doing, but nothing's turning out like I expected. I need you to show me what to do. How can I fix things?

"Do you even care about business? I know you care about people and the people who work for us are being hurt. Not to mention everybody in the country who is suffering because of the gas tax."

Backlash

"Was I hasty? Was I too stubborn? Did I make a mistake?" As she said the word "mistake", she thought how inadequate the word was to describe what was happening. *If it was a mistake, it had been a terrific one.*

"I confess I have not always tried to know Your will, Lord. Forgive me for going forward in my own way without being sure it was Your way. Help me to submit to Your will in all areas of my life."

She prayed for several more minutes, moving from self-doubt and questioning God to repentance and finally to thanksgiving and assurance. She arose and knocked the dust from her knees with a new humility.

She didn't stay long, since it was still hot in South Texas and the afternoon sun would soon be too much. Jackie returned to the stable and rubbed down Sable. Then she drove back to Houston by a different route, so as to see some country she hadn't seen in a while.

* * *

It was late afternoon before she arrived back home. Coming in the back door, she noticed the light blinking on her answering machine. Her number was unlisted, so there were only a few people who would have called. The message was from Wayne, who sounded panicked. "Bud is calling a stockholders meeting to remove you as CEO!" he said. "He's saying you are destroying the company! Please call me."

So, it had come to this. Jackie had threatened to unseat the board and now Bud was trying to get the stockholders to unseat her for failures of leadership. Unfortunately, Jackie felt like Bud might be right this time.

* * *

The Cattlemen's Arena was beginning to fill up with the gathering Axiom stockholders on a sweltering Saturday in mid-September. The huge air conditioners would use enough electricity today to power a small Texas town for a full week.

Jackie stood behind the curtains on the stage looking out at the people standing in intense groups, discussing the material in their handout, which had been hastily assembled and printed by the Board of Directors. Others were already seated, using the handout as fans, since the air conditioning could only do so much to overcome the South Texas heat, even inside the arena.

The auditorium was dimly lit with bright lights aimed at the stage so she couldn't make out the distant faces. She would know many of these people, since many of the local stockholders were also company employees or had bought stock decades ago and grown rich with the company. A feeble voice inside her told her to leave the stage and go out to shake the hands of the gathering crowd, but she didn't seem to be able to move from her hiding place behind the heavy curtain.

Across the arena, Jackie saw Bud Eldridge enter through a door that led to temporary offices available to event planners. With him was Claude Bowman. This was their show. Jackie was the reason for the meeting, but she had no control over the agenda. Her career could end today. It was amazing to contemplate, that the involvement of the James family in Axiom Oil Incorporated might end this way. She was depressed to think Bud might be right; that her stubbornness had nearly brought the company to its knees. The company her grandfather had founded and her father had made a merchandising powerhouse would be brought dangerously close to collapse by Jackie's unwillingness to go along with a new tax. Perhaps her detractors were right. Perhaps the politicians and the teamsters and the Board members were right. Perhaps she had been wrong all along, but was too bullheaded to realize or admit it.

She was like her grandfather. He was obstinate as a mule, or so Jackie could remember her grandmother saying through gritted teeth. It was a different time then. Her grandmother had no aspirations for a career. The same was true of Jackie's mother, but Jackie grew up during a time when women were told they could have it all. That meant career and family. Jackie had the former, but not the latter. Life was about choices after all. One couldn't have it all, not because convention prevented women from having a career, but because there just wasn't time to do everything.

There were probably some people here today who regretted putting a woman in charge of their company. Axiom didn't just belong to Jackie. It also belonged to these people gradually finding their places in the rows of cushioned but narrow stadium seats. "Axiom is a public company now," Bud had said when she told him she wanted to be CEO. Had she forgotten that when she took the company down the road of the moratorium? She had been elected by the narrowest of margins and the vote for the moratorium had been close as well. It was possible that the steady stream of bad news both within and without the company might sway enough stockholders that she would be given her walking papers.

The clock finally reached the appointed time and Bud stepped to the microphone to call the meeting to order. He led the stockholders through almost a full hour of review of the corporate bylaws to be sure everyone understood what they were doing. Each attendee had a copy in his handout folder. Even though Jackie had been elected by the Board of Directors, the bylaws required that the stockholders vote to unseat an existing officer of the company.

Then followed a presentation, complete with PowerPoint slides, showing the downward course of the stock price and the corresponding valuation of the company since the moratorium began. No one was surprised by the numbers, but Jackie was distressed by the impression the charts and graphs made as they lingered on the screen.

To Jackie's surprise, the next presentation was made by Alec Kincaid, the lawyer and stockholder who had attempted to lead the class-action suit against the company and Jackie herself. The suit had failed, but obviously he hadn't given up.

"We as stockholders must hold management's feet to the fire," Kincaid said, his public-address-powered voice echoing through the large space of the arena. "This moratorium was a hare-brained idea and the proof of that is in the numbers we just saw. Can we allow those numbers to keep going down just because of some sentimental attachment to the James family?"

"No!" came the answer from many voices in the arena.

"Do we have to take these losses lying down?"

"No!" the crowd roared again.

As Jackie looked out into the dimly lit auditorium, she could see that not all of the people were responding to Kincaid.

"Can we do something about it?"

"Yes!"

"Can we save this company?"

"Yes!"

"Mr. Chairman," Kincaid said, contorting himself to look behind him at Bud while keeping his booming voice close to the microphone. "I move we open the floor for nominations for a new Chief Executive Officer for Axiom Oil Incorporated!"

"Yes!" The portion of the crowd that was with Kincaid then broke out into spontaneous cheers mixed with shouts of a variety of things Jackie couldn't understand. *Maybe it's just as well*, she thought. About that time, Wayne appeared at her side. As always, he was where she needed him when she needed him to be there. His expression was tortured as if he were carrying a large weight on his back. Jackie could only smile at him weakly and return her eyes to the stage.

When Kincaid had finished, Bud announced that there had been a second to the motion and he would entertain questions from the floor. Microphones were set up and lines quickly formed. The first couple of people asked procedural questions about picky things in the bylaws, then a man Jackie didn't know came to the mic.

"What I'd like to ask everyone is this: do we know that things would be better without the moratorium? Have you looked at the stock price for Petrocom Energy Limited lately? They aren't having a moratorium, but they are closing stations and laying off employees by the thousand and their stock price is down 20 percent anyhow. They might be tempted to replace their CEO for NOT having a moratorium. The only solution to the situation is to get Congress to repeal the gas tax. And Axiom is the only one doing anything that might make that happen, led by the CEO that some of you want to replace! I say, stay the course. Vote for Jackie James today and, in November, vote against those politicians that put us in this position!"

Several hundred people then jumped to their feet and cheered, allowing Jackie to see how the other side felt and how many there were. A few more people asked questions and made impassioned speeches for one side or the other, then a woman came to the mic.

"I'd like to ask, are we going to hear from Jacqueline James today? It seems we ought to let her speak for herself."

Again, there was loud cheering. Jackie looked at Wayne and he smiled. Then she looked at Bud, who was already looking over at her with daggers in his eyes. Finally, he nodded to her and Wayne gently pushed her out from behind the curtain.

As she appeared on stage, the arena erupted and it seemed everyone was on his feet; some cheering and others jeering as she took small steps in the general direction of the rented podium with the Axiom logo affixed. After what seemed an eternity, she was behind the microphone, looking out at the deeply divided crowd. She slowly looked from one side to another as the people continued to stand and applaud or roar their defiance. Finally, she raised a small hand in a feeble attempt to get the crowd to be quiet. It took about another 30 seconds before there was peace again and everyone took their seats.

"I didn't come with a prepared speech," she began, as every eye stared at her unblinking. "So, I can't make a stirring defense of myself. It's true that things haven't gone too well since the Gulf Pride was attacked. Some of the things that have happened were not our fault, like the attack itself and the gas tax. I thought the moratorium was the way to go. Maybe I was wrong."

The only sound was the air conditioning blower as the people watched the small woman at the podium. It seemed they hadn't expected her to admit she might be wrong, because they sat motionless awaiting her next words.

"I hope you all know that I would never intentionally do anything to hurt you. I love this company and you are its owners, just like me. I thought it was the best thing to do. Some of you disagree. That's your privilege. If it makes you feel any better, I've lost three billion dollars since July 1."

If it was possible, the room got quieter.

"I only tell you that to let you know I'm in the same boat as you, and I don't like losing money either. But maybe I'm not the right person to lead the company right now. That's a decision you will have to make. I like what someone said earlier, that the moratorium is the only thing that has a prayer of changing the government's mind about the gas tax. But maybe I was wrong to push it through. If that's the case, I just want to say I appreciate the love and hard work you have shown the company that my grandfather started, and I won't hold anything against any of you."

She turned and started walking back toward the curtains beside the stage as no one moved a muscle. Then, the silence was broken by a single pair of clapping hands. Jackie turned looked out beyond the glare of the stage lights and saw a man in a white suit standing, a cane hanging from his forearm as he clapped. It was Tom Davis, smiling at her and giving her a lonely standing ovation. She returned his smile, though her eyes were filling with tears. More people clapped and stood to their feet. Soon it seemed the majority were applauding as Jackie stood looking at them with tears running down her face. Through her tears, she saw Doris and Gina, standing together, Marcus and Benny looking at her and clapping, Bret McAlister in his straw cowboy hat, and Dennis, his trademark handlebar mustache stretched by the grin on his face. Then she saw her mother, in the crowd with the rest of the stockholders! Many of them probably had no idea who she was. She had slipped in without fanfare and was standing and applauding too.

Finally, Jackie broke down and had to cover her face with her hands as she wept freely. She regained control enough to wave at them and then made her way behind the curtain where Wayne took her in his arms, his own eyes glistening.

There were a few more questioners at the microphones, then someone called question. When the motion to entertain nominations for a new Chief Executive Officer was put to a vote, it failed to receive the votes of the required majority of stockholders; a fact all the more amazing because Jackie had abstained.

CHAPTER TWENTY-TWO

It was a crisp morning in Manhattan and the moisture in the air was cold enough to make anyone who took a deep breath begin to look for the first golden leaves of Autumn as they hurried past Central Park. At the Axiom service station that became famous for giving a gallon of gas to a weeping mother three months before, Manager Jim Powers raised the blinds on the plate-glass window facing the street.

Today was the day. October 1. He could finally sell gas again.

It would cost every penny the law allowed; $6.00 per gallon for the most expensive grade, but at least he did have gas to sell. Not every station manager could say that.

It felt like the moratorium had been much longer than three months, so much had happened in that time; so much had changed. As Jim watched, two of his employees put up a large gold and black sign that proclaimed, "Gas For Sale." The signs that explained the moratorium were gone from the pumps and the padlocks were off. Presently a car rolled in and stopped at a

Gary L. Ivey

self-serve pump. Jim yielded to impulse and strolled out to the pump island.

"Good morning," he greeted the woman bent over the side of her car where the gas tank opening was located.

Surprised, she looked up. "Oh. Good morning."

"You're our first customer. In three months."

"Oh, really?"

"Yeah, welcome back." He meant it for her, but also for the whole city. Indeed, the whole country.

* * *

It seemed the entire company was breathing a sigh of relief that it was over. The tension that had been palpable in the halls of the black glass-and-steel tower for three months dissipated overnight as the green of September began to change to October red and gold. As she entered the headquarters building, Jackie actually heard people whistling in the halls again.

They were by no means out of the woods, she knew. The end of the moratorium did not mean an end of the company's financial problems. Nor did it mean an end to threats to Jackie's position as leader of the company. She had believed so strongly that the moratorium was the only way in the beginning. Others believed it had caused more harm than good and Jackie wasn't sure herself anymore. The company had suffered more than she had expected and the moratorium didn't seem to have made a difference. The gas tax was still in place, though there was some agitation in the country to repeal it and the election was just over a month away.

"Good morning!"

"It certainly is!" Jackie agreed with Doris' greeting.

Backlash

"You have a news conference today," her administrative assistant reminded Jackie, though it was hardly necessary. Charlene and her staff had been planning the news conference for a week, but her mind was already focusing on a specific evening next week.

* * *

She should have felt guilty, but she didn't. After all that had happened and was continuing to happen, she felt she deserved this indulgence. *The fact that it required a white lie and the concoction of an elaborate pretext is just part of the cost of doing business,* Jackie thought. And he had played along, pretending that there was a perfectly good reason for him to come to Houston once again. How many exclusive interviews could she give Patrick before other people saw what the two of them had yet to admit: that they were seriously attracted to each other and wanted to spend some real time together?

Even when the day finally arrived, Jackie had barely admitted it to herself and of course they had never talked about it. Perhaps she would change that on this trip. She was out of practice at the game of love, and had long since forgotten the most basic moves in the playbook. Yet at this time of her life, when she was at the top of her game — her game being her career — she should be able to say what she wanted to say.

So why was she terrified to bring up the subject when he would arrive at any moment? She, who faced down a whole tribe of "news gypsies", won over disgruntled stockholders, and shot from the hip at a Senate subcommittee, was nervous about sitting down with a man she had come to care about and telling him how she was feeling. She who won over the board of directors and the unions was afraid that the doorbell would ring soon and it would be him. And, like a school girl, she was afraid it wouldn't ring at all.

She had told him to come to her house. *Why did I do that?* she wondered. Might he get the wrong idea? Or was the wrong idea what she intended? No, she had not asked him to come to her house for any improper purpose. Her Baptist upbringing sent unmistakable messages to her conscience about that. She really just wanted to set things up like a date.

There, she admitted it to herself. She liked him and hoped he felt the same way and she wanted to have a date, so she asked him to pick her up at home. Yes, it was very "high school", with Jackie playing the part of her own father, demanding that the boy come to the front door and take her out like a gentleman. It made her feel devious and underhanded, but she somehow sensed that Patrick was complicit with her. He had agreed to come, and apparently with a plane ticket purchased by the newspaper, yet she knew in her heart that he cared less for the interview she would give him or the article he would write than for the opportunity for them to meet again, face to face.

So, she sat waiting for the doorbell to ring in a royal blue silk dress that clung to her in all the right places and her makeup was as perfect as she could make it. Again, she arrived at the conclusion she had reached several times a day since she had called him. There was adequate reason for a follow-up interview, but the real reason for having him here was so they could talk face-to-face about the "elephant in the corner" — their relationship.

She absent-mindedly straightened the items on the tear-drop-shaped, glass-topped coffee table, until she realized she was becoming her mother, so she stopped. She had already straightened and dusted and put everything just so, so that when she gave him the grand tour it would be right. She went to the kitchen and got a drink of water, not because she was thirsty, but because it gave her something to do until the doorbell rang.

And then it did. The chime was melodic and Jackie's heart responded to its rhythm. She started running, then slowed and gathered her composure, took a breath and finished walking to the front door. She twisted the deadbolt and turned the doorknob, pulling the wide door open with a flourish. In an instant, her eyes changed from smiling to questioning to shock. Standing on her porch in the soft light of the twin sconces was Arturo!

* * *

The black SUV with government plates pulled up about 10 seconds after the fancy Italian sports car rolled to a stop in front of the awning over the front door of a restaurant the inside of which neither of the men in the SUV could afford to see. They were aware of the Georgetown restaurant of course. It was frequented by some of the most powerful men and women in the world and a lot of their assistants and hangers-on.

Special Agent Devon Thacker sat behind the wheel watching as the dandy driving the sports car emerged and tossed the keys to a valet. Simultaneously, two Barbie-like women, all legs and blonde hair, struggled to exit the passenger side of the sleek, low convertible.

Thacker looked at his partner, Special Agent Sam Jorgensen. Both laughed out loud without having to say anything.

Two minutes later, just as the waiter offered Marvin Borelli the opportunity to test the wine while the two Barbies giggled, Jorgensen and Thacker strode up to the table.

"Marvin Borelli, I'm Special Agent Jorgensen and this is Special Agent Thacker. We need to ask you a few questions."

"What the... What's this about? Can't you see we are dining?"

"I'm not really concerned about that. You need to come with us now."

"Why don't you just come to my office tomorrow? Here, I'll give you my card..." Borelli reached into his jacket pocket, but in a blink Thacker grabbed his wrist and wrenched it around behind him. The Barbies involuntarily let out a high-pitched, short cry before covering their mouths with starched white napkins.

"No, you'll come with us now," Jorgensen said with no discernible change in tone.

Borelli looked through wide eyes at the tables around him and realized all conversation had ceased and everyone was watching his little drama.

"Fine!" he said, jerking his arm from Thacker's grasp. "Let's get out of here. Shall I follow you? I just dropped my car with the valet."

"Oh, no! You'll be riding in the back of our vehicle," Thacker said with a grin.

"What! What about my car!" "We'll take care of your car."

"What about us?" the Barbies asked in unison.

"We'll call you a cab," Jorgensen replied.

"This is outrageous!" Borelli said, louder than he wanted to. "Are you charging me with something? I know my rights!"

"So do we, fella," Thacker said. "Don't push your luck. It will be better for you."

"Fascists!"

"Whatever," Thacker said as he led Borelli away under the wide eyes of hundreds of onlookers.

* * *

"What…? What are you doing here?" Jackie stammered.

"I'm sorry," Arturo said. "I probably should have called."

"Yes, you should have. Ten years ago!"

Arturo tried to come close and comfort her, but she stiff-armed him.

"What are you doing here now?"

"I saw you on TV and I knew you were having difficulties."

His voice faltered a little with some emotion of his own, but Jackie's bewilderment did not allow her to comprehend it. Hot tears flowed profusely and she was helpless to stop them. She couldn't tell if she was weeping from surprise or rage. She only knew she couldn't handle this situation right now.

"You can't stay, I'm expecting someone. Any minute."

"All right. I'm sorry. I'm staying at a hotel. Please call me," he said, handing her a piece of hotel stationery with a room number written on it. He looked back at her as he turned and walked down the steps in the soft glow of the porch sconces.

She closed the door, leaning against it as if to prevent more bad news from coming in. Suddenly she wondered if she could salvage her makeup before Patrick arrived and she ran to her bedroom makeup table. Even if she could replace the elements of the face she showed the world in time, he would be able to tell she had been crying.

As she washed her face and began reapplying the thin covering the flood of tears had washed away, she became angry that Arturo would show up now, of all times. So many times she had wished he would return, reappearing from the mist into which he had vanished nearly 10 years before. He said he had seen her on the news and had decided he wanted to see her. Jackie found herself spitting out hateful whispers at the man who had broken her heart and then reappeared to ruin her evening as she sat at her makeup vanity, bathed in the warm light ringing the oval mirror.

* * *

"What's wrong?" was almost the first thing Patrick said as she welcomed him through the front door when he arrived 15 minutes later.

Jackie struggled to smile as she said, "Oh, nothing you need to worry about." But Patrick didn't look convinced and throughout the evening he appeared to worry, being more attentive and less cynical than usual. He didn't ask again and she didn't volunteer any information. There was no need to tell him anything. They went, not to the Bar T, but to an upscale Continental restaurant that Jackie knew. She insisted on paying the check, telling him that it was her town, her treat. One look at the prices on the menu and Patrick told her she had convinced him to let her have her way with the bill.

She tried to organize her thoughts as she sat eating food that was strangely tasteless, though she knew from past experience it must actually be wonderful. She had intended to bring up her feelings toward Patrick, but the sudden appearance of Arturo had thoroughly confused her feelings. As she struggled to pay attention to the conversation, Patrick watched her through eyes narrowed with obvious concern. If he had anything to say of a personal nature, the confused emotions she could not hide caused him to keep it inside.

She felt more human as the evening wore on, even managing a phony smile and a joke. He took her home in his rental car and she told him she would see him at her office tomorrow for the interview. She felt a little sorry for him as she closed her front door with him still standing on the porch.

* * *

Special Agent Thomas Shannon lowered his binoculars as yet another car drove through the brick pillars marking the opening in the fence around Paul Stoddard's acreage. He and Agent Tony Bouchet were sitting in Shannon's government-issue Ford Crown Victoria, having come over from New Orleans to be present for the take down. An intercepted e-mail had alerted the FBI to the monthly meeting of the terrorist cell. So far, the chatter on the FBI radios was estimating a couple of dozen people were assembled at the old farmhouse behind the screen of trees. The Houston FBI was there in force, waiting on side streets out of view, as well as local county sheriff's deputies the Feds had called in as backup. They would have no trouble apprehending the perpetrators meeting on this remote property, but Shannon hoped they could do it without shedding blood on either side. It was Bureau policy — and only prudent — to assume the suspects would be armed. None of the officers needed to be told that.

The agents from the Houston FBI Field Office were in charge of the arrest since it was in their jurisdiction and they had begun staking out this Stoddard guy several weeks ago. Shannon and Bouchet were there because it was originally their case. Their numbers were swelled by uniformed officers from the Baytown police.

In the weeks after the tip from the reporter about the "Mongoose" e-mails, Shannon's New Orleans Field Office had been able to identify the other members in Stoddard's cell. They had pictures of each of them from their drivers' licenses, since the digital images were stored in the state database. Each picture had been blown up to 8 1/2-by-11 on a photocopier and distributed to the officers during the briefing. Of course, during the actual arrests, it wouldn't matter who was who. Everyone on the property tonight would be arrested. None had criminal records, except for the expected traffic violations, a couple of teenage shoplifting incidents and a few arrests during demonstrations. Investigation had revealed that membership in various Environmental concern groups was the common thread that tied them all together, in addition to the "Knights of Mother Earth" blog, of course.

Shannon was certain Stoddard had been involved in the filling station bombing in Atlanta, though there was no conclusive evidence so far. Those monitoring his phone and e-mail communications had noted that there was no activity during a couple of days either side of the incident, but no one had found any activity on credit cards, passenger manifests or hotel registers in Atlanta. Stoddard had used cash almost exclusively on the Gulf Pride attack, so it was no surprise that there was no paper trail tying him to Atlanta.

"What do you make of this Stoddard character?" Tony asked his boss.

"I think he's a bit strange, but no stranger than most of the people we track down."

"I mean, this guy is a real rocket scientist, for Pete's sake, but he spends his days picking up strays!"

Shannon recalled from the file that Stoddard did have an unusual history. Working as he did for the Baytown Animal Control Shelter, he appeared blue collar, but the FBI had thoroughly investigated his background and found that he had a doctorate in mathematics from the University of California. He had worked for three years for NASA in Houston, where he had apparently shown promise, but suddenly changed direction and left abruptly about six years ago. Now he was the ringleader of a budding domestic terrorist cell. If they looked for anybody as they made the arrests, it would be Paul Stoddard.

Backlash

Several minutes had gone by since a vehicle had passed through the brick pillars. It shouldn't be long now.

* * *

Paul slipped out of the formal living room, the one room that was cleared enough to host a meeting, to the kitchen to get a bag of ice from the freezer. It was nearly 10 p.m. and the meeting was winding down. There would soon be 18 thirsty throats to quench, dry from a prolonged discussion of solar-versus-fuel-cell-versus-hybrid power. Nothing was ever settled in these loud discussions, and none of them was actively involved in research into the alternative fuels in any event. Some had participated in symbolic construction of experimental vehicles for Earth Day parades, partly to give a high school or college auto shop something positive to do, but mostly to demonstrate that alternative fuels were a reality. After all, it was just the greed of the Detroit/Oil Company/Government Complex that prevented those technologies from gaining acceptance. Everyone knew that a practical hydrogen fuel-cell car had been available for years – with water as the only exhaust! — but had been suppressed by the oil companies in collusion with the auto industry. The greedy oppressors had too much invested in the current technology to care that they were slowly poisoning the earth and its inhabitants.

He finished loading the ice into a large cooler and took several glasses of eclectic styles out of the cupboard. Paul then placed on the counter a couple of two-liter bottles of pop — one sugar-free, a quart bottle of tomato juice, a bottle of spring water and a six-pack of beer. The preferences of the group were surprisingly diverse. Whereas they were pretty much all vegetarians, when it came to beverages, they were all over the map. Most were tea-totalers who could opt for soda or juice. The ones who didn't like tomato juice might go for the diet soda, especially those who regarded sugar as toxic. But many also believed artificial sweetener caused cancer, so they might choose the sugar soda, unless they didn't like plastic bottles because they weren't biodegradable, in which case they could drink the tomato juice. The beer was for the rest, some of whom preferred wine, but they would be out of luck tonight. If all else failed, he had made sure the bottled water was free of chlorine.

Suddenly Paul heard a loud BOOM and saw a flash of light, followed by the crashing of glass and splintering of wood that sounded like it came from the front of the house. He looked up and saw lights outside. Next there were loud, threatening shouts and frightened screams in the formal living room and the sound of people running. Paul dropped the glass he had been putting ice in and ran to the back hallway. Through an open door into the formal living room he saw a cloud of smoke and armed, uniformed men shouting and pushing the members of his group to the floor. He hurried to the stairs that led down into the basement, feeling for his 9mm pistol. It was in its holster on his belt where it was supposed to be. He had taken to wearing it whenever they had a meeting to assert his authority and lend an air of seriousness to the work they were doing.

His breath was short and cold in his lungs even though the night was warm and humid. In his haste, he nearly fell down on the basement floor. He tried to think of what to do. It must be police. How did they find him? If they knew about the group and knew where he lived, then they knew about their activities. But how? They had been very careful. They had covered their tracks. Even the website was bounced off a second server to avoid being traced.

Backlash

The noise upstairs was lessening. Already the police had subdued his brave activists. The little bit he had seen told him there were too many police for him to take them on directly. Think! He had to get away where he could fight from a position of strength; where he could reclaim the element of surprise. *Could it be that the "Knights of Mother Earth" would be swept away in one night? Who were these Fascists and how did they find us?*

There was no time to consider these questions further. Paul could see feet running by the basement windows and light from bouncing flashlights dancing about the yard and through the high windows into the basement. It seemed there were men everywhere, outside and inside, with dogs barking. Then it struck him. The police had dogs, but so did he.

He waited until a couple of officers had run by the basement window closest to the dog runs in the back yard. Then he opened the window and slipped outside, crawled away from the house and rolled over the chain link fence into the pen with the big dogs. Thankfully, the dogs knew him by his scent, but they were exercised by the shouts of the police and the barking of their dogs. Paul's dogs added their voices to the racket as he unlocked the gate, releasing five of his most vicious canines. They immediately burst out of their chain-link prison and attacked three officers and their dogs. The five dogs, two Pit Bulls, two Dobermans and a Chow, attacked the German Shepherd police dogs and their handlers with ferocity born as well as bred in them. It was both beautiful and horrible as the men fell as if they had been gazelles, set upon by leopards in a PBS nature film. Dogs fought dogs in the moonlight. The police were in no condition to notice when Paul opened the other gate, releasing another 16 dogs of various breeds and sizes. They ran around both sides of the house, barking at shadows, encountering more officers and police dogs. In their terror, the police began firing their guns at the dogs, which yelped in pain and fell to the ground. Paul choked back a scream and white-hot rage momentarily blinded him as he watched from behind a kennel. More police came and more dogs died.

Paul drew his Glock from its holster and with trembling hands pointed it at the men who were killing his beloved animals, firing once, the bullet whizzing by his target, thudding harmlessly into the wall of his house. He squinted down the barrel, preparing to fire again, but he stopped, realizing that if he fired he would be discovered. Then the Fascists would return fire and he would either be killed or captured and then would be of no service to The Cause. He could see the police cars now, out on the County Road, where they had turned on their cycling blue and red lights, the need for surprise past. He could also see uniformed police and men with the letters "FBI" emblazoned on the backs of dark windbreakers in fluorescent yellow, clearly visible in the moonlight.

All the lights in the house were on now, including the basement. Armed law enforcement officers were examining every corner of his home and everything he owned. The "Knights of Mother Earth" had been subdued and shackled without warning. Realizing that all was lost, he holstered his pistol, turned and ducked under the low-hanging limbs of the old live oak and quietly climbed over the back fence of his property.

Knowing the area as he did, he was able to slip away in the darkness, between houses that had been built a mere 30 years ago on what had once been farmland belonging to his house's original owner.

At one house, in a recently added carport, he found a Ford Ranger pickup, unlocked with the keys in the ignition. Through

Backlash

the windows of the house, he could see the blue light of a television set, showing an episode of a popular police show, the residents unaware that a real police drama was taking place just over their back fence. He knew the couple who lived here only by sight, so what he did next presented no problem for him. Paul got into the pickup and turned the key, driving quickly away.

CHAPTER TWENTY-THREE

Thirty minutes later, Paul Stoddard slowed the small truck in the parking lot of a darkened strip mall and looked across the intersection at the Baytown Animal Control Shelter. He had a key to the building and wanted to go in to rest and think, not to mention collecting a few belongings from his locker. Then he thought better of it. If they knew where he lived, they almost certainly knew where he worked and might be staking out the building. He put the truck back in gear and drove away, not the least bit sorry to be leaving the Shelter for the last time.

He turned the little pickup toward Interstate 10.

He could never go back to his house either, of course. It would be hard enough for him just to elude capture and stay out of jail. He would certainly miss his home of 10 years, not to mention his books and other belongings, humble though they were. He would also miss the camaraderie of the "Knights," even though many of them were fractious and argumentative, everyone having a different idea about solutions to global problems. Perhaps more than the people he would miss the feeling of doing something tangible to benefit the Earth, something the Fascist policemen occupying his house would never understand.

But most of all he would miss his animals. Those that the police hadn't killed would go back to the Animal Shelter, where they would again be condemned to death and he wouldn't be able to save them this time. Little Neutron still had a bum leg.

By now, they would have his computer. From it they would have a complete timeline of his activity and the content of his communications with his various contacts. Panic seized him again as he thought of the people whose e-mail addresses the police would find on his computer. Paul's grip tightened on the steering wheel as anger took over from his fear. He would escape, he vowed, and would strike back, once he was back on his feet. He needed to do some things to avoid getting caught until he could get far away. He would need to change the license plates on the truck if he was to make it far, since the owner would report it stolen. Hopefully, he wouldn't notice it was gone until morning and Paul would be many miles away by then. He would have to steal a set of license plates to replace the ones that the police would be looking for. The only alternative was to steal another car, but he wouldn't do that yet.

He needed money, too. He could stop by an ATM and empty his bank account, but it would only net him perhaps $300. Added to the money in his wallet, he wouldn't have $350. He still had a couple of thousand dollars in cash left from the Atlanta job, which he was to keep for incidental expenses of the "Knights of Mother Earth", but that was secured behind the false panel in his upstairs bedroom and the police would doubtless find it. He calculated in his head that it would take about six tanks of gas to get to the West Coast.

In spite of how dark things looked right now, he could look forward to driving up the coast of California, with all its natural wonders: the Sierra Nevada, the coastal highway, Big Sur, San Francisco Bay, the Redwoods, then through Oregon and Washington to Canada. To be sure to get lost, he would go all the way to Alaska. He had always wanted to go there; the last American wilderness! And with the threat of drilling for oil in the Wildlife Reserve, perhaps he could be useful there.

But that would mean he would need much more than six tanks of gas. Perhaps he would have to stop and work for a while, before going on to his final destination. But what kind of job could he get where there would be no criminal background check? It would have to be menial and below the radar. He felt sure his Washington contact could get a new picture ID for him and maybe, with some careful planning, some cash. As long as he didn't stay in one place too long, he would be okay. These days people who were wanted by the law often showed up on TV and their neighbors or coworkers turned them in. Maybe he could work a while as a day laborer and then move on to another city when he had enough for a few meals and a tank of gas.

That was a problem in itself. The gasoline tax was having the desired effect and gasoline prices had gone up as expected. The shortage still held them up against the cap. Driving up the price of gasoline had been one of the goals of the people he was working with all along, but now he wondered how he would get the money to move himself across the country to stay ahead of law enforcement. Briefly he considered Amtrak or Greyhound, but they would make it too easy for the police to apprehend him, with their inflexible, scheduled stops. No, he must have the independence and flexibility only a private car could give. In his head, he calculated that the six tanks of gas he needed to get to the coast would take almost all of the money he would withdraw from his bank account. Would he be forced to steal gas, or money to buy gas?

He was traveling on Interstate 10 West past the bejeweled Houston skyline, which rose beautifully into the night sky. Then he caught himself and rebelled at the thought of the artificially lit buildings being beautiful in any way. He fumed for several minutes about the pretentious waste and air pollution of the city and the technological advances that molded its lifestyle.

Once past downtown, he saw a branch of his bank off the Interstate, so he exited and pulled into the parking lot in front of the ATM. He didn't immediately get out of the truck, knowing that pulling money out now would alert the police to the fact he was on the run and the general direction he was fleeing, but he couldn't think of another way. He wasn't ready to start robbing convenience stores for gas money.

So, he opened the driver's door and put on an Astros cap he found on the seat, knowing it would not completely fool the police, but wanting to do something to shield his face from the ATM security camera. He put his card in the slot and punched in his PIN, asking to withdraw all but five dollars of the current balance; just over three hundred dollars. Some checks would probably bounce as a result, but that was the least of his worries.

To his horror, the colorful ATM screen politely said in a curt female voice, "We are sorry, Mr. Stoddard. No funds are available for this account. Would you like to select another account?"

That's impossible! he fumed. Then he realized the FBI would have frozen his account before the raid to prevent him from fleeing. The money in his pocket wouldn't even buy a bus ticket and his credit card was perpetually at the limit.

He did follow through on his intention to steal some license plates, though. Conveniently, the bank had a couple of cars in the lot that were for sale; repos, no doubt. He would have called it a godsend, if he had believed in God. Using the pocket knife he always carried, he quickly unscrewed the plates from one of the cars and put them in the stolen truck. He would install them later, not wanting to be in one place too long. He did take time to put the pickup's plates on the repo, since the bank people wouldn't likely notice the switch for several days, so long as the car had a tag on it, but would notice right away if the plates were gone altogether.

He drove a little further down the street, away from the Interstate and found a pay phone. He had his cell phone in a holster on his belt, but using it would be one more way the FBI could follow his movements. *His cell phone might even be tapped*, he thought bitterly, unsure how difficult it was to tap a digital phone. He dropped a couple of coins into the slot and dialed a cell number. He hoped the owner would have his phone on. It was after midnight in Washington, D.C., so it was by no means certain that the cell phone would be turned on.

"Hello," answered a strange voice after three rings.

"Who is this?" Paul asked warily.

"You called me."

"But you're not who I was calling."

"Yeah, well, this is Special Agent Thacker. If you were trying..."

Paul slammed down the phone. He began hyperventilating and had to support himself on the shell of the payphone. They had arrested his contact! That was the only explanation for a government agent answering his contact's cell phone. *They're arresting us all!* he thought.

Suddenly, he realized this was the freeway exit that led to Jacqueline James' house. A fresh wave of anger and resentment blinded him as he remembered the disgusting capitalist who had brought him to this place!

So angry he could barely see to drive, he jumped back in the truck and drove like a madman toward her subdivision.

* * *

The ash wood flooring felt cool under Jackie's feet as she padded back to her bedroom with a fresh cup of hot chocolate. It was one of the few things that brought her comfort during the long grueling days of the moratorium and tonight, with the jarring appearance of Arturo and the laborious evening with Patrick afterward, she needed comfort food. She hoped she wasn't gaining too much weight and had considered switching to hot tea, but it just wasn't the same. She used her free hand to pull the floral-print cotton nightgown tight against her legs as she sat on the bed. She didn't turn on the television, opting instead for a short devotional from a book on her bedside table to clear her mind of the confusing events of the evening.

When the cup was empty she set it and the book aside and turned off the contemporary lamp, using the wall switch by her bed that was connected to another three-way switch by the door. The matching lamp on the other side of the king-size bed wasn't on the three-way circuit and she rarely turned it on. In spite of the stress of the past few hours, she was sleeping solidly in less than two minutes.

Time has no meaning during sleep. The passage to REM sleep, when dreams are most frequent, is not remembered, so it seems like seconds. On the other hand, the time during dreams is elastic, sometimes taking several minutes and other times

Gary L. Ivey

presenting themselves full-blown in a split second, though the dreamer may experience the dream as lasting hours.

Therefore, Jackie had no idea what time it was when she was startled awake by the sound of glass breaking. In the confusion that always accompanies being awakened from deep sleep, she looked around and was immediately shocked and frightened as the lamp on her bedside table came on, switched on from across the room by the door.

"Don't move!" a gruff voice said, angrily.

She blinked her eyes to adjust to the light. "What? Who are you?" As her eyes focused she saw a bearded man standing at the foot of her bed. His jeans and plaid shirt were dirty and gave off a musty smell. In his hand was a semi-automatic pistol, reflecting the lamplight.

"I said, don't move!"

An involuntary scream escaped Jackie's mouth and she clapped a hand over it even as she scrambled backward against her headboard. Her suddenly alert mind raced to make sense of the situation.

"Who are you?" she heard herself ask again.

"Shut up! I need to think for a minute and I might need you to help me. And don't you think about calling anybody, because I cut the telephone line. That'll keep your alarm from sending out a message, too."

Jackie was silent, trembling as she tried to take it all in. He had broken into her house, saying he might need her help, and had cut the telephone line to prevent her from calling out. She gradually calmed down as he paced around the bedroom, looking at first this and then that with disdain, sighing and sputtering.

Then she had another thought, which enabled her to stop shaking. He had said something about cutting the telephone

331

line so her alarm wouldn't send out a message, but he couldn't know that her alarm was monitored, not through the telephone line, but through her cable television connection, which was underground. When he broke the window to get into the house an intruder alert would have been sent to the monitoring company. They would attempt to telephone her to determine the validity of the alert. When they discovered the line was dead, they would send the police. *I just need to stay alive until then.*

"You said you needed me to help you?" she said tentatively.

"Shut up! I've got to think."

So she was quiet again as he continued to pace and sputter. She tried to imagine what the next few minutes might entail. Would he kidnap her? Would he just say, "Forget it" and shoot her? Would he rape her? She looked around the room to see if there was anything she could use to defend herself if things got out of hand before the police got there. Finally, he stopped pacing.

"You think you're so smart!"

"I beg your pardon?"

"You think you're so smart," he said again, and as he spoke the hand that held the pistol flailed around wildly. "With your fancy house and clothes and car. I've been watching you!"

Jackie shuddered, as she heard the echo of the message on the bombed oil platform. Suddenly she realized who this might be and her whole body became rigid. The FBI agent from New Orleans had said their main suspect for the attack was a tall, slender man with a beard from the Houston area. *This could be him!*

That thought terrified her. The way he was pacing this way and that, he might have had a psychotic break. There was no telling what he might do. She had .38-caliber revolver in the drawer of her night table, but to go for it now would just get her killed, so she sat perfectly still with the covers drawn up under her chin. Suddenly he was bending over her, a menacing scowl behind his bushy beard. Then, just as abruptly, he began pacing again.

"You are a rapist! Did you know that? You and your father, and all the wage slaves that prostitute themselves for you."

Jackie said nothing, so he continued.

"You endanger life on the Earth for years to come by trafficking in oil, which you take from the Earth, though she hasn't given you permission to take from her. You foul the ground water with your putrid fuel. You soil the air with your noxious, toxic fumes. Because of you, the sun burns hotter and life on the Earth will soon cease to exist!"

She watched and listened to his nonsensical diatribe, unable to move, as he finally took a breath and prepared to go at her again.

"Don't you see how you are a rapist? You take from the Earth, you take from people, all to enrich yourself and your friends. People have no choice but to buy your bitter, caustic products to live in society."

He had told her to be quiet, so she was, and he continued.

"You're all alike! You make technology that distorts life. It's an aberration. Human beings were not meant to live this way. It's too frantic, too complex, too pointless. The machines are taking over everything. And you're helping them."

Jackie was having trouble following what he was trying to say. "Why did you bomb our oilrig?" she said abruptly, surprising even herself.

"Who said I did that?" he demanded shrilly.

"A lucky guess. Why'd you do it?"

"To stop you from producing oil. To stop you from polluting."

Encouraged by the exchange, she continued. "Bombing one installation isn't going to end oil and gasoline production."

"It should have — with the tax, and besides, we didn't just bomb one facility."

Jackie caught her breath as she analyzed the import of what he had said. She carefully phrased her next question. "Did you know about the tax when you bombed the platform?"

He looked at her with confusion in his wild eyes, as if in his frame of mind he couldn't understand the significance of the question, but knew better than to answer.

"Well, how 'bout this? How come the FBI raided my house tonight?"

"They did?"

"Yeah, they did. Don't pretend you didn't know!"

"I didn't know. The FBI hasn't told me much." It was true enough that she hoped he might believe it. "They don't tell many people when they do something like that."

He looked skeptical, but didn't challenge her.

"If they raided your house, how come you're here?"

"I'm too slippery for them," he swaggered a little as he said it. "I got away."

"And you came here, for what?"

"To teach you a lesson."

"By threatening me with a gun?"

"That's just to make you listen," he said as he looked at the gun in his hand as if he had forgotten about it. "The lesson has to do with the Environment and technology."

"Okay, I'm listening."

"The human animal needs to be one with Nature, not exploit her," he began, as if giving a rehearsed speech. "People today are separated from Mother Earth by technology. They go weeks without watching a sunset or smelling a flower."

"And that's my fault?" Jackie dared to ask.

"You and many more like you. You rob the earth of its resources and give nothing back but fouled air and polluted water. You traffic in technologies that allow people to live such a fast pace that their lives become artificial and plastic. They are insulated from the normal cycles of life; seedtime and harvest, the rhythm of the seasons. They grow restless and unfulfilled. A hundred years ago, people lived much closer to Nature. They had control of their lives. But greedy industrialists like you have ruined that simple life and spoiled the Earth itself. To line your pockets, you have made people want things they didn't know they wanted until finally they think they must have them to live. We will all pay the price for your greed; the price will be the death of the planet!" He underlined his final words with a sweep of his gun hand.

"Is that why you were willing to kill my employees?" Jackie's question sounded unnecessarily defiant, even to her.

"We didn't plan that," he snarled, "but many more have died because of you. There is much blood on your hands; the blood of the all life on the Earth! We were beginning a revolution! We were going to roll back the onslaught of technology that enslaves us!"

"How are you enslaved?" Jackie could see the question caught him off guard and he glared at her angrily, as if the answer should be obvious.

"Because we have to use your technology to survive. It's not natural, but soon people think they have to have it and it enslaves them. People used to live close enough to their work to walk. Now they spend hours locked in their cars, commuting. They have to work harder to afford the car and the gas for it, because what used to be optional is now a necessity. We are enslaved! But we were going to change things, until your moratorium!"

"But your attack and the gas tax that resulted increased the price of gasoline. Didn't that make people more enslaved? Isn't every tax increase a reduction in freedom, taking power from the individual and giving it to government?"

He didn't answer, but started pacing again and muttering to himself. Suddenly he grabbed her roughly by the arm and pulled her from the bed. "Come on! You're coming with me! You'll be my insurance."

"What? Where?" she clutched at her nightgown to preserve her modesty as he pulled her bodily from her bed. *Where are the police?* she thought. *They should have been here long before now.* Jackie decided she wouldn't go to her death willingly. As he pulled her from her bed she pretended to slip and fall to the floor.

"Get up!" he screamed in frustration.

She didn't get up, but looked as he pointed the gun at her. For a long moment, she stared at him staring back at her, wondering if he could really shoot her. Finally, he grabbed her arm and pulled her upward, her petite frame offering no resistance.

Suddenly she was on her feet and he continued to point the gun at her head while tightly holding her left arm. He pushed her toward the door of the bedroom, but she did not cooperate at all, and he cursed her obstinacy. Subconsciously she recalled that law enforcement personnel universally advised people in such situations to cooperate with their assailants, but to her, it didn't seem the right thing to do.

As if on cue, the doorbell rang. It was the police, she knew, summoned by the silent alarm. As he looked toward the doorway questioning the meaning of the doorbell, she immediately took advantage of his surprise, swinging her fist in a wide right roundhouse with all her strength. The blow bounced off his head as if it had been an annoying insect and he glared at her.

"Stop it! You're going to answer the door and convince whoever it is to go away. No funny stuff!"

He pushed her down the hall toward the foyer and the front door, releasing her so she could open it, but keeping the pistol trained on her nonetheless. From the hallway, she saw the broken window in the library where her captor had gained his entrance to her home. She twisted the deadbolt and turned the knob as he pointed the gun at her from behind the slightly open door. On the porch, Jackie saw a single policeman holding a flashlight.

"Are you Jacqueline James?" he asked, studying her face in the harsh light.

"Yes."

"Is everything all right, ma'am?"

"Yes, no problem officer."

"We got a call that your alarm was tripped."

"Must have been a false alarm. Sorry."

"Why didn't you answer your phone?"

"I went to bed early. Must not have heard it."

"Well, if everything's okay..."

"Yes, thank you."

Just then a noise came from the hallway as another policeman announced himself, having come through the broken plate-glass window. The bearded terrorist slammed the front door in the first police officer's face, knocking Jackie to the floor and turned to fire his gun three times at the second cop just as he entered the foyer. The officer had drawn his gun, but was unable to get a shot off before he was hit full in the chest. He fell backward and lay still.

As Jackie watched, horrified, her captor ran to the window beside the front door and fired three more times, shattering the glass, after which he seemed to relax. Jackie rose to her feet and looked out the broken window to see the first policeman lying motionless on her well-kept lawn, his weapon drawn too late.

Her hope of imminent rescue was gone. She would have to find another way to survive.

Suddenly her head seemed to explode in pain and she fell to the floor yet again, realizing shortly that he had hit her with the hot barrel of his pistol.

"Damn you, woman! How did they know to come?"

Jackie was nursing her rapidly swelling skull and just looked at him sullenly.

"Get some clothes on! We're getting out of here," he shouted.

He grabbed her by the arm and pushed her toward the hallway and her bedroom where this ordeal had started. She had to step over the policeman, seeing that a pool of blood had formed under him on the light-colored wood floor. She couldn't be sure if he was dead, but she knew better than to ask if she could examine him.

"Are you going to give me some privacy?" she asked when they had arrived at the door to her walk-in closet.

"Hell, no! Just put on something over your nightgown."

Jackie stepped into the closet to select something to wear. She moved slower than she needed to, trying to think of a way to let someone know what was happening or how she might end her captivity herself. She knew that the distance between the houses in this exclusive neighborhood, coupled with the tremendous quality of the double insulated windows and well-insulated walls in the sturdy houses, made it nearly impossible that someone heard the shots and reported them as such. It was a lot more likely that her neighbors, if they heard anything at all, simply rolled over and went back to sleep, not wanting to involve themselves in the problems of other households in their block. The police officers would be missed and someone would be sent to find them, but how long would that take? She thought of the .38-caliber revolver in her nightstand and wished that she had another one in her closet.

After donning some old jeans and a denim shirt, she pulled on a pair of running shoes and tied the laces.

"Don't forget your keys. We're taking your car. And get your purse. We'll need money."

Jackie wordlessly obeyed. To get her keys she would have to go to her nightstand. Out of the corner of her eye she watched him watching her as she walked toward the bed.

"My purse is on the table right there," she said, suggestively pointing to an oval table by the window. She watched in amazement as he turned his back to her to pick it up. She had very little time. She grabbed the devotional book from her bedside table and, while his back was turned, threw it through the doorway and down the hallway, where it bounced and ricocheted making a frightful racket. Startled, he turned toward the door. Jackie reached for the lamp on the nightstand and pulled its cord from the wall socket, plunging the room into darkness. Remembering where he had been, she swung the ceramic lamp by its shade directly at the point in 3-D space occupied by his head. The lamp shattered noisily and she heard an involuntary groan and the sound of a heavy metal object striking the wood floor. She then dove at his midsection and they both went down, with him stunned and bewildered and her thrashing to find his hands in the dark. She wrapped the electrical cord around first one then the other of his hands, then around one of his feet as if he had been one of her rodeo calves.

When she had tied him up and he discovered he couldn't immediately free himself, he roared in anger, but she was off him by then, to the drawer of the nightstand where she retrieved her .38. In the moonlight coming through the sheer drapes, she saw his shiny gun lying on the floor. She swooped down to get it and then hopped over the king-sized bed, easily finding the switch to turn on the other lamp.

There he was on the floor with a large red welt on the right side of his face, sputtering and cursing and straining at the knots in the lamp cord that still had the shattered lamp on one end of it.

"Be still," she shouted, pointing her .38-caliber Colt at him menacingly. "I come from a long line of cowboys and Indians and I won't hesitate to use this!"

The fact was she had never pointed a loaded gun at another human being in her life, but then she had never in her life been held at gunpoint for almost an hour, either. She walked around the bed and picked up her purse where he had dropped it, keeping the gun trained on his bulging eyes. With her other hand, she extracted her cell phone and dialed 911 with her thumb.

CHAPTER TWENTY-FOUR

The red flashing light was a sudden, unexpected clash with the white headlights of the cars in John Watson's rear-view mirror. What was this about, he wondered? He knew he hadn't been speeding. He pulled the car off to the side of Independence Avenue after he got across the bridge, hoping there was some mistake and he would soon be on his way home from his late dinner out.

The dark unmarked SUV stopped behind him, and an officer emerged without turning off either the red flashing light or the piercing headlights. In his side mirror, Watson saw that he was dressed in a suit instead of police blues, but he didn't have time to wonder about it.

"Mr. Watson, could you come with me, please?" the man unfolded a badge with large block letters that said "FBI."

"What's this about?" Watson asked, a bead of sweat forming on his upper lip in spite of the chilly October dampness of the tidal basin.

"We need to ask you a few questions. My partner can bring your car."

On cue, another dark-suited FBI-type man appeared in Watson's rear-view mirror.

"Am I under arrest?" Watson was beginning to be alarmed.

"We just need you to come with us."

His tone didn't leave Watson any options, so he got out of the car and entered the FBI vehicle by the back door the agent held open for him. He was now sweating from under his collar down the middle of his back. *What could this be about?* he wondered desperately.

* * *

He was taken to a nondescript building a block off Pennsylvania Avenue. It wasn't the Hoover Building, but it did say "FBI" on the wall behind the guard's desk inside the front door. Watson supposed the FBI must have other offices in Washington besides their National headquarters, though he'd never thought about it. The agent, who had identified himself as Special Agent Samuel Jorgensen, led him to a room with four blank walls painted institutional-pea-soup green. The only furniture was a table and three equally institutional chairs.

"Mr. Watson, we need to ask you about 'Mongoose'."

Watson swallowed, wondering how they knew, how to tell them as little as possible, and more importantly, how to convince them that he really knew very little.

"I'm not sure I know what you mean."

"Yes, you do. We already got a warrant and saw what's on your computer. Now suppose you just tell us what you know."

They have seen my computer? How long have they been watching me? Are my phones tapped? He thought back over his communications and meetings. *What had tipped them off?*

"I got a few e-mails. I just figured it was some crackpot."

"Um-hmm. You're familiar with the attack on the offshore oil platform last spring?"

"Yes, of course, but I believe it was an industrial accident."

"Yes, we know, because you've written several articles about it," Jorgensen nodded to a file laying on the table that he didn't open, but Watson could see several dog-eared newspaper clippings sticking out of it.

"In my capacity as Science and Environment Editor, yes."

"When did you learn about the attack?"

"The next day, I suppose, from TV."

"You didn't have prior knowledge of the attack?"

"No, how could I?" As soon as he said it he knew he was caught. If the FBI had his computer files they would be able to see from the date and content of the Mongoose e-mails that he had known something was about to happen. Sure enough, Agent Jorgensen reached inside the file folder and took out a sheet of paper and laid it in front of Watson.

"This e-mail came to you six days before the attack. It says that an attack is imminent. Why didn't you notify someone?"

Watson felt the sweating start again.

* * *

Paul Stoddard had been handcuffed and taken to jail an hour ago. It had seemed like an eternity that she had kept her revolver pointed at him until the police arrived and she could relax. Later he would be put on trial in Federal court and Jackie would have to testify. Then he would certainly be convicted and sent to Federal prison for life, if he was lucky. With the police had come EMT's who applied first aid to the bruises on her head where the pistol barrel had struck her, but only after tending to the two policemen, one of whom was dead at the scene and still lying in the hall, covered with a sheet.

The other was rushed to the hospital in critical condition, Jackie assumed.

Special Agent Thomas Shannon and his partner had been contacted by the Houston police and were now sitting on the sandstone-colored, leather couch in Jackie's living room, each holding a cup of hot tea she had made for them. Other officers from the Houston field office and the Houston Police Department were taking pictures and gathering evidence all over the house. Still others were nailing a piece of plywood over each of the broken plate-glass windows and cleaning up the jagged shards on the floor.

Putting together what they knew with what she was able to remember of the things Stoddard had said to her, the FBI men were listing the new charges they would bring against the eco-terrorist: resisting arrest, grand theft auto, breaking and entering, attempted kidnapping, assault with a deadly weapon, and the assault and murder of the policemen.

"It might interest you to know that other arrests were made tonight as well," Agent Shannon said.

"Oh really?" Jackie replied. "Other than Stoddard's gang?"

"Yes, in Washington a couple of people were arrested — a lobbyist and that reporter who got the e-mails is being questioned. There are others we don't quite have enough information to charge, but we hope to get them yet."

"So Stoddard's group didn't act on its own?" Jackie asked.

"Oh, no. It appears that the funding came from Washington through the lobbyist. Some of the money probably came from donations to environmental groups where the members didn't know they were contributing to terrorism. There may even be political campaign money involved."

"You mean political contributions funded an act of terrorism?"

"We can't prove that yet, so don't say anything to anybody."

"Wow! That's incredible! Was it all about the gas tax?"

"It appears that was a big part of it. The attack was supposed to provide an excuse for punishing the oil companies and raising a big pile of cash." He looked at his watch and stood up. "Thank you, Ms. James. I'm glad you're okay. We'll need you to give us a formal statement later."

After what would be the first of many interviews by the Police and FBI, Jackie went to the kitchen, seemingly the only room in the house where law enforcement personnel weren't working. She picked up the telephone and began dialing, then remembered that the line had been cut. So, she got her cell phone and dialed the number to Patrick Garrity's cell phone.

"Yeah?" a groggy male voice answered. It was four a.m.

"I'm sorry for calling so early, but I had to talk to you."

"Jackie?"

"A horrible thing happened tonight..." and then she lost it. She had kept her composure pretty well through the ordeal with Paul Stoddard, the shooting, his arrest and the debriefing for the FBI. But now she let down and the tears came in a torrent.

"Jackie, what's wrong? What happened?"

"The... the police and the FBI are here. The leader of the terrorists was here tonight...."

"What? What do you mean? He was where?"

"Here in my house. He broke in and held me at gunpoint. And he shot two policemen."

"Oh, my God! Are you okay?"

"Yes," she started to get control of herself, sniffing in mid sob before going on. "He broke in while I was sleeping."

"Where is he now?"

"The police took him to jail."

"I'm on my way."

"You don't have to…" she started to say, but he had already hung up.

* * *

Patrick was alarmed by the ambulance in the front yard and the many police and FBI vehicles on the driveway and on the street. More alarming was the gurney being wheeled out the front door as he was trying to go in. The person on the gurney was completely zipped up in a black body bag. Once inside, he was startled by Jackie's appearance. She was dressed in a wrinkled denim shirt, her hair was tousled and her forehead bandaged.

"Did he hurt you?"

"No. I mean, he hit me with his gun but it could have been worse," she answered as she led him to the kitchen. "It was terrifying when he shot the policemen, but then I hit him with a lamp and hogtied him with the cord."

Patrick laughed a relieved laugh then. "I wish I could have seen that!"

"I'm so glad you're here, now," she sighed.

"Yes, me too."

"So, I guess everyone that wants to hurt me has been arrested!"

"Who else has been arrested?" he asked as they sat down on the couch.

"Well, I guess they got Stoddard's entire cell group. They were based just over in Baytown. Also, in Washington they arrested a lobbyist for some environmental group. Apparently, the money came from them. And I'm afraid your colleague, the Environmental reporter, has been taken in for questioning."

"Oh no! Will he know I turned him in?"

"Only if the FBI tells him."

"I hate that."

"Well, if he was helping the terrorists, he needs to be arrested. You did the right thing."

"It just makes me feel bad. Anyway, I'm glad you're all right."

"And, I don't really know much about it, but you might want to start digging into a political connection."

"What do you mean?"

"I don't know anything really and I'm not supposed to tell anybody what I do know. Talk to Special Agent Shannon for the best info on all that, but I'll give you an exclusive on my little adventure."

"That's great." Patrick had forgotten that he was here to do an interview. His trip and the resulting article wouldn't feel so contrived now.

"Thanks for being here for me," she said as she leaned over and put her arms around him. It felt natural as he held her close with his arm across her back, his hand occasionally caressing the softness of her denim shirt. They stood together in silence with just indirect halogen lamps softly illuminating the kitchen.

Finally, she spoke. "Patrick, can I ask you something?"

"Of course."

"Do you like me?"

He smiled at the simplicity and vulnerability the question revealed. "Of course, I like you."

"I mean, are you attracted to me, as a woman?"

* * *

Patrick didn't answer immediately. Jackie was the CEO of one of the world's largest companies and had scores of people that took orders from her. She lived in a large house in an exclusive neighborhood. Yet, at a time like this, she was just a woman, looking for some reassurance; looking for love and caring.

"I was wondering how I could bring that subject up myself," he began. "Yes, I am attracted to you. I was attracted to you the first time I saw you, but I didn't dare hope you would want to spend time with me."

"What? Why?"

"Isn't it obvious? You run in some pretty heady circles. High finance, leading a Fortune 20 company, and you are personally wealthier than some of the nations of the Third World!"

"I am not!" she protested with her first genuine smile since he had arrived.

He was partly kidding, but he had made his point.

"Those things don't matter to me," she said. "I like who you are and I like how I feel when I'm with you. That's all that matters, isn't it?"

"I'd like to think so," he said, not sure what to say next. "I just didn't know if..."

When he didn't finish his sentence, she said "I know it isn't easy to form a — friendship — long distance as we are but, if it's okay with you, I'd like to see more of you."

He felt a flood of unexpected emotion, but he smiled broadly and took her hand. "I'd like that — a lot."

* * *

The police and FBI still had work to do as the sun came up and Jackie decided she had to get out of there. She ran the police out of her bedroom long enough to get dressed and pack a bag to take to her mother's house. When she was ready, she led the way in her BMW and Patrick followed in his rental car.

She opened the back door of the Tudor mansion and Patrick followed wide-eyed into the cavernous back hallway and finally to the sprawling kitchen. It was still early and no one was stirring. Soon Jackie was busy and had filled the kitchen with the smell of brewing coffee. Her back and head ached from the misadventures of the night. From the well-stocked pantry, she found some pastries that would serve as breakfast.

"How are you doing?" he asked her as she took the food to the table in the breakfast nook where he was sitting, looking into her dark eyes for the truth, regardless of what she might say.

"I'll be okay. I'll be busy today, cleaning up after last night."

He ignored the surface meaning of the words and acted on what he saw in her eyes, standing and pulling her close to him, her small frame nearly disappearing in his embrace. He held her until she quietly wept, releasing the stress she felt behind her brave words. After a full minute of allowing her to relax and let out her tension, he relaxed his arms and took a step back. She lowered her head, embarrassed by her tears. She wiped her eyes on her sleeve and turned back to the Italian marble countertop.

"Coffee's ready," she said, pouring two large cups.

"Great."

They sat at the breakfast table and nibbled sweet rolls and slowly sipped their coffee.

"I won't be going in to the office today," she told him. "I need to be home for the glazer and the telephone repairman, so we could do the interview right after breakfast, if you like."

"Okay. My flight back to Washington isn't until late afternoon."

She was glad he didn't have to rush and wished he could stay longer. But the danger was past and he had a job to do, so she said nothing.

After breakfast, he used a pad she borrowed from the desk in her father's library to take notes as she told him in detail what had happened overnight. He would get other information for background from the FBI, as Jackie had Special Agent Shannon's cell phone number.

Jackie introduced Patrick to her mother after the interview. She didn't identify him as anyone special because she hadn't had time to decide how she would designate him. It was too early. The knowing look in her mother's eyes told her that she knew he was more than just some reporter off the street. It gave Jackie a new appreciation for her mother's perceptiveness.

They returned to her house by late morning as the law enforcement personnel were finishing up their work and melting away. From her mother's house, she had called several numbers for people to come and fix her phone line and the broken plate-glass windows, but it would take a little time for them to arrive.

When the time came for Patrick to return his rental car to the airport and return to Washington, he paused at the door for an awkward moment as she looked up at him, her words brave as always, but her eyes telling him she didn't want him to go. A wave of emotion washed over her as he leaned over, gently, tentatively touching his lips to hers. She was overjoyed and leaned forward and reached her hand behind his neck to help her press hard in answer to his kiss. He let her pull away when she was ready, her glistening eyes locked on his.

"I'll call you when I get to Washington."

"I might have a phone by then," she laughed, relaxing from the intensity of their first kiss, then growing serious again. "Thanks again for coming to my rescue."

"I didn't come in time to rescue you."

"But you let me cry on your shoulder," and she came close to tears again. "I wish you didn't have to go."

"You'll have to come to Washington."

"Absolutely."

"I'll take you to my favorite steak-and-potatoes place, no cowboy boots allowed."

"That's a date. You need to go or you'll miss your plane."

"Yes, I guess so. Take care of yourself," he told her. "You're important to me."

"And you are so important to me, but you'd better go or I may change my mind and not let you."

He left by the front door about 12 hours after he arrived and she knew that much had changed in her life.

* * *

Senator Nathan Taylor's face drained of all its color when he saw the headline in the Washington Herald. Front page above the fold, it declared, "20 ARRESTED IN ECO-TERRORISM PLOT." The byline read "Patrick Garrity." The article even had a mugshot of Paul Stoddard, with one side of his head bruised and swollen.

The body of the article brought much more bad news.

"A homeland terrorist cell was rounded up in a late-night raid in the Houston suburb of Baytown night before last. Nineteen members of the 'Knights of Mother Earth' were arrested when they gathered for their monthly meeting. They were charged with carrying out the attack on the Gulf Pride offshore oil-drilling platform in the Gulf of Mexico last May.

"Two Houston police officers were shot in the subsequent pursuit of the ringleader of the terrorist cell, Paul Stoddard. One officer was killed and the other hospitalized in critical condition.

"The arrests were made after an exhaustive FBI investigation into the incident which ranged from Houston to New Orleans to Washington D.C. It is believed that funding and other support for the 'Knights' may have originated in the Nation's Capital.

"Paul Stoddard, leader of the 'Knights', initially eluded capture, but was apprehended in Houston later that same night (see sidebar)."

Taylor glanced at the sidebar and was dismayed to see the heading: "AXIOM CEO OVERCOMES ECOTERRORIST COP KILLER." Taylor shuddered to think what the popular reaction would be to that news. He continued reading the main article and his concern increased exponentially. Though he hadn't known Paul Stoddard's name, he knew everything else the article conveyed about him. It had been foolish for him to try to kidnap the Axiom Oil executive, but he was only able to do that because the FBI failed to capture him at his house. The classless functionary would probably sing like a canary in custody. Thankfully, Stoddard didn't know about Taylor. What he read next caused Taylor much more alarm.

"Also arrested night before last in Washington was Marvin Borelli, a lobbyist for the Environmental activist groups. He was charged as the mastermind of the terrorist incident.

"Sources in the FBI say the agency has been investigating for several weeks and indicate more arrests may be made in the near future."

This was a disaster. Taylor counted on Borelli to handle these issues and keep his name out of his activities. *How could this happen and I hadn't heard*, Taylor wondered? *What would Borelli do if faced with a trial and conviction? What would he say if offered a plea deal?* The article continued.

"Although Axiom Oil Incorporated, owner of the Gulf Pride oil platform off the coast of Louisiana, claimed from the beginning that the explosion was an act of terrorism, many had questioned the company's version of events, believing the explosion to be an industrial accident resulting from negligence. One oil field worker died in the incident. It appears now that there was indeed a terrorist attack that resulted from a wide-ranging conspiracy.

"Members of the House of Representatives say they will begin an investigation into the timing of the 'Petroleum Independence Act' which levied a new gas tax and precipitated the Axiom moratorium on gasoline sales. 'The gas tax bill was promoted as a measure to help avoid ecological accidents,' said Carl Kellerman (R-CO). 'Now we know the incident in the Gulf of Mexico was not an accident at all, and that throws suspicion on the motivations behind the bill.'"

Taylor suddenly found he couldn't breathe. Then he began to relax, telling himself he had been through situations like this before. He could certainly handle a member of the House from a Podunk district in Colorado. He just needed to keep quiet until he was required to speak, then he would use all the authority of his office to shout down those who would undoubtedly array themselves against him, smelling blood in the water. He had weathered this kind of storm before.

* * *

Patrick was amused but hardly surprised to see the national media outlets turn on a dime and begin reporting the arrests as the natural culmination of the story they had been reporting all along. His article had sent scores of news outlets across the country scrambling to get up to speed on the eco-terrorism angle.

John Watson had been released after questioning, but he was a changed man. Before, he had been almost giddy, reporting the trials of the oil companies. Now he was subdued and quiet. Patrick had chosen not to include Watson in the article, partly because none of his FBI sources had volunteered the information and he didn't want to unnecessarily call attention to his own knowledge of Watson's involvement. It was not generally known at the Herald that Watson had been questioned at all. Patrick still didn't know what Watson's actual involvement was. If he was materially involved, it would come out soon enough, he reasoned.

Meanwhile, Patrick discreetly pursued the political involvement angle. Jackie hadn't known enough or hadn't been willing to share enough detail to tell him where to look exactly, but he knew the "usual suspects." Special Agent Shannon hadn't been at all forthcoming when Patrick asked him if there was a connection to any Washington politicians. Patrick had tried to point out to Agent Shannon that he owed him a favor, since the case might still be unsolved without Patrick's turning over John Watson's emails, but Shannon wasn't buying. He would return the favor some other time when it wouldn't jeopardize an investigation, he had said. Patrick made noises about being frustrated by Shannon's refusal to share information, but silently noted that Shannon had inadvertently confirmed that politicians were being investigated. His reaction had been vehement enough that Patrick knew he was concealing something and it would only be a matter of time until he ferreted it out.

He pushed the "Intercom" button on his desk phone and punched the number for one of his political reporters. "Anne, could you come in here, please?" he asked when a female voice answered.

Momentarily, a 30-something woman with close-cropped, straight black hair and thick, dark mascara breezed through Patrick's door and plopped down in the chair in front of Patrick's desk. She was about 32, with a deceptively avante garde exterior that masked her no-nonsense intellect.

"What's up?" asked Anne Falk, one of his best political reporters.

"What are you working on?"

"I'm caught up. What've you got for me?"

"How many Senate pages do you know?"

CHAPTER TWENTY-FIVE

This coarse prison jumpsuit is a far cry from my usual tailored Armani, Marvin Borelli thought bitterly, as he sat in the interrogation room, waiting. He had spent two nights in jail in Alexandria, Virginia. Marvin wondered what was taking so long. Time moved so slowly here he had to keep reminding himself it had only been two days.

The indignities of those two days had been beyond anything he could have imagined: the strip search; the rough handling and questioning by people with intelligence and breeding so inferior to his own; the cheap, institutional furniture and cold hard floors. And that had just been the insults of his arrest. Once he was taken to lock-up the real outrages had begun: the cell barely large enough for the steel cot and exposed stainless-steel commode, the rough concrete walls and incessant noise — cries of anger and pain from inmates for God-only-knew what reasons, all night and all day, reverberating through the concrete and steel halls. And the food — it was scarcely worthy of the maggots Marvin was afraid he would find in it. For a man with his background, his culture, it was just too much.

He was confident that his lawyer, with the backing of powerful Senators who owed Marvin Borelli a return of favor, would have him out of there soon. But why was it taking so long?

He again fought back the numbing, cold fear that he would never admit. Not fear of prison so much, though that was fearful enough, but more a fear of the repercussions that would descend from everything coming unraveled. He had been very careful to not let those providing the funding know exactly what he was doing. And those who actually carried out the missions had no idea where the funds had come from. The fear came from the fact that Marvin knew everything about everything and he was confined. What measures would be taken to get him to tell what he knew?

Of lesser immediate concern was the long-term impact this would have on the Cause. It was well known that he lobbied for specific, high-profile Environmental organizations. He was not directly employed by any of them, but they depended on him to funnel their considerable money to influence lawmakers and bureaucrats to grease the wheels of progress in the vital work of saving the Earth. They couldn't have known of his tactics and the alliances he had made, but they would know now. His contractor status would almost certainly be gone, even if he was fortunate enough to be exonerated, and with it would be gone the parties, the starlets, the cash.

After what seemed like hours, but may have only been a few minutes — how could he tell without his Rolex or even a clock on the wall? — two men came through the door and sat down across the table from Marvin, the younger carrying a plastic suitbag.

"Hello, Marvin," began his attorney, Joseph Panckowicz, a tall dignified man in a pin-striped suit with a full head of regal white hair. When he smiled, the corners of his mouth lifted the folds of his once-handsome face like the opening of a theater curtain.

"Your arraignment is set for tomorrow morning at nine. I've brought you a suit." Panckowicz gestured to the law associate at his elbow, gripping the plastic-wrapped outfit with fear showing in his eyes. The young man with the close-cropped hair timidly pushed the outfit across the table toward Marvin, looking at him as if he was accused of murdering his family with a chainsaw.

"Why can't you get me out now?" demanded Marvin. "I've been here two blasted nights already!"

"You'll be out after your arraignment tomorrow, I promise. The authorities aren't very flexible where you are concerned."

"Can't you threaten them, get a court order or something?"

"I'm afraid those tactics aren't working. You have been charged with serious crimes and the judge isn't open to cooperation." Panckowicz pronounced the last word as if it was code for something he preferred not to reveal. "Be a little patient and, for God's sake, keep your mouth shut. You'll be out of here before you know it."

Marvin accepted the chastening from his experienced, $500-an-hour attorney and stared at the chipped paint on the tabletop, fearing that he was in for a long, difficult ordeal, despite his attorney's assurances of his impending release.

* * *

Jackie finally called Arturo and they agreed to meet for coffee. She didn't want him to come to her house. A neutral place would be better. As they made small talk, she looked at him sitting across from her in the booth at the bistro she had selected, really seeing him again for the first time in many years. She had been too distraught when he had showed up unannounced that eventful night. He had acquired some gray hair mixed with the black. She supposed she would have some too, but she wasn't about to let the color wear off to find out.

"I was concerned about you," he said, hardly looking her in the eye. "I saw you on TV. It looked like you were having a lot of trouble."

"Yeah, well. Things have pretty much stabilized now."

"You have every right to be angry with me."

"Okay, tell me what happened. Why did you leave? Where did you go?"

He still only glanced at her as he answered. "It was getting to be too much: the wedding, the plans, your mother. I got scared, I guess."

"Scared of what?"

"Your life is so different from mine. Your family is so wealthy."

"You're not poor," she argued. Arturo's father was an importer of goods from South of the Border who had done quite well for himself. It was nothing like the expanse of Axiom's holdings of course, but a respectable personal fortune nonetheless. "You know that's not important to me anyway."

"Well, I'm sorry that I did that to you. Once I left, I couldn't come back to face you. And so, the years went by...."

She saw he did appear genuinely sorry. Her own pain and anger had decayed with time and been replaced by the exhilaration of her budding relationship with Patrick. She could only pity Arturo.

"It was a long time ago," she began, forgetting the hot words she had spent years planning to say if she saw him again. "I've moved on. Perhaps everything turned out for the best."

She was surprised to see hurt in his eyes. She had never considered that he might have spent the years regretting his departure. Now that she was letting him off the hook, he seemed to want something — but what?

"So, you're okay?"

"I'm better each day than the day before," she asserted, realizing the truth of the words only after they were spoken.

* * *

The mid-October air was crisp and frosty. Senator Taylor's breath shot out of his mouth in little puffs of fog as he spat out the words of a speech that was pretty much a rehash of campaign speeches he had given thousands of times before. There were fewer people than expected at the rally in Burlington. Nathan Taylor's campaign chairman had hastily put together four get-out-the-vote rallies, because the polls were showing an alarming downtrend in approval of the senior senator from Vermont. Taylor still regarded the effort as a bother and unnecessary, but his strategists insisted.

Vermont had a grand total of 14 counties and a population of only 600,000. That was only a little more than one-third the number of people who lived in Manhattan. Over the years of public service, Taylor had become intimately familiar with each and every postcard village in each and every county of the tiny state, with their white-steepled churches and shuttered Cape Cod houses that had scarcely changed in 300 years. The trees were just beginning to lose the glorious red and yellow leaves that made New England a haven for artists as well as a favorite destination for senior-citizen bus tours.

"And finally, let me say to my fellow Americans from the Green Mountain State, I will do as I have been doing, representing your interests in Washington for another term. Thank you for your loyal support over all these years."

"Hey Senator, what's the connection between your gas tax and the attack on the oil platform?"

Taylor's eyes grew wide with shock at the heckler's question as he searched the crowd for the source of the impertinent interruption. Then his eyes narrowed and grew as cold as the New England afternoon.

"Now, now. Let's focus on the needs of the American people..."

"We need a tax cut, that's what we need!" another voice said. Suddenly several voices began calling one thing or another. Taylor's supporters tried to shout down the hecklers. "Please, let's calm down," Taylor said over and over again, to no avail.

"We need gas! We need gas! We need gas..." several people began to shout. Taylor was unable to regain control. Burlington police waded into the crowd and began to remove the protestors.

* * *

The printing press at the Washington Herald was three stories high and a hundred feet long. The three-foot-diameter rolls of newsprint were loaded at the front end of the press with more rolls close by to provide plenty of paper for the expanded edition that always came out after a national election like the one happening today, November 7. Soon, ribbons of newsprint would fly through the marvelous blue machine, up, down and through, impressed by several huge ink-drenched drums until, on the other end, it was cut and folded into thousands of identical sections of the newspaper with its ten columns of type, colorful charts and photos of winners and losers.

But for now, the press was quiet, awaiting the finished layouts from Paste-up. It was seven p.m., Eastern time, and just four on the West Coast. Many polls would stay open another three hours in the Pacific time zone and five hours in Hawaii. In the Political News Department of the Washington Herald, telephones, printers and fax machines kept up a continuous white noise that was largely unheard by the reporters except when it was their own phones ringing. E-mail, text and IM traffic was even busier, but much quieter. The entire staff was still at work and would probably pull an "all-nighter", as was customary when a National presidential election was held.

In his office, Patrick Garrity watched Fox News out of the corner of one eye, while scanning the running wire copy from Associated Press on his computer monitor. About once a minute, one of his reporters stuck his or her head in his door to relay some tidbit of information they had gleaned from some source they thought he might be unaware of. In fact, there was little that Patrick missed, even when information was coming as fast and furious as it did on Election Day.

He was hoping to leave to grab a quick dinner at the Blue Ribbon Grill soon, because Jackie was in Washington. He had explained that he would be very busy until the election was over, but figured he could get away for a half hour.

"You need anything? I'm going to the breakroom," said Anne Falk, one of Patrick's reporters.

"Yeah, Pepsi please."

"Breakfast of Champions," Anne winked at him and was gone, almost running into Jed Thompkins, another reporter whose thick glasses and tendency toward clumsiness made Patrick think of Mr. Magoo.

"Pat, I got something here. I think we've got an upset brewing in Vermont."

"Yeah, I've been watching it," Patrick answered as he fumbled through a sheaf of printouts showing election results from the AP wire. It was too early to tell about trends, but Patrick knew there had to be panic in some campaign offices across the country.

"The polls are now closed in Vermont," Jed continued. "And it appears the news isn't good for Senator Nathan Taylor."

"Yeah, that is a surprise! Everybody figured his seat was secure." He had been unopposed for the Democratic nomination and the Republicans had put forward a lackluster candidate, not expecting him to be able to win against the veteran Taylor.

"The real surprise is that early returns look like the front runner is Daniel Conte," Jed said with one eyebrow slightly raised.

"The Libertarian?" Patrick chuckled, "I guess the independent Green Mountain State couldn't bring itself to vote for a Republican, so it's going for the dark-horse Libertarian." It was extremely rare for a Libertarian to win a seat in Congress, much less the Senate, so Patrick wondered what it might portend. It might be a vote against Taylor because of the gas tax, which was just as well, since Patrick was almost certain there was already an investigation of Taylor's possible complicity in the attack on Axiom's oil platform.

"Jed, tomorrow after things settle down, after all the raw results are tabulated and reported, I think I'd like you to compare lawmakers' votes on the gas tax with the winners and losers in the election. That might be interesting!"

Jed looked off into the distance through his thick glasses as he pondered Patrick's assignment. "You got it," he said finally, almost colliding with the door facing on his way out of Patrick's office.

* * *

Not too far away, at Blair House, supporters of President Robert Ryles were watching several rented televisions tuned to various channels, as ABC, CBS, NBC, FOX News and CNN chronicled the incoming returns. At this point, the numbers the networks reported were not actual counted votes at all, but the results of exit polling. The actual results of voting wouldn't be available for several hours, in some cases until tomorrow night. The pressure the news agencies felt to beat each other in calling the various races had led them to treat exit polls as if they were the actual results, even though the polling organizations only questioned a fraction of the voters and people could easily lie to pollsters. Ryles suspected many did.

That's why he wasn't particularly worried yet. As he sat in the living quarters of the White House, preparing for the hour when the Secret Service would accompany him and his family on the short limo ride to Blair house, he took notes on percentages being reported for each state. He would have preferred that the televised results show a stronger move in his favor across the country, where the vast majority of polls were still open. Unfortunately, there were already some disappointing results.

With all polls closed on the Eastern Seaboard, it appeared he might be losing key states like New York and Florida. ABC, CNN and CBS had already declared them for his opponent. He had written off Massachusetts, Vermont and the District of Columbia long ago, but he had hoped for big wins in the Empire and Sunshine states. Ohio, Indiana and Georgia were still too close to call. West Virginia, New Hampshire, and

Delaware had been declared by the media for Ryles, but their populations, and therefore their number of electors, was small. Ryles consoled himself with the knowledge that he was from the Midwest. *Surely, we can look forward to better news as the returns began to come in from the Mississippi Valley and Plains states.*

The First Lady, the Ryles' grown children and their families were scattered through the living quarters of the executive mansion, shadowed as always by Secret Service agents who dutifully radioed their every move to the central command post. Aides came and went with hurried questions needing Ryles' answer or approval.

* * *

A similar scene was taking place in the suite Vermont Senator Nathan Taylor had rented on the top floor of the Capitol Plaza Hotel in Montpelier. Taylor was also keeping track of returns, though he had a much smaller universe to keep track of than President Ryles.

With a "living room" and two bedrooms, the suite was large enough for some of his Washington staffers and top campaign workers to crowd around the heavily laden buffet table and the 32-inch television that was permanently installed in the living room of the suite.

Senator Taylor and his family were relaxing in the larger of two bedrooms where Taylor's wife, their two sons, Nathan Jr. and "Chip", plus their wives and children, were gathered for the victory celebration as they had been many times before, going back to the time the sons were small. Another TV was being flipped from channel to channel as dictated by Nathan Jr., who currently possessed the remote control.

Backlash

In the back of Taylor's mind, an ugly thought crouched as if preparing to spring into the light. He could ignore it most of the time, but tonight, in spite of himself, the thought was pushing its way forward. There was increasing concern among his supporters about his relationship with Marvin Borelli. It was impossible to deny that he knew Marvin and had spent time with him. What was not widely known was that much of the language in the Petroleum Independence Act had come from Borelli's draft. And now, Marvin sat in jail, his attorney preparing for a trial concerning the funding of the attack on the offshore oil platform. Taylor hadn't known the Texas activists that had carried out the plot, but he certainly knew it had been planned and funded by Borelli. The FBI had been deferential toward Taylor, but they had been asking staffers about his appointments and movements on certain dates, he had learned. Almost as worrisome were questions coming from various press outlets.

Downstairs in the Governor's ballroom, the faithful campaign volunteers and loyal supporters of the senior senator from Vermont had been camped out much of the afternoon and evening. They talked and laughed and grazed the buffet table. A red-white-and-blue banner behind the hotel podium optimistically proclaimed, "Six More Years of Responsible Government." Red-white-and-blue balloons rested in a net tied to the ceiling, ready to be released when Senator Taylor came down to announce the presumed victory. The press was there as well, TV lights casting long shadows against the red-and-gold wallpaper.

As time dragged on, the crowd grew less boisterous and listened more closely to the poll results on the televisions placed strategically around the banquet hall. In past years,

Senator Taylor had come down to announce his victory much earlier.

* * *

The volume was up on the TV so the patrons could hear the election returns. Jackie was finishing a Blue Ribbon Grill steak that was much too big for a woman her size, but that was reason enough for her to insist on finishing it. She was in Washington to see Patrick, who had to go back to work on election coverage as soon as they finished eating.

Patrick had warned Jackie that he would be busy, but she had said that was okay. They were both busy people and it would be difficult at best to grow their friendship long distance. It was her turn to come to him and she hadn't wanted to pass up the opportunity.

She had agreed to meet him there, but knew she would probably finish the meal alone. She was just thankful he could get away at all. They had been talking regularly on the phone and by e-mail since his visit to Houston when the terrorists had been arrested. Patrick had been a rock during the turmoil of that couple of days. His responsibility contrasted starkly with Arturo's disappearance and years-long silence, yet Jackie was surprised how easily she had sent Arturo away. Now she almost didn't understand why she had obsessed about him for all those years.

"Dessert?" Patrick asked as Jackie took a deep breath and laid down her fork, knowing that he needed to get back to work.

"No, I don't think so tonight!" she said, patting her midsection. "Early returns don't look good for the president."

"So, I see," he answered, glancing at the running totals at the bottom of the TV screen. "Same for the sponsors of the gas tax bill. I already have my team working on comparing wins and losses with the votes on the bill. Should be interesting."

"I'd be surprised if you found much correlation."

"We'll see. If there is a correlation, my hat will be off to you."

"To me? Why?"

"Because you will have changed the world."

"What?"

Patrick drew himself back with a mock air of authority, "I predict that the main supporters of the gas tax will be defeated tonight, and when the new Congress convenes, not only will the effort to nationalize the oil industry be forgotten, but the Petroleum Independence Act will be repealed!"

Jackie was amused by his pomposity, but he probably did know what he was talking about. "I hope you're right," she answered, "for everybody's sake."

"And I further predict," he continued, milking the attention, "that Axiom Oil Incorporated's stock price will soar beyond its previous lofty heights!"

"Hear, hear!" said Jackie, with mocking polite applause.

"I may even buy some myself."

"Well, you better buy it quickly because it won't be this low for long!"

"From your lips to God's ear!" Patrick said with a flourish.

Jackie smiled and looked down.

"Look," he continued, gesturing with his fork toward the TV. "Nathan Taylor is finished. It was his bill. Everybody thought he was a lock. But Vermont is going to a Libertarian. You did that."

"Don't be silly. He did it to himself. Or maybe they just got tired of him."

"No, I know how these things work. Besides, losing an election will be the least of his worries if the FBI can implicate him in the conspiracy. Maybe people would have reacted and removed him for the gas tax anyway, but I think it's because you stood up to him and people like him. That's how you changed the world. You made people think about the overreaching of government." He raised his iced tea glass. "I'm glad to know you, Jacqueline Marie James."

"Thank you," she replied in surprise and raised her own glass to meet his. "I'm glad I know you, too," was all she could manage to say.

Too soon he had to go back to work. With misty eyes, she embraced him and they kissed the briefest tentative kiss that held so much promise of what could come after. Jackie sat back down after he was gone and ordered a cup of coffee. She sipped it slowly and smiled involuntarily.

She didn't think she had changed the world. It took much more than she had done to do that. Perhaps she had changed some minds, but she was sure that there were many more who would still like to harm her, her company and the people who depended on it. Maybe it would be more accurate to say she had "made a difference." There was a kind of irony in that, since she figured those who had meant to harm her felt they were trying to make a difference, too. They had tried to use the iron power of government to force the population of the country into their mold. People in the government had abused their power to hurt people in the name of Environmental Concern. But if Jackie had made even a few people aware of the potential for abuse of power that was always present in government, then she had made a difference.

"Power corrupts, but absolute power corrupts absolutely", went the saying. Some people probably thought Jackie had too much power, but she knew that the gas tax episode had demonstrated that there were people with much more power than she. She was glad that some of them were being held accountable, if only through lost elections.

That change would come to her industry in the future was certain, just as it had in the past, but it would come in such a way that wouldn't endanger people's livelihoods and security. Advances in technology would continue moving them toward cleaner fuels and cleaner processes, as had been happening for 100 years, *and that is a good thing, of course,* Jackie thought.

Tomorrow, when the election dust had settled and Patrick had finished his all-nighter, they would meet again, if only briefly before she had to return to Houston and work. Her emotions were decidedly mixed about leaving, but for the first time in months, there was reason to hope.

THE END

STUDIO IV PRODUCTIONS 2017

GET THREE FREE CHAPTERS of *Backlash 2: Justice Denied*, the second book in the *Backlash* series as well as receiving information about other future releases from Gary L. Ivey when you join his email list at **www.backlashbook.com.**

Backlash 2: Justice Denied

The gas tax still needs repealing; the fate of Axiom's employees and customers is at stake. Congress passes the repeal, but a judge stands in the way.

Attacks against the company continue, this time on Wall Street as well as Main Street.

How can Jackie keep her company together and find out who is behind the attacks?

How will she cope with a betrayal by someone close to her?

Want more?

Check out **www.garyivey.com** for blog posts about freedom and the free market.

Follow Gary L. Ivey on Facebook at **www.facebook.com/GaryIveyAuthor/** and on Twitter **@gary_ivey**.

Watch for future books by Gary Ivey

Thine Is the Kingdom

It was a time of triumph, but also a time of crisis when Israel's first monarchs established the kingdom.

With great power comes great responsibility. Follow the ascendancy of God's people during the reigns of Saul, David and Solomon through the eyes of fictional as well as real Bible characters.

To be notified about publication of *Thine Is the Kingdom*, join the email list at **www.backlashbook.com** or **www.garyivey.com**.

About the Author

Gary L. Ivey wrote *Backlash* while living in Georgia but has since moved to the state of Hawaii to be near children and grandchildren.

He is originally from Oklahoma and has also lived in Texas, Mississippi and Alabama. He met his wife in Louisiana.

His father worked as a middle manager in a large oil company for 31 years and still receives a pension check every month. Though not claiming to be an expert, Ivey grew up learning about the oil business and its place in the national economy without really trying.

His belief in the importance of the free market economy to the free people of the United States and that free-market capitalism is the best system to alleviate poverty in the world led him to write *Backlash*.

An entrepreneur himself, together with his wife of 45 years, he has owned a web development company for nearly 20 years. Before that, he owned a video production business and before that worked as a magazine editor and pastor.

Besides writing, Ivey likes to write, play and listen to music in a variety of styles.

www.ingramcontent.com/pod-product-compliance
Lightning Source LLC
Chambersburg PA
CBHW071204250626
47159CB00001B/191